The Kennedy Boys

Saving Brad

The Fifth Novel

SIOBHAN DAVIS

www.siobhandavis.com

Printed by Createspace, an Amazon.com Company
Paperback edition © November 2017

ISBN-13: 978-1978102781
ISBN-10: 197810278X

Editor: Kelly Hartigan (XterraWeb) editing.xterraweb.com
Cover design by Robin Harper https://wickedbydesigncovers.wixsite.com
Cover photo by Sara Eirew Photographer
Formatting by The Deliberate Page www.DeliberatePage.com

Note from the Author

While this book is a standalone title in the Kennedy Boys series, it is advisable to have read the previous books as that is where we were first introduced to most of the characters in this book. Forgiving Keven is the next release, slated for publication in early 2019.

Due to some heavy subject matter, sexual situations, language, and possible triggers, this book is not suitable for anyone under the age of eighteen.

Rachel, our female protagonist, has only recently immigrated to America. Her word choices, speech patterns, and colloquialisms are Irish English, and I have enclosed a glossary at the back of this book which might come in handy as you read!

For readers who are up to date with this series, we meet Brad and Rachel in *Saving Brad* as they are both starting their sophomore year at their respective colleges. I know many of you are Team Brad, and your enthusiastic feedback is the main reason why this book was brought forward in the series. I hope you enjoy reading it as much as I enjoyed writing it.

Prologue

August–Nantucket

Brad

"You remember Rach, right, Brad?" Faye gestures toward her friend who is currently engrossed in conversation on the other side of the patio with a newly engaged Lana and Kalvin. They've just returned from visiting the house Kal bought his fiancée as a surprise engagement present.

Hell, yeah. Of course, I remember her. "Sure." *Play it cool, dude.* "Hard to forget mouthy little Red." Except she's dyed her hair since the first time we met, and her bright red locks have been replaced by rich chocolaty-brown strands that beg to be touched.

Faye scowls. "I hope you're not going to be rude to her again."

Uh-oh. Recalling our chat from an hour ago, I realize it's a bit late for that. But that's not what Faye is referencing.

The first time I met Rachel was when she sprung a surprise visit on Faye, at Wellesley, with their other friend Jill, more than a year and a half ago.

I was only rude to her about ninety-five percent of the time.

The other five percent ... well, let's just say I definitely wasn't rude then and leave it at that.

I smother my smirk before Faye notices. "Don't worry. I'll play nice." I send her a toothy grin, and she narrows her eyes suspiciously.

Considering Faye never said a word to me after her friends returned to Ireland, I think it's safe to assume Rachel didn't tell her what went down between us. I thought girls told each other everything, and I'd been expecting a shakedown that never happened.

Thoughts of that night wander through my mind, and not for the first time.

It was one of the hottest experiences of my life.

We'd been out in Boston earlier that day. After dinner in the city, we came back to the house and watched a couple of movies. Rachel and I had been knocking back beers at an alarming rate, as if it was an implied competition. Ky had been pawing at Faye relentlessly all day, and I'd just about reached my limit. Excusing myself, I'd lied and said I was tired, but I didn't head to bed. I stepped outside, oblivious to the cold winter night air because I was so consumed with thoughts of Faye and the caustic pain ripping my insides apart.

My heart throbs painfully in my chest, performing that horrible twisty thing it does every time I think of her—the girl I want and can never have.

Speaking of.

"Earth to Brad." Faye clicks her fingers in my face. "Where'd you go? I've been talking for, like, the last three minutes, and you haven't heard a word I said, have you?"

"Sorry. Drifted off."

She takes a step closer, and I instinctively take a step back. Defensive mode is the only way I can tolerate being around her these days. The urge to sweep her into my arms and kiss the living daylights out of her hasn't faded. Out of the corner of my eye, I spy Ky watching me with hawk eyes.

He knows.

He knows it hasn't gotten any better.

That I'm still lusting after his woman.

Wrong. Still in *love* with his woman.

The tiny cracks in our relationship are spreading, and I'm waiting for him to detonate. Can't say I'd blame my best bud. He's been unbelievably mature about the whole situation, but I know I'm stretching his patience to the limit. It's been almost two years, and I should be over her. God knows I've screwed enough girls in the intervening period, but trying to fuck her out of my head isn't working.

Nothing is working.

I'm still in love with my best friend's girl. His one true love. The girl who will always be by his side.

I'm pathetic and weak, and I hate myself for it. Every day my self-loathing intensifies until I think I might burn from the inside out.

Faye sighs, dragging me back into the moment. "Are things ever going to be okay with the three of us?" Her bright smile has evaporated.

I could lie but what's the point?

She knows how I feel.

He knows how I feel.

It's the unspoken elephant in the room. This constant wedge between us. I don't know how much more of the stress I can take.

"I'm trying," I answer honestly.

She shakes her head sadly. "No, you're not. Not really." I arch a brow. "I know you're screwing all around you, but you always pick the wrong girls, and I'll bet you're doing that on purpose."

"Don't try to psychoanalyze me," I growl, irritated all of a sudden. "You don't know what I'm feeling."

Bravely, she touches my arm. "You're right. I don't, because you keep shutting me out. Shutting Ky out."

"Because I have to!" I run my hands through my hair. "I can't talk to you about it, and you know why."

"You need to widen the field. Look for a nice girl, not one of those groupies who hang off your every word. That's not you. I know it isn't."

"Faye, I'm nineteen, on the football team at Harvard, and as horny as the next guy. No guy goes to college to find their soul mate. They go to party and fuck as many girls as they can before they settle down. There is nothing wrong with what I'm doing, and you and Kyler don't get to lecture me on my lifestyle, so butt out."

Shucking her hand off, I walk away, not giving a shit that it's rude to bail without warning. I need to blow off some steam—to calm the insanity brewing to epic proportions inside my head. I stomp down to the beach, veering left away from the party in full swing on the other side of the sandy strip.

I drop down onto the sand and rest my head on my knees. What an epic fuck-up. Shit. I let out a frustrated roar. Way to act like a total immature ass.

I need a distraction, so when my mind returns to that night with Rachel, I welcome it.

I was out on the patio, feeling sorry for myself when she joined me. "What do you want?" I snapped.

She faced the picturesque gardens as she spoke. "She's completely and utterly in love with Ky."

I sighed. "I know."

She turned around to me. "So, do something about it, because you're wasting your time if you think she's going to ever leave him."

"Don't pretend you know what I'm thinking or what I should do."

"You're an idiot." She barked out a laugh. "A guy like you has tons of options. Find someone else. Get laid. Find a life that isn't so centered around the Kennedys and this house. Take control of your own life. You dictate where you go and who you spend it with."

"You make it sound so easy." And, suddenly, I'd wondered if we were even speaking about me anymore.

She paused considerably before replying, and I swore tears appeared briefly in her eyes. "I know it's not easy. Nothing that important ever is."

"How do you do it?" I risked asking, looking at her with a fresh perspective.

Her pretty brown eyes glistened with pain. "I'm still trying to figure it out, but I think I'm getting there."

"How?" I whispered, moving closer to her. I stared deep into her eyes, like they might hold the key to eradicating my misery.

She peered up at me, contemplating how much to tell me. Right then, Rachel was an open book, and the pain I witnessed was all too real. That girl was hurting. "I drink and I fuck, usually in that order. It's the only time I can blank it all out."

My eyes popped wide in surprise. Not at what she told me. I'd seen enough the night before to verify that statement. I was startled she was being so honest. We were virtual strangers, and she owed me nothing. "Does it help?"

Her hand landed on my arm, and tingles danced over my skin even through my shirt. "Yes and no." She moved closer and her chest brushed against mine. "It dulls the pain in the moment." Her hands slid up my chest, and my arms wrapped around her waist. My heart started beating faster. "And in that moment, it feels fucking great. Not to think about any of the crap. Just to feel"—she looked off into space—"normal. Even if it is fleeting, delusional."

"You want to feel like that now?" I whispered, fixating on her mouth so there could be no misunderstanding.

"You don't even like me."

"You don't like me."

"True." She smiled as her small hands crept around the back of my neck. "You're a dick."

"Do you like most of the guys you fuck?" I pulled her closer against my body, ensuring she felt the straining bulge in my pants.

She thought about that for a bit. "No. Almost never."

I grinned. "Well then, I don't think we have any problem. Do you?" A slight frown appeared on her forehead, and I instantly knew what caused it. "Don't go there. You've already said it. She loves him. She wouldn't care about this."

"She cares about you."

"Please. Don't." My tone was effusive with pleading. Now that the seeds had been sown, and my body was on board with the plan, if she backed out, I would be in a whole new world of pain.

Removing her hands from my neck, she slid one down the narrow gap between us, palming my erection. "You need this? You need me?"

"Yes," I growled, pushing into her hand.

A steely resolve etched across her face. "Fuck me, Brad."

And I did.

And it was the hottest sex of my life.

Pushing her up against the wall, ensuring we were out of sight of the windows, I tore her panties away as she popped the button on my jeans. Our mouths meshed in a frantic marriage of pain and lust and anger and despair. She tasted of beer and mint, and her lips were as soft as silk as they moved effortlessly against mine. My fingers plunged into her wet warmth, and she moaned low under her breath, already as worked up as me. Shoving my jeans and boxers down, and quickly rolling a condom on, I thrust into her hard, over and over, while she dug her nails into my back. I captured her moans with my mouth and held her legs firmly around my waist as I fucked her. My hand was rough as it kneaded her breast through her dress, and I could feel her body on the brink of losing control. "God, Brad. Don't stop. Fuck me harder. Do it. Harder. Faster," she gritted out, and I damn near exploded on the spot. When she came, her entire body shuddered around me as she whispered my name in my ear. My release followed and I continued pumping until I was completely spent.

I'm hard now just thinking about it.

After we screwed, we just walked away without acknowledging what we'd done. She left the next day without even saying goodbye. I'd like to say I haven't thought of her in the interim, but there's no point lying to myself.

I have thought of her often.

Wondered what kind of pain tortures her.

Wondered how many random guys she's fucked since I last saw her and whether it's brought her any measure of peace.

I bark out a dry laugh as realization dawns. Unwittingly, I've been following her advice. Getting drunk and getting laid, but she's right. It's a momentary escape from the pain. Once it's over, the usual heartache returns. Only this time, the heartache is joined by a new layer of guilt and self-revulsion.

Does she feel that too?

Does Rachel hate herself as much as I hate me?

She's moving here now. She's transferred from her college in Ireland to the Massachusetts College of Art and Design. Alex Kennedy, Ky's mom, helped set everything up.

As Faye's best friend, and new roomie, Rachel is going to be a more permanent feature in my life. Not that I need any more complications, but I guess I'm about to discover the answers to my questions.

Chapter One

Three Weeks Later

Brad

Faye's stunning blue eyes swim to the forefront of my mind and I groan. *Not now. Go away.* It's bad enough I'm in love with my best friend's girl, but the fact she plays a starring role in my daily fantasies makes me feel like some sick pervert. Ky would cut my balls off if he knew the extent of my obsession. Honestly, it's getting to the stage where I'm starting to genuinely worry about myself. Nails dig into my ass, and I thrust harder, grunting as a wave of pleasure courses through me.

"Who the hell is Faye?" the blonde underneath me asks with a growl, clearly pissed.

"No one ..." *Fuck, what's her name? Cassie? Carla? Kayla, that's it, I'm pretty sure.* "Kayla. Sorry, baby. This is so good." I thrust in harder to drill it home. *See my point?* I'm totally losing it if I'm calling out Faye's name as I'm nailing some other chick. My own thoughts make me a little sick. *How has it come to this? How have I sunk so low?*

Her eyes roll in her head, and her back arches off the bed. "That *is* good, *baby*. And my name's Callie, asshole."

I pull her up onto my lap, bracing one arm against the headrest as I thrust my hips up to meet hers. I kiss her passionately, greedily, focusing one hundred percent on the hot blonde who is currently giving me the ride of my life. We went at it half the night, and I must've fallen asleep before I could kick her out. Not that I'm complaining. A morning quickie is a rare treat. My head dips, and I suck her nipple into my mouth. She screams my name out at the exact same moment the door to my bedroom swings opens.

"Ho. Lee. Crap!" a familiar voice shrieks, and I rip the blonde off me faster than a bloodsucking leech. "Shit, sorry, Brad. I didn't know you had company." Faye shields her face with her hand, quickly looking away. Her cheeks have turned bright red. You'd swear she was some virginal innocent by her obvious embarrassed expression. Except I share this apartment with her boyfriend, and I've heard them plenty of times in the throes of sex. Judging from the sounds emitting from his bedroom, and the way Ky's headboard bangs wildly against the wall, I'd say Faye is used to being well and truly fucked.

And now my mind has totally gone there. Great, just what I need. My dick starts hardening again, and I reach down, covering the evidence with my hands. The blonde grabs the sheet up under her chin, and her eyes beseech me to handle the situation.

"Faye, babe," Ky says, approaching from behind her. The blonde's eyes narrow suspiciously. Ky peers into the room, roaring with laughter as his hands snake around Faye's waist. He leans his chin on her shoulder. "You turned voyeur or something?"

She slaps his arm. "I didn't know he had someone in here."

"Eh, hello." I gesture toward Callie. "Do you mind getting the hell out of my room."

"Of course, bro." Ky starts backing Faye out into the narrow corridor. "But make it snappy. Rachel's flight lands at eleven, and we want to get there early in case it arrives ahead of schedule."

Dammit. I had totally forgotten today was the day. *Could this day get any worse? And why the hell did I agree to go with them?* I snort. I know why. Because Faye turned the charm on, and I relented straightaway. I'm wrapped around her finger every bit as much as Ky is.

They close the door, and I return my attention to Callie, my cock straining with renewed arousal. "Where are you going?" I reach for her as she swings her legs out the side of the bed.

"Home."

I pat the mattress. "Come back to bed. We have enough time to finish."

She plants her hands on her hips, standing before me stark naked, and damn, if it isn't hot as hell. She has a rocking body, and she isn't afraid to show it off. "I'm no longer in the mood."

I stand up, moving toward her with intent. "I can fix that in two seconds."

She thrusts out a palm, slamming into my chest and holding me at arm's length. She looks down at my hard erection. "I'll bet you could, but I'm not some dumb bimbo." She points at my dick. "That's not for me. That's for *her*." She spits the word out like it's poison.

"Ah come on, don't be like that." I make an attempt to pull her into me, but she's having none of it.

"I didn't want to believe everything that's said about you because I've seen how you are in class, and I couldn't reconcile that person with the rumors. But it turns out the rumors are true. You're a total douche, Brad, and nothing would entice me between the sheets with you again. Now, let me go."

I lift my hands in a conciliatory gesture. "Fine. Your loss." Guess I'll have to rub one out in the shower now.

She angrily pulls her clothes on as I grab a pair of sweatpants off the floor and tug them on. Yanking the door open, she stomps into the living area and I rush out after her. She's glaring at Faye, and Faye stares at me in confusion. "Call me some time," she says to Ky, roaming his body with hungry eyes. "I have a feeling you'll be in need of new female company soon." Casting another glare at Faye, she storms out of the apartment leaving a mess in her wake.

"What the hell is that chick's problem?" Faye asks Ky, her fists clenched into balls of fury at her side. "What a bitch! She hit on you right in front of me." A red flush creeps up her neck, and her eyes blaze with unconcealed anger.

"Babe." Ky draws her into his arms. "Ignore her. She's obviously sore because you interrupted, and clearly, she didn't get her rocks off." He levels an amused look my way.

"Neither of us did," I growl. "Thanks for that by the way." The amused expression drops off Ky's face, and his uber-protective mode cranks up a notch. He's getting ready to chew me out. Not that he needs to. Faye is more than capable of standing her ground, but Ky loves to go all alpha-protector. "Sorry," I add quickly, before he can lay into me. "It's not your fault I lost track of time."

"I was going to say I'm sorry for ruining your fun, but after the way that bitch acted, I think I've just done you a massive favor, Brad," Faye proclaims.

Well, fuck me. Can my warped life get any more warped?

"Why did Rachel go back to Ireland anyway?" I ask from the backseat of Ky's Range Rover en route to Logan Airport.

"She had to pack up the rest of her stuff, and her parents wanted to talk to her about something," Faye confirms, shifting around in the passenger seat so she's facing me.

"And she's really moving here for good?" I look absently out the window as Ky takes the exit for the airport.

"Yep." Faye can't contain her excitement. "It's going to be so cool having her here. And the apartment she bought for us to share is incredible. It's in a fabulous building only minutes' walk from Harvard. She got the best unit on the top floor, and we have our own rooms with walk-in wardrobes and en suite bathrooms and our own outside decked area. And they have this amazing communal rooftop deck too, parking, Wi-Fi, twenty-four-hour concierge, and even a gym," she gushes, sighing dreamily. "It sure beats living in the freshman dorms."

"Breathe, babe." Ky pins her with an amused look. "And you *wanted* to live in the dorms last year."

She twists around in her seat, the leather making a squelching sound in the process. "I know, and I'm glad I experienced it, but I'm happy to be moving out and moving in with someone I know and trust."

Ky squeezes her thigh. "Me too, and I'm glad you're away from Becca. That girl gave me the creeps."

Faye's roomie last year took more than a little liking to Ky. It didn't seem to matter that he was besotted with his girlfriend—she pestered him all of fall semester to the point of harassment. Ky threatened to report her and organized a transfer for Faye to a single dorm, and, thankfully, that was the end of her interference. But it added a lot of unnecessary drama to our freshman year.

Faye shudders. "I know. That girl was genuinely scary."

"It's behind us now." Ky looks at her so adoringly—in what is his usual way—and a pang of envy has a vise-grip on my heart. It's so difficult to be around them, and that whole situation with Becca meant Faye spent an inordinate amount of time in our apartment those first few months, which only added to my torture. I enjoyed a lot of hookups and one-night stands in the early Harvard days. Anything to not have to return home and listen to my friend banging the hell out of the girl I love.

While Faye and Ky returned to Wellesley for summer break, I chose to stay in our apartment, needing the headspace. One of the guys from the football team moved in with me, and we spent the summer partying up a storm, only toning things down the last few weeks once early practice sessions started up. Coach takes a dim view of excessive partying, and I've been privy to more than a few lectures over the course of the last year. Still, it's hard for him to find fault when I'm keeping good grades and playing well.

Faye stretches over the console to kiss Ky, and bile swims up my throat.

Closing my eyes, I rest my head against the window, praying to God to release me from this hell.

"I've a good feeling about this year. Our sophomore year is going to be great. For all of us," Faye says softly. My eyes fly open, just catching the hopeful look she sends my way. I pray she's right, because the prospect of spending another year locked in this awkward love triangle doesn't bear thinking about. I don't think I'll survive another year of the same. There is only so much a guy can take before he cracks.

Faye returns Ky's adoring gaze, reaching across to tenderly caress his face.

My heart aches again, and I slump a little in my seat, awash with a whole array of conflicted emotions. Sometimes, I wish I could just remove my brain and all the accompanying futile thoughts and enjoy the nothingness. The complete and utter silence that would be a welcome relief.

Rachel's flight has already landed by the time we park, and we race through the airport to reach arrivals before she walks out.

About two minutes after we arrive, she emerges through the gate looking even more beautiful than I remember. Her gorgeous dark hair is loose and flowing in thick waves down her back. She is wearing fitted skinny jeans that hug her curves in all the right places and a flimsy white blouse over a snug white lacy tank top. Moving confidently in her strappy stilettos, she removes her large sunglasses, propping them on top of her head as she notices Faye running toward her. The girls hug as Ky takes ahold of Rachel's suitcase, returning to my side.

"You doing okay?" He glances sideways at me.

"I'm fine," I say, more harshly than necessary.

He levels a serious look at me. "What was up with the girl earlier?"

I shrug. "Who knows? We weren't doing much talking."

He scrubs a hand over his cheek. "I know things are rough, man, but screwing your way through campus again this year isn't the answer. And it's not who you are."

"I don't give you advice on your love life, so don't try to inject yourself into mine," I hiss. "I'm sick of everyone trying to tell me what to do. It's my life, and I'll live it the way I want to."

He sighs, and I watch as the girls loop arms, heading in our direction. "That's bullshit, man, and you know it. Fine if you don't want to confide in me. I get it. But at least confide in *someone*."

What's the frigging point? Talking about it isn't going to solve the issue. I have no clue how to fix this clusterfuck I find myself in. I should never have suggested I act as Faye's fake boyfriend during senior year of high school. That's really when all the problems started. I was already attracted to her looks and her personality, so putting myself in that position was a recipe for disaster. But I thought I was helping Ky out. His troublesome ex was blackmailing him, and he was concerned she would target Faye if she knew he was falling for her. So, we agreed the best form of protection was to pretend I was her boyfriend, to hide her true relationship.

By the time our fake relationship was over, I was already head over heels in love with her. I should never have allowed my heart to become invested, but it was difficult to remain detached when we spent so much time together. We were going through similar things at the time, and we connected in a way I've never connected with any girl before. She became a good friend. And so much more. While Faye had a strict no-kissing policy in place, we held hands and were openly affectionate for months. She stole my heart before I even realized it.

And let's not forget the two times we had kissed before she cemented her relationship with my best friend. I can still remember how soft her lips were. How good it felt to hold her in my arms.

Reliving those memories is killing me, but I must love torturing myself, because I can't stop thinking about her. She's the only girl I want even though I know she will never be mine.

And I hate that there's constant tension in my relationship with Ky. We've known each other since we were two, and this is driving a wedge between us. Ky and I used to be able to talk to each other about anything, and I miss it. He's the brother I always wished I had—not to disparage my two sisters whom I miss so Goddamned much—but, growing up, Ky was my de facto brother, and I never thought the time would come when a girl came between us.

And it's not like this is an isolated case.

Addison was the first girl to drive a stake through the heart of our friendship, and our relationship never had time to recover from that fuck-up before this new one kicked off.

The girls land in front of us. "Look who came with," Faye says to Rachel, wiggling her eyebrows as she stares at me.

I jerk my chin up, shoving my hands in my pockets. "Red."

Her lips purse before speaking. "Dickhead."

And I am a dickhead. I know she doesn't like to be called that, and it's not exactly fitting any more considering her hair is no longer the garish red it was when we first met, but I know it pisses her off, and I want her to stay mad at me. Rachel has some stupid notion in her head that we can be friends, and I'm determined to quash that idea before it takes root.

Friendship with a girl as hot as Rachel would only lead to sex, and I don't go back for seconds.

Chapter Two

Rachel

That guy is such an asshole. He's the only potential blip in this otherwise stellar plan of mine. I honestly can't fathom how Kyler has been best friends with Brad since they were little kids. How they're practically like brothers, according to Faye. Brad has a major chip on his shoulder, and he doesn't seem to care who knows it. Well, I came here to get away from that kind of shite and no one is going to drag me back to the gutter. Not even a guy as fit as Brad.

The guys are leading the charge in front of us, giving me ample opportunity to ogle the asshole without his knowledge. My eyes drop from his broad shoulders and muscular back—which flexes and rolls under his clingy shirt as he moves—to his shapely ass, and I have to fight the urge to jump him from behind. There is no denying how utterly gorgeous Brad McConaughey is. With his cropped blond hair, stunning blue eyes framed by lashes that should be illegal on a guy, and the chiseled lines of his tanned face, Brad is temptation on a stick. He has that all-American golden boy good looks I used to swoon over when I was younger. He's like the US equivalent of Niall Horan, albeit a moodier, crankier version. Not that I know Niall Horan personally or anything, but he always comes across as a total sweetheart. Looks, talent, humor, intelligence, and a good heart. A winning combination if ever there was one. Although, I'm kind of protective over our homegrown talent, so I might be biased.

Faye digs her elbows in my ribs, breaking through my inner Niall swooning. "Were you even listening to me?"

"Nope." I grin at her, linking my arm more firmly through hers. "I was just daydreaming about Niall Horan."

"Random dot com."

I snort. "I was thinking that Brad could be like the US Niall Horan if he wasn't such an ass."

Quick as a flash, Brad spins around, eyeballing me with a smirk. "You think I look like Niall Horan? All the ladies love Niall, or so I've been told."

"And your point is?"

We come to a standstill in front of Kyler's car.

"The ladies love me too, Red. And I think you have an inkling why."

He winks, and it's so wrong.

All of it.

The sleazy comment, the sly reminder that he's been inside me, and the shady wink. I often get a sense with Brad that he's playing a part. A role he's not entirely comfortable with, which is why he can't pull it off most of the time. I roll my eyes. "Modest much, dickhead?"

He barks out a laugh. "If you've got it, flaunt it." He leans against the side of the car as Kyler loads my case in the boot. Out of the corner of my eye, I see Faye sadly shake her head.

"It's college. A hard dick is a hard dick. A lot of girls don't discriminate."

The corners of Kyler's mouth turn up as he closes the boot. He shares a knowing look with Faye, taking her by the hand and helping her into the passenger seat. When he leans in and kisses her, I silently swoon. I'm so happy for my best friend. She's found herself a good guy, and they are crazy in love. Even though I don't believe in it for myself, I'm thrilled she is in such a good place in her life. Faye has had her fair share of demons to battle, and she gives me hope. If Faye can pull through it, then so can I.

"A lot of girls or just you?" Brad teases, pushing off the car and opening the back door for me.

Our chests brush as I slide into the seat, and a flurry of delicious tingles spreads over my skin. Resting a hand on top of the car, he leans in, arching a brow as he waits for my reply. I purposely keep my eyes locked on his face, ignoring those lick-worthy biceps of his. Even though the urge to wrap my arms around the rock-solid definition in his upper arms is almost too much to resist, I won't give him the satisfaction. His ego's through the roof as it is, and my Niall comment didn't help.

The last time we spoke, three weeks ago in Nantucket, he made his feelings blatantly clear. He hates me so much he doesn't even want to be friends. I've tried not to let the crushing rejection hurt, but I'd only be lying to myself if I said it didn't gut me. I'm attempting to turn over a new leaf, to start a clean new chapter in my life, and his hurtful words chipped away at my fragile self-confidence. But I'm determined to rise above it. Screw him. I don't need him in my life anyway. "I hate to disappoint you, lover boy, but I'm not in the minority when it comes to opinions on sex. Plenty of girls enjoy casual sex without attachment. Like I said, when you need to fuck, a dick is a dick is a dick."

Faye splutters from the front seat. "Christ, Rach. When did you get so cynical?"

"You call it cynical. I call it realism."

Brad scoots in the back alongside me as I buckle myself in. "But you're forgetting the most important thing, Red." He smirks. "All dicks are not made equal, and it's how skillful you are with your tool that counts."

Ky cracks up laughing in the front seat while maneuvering the SUV out of the car park.

"Okay, I'll concede on dick size. A juicy big cock is nice." Faye makes a strangled sound in the back of her throat. "Riding a tiny pecker is no fun, but, size aside, guys can be taught how to use their dicks correctly. It's not rocket science."

He pins me with an intense look. "It sounds like you have lots of personal experience."

And just like that, he transforms a jokey conversation into a serious one. All the blood drains from my face. I had to put up with a lot of this shite back home, and I'm not going to deal with the same crap here. Especially not from him. "Are you calling me a slut?"

He holds my gaze. "I'm not the one who used that word."

Faye gasps.

"So, let me know if I got this straight. It's okay for you to act like a manwhore around campus and everyone will pat you on the back and tell you 'you the man,' but a girl who indulges in casual sex is a slut and deserves to be stoned for her deviant ways?" I glare at him, putting the full weight of years of hurt behind it. "Have I got that right?"

"I don't make the rules, Red. Things are the way they are, and I think you're getting your panties in a bunch for no good reason."

"You would say that. You're a class-A jerk."

"Do you always resort to insults to try and win an argument? I hate to break it to you, but that's a proven sign of lower intelligence."

I curl my hands into fists at my side. "And any guy who throws that accusation around just to one-up a girl who is clearly anything but stupid is an arrogant motherfucker."

I was going to add "with a small dick" onto the end, but I stopped myself in time. That is something I know categorically isn't true, and there's no way I want to introduce that particular subject to the conversation. I'm not sure why I kept the fact I slept with Brad from Faye, but it isn't something I want to dwell on or discuss at this juncture. I made a solemn promise to myself to leave the past behind when I left Ireland, and I'm not about to renege on that deal.

My sanity depends upon it.

My *future* depends upon it.

"Can you two just stop? Please," Faye beseeches. "You're making my head hurt."

I send one last glare Brad's way, before squishing over in the seat until my body is crushed against the door, putting as much distance between us as physically possible.

"Oh my God, Faye!" I screech when we enter the apartment, dropping my handbag on the floor by the fireplace as we step into the open living space. The place is virtually unrecognizable. It was just a bare shell when I signed the contract, and now it is fully furnished. Faye has obviously gone to considerable lengths with the interior styling, and I couldn't love my friend any more than I do in this minute. She has no idea how much something like this means to me.

The living room is all soft couches in muted grays and lilacs with matching rugs, pictures, and other accessories. Floating gossamer curtains frame the wide window at the far side of the room. "You have done an amazing job, girlfriend. It's stunning. I love it."

I trail the tips of my fingers over the expensive-looking walnut table as I pass by the dining area and into the kitchen. The white gloss cupboards are clean and new despite the overuse they have no doubt already been subjected to. Faye and Ky have been living here the past week, coordinating the fit-out. Faye loves to cook, and I'm sure she has given the kitchen a thorough workout by now. I smile when I spot the far wall devoted to Hewson. There must be at least twenty photos of the little guy pinned to the corkboard. I inspect them more closely, smiling at his adorable little face. "He's so cute he almost makes me broody."

"I know. Me too. I just love him so much." Faye has that dreamy quality to her voice that is always evident when she talks about Kyler's nephew. The pair of them dotes on him.

Kyler almost chokes on his bottle of water, and Brad slaps him on the back.

I open the side door to our private deck, admiring the little wicker table and two chairs. Two narrow loungers reside on the other side, and a massive cream-colored plant pot is crammed to capacity with colorful flowers.

"Let me show you your room." Faye tugs on my elbow, pulling me back inside as the boys drop down on the loungers, stretching out their long limbs.

"Well, what do you think?" she asks, nervously chewing on the side of her thumb. My gaze roams the room, skimming over the king-sized cream leather bed, the sleek glossy furniture, and the beautiful cream, gold, and duck-egg blue bedspread and matching curtains. A soft beige carpet is underfoot.

I spin around, pulling my best friend into my arms. "I love it. It's perfect. Elegant and understated."

She eases back, frowning a little as she scrutinizes my face. "Why the worry lines?" she asks.

"I thought I told you to take the master suite? It makes more sense for you to have the bigger room. You are the one with the boyfriend after all."

"Rach, you own this place. I didn't feel comfortable taking the master bedroom."

That's Faye all over. "You're an idiot." I lightly punch her in the arm. "We've talked about this. It doesn't matter who bought the place. It's only money." I can afford to be flippant about it now. My whole attitude to money changed after my parents won over eighty million euro on the lottery. Before then, I would have shared Faye's opinions, but now I have more than I need, so I refuse to let it get in the way of anything. Faye has a generous allowance from her recently discovered bio dad, and the Kennedys are loaded, so money is not an issue for her either, but I sense she's still struggling to come to terms with that.

As if on cue, she rolls her eyes. "I can't believe you've done a one-eighty. You were such a tight wad in school." She holds up a hand as I open my mouth to speak. "I know. I know. It's because you didn't have much money back then, and now you have loads, but I don't get how your attitude has changed so fast."

"There are more pressing demands on my headspace than money, Faye. That's why. It's one less thing to worry about and I'm not going to feel guilty for it. Mum and Dad gave us ten mill each and I'm more than set up for life."

She nods. "You still should have let me pay half. James and Dad were more than happy to cough up my share." James is Kyler's dad and Faye's uncle. Although, they only found out a couple years ago that James isn't actually his bio dad. That's a whole other story.

"I need to have somewhere I can call mine even though"—I rush to reassure her—"this is totally your place too." It's hard to articulate my feelings, and I mean every word. This apartment is as much hers as it is mine, but it was important to me that my name was the only one on the deed. I need to make roots. To forge a new path in life. To forget the past, live in the present, and look forward to the future. It's hard to explain that to anyone when they don't know the secret I've been hiding these last six years.

Faye swallows noisily, and we stare at one another. I know it's on the tip of her tongue. To ask me, as she does periodically from time to time, if I'm ready to talk about it. She knows something happened to me, but she has none of the specifics, and I intend to keep it that way.

I can't tell her.

Can't tell anyone.

I'm too ashamed.

I swing into deflective mode. "My parents are getting divorced."

Her eyes pop wide. "What?"

I perch on the edge of the soft bed. "That's what they wanted to talk to me about. It's a joke." I shake my head as a sour taste fills my mouth. "Dad is shacked up with this gold digger who is barely older than me, and Mom is indulging all her cougar fantasies with her gym instructor. Apparently, they have fallen out of love and want to move on in their lives, blah, blah."

"I'm so sorry, Rach. Does your brother know?" I nod, not wanting to get into a conversation about Alec. "How are you feeling?" She sits down beside me, wrapping her arm around my shoulder.

"I'm not really sure yet," I admit truthfully. After years of pretending I don't have any feelings—it's been my main coping mechanism—I'm terrified to open that door. Afraid all the pent-up emotions from my past will jump out and swamp me, drowning me in a sea of things I don't want to think about let alone feel.

Relocating to America is my big attempt at taking control of my life. Already, I can breathe easier here. There is less looking over my shoulder. The sense of relief that I've done it, that I've followed through, is monumental.

I just hope it's enough.

That the distance is enough.

That I can finally live my life without fear.

Because I'm done being a victim.

I'm a survivor.

And it's finally time to start living my life.

Chapter Three

Brad

It's the next morning, and I'm standing in line in the local coffee place waiting for Ky to show up when someone taps me on the shoulder. I turn around, wracking my brains, when I spot the blonde from yesterday. Shit, what was her name again? "Hey."

"Hey, asshole." Her lips curl into a snarl.

What is it with chicks calling me derogatory names? Rach had a choice collection for me yesterday, not that I didn't deserve some of them. I was out of line with my insinuations, but what she doesn't know is that it's deliberate. I need her to continue hating me, because she's far too fucking tempting otherwise. I've already jerked off twice thinking about her, which is causing a certain degree of confusion in my muddled mind.

"I'm not interested in talking to you if you're not going to be nice." I move to turn back around, but she applies gentle pressure to my arm, stalling me.

"I know who she is."

I quirk a brow. I haven't a clue what she's talking about.

"Faye."

That one word sends chills up my spine. I shove her hand off. "What the fuck?"

She shrugs nonchalantly. "I'm just letting you know I know who Faye is."

The line moves as the door swings open, and Ky steps inside. I inwardly curse. I don't know what her agenda is, but the last thing I need right now is Ky discovering I called out Faye's name while I was boning some random chick. I jerk my chin up, gesturing to the empty table in the corner. "Grab that," I holler. "I'll put your order in."

The girl spins around, watching Ky weave a path through the busy café. Slowly, she turns around. "Interesting. Very interesting."

I lean down, putting my face in hers. "I don't know what you think you know, but you're mistaken. Faye is my best friend's girlfriend, and there is nothing going on with me and her. She's over at our place all the time, and I was drunk the other morning. It was a slip of the tongue, and it meant nothing."

"Whatever you say, asshole." She folds her arms, leveling a stubborn look my way.

I narrow my eyes. "If you do anything to cause problems between them, I won't hesitate to take you down. Consider this a warning."

She shoves her middle finger up at me, all brazen like. She starts backing up toward the door, sneaking glances at Ky as she does. "Whatever you say, asshole!" she yells, before pushing her way outside.

I curse under my breath as I watch the confusion spread across Ky's face. The line moves, and I prop my elbows on the counter while I place our orders.

I hand Ky his coffee, taking the seat across from him. "What's her beef?" he asks straightaway.

"Told you already, I don't know," I lie, "but I hope she's not going to become a problem."

"It's par for the course when you screw around. You're bound to meet a few whackos." He blows on the top of his coffee before taking a sip. "All set for Monday?"

The first semester officially starts on Monday, and, contrary to popular opinion, I'm actually looking forward to getting stuck into my studies, especially now I've chosen business administration and management as my major. It's good to have a dedicated focus. Although my schedule is heavy between classes and football, I welcome it. There's less time to think. Harvard suits me so well in a lot of regards. It isn't one of those colleges where football is king and the players are treated like immortals, and I like that. We have decent support at our games, and the team enjoys a certain notoriety, but not every person knows who I am on campus, and I can go about my business largely under the radar. Plus, the professors are excellent, and no one frowns upon you if you take your studies seriously.

I need to graduate with strong results. I know I'm a decent football player, but so are a lot of guys on the team. More than thirty-five ex-Crimson players have been drafted or signed professional contracts with the NFL, but the competition is always fierce, and the odds are slim. I can't count on a professional football career. While it would be a dream come true, I've had a dose of reality these last few years, and nothing is guaranteed.

Thanks to my quasi-orphan status, I'm on a scholarship, and I need to maintain good grades. Usually, you have to find some kind of work if you are on a scholarship here, but I'm exempted due to my football commitments. I have minimal spare time, so I've had to take out a few student loans to cover the rest of my expenses. I prefer that though, and even if I graduate with a mountain of debt, I'd hate to be saddled with work on top of my other responsibilities. Having a job would've given me zero time for partying, which is the only way I'm managing to retain a grip on my sanity in light of my whole unrequited love scenario.

I lean back in my seat, stretching my legs out and crossing my feet at the ankles. "Yeah. I'm ready for Monday. I took some extra classes during summer break so I'm ahead."

"Cool. Have you heard anything from your family?"

Piercing dagger-like pains stab me all over. "Nah, man. Same ole, same ole." I'm downplaying it but Ky knows me too well.

"Shit, bro. I hate that. Are you sure you don't want me to get my parents on the case? I know they could do something."

This is, like, the millionth time he's offered, and I'm really grateful that he wants to help. But no one can. It's an impossible situation. "Thanks, dude. I know you want to help, but it's too risky. I don't know if the Feds are still keeping tabs on me, and I can't take that chance."

I only discovered the Feds were watching me when Faye was kidnapped during senior year of high school. Ky and I had taken off after her, making a botched rescue attempt. If the Feds hadn't shown up, I'm not sure what would have happened. Turns out, they'd been following me for a while. Hoping my renegade parents would reach out to me and they'd have a lock on their whereabouts. But my parents haven't contacted me since they fled abroad over two and a half years ago.

"I thought Kev confirmed they weren't?" Ky responds, taking a big slurp of his drink.

Keven Kennedy has mad hacking skills, an expertise his family—and me by extension—have had cause to lean on a lot in the last couple years. On many occasions, I've been tempted to call him and ask him to search for my family, but I've always stopped myself. While Kev has considerable ability, I still can't take the risk. My family's lives depend on them staying hidden. Still it sucks that I don't even know where they are or what they've been doing these last few years.

"He did, and while I'm not doubting your brother, I'm still being cautious. You never know with stuff like this. The government wants to catch my dad real bad. It's an election year, and it'd make them look good."

"It sucks, man."

"Tell me something I don't know."

We are both quiet for a bit. Thoughts of my family always make me melancholy. It's been so long since I've seen them, and I miss them so much. I hate feeling like this. Aimless, lost, alone.

"Hey, speaking of Keven. It's his twenty-first next week and Mom's throwing a party at the Boston Merrion Hotel on Saturday. You're coming, right?"

"Sure. Wouldn't miss it. Thanks for the invite." He rubs his prickly jaw, looking pensive, and I know he has something on his mind. "Out with it."

"What's going on with you and Rachel?"

I drain the last dregs of my coffee before I reply. "Has she said something is going on between us?"

He shakes his head. "No. Let's just call it intuition."

I may as well come clean. I shrug. "We fucked once. The first time we met. It's no biggie."

A sly smile spreads across his mouth. "You dirty dog, McConaughey. You kept that one quiet."

"It was in the middle of all that shit that was going down. It didn't seem important." That's only a half-truth, though. I didn't want it getting back to Faye that I'd had sex with one of her best friends. I was still harboring hope she'd pick me, and I didn't want it influencing her decision. But that ship has long since sailed, and I figure it's only a matter of time before Rachel fills her in.

"You got feelings for her?"

"Nope." I pop the P, rubbing a thumb across my lower lip.

He surveys me astutely. "Okay. Well, you should know she was with Kev when we vacationed in Ireland last year. I don't know exactly what went down between them, but she asked Faye for his number last night."

I shrug, feigning indifference. "None of my business."

If that's really the case, why is there such a sick feeling in the pit of my stomach?

"Party at Noah's tonight," Ryan says as we walk out of the locker room together. My hair is still damp from the shower, and my legs ache from the extra ten laps coach made me run for arguing with him in front of the team. "You game?"

"Sure." I fling my duffel over my shoulder as we step out into the corridor. The usual groupies are loitering in the lobby, alongside some of my teammates' regular fuck buddies and a few of the guys' girlfriends. I wave to a couple of the girlfriends as Ryan and I walk past.

"Brad! Wait up!" a voice calls out from behind me. Ryan and I turn around, watching a good-looking brunette jog toward us. Her tits are bouncing up and down, capturing both our attention.

"Nice," Ryan murmurs under his breath. "She one of your regulars?"

"I don't have regulars."

"And why is that?"

"I don't have time for a relationship or clingers-on," I lie.

"Hey." The brunette smiles as she comes to a standstill in front of us. She's gorgeous, and she knows it.

"Hey," I reply coolly, wracking my brains to see if I know her. She doesn't look familiar, but that's nothing new. I'm usually completely smashed by the time I take a girl to my bed.

"I was wondering if you were going to the campus party tonight? And if you wanted to hang out?" With the way she's currently eye-fucking me, it's obvious hang out is a polite way of asking for a hookup.

"I'm out of here, man," Ryan says, slapping me on the back with a knowing look. "Catch you later."

"Noah's place?" I ask, leaning against the wall.

"Yes. That's the one." Her eyes spark with hope and desire.

"Have we met before?" That's code for "have we fucked before?" because it's not like I can ask her outright; I'm not a total douche.

"Not really. I'm in your math class, but I don't think you've noticed me. I, on the other hand, have definitely noticed you." The look she gives me is suggestive in the extreme. My brows nudge up in amusement. This girl has balls, and I admire that. She steps into me, placing her hand on my chest. "I just broke up with my boyfriend, and I'm looking for some fun. I heard you're the right guy for the job."

That kind of comment is like the playboy's holy grail. But I'm role-playing, at best, so, it's no surprise I feel strangely empty at her words. I'm debating my reply, when Coach barks out my name. My head swivels. He is standing outside the door to the locker room with his arms folded sternly across his chest, staring at me. He wiggles his fingers in a "come hither" manner.

I maneuver around the nameless girl. "Gotta go."

"What about the party?" She pouts, and it's not a good look on her.

"I'll think about it," I throw out over my shoulder as I sprint toward Coach.

"Take a seat," he says, flopping into the chair behind the desk in his office. I prepare myself for a lecture. "Two things." He eyeballs me. "Firstly, I welcome suggestions from players, but there's a correct way to pitch ideas to me. Arguing with me in front of the team is *not* the way to get my support. I liked your idea, and I'll consider it, but, in future, ask to meet with me in private, and we can discuss it in a professional manner."

"Of course, Coach. I apologize if I was out of line."

He nods, leaning forward and propping his elbows on the desk. "Secondly, get your head in the game."

My eyes pop wide. I'm always focused on the field, and I've never given less than one hundred percent. "My head is in the game, sir. I don't understand."

He sighs, as if he's already grown tired of this conversation. "The girls, the booze, and the partying, McConaughey. They've got to go. I'm not saying you can't have fun or that you can't have a girl, but try and find one you like and just stick with her?"

Huh. I want to tell him I've been there and bought the T-Shirt only to have it ripped right off my back, but I don't think he wants to hear about my romantic drama. "I'll tone it down, sir," I promise.

"Make sure you do. I know I don't need to spell it out for you. This is an important year. This is when scouts really start to take notice. If you want to play in the big leagues, you have to get your act together. NFL coaches do not want players they have to babysit or troublesome PR nightmares. They want professional athletes with leadership potential who are serious about a sports career. You are starting to make a name on campus for yourself and not for the right reasons. If that's happening here, you've got a problem. You hear me, son?"

I gulp, and my Adam's apple jumps in my throat. "Loud and clear, Coach."

His expression softens. "I know you've been dealt some heavy blows, and I admire you for fighting for your dreams, but you've got to push those lingering demons aside before they rob you of the future you want. You are not your father, and you are not responsible for his crimes. You didn't steal client's money. Your father did. You didn't force your family to flee the law. Your father did. You haven't done anything wrong, and if that guilt you're shouldering is because of your father, let it go. No one blames you for that."

That's easier said than done. While my family situation weighs heavy on my mind, and there isn't a day that goes by where I don't worry about my mom and my two sisters, the guilt I'm carrying isn't connected. That's all thanks to the mess in my head over Faye, but Coach doesn't need to know that. He doesn't understand I lose myself in drink and girls to forget the one girl who means something to me.

"Okay." He slams his hands down on the desk before standing up. "Get out of here, and get your head screwed on correctly. I don't want to have to talk to you about this again."

Chapter Four

Rachel

It's Monday morning, first day of classes, and I'm a bundle of nerves, but I'm doing my best to disguise it. I drop into a seat in the lecture hall alongside a girl with chin-length strawberry-blonde hair sitting by herself. She looks up at me and smiles.

"Hi, I'm Rachel."

"You're Irish? That's awesome." Her face lights up. "My cousin is going out with an Irish girl, and she has the cutest accent ever."

I rein in the eye roll. "What is it about Americans and the Irish accent? The amount of times I've had that said to me since I moved here is ridiculous. Back home, there is nothing special about the way I speak."

"It's the novelty factor, I guess." She crosses one leg over the other. "And there's a lot of Irish descendants in Boston." She thrusts her hand out at me. "I'm Lauren, by the way. I'm a newbie. Just transferred from the University of Illinois."

"No way!" A genuine smile graces my lips. "I just transferred from the College of Art and Design in Dublin."

"Awesome! We can be newbies together!"

I smile. "Sounds good." And it does. Apart from Jill and Rachel, I haven't had many female friends. A few girls I hung out with from school disowned me a couple of years ago, not wishing to associate with my new party girl image. And the friendships I made in college last year were fun but nothing permanent. I haven't heard from any of those girls since I left Ireland, although I haven't reached out to them either.

As Lauren and I chatter away, it's as if we've known each other for years, and instinctively I know we're going to be the best of friends.

"She's so lovely, and we just clicked instantly," I tell Faye after leaving our yoga class later that night. "It's nice to have someone in the same predicament as me. Especially because a few of the girls in class seem like total cows and really competitive."

"Tell me about it. You know I've dealt with my fair share of mean girls. Ignore them. It's the best course of action. They'll soon move on to someone or something else."

"I couldn't give a shit really." Truth. "But having a friend helps. Lauren moved here because of her boyfriend. He's a junior in Harvard. He's studying computer science, and I was wondering if Kev knew him."

"That'd be cool if he did. We could all hang out together."

"I can't wait for you to meet her. I think you'll like Lauren too."

"I could use more female friends. I still find it difficult to trust anyone. Last year, so many girls tried to use me to get to Ky or Brad or one of my cousins. It was exhausting and it pissed me off, so I've given up trying to make friends with anyone in class."

"That sucks, girlfriend." I loop my arm through hers. "But it's your fault for falling for such a hottie. Girls will always want your guy."

She groans, pushing wisps of damp hair off her sweaty forehead. "Don't mention the war. Brad hooked up with this total bitch the other morning. Before she left, she totally eye-fucked Ky in front of me. I wanted to claw her eyes out."

"No way! That is so uncool. Who does that? Screws one guy and then eyes up his best friend as she's doing the walk of shame?"

Faye opens the door to the smoothie bar, and I follow her in. We join the long queue. "Well," she says, looking a little guilty. "I may have inadvertently contributed to that." I send her a curious look. "I walked in on them having sex, and she stormed out shortly after that, so I guess she had reason to blame me but not to ogle my boyfriend and tell him to call her sometime."

I choke on a laugh. "Oh my God. You caught him screwing? For real?"

Her face scrunches up. "Please don't remind me. It's like the images are imprinted permanently on my brain."

"It can't be that disgusting. Brad's a total ride." The words slip out before I question the wisdom of them.

Her gaze bores through me. "If I didn't know better, I'd say you have a bit of a crush on Brad."

I snort, moving up the line. "Puh-lease. As if. The guy's a jerk. I don't crush on jerks."

Or anyone.

That would imply having to indulge certain feelings, and I really try to avoid that at all costs.

She tilts her head to the side, looking contemplative. "He's really not. Underneath, he's still the same sweet guy I met when I first moved here. Don't let him fool you otherwise. He's going through some stuff, and the last couple years have been hard on him. I don't know why he acts like that around you."

I pull my invisible bravery hat on. "I have a theory about that."

"Okay. Let's hear it."

I clear my throat and then release a flurry of words. "I think it's because we fucked, and he regrets it, and he most certainly doesn't want you finding out about it."

Faye is rooted to the spot, her mouth hanging open. "Wait? What? You slept with *Brad*?" Her brow puckers. "When did this happen, and why am I only hearing about it now?" A hurt look is etched on her face, and I feel like a crappy friend.

The line moves forward and so do we. "Look, don't get mad. I was going to tell you, but then you were going through all that stuff, and things were already awkward enough between you, Ky, and Brad, and I didn't want to add to that. I didn't deliberately decide to hide it from you, and it wasn't like it was planned or anything. It just happened."

"You still should've told me. Damn, Rach, you keep far too much stuff locked up inside. It's not healthy, and it's going to come back and bite you one of these days."

Tension ties my shoulders into knots. Not this again. Deep down, I know Faye is right, but it's baby steps for me. One thing at a time. "I'm sorry, and I'm telling you now." I fill her in on what went down that time we visited the Kennedy house in Wellesley. She listens without interruption, as we inch farther up the line.

"That sounds really hot," she concurs, when I've finished talking. There's a wicked grin on her face as we sit across from one another, sipping our smoothies.

"Believe me, it was. Best sex of my life." My core throbs in remembrance. Or it could be misuse. It's been a while, but that's by choice.

"So how do you feel about him now?"

"I hate him."

Her lips twitch. "No, you don't."

I stretch across the table, putting my face in hers. "Yes. I. Do."

She leans back in her chair. "What aren't you saying?"

"I talked to him in Nantucket. Made a peace offering, and he rejected me outright. He was actually really mean." A tightness invades my chest with the memory.

She frowns. "That doesn't sound like Brad."

"You think I'm making this shit up? He made his feelings very clear. He doesn't want to be my friend, to have anything to do with me."

She goes quiet. "I think that might be my fault," she says after a bit.

"How do you figure that?"

"Because of the way he says he feels about me."

"The way he feels about you, you mean."

She shakes her head. "Brad doesn't love me, not like that. He just thinks he does."

I look idly out the window. "I don't know him well enough to agree or disagree with you. He just doesn't like me." I shrug, even though it hurts to admit it, and I can't figure out why I even care. Other people's opinions of me usually just float over my head. You have to be in touch with your emotions to actually care what people think of you either way. But with Brad it's different. I just haven't worked out why.

"That isn't it. Trust me. I know the guy. There is no reason he would have for hating you. I'm telling you, this is tied up with me. I bet he feels something for you, and he isn't ready to face up to what that means." She sighs. "God, I wish there was something I could do. This is tearing us all apart, and I know it's charging toward some kind of tipping point. I'm scared of the fallout. I already feel guilty enough."

"Faye, you have nothing to feel guilty about. You never led him on. You were up-front with him the whole time, and he knew how you felt about Ky."

"I still kissed him twice, and I never should have done that. It gave out mixed signals."

I sip my drink. "That's water under the bridge now. It's been years, Faye. Brad knows the score. If he hasn't moved on, that is on him, not you."

"What are you going to do about him?"

I slurp my drink before replying. "Keep out of his way as much as possible. I don't want to add to your burden, so I'll try to be on my best behavior whenever I'm around him. It'll be challenging, but I'll give it my best shot. It's just, sometimes, he makes me so mad I could spit."

"You sure you don't have feelings for him?"

"When have you ever known me to catch feelings? Chill. Don't worry. It'll all be cool."

Faye leaves the smoothie bar before me. I've arranged to meet Keven outside to ask him my favor, and I don't want her around to overhear our conversation, so I told her he's running late and shooed her out the door. I'm standing at the corner of the building, waiting for Kev to show his face, when a conversation drifts my way.

"I'm telling you, there's something going on there. Something Brad doesn't want me to discover. He basically threatened me, and no one does that unless they have something to hide," a female voice says. I inch closer to the wall and take a quick peek around the corner. A blonde is standing with her back to me, talking to two dark-haired girls.

"Why do you even care? So what if he's hiding something," the taller brunette asks.

"Because I can't stand cheaters," she hisses.

"Or you want to dig your claws into Kyler Kennedy?" The shorter brunette smirks.

Blondie tosses her long hair over her shoulder. "I'd be doing Kyler a favor. I'll bet he wouldn't be pleased to know his best friend calls out Faye's name when he's in the middle of sex with another girl."

What the ever-loving fuck?

A hand lands on my shoulder, and I jump about ten feet in the air.

"Sheesh, Rachel. It's only me," Kev says, as I struggle to recalibrate my breathing.

I slap his massive arm. "You scared the hell out of me, Kev. Didn't your mum ever tell you not to sneak up on unsuspecting girls?"

"Sure. Same way I figure your mom told you never to eavesdrop on other people's conversations."

"How much of that did you hear?" I level him with a somber look.

"Enough to know Brad is more fucked in the head than I realized." He reclines against the wall, folding his arms across his very impressive chest. A chest I've been up close and personal with.

"I know, but you can't say anything. Let me talk to him."

"I didn't realize you two were close."

"We're not. He hates me, but I'll make him listen."

Kev's eyes drill into me. "I'm sure he doesn't hate you, Rach. That's a virtual impossibility. You're far too pretty and sweet."

My insides turn to mush. "That is one of the nicest things anyone has ever said to me."

He quirks a brow. "That's sad, if it's true. You're a gorgeous girl, Rachel, and you should've been told that a thousand times."

My cheeks turn red, amazing myself. I cannot remember the last time I blushed. Probably before I turned thirteen, when I was still innocent.

Kev grins. "Aw, you're so cute when you're blushing."

"Shut the fuck up. And don't tell anyone." I grin back at him. "I've a rep to maintain."

"These lips are sealed."

Talk of his lips brings memories of our time together to the forefront of my mind. We spent a lot of time making out the summer before last when he visited Ireland with Faye, Ky, and the rest of the Kennedys. Those were some fun times.

His expression turns more serious, and I'm guessing he's worked out where my mind just went. "Look, Rachel." He smooths a hand across the top of his cropped hair.

I hold up a hand. "No need to say it, Kev. I'm not looking to pick up where we left off in Ireland. I'm not in the market for a boyfriend or a hookup, so stop looking so worried."

His shoulders visibly relax. "We were good together, but it was a one-time thing. I don't do relationships either."

"We're cool, Kev. Honestly. Don't sweat it." I swat his arm. "It's like I told you that time we talked. I need a do-over, and you helped, you know."

He looks surprised. "I did?"

I nod. "Yeah. You ultimately led me on a path to this point, so I guess I owe you."

"You don't owe me a damned thing. Just be happy. You deserve it."

My cheeks flush again, throwing me for a loop. "I, uh, thanks."

He grins again. "I did wonder when you asked to meet up."

"Oh, yeah." I clutch onto the lifeline. "About that. I need your help."

Taking my elbow, he steers me away from the building, only stopping when we reach an empty bench. He looks all around before nodding for me to sit down. "Okay. What's up?"

I fish the documents out of my bag, handing them to him. "First up, this is a paid gig." I thrust a wad of cash at him.

He swats my hands away. "I don't want your money."

"You're taking it." I open his palm, shoving the money in, and closing his fist around it.

He takes one look at the fierce determination on my face and relents. He pockets the cash and eyeballs me. "What do you need me to do?"

"I need two things. I need to be invisible, and I want you to track someone for me. It's all there in the paperwork." His penetrating gaze unsettles me. "Stop looking at me like that. If you don't want the job, I'll find someone else to do it." I reach over him to snatch the documents back, but he lifts them over his head.

"Calm down. Of course, I'll take the job."

Air whooshes from my lungs in grateful relief. Silence engulfs us as he examines the paperwork. When he notices the name, his head lifts. My eyes dare him to pry at his peril. We stare at one another, and I thrust my shoulders back, confidently holding my own. He continues scrutinizing my face, and a line of sweat glides down my back.

One of the main reasons I approached Kev to do this—besides his mad IT skills—is because he can be trusted to keep my confidence, and he won't ask questions. The guy is uber-private, and I know he'll be discreet. But if he makes a liar of me now, all bets are off. I'll find someone else who will do it, no questions asked.

"I can do this," he finally confirms. "It might take a couple of weeks as I've already got a heavy workload with college and other stuff. Which is more important to tackle first?"

I mull it over. "Hide me, then track him."

"Consider it done." He stands up, extending a hand toward me. I let him pull me to my feet. "I'm not going to ask because I know you don't want me to, but if you're in trouble, I want you to know you can come to me. About anything. At any time."

Tears prick my eyes. "Thank you," I whisper, suddenly choked with emotion. I haven't told Kev anything, yet he can tell this is serious shit. "I've never had anyone to call."

Quick as a flash, he pulls me to him, wrapping his warm, muscular arms around me. I nuzzle into his body, struggling to breathe over the pressure in my chest. He rubs his hand up and down my spine, and, gradually, I calm down. I shuck out of his arms. "Thanks, Keven. You're such a nice guy."

"Ssh!" He puts a finger to his mouth. "Don't ever repeat that statement in public. You're not the only one with a rep."

I laugh, and his expression softens. "I'll keep in contact with you via text, but the messages will be cryptic."

"I understand." Faye told me he's messed up in all kinds of crap, and I'd rather not know. I've enough of my own crap to sort through.

"In terms of the tracking, do you want a weekly or monthly report?"

I shake my head. "Neither. The only time I want to hear from you is if he steps foot on US soil."

"Understood."

"Thanks, Kev. I really appreciate this."

"I'm glad to help."

He won't let me walk home by myself, even though it's only five blocks away, insisting on driving me.

As I wave him off outside our building, a spreading warmth heats up all the frozen parts inside me. I've never had anyone I could confide in or call upon before. Knowing Kev is on my side, even without having the facts, helps relieve some of the anguish and fear. As I skip into the building, a surge of hope bubbles to the surface.

I'm taking back my life, and I'm no longer alone.

Chapter Five

Brad

To the birthday boy," Faye says, raising her glass in a toast. The rest of the Kennedy brothers, Melissa, Lana, Rachel, and I lift our glasses. It's Saturday night, an hour before the party officially starts, and we are enjoying a few drinks while Alex and James Kennedy rush around the grand ballroom of the Boston Merrion Hotel with the event planner, making sure everything is perfect.

We played our first game of the season this afternoon, and it was a landslide victory. We beat URI fifty-one to twenty-two, so I'm definitely in the mood for celebrating.

While most of us aren't legal yet, James organized a few buckets of beer, wine, and vodka on the down low. The bartender sends surreptitious glances our way every now and then, and judging by his frown, he isn't happy, but I guess no one wants to challenge the mighty Kennedys, and I'm guessing money has changed hands. And it's a private function, so it's not like we're deliberately flouting the law by drinking in public.

"To Kev," Kal says, as everyone chinks glasses. "My hero. When I grow up, I so want to be a badass, mean, and moody gray-hat just like you."

Lana pinches Kal's arm, as everyone else either laughs or groans.

"You're an idiot." Kev shoves Kal good-naturedly. "I sympathize, Lana." He sends his sister-in-law-to-be a benevolent look.

"Thanks. I need all the sympathy I can get," Lana teases, shooting Kev and Kal a wide grin.

Kal snakes his arm around his fiancée's waist, holding her close as he kisses her quickly. They are giving Ky and Faye a run for their money in the PDA stakes, but I'm happy for them. They've had their own fair share of crap to deal with, and it's good to see them come out on the other side of it.

Kev trails behind Rachel as she rushes to the door with a squeal. Discreetly, I cast an eye over my shoulder. She's wearing a figure-hugging red, knee-length dress that showcases her rocking body to perfection. I've been hiding a massive boner since she arrived. I can scarcely take my eyes off her, which is problematic for a whole heap of reasons. I watch as she greets a pretty girl with strawberry-blonde hair, pulling her into a hug. Kev is laughing with the guy she arrived with—a tall, skinny, nerdy-looking dude.

"She looks fucking hot." I twist my head around. Kent's eyes are dark with lust as he stares at Rachel.

"She's way out of your league." I raise a bottle of beer to my lips. "Don't bother wasting your time." I know Kent has hit on Rachel a few times, and she's always knocked him back. Kent is one of the triplets, and although they turn eighteen in a couple months, he's too young and too immature for Rachel. I don't need her to tell me that.

If I've a chip on my shoulder, Kent has a boulder on his.

"Is that a note of jealousy I detect?"

"Nope."

"So, you don't care that Kev seems to be staking a claim then?"

I jerk around at that, watching with bile in my mouth as Kev takes Rach's hand and pulls her into his side. She snuggles into him, and I feel like puking.

Kent sniggers. "Yeah, thought as much. You haven't taken your eyes off her since she showed up. Man up, Brad, or you'll lose her."

I almost choke on my beer. "I think I've heard it all now. The day I take romantic advice from Kent Kennedy is the day the world ends."

"Hardy, har." He elbows me in the ribs, swiping my beer and draining it in one go. "I bet I've had more girls than you."

He probably has. "Don't be so crude, Kent, and it's not a competition."

"Hell yeah." Kent smirks, looking at something over my shoulder. He rubs his hands gleefully. "Now it's time to get the party started." He smiles devilishly at the girl who lands in front of him.

"Hey, sexy." Faye's half-sister, Whitney, purrs as she runs her hands up Kent's chest. "Were you waiting for me?"

"You betcha, gorgeous." He slings his arm around her shoulder, grinning like he just won the lottery.

"I know you." She gives me the once-over with a mischievous smile.

"I'm Brad. Ky's friend. We met at the Kennedy house one time."

"Oh yeah. Now, I remember."

"You look different." The last time I met her she was younger, still a kid. She had really long blonde hair with bright pink strips in it. Now her hair just about brushes her shoulders and it's a dark purple color. She's taller, and with the amount of makeup on her face, and the barely-there dress that is molded to her definitely-not-childish curves, she could easily pass for nineteen or twenty, although I know she's at least three years younger than that.

Faye yanks Whitney out from Kent's protective embrace, pulling her into a monster hug. "Hey, Whit. How are you? I'm so glad you could come."

Whitney extracts herself from her big sister's embrace, wrapping her arms around her waist self-consciously. "God, you are so uncool. Who does that?"

A glimmer of hurt flashes across Faye's face, and my blood boils. "Don't be such a bitch." I stand up, walking to Faye's side. "You should be glad your sister is happy to see you."

"Butt out, butthead." She pouts, and Kent snorts with laughter.

Faye shakes her head, and my eyes lock onto the long, elegant column of her neck. She's wearing her hair up tonight, and she has a gorgeous black and gold dress on that hugs her curves to perfection. Her stunning long legs are encased in towering sandals, bringing her at eye level with me. Lightly, I touch her arm. "You okay?" She turns to face me, and I suck in a breath. Her stunning blue eyes are heavily made up, and she looks even more gorgeous than usual.

"I've got this." Ky appears on her other side, drilling me with a subtle look that says "back the hell off."

I didn't realize when I declared my feelings that I was condemning my friendship with Faye too. The only time I get to talk to her is when Ky is by her side, and that just makes everything awkward, so we don't talk much. And I miss her. We were good friends our senior year, and we helped each other through stuff. Now, I feel like I'm not even allowed to be her friend, and that sucks.

I take a couple of steps back, swipe another beer, and drain it in one go. When I reach for another, I notice Faye frowning. I feel a drunken coma coming on, and I don't need any bystanders. "I'm going to stand by the bar," I say to no one in particular.

"Hey, I'll come with." Kal pecks Lana on the lips and saunters over to me, slapping me on the back.

He doesn't say a word until we're propped against the counter of the bar watching the band rehearse on the other side of the room. More guests are starting to arrive, but the room still looks half empty. Knowing the Kennedys though, they will have invited half of Boston, and it won't take long for the place to fill up. "What's up?" Kal asks, eyeing me shrewdly.

"Nothing much, bro. How's Hewson?"

His entire face lights up at the mention of his young son, and he removes his cell from the pocket of his pants. "Here." He pulls up some pictures. "This was him last week when Lana and I took him to the park."

Hewson is captured on a swing midair, and his head is thrown back in laughter. "Man, he's getting so big."

"He's nearly one and a half now," Kal proudly admits. "He's a cool little dude even if he is like a wannabe demon when he doesn't get his own way." He chuckles.

"Sounds like he's taking after the Kennedy side of the family," I tease.

"No doubt about it." Kal grins. "He's my mini me in every conceivable way."

"Don't let Lana hear you taking all the credit."

"She'd agree with you. He's like a clone of me. It's incredible. There are some days when I still can't believe he's a part of me. It's humbling."

"Shit, bro. When'd you go and get all grown up?" I tap my bottle against his. Kal has always felt like my little brother, as much as he is Ky's.

Because there isn't that much of a gap in our ages, we tended to hang around quite a bit outside of school.

"Don't be fooled. I'm still a big kid at the best of times. Lana likes to say she has two kids to look after." He laughs.

"Have you set a wedding date yet?"

He shakes his head. "Nah. No rush, dude. We want to finish college and put down some permanent roots before we do that." Lines crease his forehead as he looks over my shoulder.

I follow his gaze, noticing the eldest Kennedy brother, Kaden, greeting a cute redhead at the entrance to the ballroom. I've seen him with her before, but I can't remember her name. Kade's wide shoulders are even wider, and his bulging biceps are straining the material of his shirt. "Someone's been hitting the weights."

Kal snorts. "I think Kade is taking this crap with Kev to a whole new level."

"What? They're still not talking? And you think he beefed up to piss Kev off?" That seems far too juvenile for Kade.

"Who knows?" He shrugs. "They talk but not like they used to. They were always tight, but since they got into that fist fight in Ireland, they've been at each other's throats. They're not even rooming together anymore." Kal scowls again.

"What?"

"I can't believe he's still with her. I don't know what he sees in Tiffani."

I skim my gaze over the redhead's body, focusing on her awesome chest. "I can see two reasons." She turns around, showcasing a pert ass. "Make that three." I smirk. Kal stares at me like I've just sprouted horns. "What? Has monogamy turned you into a pussy, too?"

"Dude, there's some weird shit happening here. I think you've morphed into me, and I'm acting more like how you used to. You know, when you were decent." He pins me with a knowing look, and I snort. An excited glint appears in his eye. "It's like that movie, you know the one with Lindsay Lohan in it, where she switched bodies with her mom." A huge grin appears on his face, and he clicks his fingers as the memory comes to him. "Bro, we're exactly like that. It's our own version of *Freaky Friday*."

"If that's the case," I say, taking a swig from my bottle, "I guess it'll be me taking Lana to bed later then." His face pales, and I bite back a laugh. "Just think about that when you're fucking her. That it's really me boning her. Me with my hands all over her gorgeous body." I wink at him, watching as his face turns even paler.

"You're a twisted bastard, McConaughey." I send him a smug grin. "Takes one to know one, asshole."

Girlish giggling from behind has us both turning around before Kal can come back with a retort. Lana, Faye, Rachel, and Melissa—Keaton Kennedy's girlfriend—are all huddled over a phone, laughing. Kev appears behind Rach, placing a hand on her bare shoulder as he leans over to look. A muscle ticks in my jaw, and all trace of good humor evaporates.

"Nothing's going on with them," Kal offers up, astutely assessing the situation.

I take another swig of my beer, my eyes never leaving Rachel. She is looking up at Kev, saying something to him, and she's giving him the biggest smile ever. A sour taste builds in the back of my throat. "None of my business," I say through gritted teeth.

"I see how you look at her. And I see how you still look at Faye when you think no one is watching." He scratches the back of his head. "I'm here if you ever want to talk about it."

Well, damn. That's not something I ever expected. I can't ever remember having a serious conversation with Kal. He really has matured. "Thanks, man, but there's nothing to talk about."

"You're a good guy, Brad, and you deserve to be happy. If Rachel could be that for you, don't mess it up."

"She appears to be already taken."

"Kev isn't interested in her like that. They're friends. Nothing more."

Huh. Could've fooled me. The guy can barely keep his hands off her. Not like I care, anyway.

I lose count of the number of beers I knock back in the next couple hours. When the familiar numb feeling crawls over me, I finally start to relax, loosening the top button of my shirt as I make my way back over to our table. The party is in full swing now. The ballroom is packed to capacity, and the dance floor is hopping as Kev's college friends rock it out alongside members of his family and his parents' friends.

I've only just dropped into a seat beside Ky when Faye's voice projects around the room. "Can I have everyone's attention please," she asks from her position on stage. "And I need the birthday boy up here right now." A few of Kev's friends holler, nudging him toward his cousin.

"What's going on?" I ask Ky.

"Oh, man, this is going to be so funny. Kev is going to kill her." He snorts, poking me in the ribs. "Just listen and watch."

"In Ireland, we have a tradition when you turn twenty-one, and it's something that I think Keven will get a kick out of." She purses her lips, struggling to contain her mirth. "Come here, big fella. Don't be shy."

We get up and move around the side of the room. Kev walks toward Faye with a dark look on his face, and I can't help laughing. He looks like he's walking the green mile.

One of the waiters places a chair in front of the stage. Faye steps down beside it, still clutching the mic and grinning like crazy. When Kev arrives, she shoves him down into it. "Now, I need twenty-one girls to give our birthday boy twenty-one kisses." Kev eyeballs Faye, but the corner of his mouth twitches. The crowd roars their approval.

"Oh, yeah. I'm so doing this on my twenty-first," Kent says, materializing beside us with Whitney in tow. She stomps on his foot. "What the hell, Whit?" He bends down, rubbing his sore foot. He glares at her. "That fucking hurt. And stop being a baby. It's not like we're fucking exclusive or anything. Chill out."

"You're a jerk," she hisses.

"Whatever." He throws his hands in the air.

"Those two are a disaster waiting to happen," Ky mumbles.

"Okay," Faye calls out, reclaiming our attention. A big group of girls are eagerly awaiting direction. "Line up in a row, one behind the other." Faye leans down, talking quickly to Kev. She nods before straightening up. "Rach? Girlfriend, up here." She gestures with her fingers, and Rach strides through the crowd with her head held high drawing the attention of every male in the room. My eyes are like heat-seeking missiles tracking her every step. They huddle in conversation, and then Rach arches a brow before swinging her gaze on Kev. He pulls her down, whispering in her ear. I'm dying to know what's going on, but I don't want to ask the question and have Ky questioning me about her again. Rachel nods and then moves to the very end of the line.

The band starts playing, and slowly the girls move up to Kev, offering kisses. Most just kiss him on the cheek; a few give him quick pecks on the lips. A couple seize the opportunity, kissing him deeply before he can pry them off. From his relaxed wide-legged stance and the smug grin on his face, I can tell he's enjoying this.

"Well, dammit all to hell," Ky exclaims, folding his arms. "I think this may have backfired. He's fucking loving this."

"No shit, Sherlock," Kal says. "As if any dude is going to complain about twenty-one girls lining up to lock lips." Lana elbows him sharply in the ribs, sending him a pointed look. He plasters an obviously fake indignant look on his face. "Except me. I would kill Faye stone dead if she tried that on me."

The line is dwindling, and my nerves are stretched thin. Faye plants herself in front of Rachel and I watch them giggling. Faye leans down, and kisses Kev on the cheek. My heart is in my mouth as I watch Rachel step up to him. He pulls her down into his lap, and a chorus of wolf whistles rings out across the room. I run my hand around the back of my neck, wanting to look away but conscious of Ky's observant gaze. He's watching my reaction, and I'm not going to give him any ideas. I know he's trying to pawn me off on Rachel in the hope I'll forget about Faye. I'm not stupid. It's what I'd do if I was in his shoes.

Kev's arms snake around Rach's back, creeping up her spine and winding into her hair. He pulls her face to his and melds his lips to hers. The crowd goes wild as he kisses the shit out of her. My stomach lurches to my toes, and I grind down on my molars, feeling far too much for the amount of beer I've consumed.

Eventually, he stops molesting her mouth, stands up, and takes her hand. Alex and James walk to their son, handing him a gift-wrapped box, and Rach discreetly steps to the side. Her eyes zone in on my mine from across the room, and we share a loaded look. Ky watches silently, and that should be enough to make me look away, but it's like I'm frozen in time. My eyes refuse to look at anything or anyone but her.

And she doesn't break eye contact either.

Not until Kev turns around, stretching his hand out and motioning her forward. I turn around and grab another bottle of beer from the bucket, having seen enough.

Another couple of hours go by, and I'm starting to see double. I'm being an unsocial prick, sitting at our table, drinking, and watching everyone else having fun on the dance floor. A shadow looms over me. "Can I talk to you?" Rachel asks, and I tilt my head up. She takes the seat beside me without waiting for a reply.

"Where's your boyfriend?" I snap.

"I don't have a boyfriend."

"So that wasn't your tongue shoved down Kev's throat earlier?" My mouth pulls into a sneer.

She sends me a short, biting smile. "Oh, no, it was. My tongue was most definitely in his mouth."

I growl, grabbing my beer and knocking it back. Little worry lines crease her brow as she watches me. "Like I care if you have a boyfriend," I mumble after a bit, more to myself than her.

She sighs again. "Keven is not my boyfriend, nor is he ever likely to be, so stop being such a grump."

I harrumph. "I think you need to tell Kev that."

"Not that it's any of your business, but Kev and I are just friends. He wanted me to pretend to be his girlfriend at the party because there's this girl here from his class who won't leave him alone. He slept with her once, and she refuses to go away or something. I don't know, and I don't care. Forget about that. I need to ask you something."

I put my drink down and look into her eyes. A little amber fleck twinkles in the middle of her rich brown eyes, captivating me. I've never noticed it before. Her lips part gently as she rakes her gaze over my face. It's like being stripped naked. The intensity burns the skin off my bones. I should look away, but I'm enraptured by her. She pulls on her lower lip with her teeth, and it's like a shot of pure, raw lust has been injected into my bloodstream. Memories of fisting my hands in her hair as I fucked her swarm to the forefront of my mind, and I'm getting hot. My cock twitches in my pants. Before I know what I'm doing, my hand is cupping her face. "You look really beautiful tonight." I rub my thumb across her bottom lip. "Your mouth is so sexy."

Wait. What the fuck am I saying? What the hell am I doing? I drop my hand from her face, averting my eyes.

"You're hammered." She sighs.

"What?" I jerk my chin up, watching as she shakes her head.

"Drunk. Smashed. Two sheets to the wind. Totally fucking useless to me." She rolls her eyes.

That raises my hackles. "Excuse me?"

She stands up. "I'll talk to you when you're sober."

I rise, gently taking her arm. "I'm perfectly fine. You can say what you need to say now."

She looks down at where my fingers are curled around her lower arm. I remove them immediately. "You are about as far from fine as a person can get."

"You, of all people, have a nerve to judge me," I spit out.

"In case you're too drunk to notice, I'm completely sober. I've been drinking mineral water all night."

I snort. "Sure, you have. And I'm Mother Teresa."

"Fuck you, Brad."

My eyes darken as I stare at her. "In your dreams, Red."

"In my fucking nightmares, more like." She folds her arms across her chest, and the movement pushes her tits up higher in her dress. I wet my lips as I gape at her gorgeous chest. Rachel has a great rack—even if I didn't get my hands on her naked flesh that time we fucked. But I felt her through her thin dress and she's perfect. A decent handful but not too much. My eyes are glued to her chest, and it hasn't skipped her attention. Her eyes narrow to slits, but I don't care. The lure of all that luscious creamy skin is too much to resist, and I lean forward and kiss her.

I get one brief kiss in before she pushes me off. Searing pain rips across my cheek as she slaps me. "Don't you dare touch me when you can barely stand up straight. And, for the record, I don't have a boyfriend because I don't want a boyfriend. And that extends to casual hookups and you too."

Then she turns on her heel and storms off, leaving me looking like a complete idiot.

Chapter Six

Rachel

A few hours later, I'm in my pajamas, making tea and toast, when the front door clicks open and shut and Ky wanders into the living room. Faye slides off the kitchen stool and goes to her boyfriend, wrapping her arms around his waist.

"Did you get him home okay?" I ask, taking a third mug out of the overhead press.

"Yeah. He was totally smashed, but I managed to get him back to the apartment and put him in bed. He was snoring when I was leaving."

"Maybe you should stay there tonight," Faye says, although I'm sure that's the last thing she wants. "What if Brad pukes in the night?"

"It would serve him right to choke on his own vomit." Ky presses a kiss in Faye's hair. "He was way out of line tonight."

I carry two mugs in my hand as I walk around the other side of the counter. I hand them to Faye and Ky. "Yes, he was, but it's not a big deal."

"Try telling that to Kev."

My brows nudge up. "You do know your brother and I are only friends?"

"I know. Kev told me what you agreed to do, but that doesn't mean he was happy about the way Brad treated you. He wasn't, and neither am I."

I walk back to the kitchen as the toaster pops. "I appreciate you both looking out for me, but it's no biggie. I'm more worried about Brad. He was in a right state."

Faye pins me with a knowing look. I stay quiet as I butter the toast. I place the plate in the center of the marble island and pull myself up onto a stool. "I know what you want to say. That's the way I used to get, right?"

Faye takes the stool beside me, and Ky sits down across from her. "Yeah. I've seen you like that before."

I chew on my toast, thinking back to how out of control I was. "I've been like that way more than you've ever seen," I admit, being wholly truthful for once.

"I'm glad you're not doing that anymore. Jill and I used to worry about you so much." Mention of our other friend brings a tsunami of guilt to the surface. I haven't been a very good friend to her lately, and she was only trying to help.

Ky is quietly eating and drinking as he listens to us talking.

"I know you did. I used to worry about myself." I level an earnest look at her as I take a gulp of my tea. "I'm trying to get my head on straight now. I didn't like the person I was when I drank, so I'm determined to stay in control now." In fact, I think I was a borderline alcoholic or close to the point of no return. Now, two drinks is my safe limit, and I'm sticking to that.

Faye reaches across the counter, squeezing my hand. "I'm really proud of you, Rach."

Her words fill my heart with happiness. "Thanks. I'm proud of me, too." It hasn't been easy. For so long, drink and sex were my crutches. My way of escaping reality, and I lived for weekends when I could get out of my face and forget my life. But it was only delaying the inevitable. It was only ever a temporary release. So, I know, more than anyone, what Brad is feeling, and I feel for him. I do. Yes, he's a dickhead, and he knows how to wind me up until I'm seething, but he's in so much pain, and he's lashing out.

I'm furious with him for earlier. Getting all jealous and then trying to kiss me in front of everyone when he was drunk. The old me would've had no issue going there with him, but I'm changing. I want guys to respect me. To respect my body. Sex is a whole other minefield I'm trying to decipher.

I'm not destined to fall in love. I know that's not in the cards for me, that I'm incapable of sharing every part of myself with someone in such an intimate way, and I've resigned myself to that fact. It is what it is.

Maybe, at some point in the future, I'll want to give it a go, but, for now, I don't want a relationship.

However, there's a part of me that wants to help Brad. Because, from what I've seen, he doesn't have anyone else. Ky would be there for him if he could, but their situation is impossible, and there's no way the two of them can have an honest conversation when Brad is convinced he's in love with Faye. I saw him tonight, watching her. He has feelings for her all right, and I don't want to get mixed up in the middle of that, but it doesn't feel right leaving him by himself.

I've been there, and it's the loneliest place on the planet.

Waking up with one hell of a hangover and dealing with the solitude and the return of all those thoughts you want to banish so badly is the worst thing on Earth.

Besides, I still need to ask him about what I overheard outside the smoothie bar on Monday, so I can kill two birds with one stone.

"I'm going to go to your place and keep an eye on Brad. I don't think he should be left alone." Faye and Ky exchange a knowing look. "I've been in his shoes, and I know what it's like to wake up hungover, sick, and by yourself. I'm looking after him as a friend, nothing more, so you can forget any matchmaking ideas. I'm not interested in Brad like that."

"Sure, you're not, little liar," an inner voice taunts as I climb off the stool and walk to my room to get dressed.

The smoke alarm is going off as I turn the key in the lock and step into Brad and Ky's apartment thirty minutes later. "Shit!" I race into the kitchen. Brad is slumped over the kitchen table, fast asleep, snoring, and completely oblivious to the swirling smoke quickly filling the airspace. I swat my hands through the smoky cloud as I make my way to the cooker. A deep-fat fryer is on the hob and the hob is *on*.

The whole place could have gone up in flames.

I shudder, horrified at the images playing in my mind.

Wrapping a damp cloth around my hand, I turn off the cooker. Flames are licking the base of the deep-fat fryer as I grab the extinguisher off the wall and spray it all over the hob. I only resume breathing when all the flames are out. Very carefully, I carry the offending item outside to the balcony with the damp cloth protecting my hands. Placing it on the ground, I turn back inside, coughing profusely. I leave the double doors open to help clear out the smoke. My eyes are stinging, and my throat is dry and achy after only a couple minutes in this environment.

Brad is moaning and clutching his head in his hands when I walk back into the kitchen. The smoke alarm is still going off, so I run to it, jumping up and waving a cloth back and forth underneath the device until it finally stops. My ears offer up grateful thanks.

"What the hell?" Brad croaks, looking around in confusion. He is sitting at the kitchen table in only a pair of boxers, but I'm too fucking angry to consider all he's got going on.

"You nearly set the place on fire!" I screech, and his hands automatically cover his ears.

He looks up at me in confusion, his brow puckered. "What are you doing here?"

"Saving your sorry ass!" I sag in the chair alongside him, suddenly drained. "Shit, Brad!" I shake my head, looking at him through a new lens as my anger gives rise to concern. "You could have died if I hadn't decided to come check on you. Others could have died."

His face turns a sickly green color, and he pales at my words. Jumping up, he knocks his chair to the ground and lunges for the sink. A pang of sadness washes over me as I watch him throw up the contents of his stomach. It's too close to home. *How many times was I alone puking by myself after purposely overindulging?* An acute twisty pain spears me on the inside. *How easy would it've been for me to make a similar mistake to Brad? To be so drunk, and out of it, that I'd put the fryer on the hob instead of plugging it in?* Too easy. That's the scary truth of the matter.

I get up and move to his side, rubbing my hand gently up and down his back. I grab a wad of kitchen towel and hold it out to him. He takes it from me, looking up as his stomach expels for the last time. The look of sadness and vulnerability in his gaze almost undoes me. The only other time I've seen such a tortured soul is when I've looked in the mirror. His eyes fill with tears, and I don't hesitate, pulling him to me and wrapping my arms around his waist. He clings to me, and his head drops to my shoulder. His body trembles against mine, and silent tears tumble down my cheeks. I don't know if I'm crying as much for me as I am for him, because my head and my heart are aching so badly I can't make sense of my emotions at the moment.

After an indeterminable amount of time, his body stops trembling, and he lifts his head. He looks into my tear-sodden eyes and then presses his forehead to mine. I almost pass out from the noxious fumes, but I consciously hold my breath and give him a minute before easing out of his grasp. I take his hand. "You need to sleep this off. Come on."

I lead him to his bedroom and help him back into bed. I fix the covers over him and clear a space on his bedside locker. "I'm going to get you some water and tablets. I'll be right back." I touch his cheek and offer him a small smile.

When I return, he is already fast asleep. I leave the tablets and water by his bed, crouching down to look at him as he sleeps. He looks so innocent, so young and untroubled like this. And so gorgeous. Brad McConaughey is a lot of things, but there is no denying he's a beautiful man. His hair is much shorter than when I first met him, but that cropped look suits him. He has the face to pull it off. With his long lashes, stunning blue eyes, and carved face, he could easily model. If his football career takes off, and he becomes a celebrity, I can see him gracing the front cover of magazines and not looking out of place.

Very quietly, I tiptoe out of his room and make my way to Ky's room where I promptly conk out the instant my head hits the pillow.

Sunlight is streaming through the open window when I wake sometime later. Rubbing my eyes and fighting a yawn, I reach for my phone, startled to see it's after eleven already. My throat feels like someone took sandpaper to it. After a quick trip to the bathroom, I pad to Brad's room and peek in. He is on lying on his other side with his naked back facing the door. The covers are all tangled up in his legs, and he's snoring loud enough to wake the whole neighborhood. I must have been in quasi-coma mode not to hear that ruckus during the night.

I head out to the kitchen, surveying the damage to the hob. After I've cleaned it up, it looks in working order, except for the spot where the fryer had been. That is covered in congealed melted plastic, and there's no way I'm tackling that.

I pull out a griddle pan and fry up some bacon, mushrooms, and tomatoes on one of the rear rings.

I have just dished up two plates when Brad wanders into the kitchen, still in only his tight-fitting black boxers, not bothering to conceal the sizeable erection he's sporting. He is yawning and running a hand through his hair when he stalls the minute he spies me. His eyes startle in confusion. "Rachel." His voice is hoarse. "What are you doing here?" His gaze drops to my sleep shorts and down my bare legs and feet.

I carry the plates to the table. "You don't remember?"

Slowly, he shakes his head, and I can clearly spot the confusion mixing with panic in his eyes. I smirk, knowing full well where his head has gone. "Sit, eat, and I'll explain."

Air expels from his mouth in a loud rush as he walks cautiously toward me.

I laugh. "Relax, we didn't sleep together although you did drunkenly kiss me at the party."

He groans, looking embarrassed. "Unfortunately, I remember that part of the night. I, ah, sorry about that. I was being an asshole." Like a naughty little boy, he looks up at me with a pleading face.

"I've already forgotten about it. Please just sit down and eat. You need to get some food into your system."

We eat in silence for a little while before he puts his cutlery down and clears his throat. His eyes dart between me and the open French doors. "Why is the deep fryer out on the balcony?"

"Because it was on fire when I arrived."

His face drops. "What?"

I nod. "You were fast asleep in the kitchen, the fryer was on the hob, and the smoke alarm was going off when I arrived. You were totally out for the count." I push my half-eaten plate away, my appetite vanquished. "You could have died."

His Adam's apple jumps in his throat, as he fixates on the fryer. Turning around, he looks at the stove and then up at the ceiling. My eyes follow his movement, and I gasp. There's a dirty, smoky mark on the ceiling in the shape of a giant mushroom cloud. "Oh my God." His voice is strained. "I ... I don't even remember putting it on." He clamps a hand over his mouth. "Thank you," he whispers, after a minute. "I don't know why you're here, but thank you."

I nod. "I didn't think you should be by yourself, so I took Ky's keys and grabbed an Uber. I can't even think about what would've happened if you'd been here alone." And, the more I think about it, the more annoyed I'm getting with Kyler. Yes, I know things are awkward as fuck between them, and he can't bear to be away from Faye, but Brad is still his friend, and he should not have left him alone last night. Not when he was clearly incapable of looking after himself.

"Why do you care?"

I pin him with a frank look. "You know why." We stare at one another. "I've been drunk and alone. I've puked in the kitchen sink too many times to count. I could have set the house on fire. I had no one looking out for me either."

A muscle pulses in his jaw. "I don't mean to be rude, but I'm not your responsibility, and I'm a big boy. I fucked up, but that's all on me."

I level an incredulous look at him. "It was more than just fucking up! You could've died! This is serious, Brad, and I know what I'm talking about." I glare at him. Maybe he's still drunk, or he's lost too many brain cells to alcohol, but I'm not taking this bullshit.

"I know it's fucking serious! I know I need to get my shit together," he seethes, leaning across the table. "But it's my life, and no one asked you to get involved."

I stand up, seeing red. "You are the most ungrateful, stupid, idiotic dickhead I've ever met! And you infuriate the fuck out of me!" I scream.

He scrubs a hand over his unshaven jaw. "Look, Rachel, I—"

"No." I raise a palm in front of his face. "I don't want to hear it. I'm the fucking insane one for even worrying about you in the first place. You can set your grouchy ass on fire the next time, and see if I care."

I stomp toward the bedrooms, spinning around as I remember the main reason why I came here. "By the way, I overheard some girl outside the smoothie bar telling a couple of her girlfriends how you called her Faye when you were fucking her. It sounded like she was planning on making trouble. I wanted to give you a heads-up, because if you don't sort that shit out and she does anything to hurt my friend, I am holding you personally responsible."

He angles his head to the side. "I've dealt with that. She won't cause trouble."

I snort, shaking my head. "Yeah. That's reassuring. Not." I glower at him.

"She won't be a problem!" he yells. "And it's none of your business so butt out."

"Next time I even consider coming here to check on you, I'm going to give myself a lobotomy," I toss out before flouncing to Kyler's room to get dressed.

I don't see Brad again, even though I had half-hoped he would cop the fuck on and apologize for his assholery ways, but it didn't come to pass. That jerk is the most stubborn man I've ever met.

As I pull the door shut on their apartment and start pounding the pavements home, "Dickhead, dickhead, dickhead" is my constant silent mantra. Never again, I promise myself. I am never putting myself out for that dickhead again.

Chapter Seven

Brad

Ky rips me a new one when he returns home late Sunday night, and I let him. There isn't anything he says that I haven't already said to myself. Last night was the wake-up call I needed. I need to get my act together before I permanently fuck things up.

The rest of the week passes by quickly and uneventfully. I avoid all parties and social activities and focus on classes, study, and football practice.

It's Saturday, and we obliterated our opponents in the game earlier, and everyone on the team is buzzing—our season is off to a flying start. I'm crawling the walls and in desperate need of a change of scenery by now, so when Ryan confirms that Noah is hosting a celebratory party for the team at his place, it takes me all of two seconds to agree to attend.

The place is crammed to the rafters when we arrive, and we make a beeline for our crew. As usual, a group of girls are surrounding the football players. Normally, I'd pick a chick early in the night and go back to her place, but I'm not feeling it tonight. I've been in a weird funk all week. I'm determined to end the night relatively sober, so I'm sipping my beer instead of chugging it back like usual.

I ignore the busty blonde trying to catch my eye and close ranks around the guys, keeping her out. Ryan chuckles. "What's gotten into you?"

"Nothing. Just not in the mood tonight."

He places his hand to my forehead. "You running a fever or something?"

I swat his hand away. "Funny, I could ask you the same thing."

"Chels and I have agreed to date, and I promised her we'd be exclusive, so I've got a reason."

"No shit?" All Ryan did the last semester of our freshman year was complain about how clingy Chelsea was.

He scratches the side of his head. "You know she lives in the adjacent town to mine, so, we hung out a bit this summer, and I changed my opinion of her. I like her and the idea of sticking with one girl for a while. These groupies are starting to piss me off."

"Christ. If anyone has a fever, it's definitely you."

He laughs, tipping beer into his mouth. "Maybe." His gaze roams over my head, and a sly smile coasts over his lips. "Hey, isn't that the girl you were talking to after practice last week?"

I turn around, catching sight of the gorgeous brunette heading my way. "Yeah."

"You hook up already?"

"Nope." I take a decent-sized mouthful of my drink. "She's on the rebound and wanted me to be her fall-back guy. Her assumption that I'd readily agree pissed me off."

Ryan chuckles. "Dude, what's crawled up your butt? Last year, you wouldn't have given two shits about that."

"Yeah, well, I'm reassessing a few things."

"Hi, Brad." The brunette curls her fingers around my biceps, smiling up at me. "Remember me?"

She's wearing a tiny tank top that leaves little to the imagination. Her skintight jeans mold to her form, and there's no denying she's a gorgeous girl. She licks her lips as she leans up on her tiptoes and presses her mouth to my ear. "I was hoping you'd had time to consider my proposal."

I'm not really feeling it, but it's been two weeks since that disaster with Kayla or Callie or whatever the hell her name was. And all week I've been rubbing one out in the shower with fantasies of Rachel playing in my mind, which is something I don't want to encourage. Maybe I need to get back in the saddle.

I smooth a hand over my head, staring at her lush mouth. “I might be open to persuasion.” Excitement lights up her eyes. “If we do this, it’ll only be a one-time thing.” I make sure to be up-front about that every time.

She nods her head enthusiastically. “I’m totally cool with that.” Yeah, that’s what a lot of the clingers say.

Ryan has a knowing grin on his face. “Shut it,” I say, taking the girl’s hand and leading her out to the corridor. I press her up against the wall and lean in. She looks up at me expectantly, her hands snaking around my neck. My fingers tangle in her hair as I angle my head and lean in. Her mouth is soft and welcoming against mine, and I kiss her gently at first. Her delicate floral fragrance swirls around me, and I grip her hips, drawing her body flush against mine. She gasps into my mouth. I deepen the kiss, grinding my pelvis against hers.

Her fingers dip under my shirt, and her hands start exploring. As we kiss, a million thoughts swarm my mind. I try to focus, but my mind keeps wandering, and I’m merely going through the motions. She’s gorgeous, and a great kisser, but I’m not feeling this. Not feeling it at all. All the little raspy sounds she’s making are irritating the fuck out of me, and there’s literally zero action happening down south. That’s never happened to me before, and it’s frustrating. Irked, I kiss her harder, delving my hands back into her hair. An image of Rachel wrapped around me, digging her nails into my back, and writhing against me crawls into my mind, and I rip my lips from the brunette, falling back as my dick finally sparks to life.

“What’s wrong?” she asks, pouting.

I exhale noisily. “Sorry, but I’m not into this.” Her eyes drop to my crotch, and she smirks. Her arrogance fucking pisses me off. I lean in, my jaw drawn tight. “Sorry to disappoint you, but that’s not for you. There was zero life in my dick the entire time I was kissing you.”

She narrows her eyes, and her lower lip wobbles. Now, I feel like utter crap. Just ’cause I’m all fucked up doesn’t mean I have to take it out on her. “Look, it’s not you, okay. You’re gorgeous, and at any other time I’d be down for this, but the timing is off. Besides, you look like a nice girl. You should find someone other than a football player as your rebound guy. Better yet, go back to your boyfriend.”

I'm horrified when tears well in her eyes. "Yeah, it's not me, right, as if I'm going to fall for that. All the girls said you were a dead certainty. That you screw any female with a pulse." She pushes off the wall, furiously swiping at the falling tears. "I'm the one girl on campus you don't want to screw, and I'm basically on my knees begging? Go fuck yourself, asshole. I'm far too good for the likes of you anyway."

She shoves past me, bumping into someone as she goes.

"What did you do to her?" Ky asks, lounging against the wall and eyeing me warily.

"Told her I wouldn't fuck her. Apparently, I screw anything that moves, so the rejection didn't sit well with her."

Ky arches a brow. "You turned down pussy?"

"You don't have to act so surprised."

"It's not exactly your usual M.O."

I shrug. "Maybe I'm sick of whoring my way around campus."

Ky straightens up, mumbling something under his breath that sounds suspiciously like "about time." He bores a hole in my skull. "What's going on with you, bro?"

I sigh, leaning my head back against the wall. "I wish I knew."

Ky moves over beside me, mirroring my position. "We haven't spent any time together in ages. Why don't we hang out tomorrow? Want to head to the track?"

This is the first time in months he has expressed interest in doing something without Faye tagging along. And I haven't been to the Middleborough motocross track in months. There was a time it was like our second home, but these days, I have zero free time to indulge my hobby. I pick my head up. "Yeah, let's do it, man."

We head back into the party, and I stifle a groan when I spy Rachel with Faye along with that girl and her boyfriend from the night of Kev's twenty-first.

"Yay!" Faye exclaims when she sees me, like I'm her favorite person in the world. "We were hoping you'd be here. You've been laying low all week."

"Yeah, well. There was good reason for that." Out of the corner of my eye, I spy the brunette I was just kissing in a huddle with a few girlfriends. They all throw daggers at me, but I pretend not to notice.

Ky doesn't move to his girlfriend's side, which surprises me. He is usually stuck to her like glue at these things. Faye introduces me to Lauren and her boyfriend, Gavin, who it seems is in class with Keven. Rachel gives me a curt hello and then proceeds to ignore me. Ky and I chat about crap, and it almost feels like old times.

"Well, if it isn't the asshole extraordinaire," a female voice pipes up from behind me, sarcasm dripping off every word. Rachel visibly stiffens. I angle my head, inwardly cussing when I lock eyes with Callie.

"Trying to have a private conversation here, Kayla. Run along now." I glare at her before turning away again.

"My name is Callie, asshole."

"And mine's Brad, but you know that too." Having made my point, I take a swig from my beer as Ky silently surveys our exchange. He has that neutral expression on his face. The one that means he's calculating behind his indifferent mask.

"You're Kyler, right?" she asks in a sweet tone of voice, eyeing him like he's her next meal. I catch Rachel's eye, and she's silently imploring me to do something. Very gently, I take Callie's arm. "Let me help you find the door."

"Get your hand off me," she slurs, swaying on her feet a little. "I'm saying what I came here to say."

Reluctantly, I let her go. "Don't do this. Please. Let's go outside and talk."

She snorts in a most unattractive fashion, before straightening up, shooting me a superior look. "Yeah, I don't think so, asshole." She raises her voice, and turns toward Kyler again.

Rachel rounds our group, hissing in my ear. "Do something! Just drag her out of here! They can't hear it like this!"

"I can't force her to come with me against her will, and she'll only shout it out anyway," I whisper back. "There's no stopping this."

"I think you should know, Kyler," she bellows out, successfully capturing the interest of the room. "That your best friend imagines he's fucking your girlfriend when he's with other girls. He called me Faye several times during sex."

She's lying. It slipped out once, but I'm not going to win any brownie points by publicly correcting her. It's still one time too many.

"I can't help wondering if it's more than just his imagination though." Callie sends a suspicious look in Faye's direction. Faye has turned the color of milk, and she looks like she wishes the ground would swallow her whole. She hates being the center of attention, and the entire room has muted, watching the drama with bated breath. "How much do you trust your girlfriend, and is that wise?" She peers adoringly at Ky.

"That's enough." Rachel places herself in front of Callie, glaring at her. "You're a poisonous little bitch, and no one believes your lies. You think you're the first girl to spread rumors in an attempt to dig her claws into a Kennedy? This is old news. No one believes you, so just fuck off before you embarrass yourself even more."

"I'm not lying!" Callie roars.

"Tell that to someone who actually gives a crap," Rach coolly replies, and I want to kiss the fuck out of her feisty lips. She's handling this perfectly. "You're pathetic. I feel sorry for you."

"Time to go, Callie," Noah says, appearing beside her. He nods at me. "Let me escort you out." She doesn't go quietly, continuing to mouth off. Hushed murmurs filter around the room as everyone waits for our reaction.

"I'm sorry about that." I can't even look at Ky or Faye.

Ky slaps me on the back, more firmly than necessary. "Everyone just act normal," he commands in a low voice, grinning at me as if he found this amusing. "I'm not airing our dirty laundry in public or giving any weight to those rumors."

Rachel returns to Faye's side, whispering urgently in her ear. Lauren and Gavin don't know where to look.

Ryan saunters over with Chelsea hanging off his arm. "She's a crazy bitch, and she's been mouthing that crap all week to anyone who'll listen. Don't pay any attention to her." His worried gaze flits between Ky and me. "Hey, did you hear ..." I tune him out as he starts talking game stats and strategy, not that I'm ungrateful he switched the subject, but all I can think about is how the hell I'm going to explain this to Ky.

Twenty minutes later, Ky eyeballs me, speaking quietly. "I think it's safe to leave now, and you're coming with us."

I wet my dry lips, nodding and wishing I'd consumed a bucket load of beer. I have a feeling I'm going to need it for this conversation.

No one really talks as we make our exit, not until after Lauren and Gavin have said their goodbyes and we are back in our apartment.

The second the door shuts, Ky rounds on me. "Is it true?"

There's no point lying. "Partly."

"Explain that," he demands.

I can't even look at Faye as I confirm it. "I called her Faye once. It was unintentional. I was drunk, and it just slipped out. I'm sorry."

Ky grabs tufts of his hair and starts pacing the room. The rest of us are afraid to even breathe.

I finally glance at Faye. She looks really upset, and I don't blame her. "I'm really sorry, Faye. The last thing I want is to embarrass or upset you."

Ky shoves me. "Don't fucking talk to her! Don't even look at her!" He's close to losing it.

"Babe." Faye moves to his side, pulling him away from me. "I think we should go. Brad didn't mean it, and—"

"Of course, he fucking meant it!" Ky roars, and she flinches. "Do you not see how he looks at you?!"

Faye prods a finger in Ky's chest. "Don't you fucking shout at me! Just stop it. Stop this or I'm leaving."

He throws his hands in the air. "I might've known you'd take his side."

"Are you for fucking real?" she screams. "You're acting like an idiot and all because some bimbo wanted to cause trouble." She grabs her purse from the table. "Well, congratulations, bimbo," she yells, looking at the ceiling. "You win!" She whirls around to her boyfriend. "Happy now? I'm going home, and you're not coming with me. Not when you're in such a foul mood. I've had about enough of this shit to last a lifetime." She storms out of the apartment, and Rachel runs after her.

"We're not done talking about this," Ky fumes, jabbing his finger in my direction. "But I'm not letting her leave by herself." He races out after her, and I collapse on the ground.

"I told you to deal with her," Rachel says, materializing a few minutes later. "I just knew she was trouble."

"I thought you were gone."

She sinks down beside me, pulling her knees to her chest. "Oh no. I'm not getting in the middle of that. I'll just wait here for an hour and then go home. Hopefully, he's cooled off by then."

"You can stay the night here. I don't mind."

"Yeah, I don't think so." Her lips curve into a sneer.

A muscle clenches in my jaw. "I didn't mean anything by that."

"Sure. You were just offering out of the goodness of your heart."

I hop up, incensed. I've taken enough crap from girls tonight. "You know what, Rachel. I really couldn't give a shit. Stay here or leave. Makes no difference to me. If I wanted to fuck someone tonight, I had plenty of offers. I certainly don't have to lower my standards." I send her a pointed look, even though it's a low blow and a total lie.

She scrambles to her feet, her cheeks inflamed. "You are officially the world's biggest dickhead, and I wouldn't fuck you again even if my life depended on it."

"Yeah, I seem to recall you telling me that before. Sounds like you're trying real hard to convince yourself of that. Isn't that right, Red?" It's like enraging a pit bull.

She pokes her finger in my chest, and steam is practically billowing out of her ears. Her skin is flushed red, and there's a thunderous look in her eyes. Yeah, I've definitely poked the beast. "In case that's too complex for your simple brain"—she spits out the words—"I hate you. I fucking detest you. I cannot even stand to be in the same room as you. I am done with this shit. Stay the hell away from me."

Because I'm an idiot, I smirk.

Her hands ball into fists, and I think she might actually hit me.

Instead, she emits a roar of frustration and stomps to the door, slamming it violently behind her.

Chapter Eight

Rachel

I hope Ky kicks Brad to the curb. I hope he ends up miserable and alone. I hope he gets crabs and his dick falls off. I hope he drinks himself into a coma and never wakes up. Okay, I take that last one back. That's taking it to extremes. I don't want him to die. I just want him to stay the hell out of my life. He's ruining my do-over. All week, he's been hijacking my mind, and I hate it. He's making me think about things I don't want to think about. Making me feel things I don't want to feel.

I try to wipe the murderous look off my face as I pass a couple in the lobby. Pushing the door open, I suck in a greedy mouthful of air, internally talking myself off the ledge as I slow my pace. The street is deserted, and apart from the glow from the street lamps, it's pitch dark. I lean against the wall and pull out my phone, calling up the Uber app. I try to rein in my anger as I wait for the driver. Brad gets under my skin like no one else, and I'm so confused by the torrent of emotions I feel.

The door slams, startling me. Brad appears in my line of sight, and I groan. His facial features relax when he sees me.

"Fuck off," I hiss before he's even reached me.

"What are you doing, Red?" he asks in a breathless voice.

What's it look like, dickhead. I think it, but I don't say it. Instead, I choose to ignore him, humming under my breath and looking everywhere but at him. It's super childish but hugely satisfying.

"Rachel? Do you need me to call an Uber, or have you already done that?"

I whistle a tune, looking at my feet this time.

"That's very immature," Brad says, and I lift my head up, whistling in his face.

His face turns red, and he looks like he wants to give me a few slaps. "I just wanted to make sure you got home safely, but if you want to act like you're five, that's fine. I'm not going anywhere, but I'm more than happy to stand here and ignore you too."

He folds his arms and leans his back against the wall. The movement stretches his shirt across his chest, and I hate that my treacherous eyes involuntarily scan his ripped chest and abs. He catches me looking and smirks.

That smirk of his holds prime position on my Top Ten list of Most Annoying Things. Seriously, every time he smirks, I want to kick him in the nuts. Or make him eat a fist sandwich. My hands tighten into balls, and I really think I could hit him. I mentally count to ten, praying for patience I know I don't possess. "Go away, Brad. I'm not your responsibility," I snap through gritted teeth, tossing his own words from last week back at him.

"I don't give a crap what you think. I'm not leaving any girl out on the sidewalk at this hour by herself. You can hate me all you want. I don't give a flying fuck."

"I swear you were put on this planet just to irritate the crap out of me."

"Touché, sweetheart." He taps his fingers off his forehead in mock salute.

"I'm not your sweetheart, your Red, or your anything!" I stomp my foot in annoyance. It was either that or smash my fist in his face.

He shrugs, attempting to smother a laugh, and that only riles me up further. He knows he's getting to me, and I hate that I'm falling into his trap, but I'm too enraged to think logically. "I can't believe you just stomped your foot. You're really indulging your inner child tonight."

"Shut. Up. Dickhead." I push off the wall, scrunching my hands in my hair. I'm feeling too much, and that's never a good sign. "And you can't talk considering you have the attention span of a gnat and a brain that's ruled by your dick."

His mouth twitches. "You're hot as hell when you're mad."

I round on him, jabbing my finger in his chest. "No! You don't get to do this."

He acts all innocent. "Do what?"

"Flirt with me! I won't allow it!"

He laughs. "I'll flirt with you if I like, and there isn't a damn thing you can do about it until the Uber gets here." His eyes smolder as he zeroes in on my mouth. His tongue darts out, and he licks his lips in a deliberately suggestive manner. "The feistier you are, the more you turn me on." My throat runs dry, and an almost painful ache starts throbbing in my core. I want to punch myself in my greedy, needy vagina.

No, no, no, no. Hell no. This is not going down.

I don't want him.

And I'm *not* remembering the explosive orgasm he gave me last time we shagged. I'm not remembering how intense it felt when he was inside me. I'm definitely not remembering that.

"I like that," he murmurs, and the seductive quality to his voice has me biting down hard on my lip. It's either that or do something ridiculous like moan.

"Like what?" I snap.

"The way you're feeling me up." He smirks again, and the urge to punch his lights out is almost overpowering.

"I'm not ..." I trail off as I zone in on my hands, gliding up and down his impressive chest. *How the fuck did that end up happening?* I step away, pulling my phone out with trembling hands and start pacing the pavement. I need to get away from him before I do something stupid like jump his annoyingly sexy bones. *Where the hell is my Uber?* My knees are like jelly, and I'm feeling all hot and bothered underneath my clothes. I hate that he has this effect on me. Hate it.

No guy has ever made me feel so much with so little.

I usually pride myself on my lack of feeling, and Brad is really messing with my mojo.

"Rachel."

I lift my head up and draw in a gasp. He is stalking toward me with the darkest, most lust-filled expression in his eyes. *How the heck am I expected to resist him when he looks like that?*

I hold out a hand. "Stop right there, mister, and don't come any closer."

He shoots me a wicked grin. "Or what?" he asks, tilting his head to the side in a cocky manner. "What will you do to me if I close this gap and shove my hand in your panties? What will I find if I push my fingers inside you? Are you wet for me, Rachel? Do you want to fuck me as much as I want to fuck you right now?"

My eyes flit to his jeans, and there's no way I could miss the giant swell of his erection. My knees almost buckle from under me. He takes another step forward, and I take another step back. "Stop. Don't take another step." I cringe at the sound of my hesitant, breathless voice.

"You're the girl who told me the best way to numb emotion was to do this. Get drunk and fuck. I'm not that drunk, but I want to fuck. I want to fuck you. We can fuck against the wall again, but I'd rather not give any of my neighbors a show." He holds out his hand. "Come on, Rach. Don't think. Let's just do this. We both need the release."

His hand levitates in the gap between us, like a predator dangling candy in front of a child. My core pulses with need, and the devil on my shoulder is screaming at me to screw him. He must sense the confusion in me. Slowly, he lowers his other hand, rubbing his palm up and down his arousal.

Holy shit. I'm in deep doo-doo with this dude. He's twisting my insides into knots. Making me want things I shouldn't want.

He watches me watching and his chest swells. "I'll make it good for you, Rach. Last time was too quick. Let me make you feel good. Let me worship your body all night long."

Oh, *hell*.

That sounds good.

Too good to pass up.

All the fight leaves me. My greedy vagina wins out. The inner devil on my shoulder squeals with joy as I fling myself at Brad. His strong arms go around my waist, and his mouth crashes down on mine without hesitancy. We devour one another like we can't get close enough. His mouth is soft and warm gliding against mine, his tongue demanding as he parts my lips and delves inside. My heart is beating ninety miles to the hour, and I think I'll die if I don't get my hands all over him. Every inch of his rock-hard body is pressed against mine, igniting every cell, every nerve ending, with liquid lust. I have never been this horny. Never craved a guy as much as this, especially not when I've been sober.

Sex and me have a weird, complicated connection, but, in this moment, I feel almost normal. And I'm not sure what I think about that. All I know is I want to stop thinking and just feel this. Feel Brad worship every inch of my body. I whimper in the back of my throat

"Upstairs. Now," he demands, breaking the kiss and taking my hand.

I keep my head down as we race through the lobby.

The second the elevator doors close, Brad is on me, his mouth plundering mine with the same fervent need. His hand creeps under my dress and into my knickers. He thrusts a finger inside me, and I cling to his shoulders, digging my nails into his toned flesh as I cry out. "As I thought. You're fucking dripping, Red."

The elevator pings, and I stagger out of the lift as if in a daze. Brad keeps a firm hold of my hand as he practically sprints to his apartment. The warmth from his hand seeps into my skin, heating me all over.

He fumbles with the keys, cursing when they drop to the floor, and I smile. He's as flustered as I am, and that's good to know. That I'm not in this alone. I'm purposely not engaging the rational side of my brain because my body will kick the shit out of me if I quit this now. I couldn't run away even if my mind demanded it. My body craves him like I've never craved a guy before.

The instant Brad pulls me into the apartment, he attacks me all over again. My back slams into the door as he backs me into it. His hands fist in my hair, and he angles my head, melding his mouth to mine. His tongue swirls into my mouth, and I groan. I yank his shirt out of his jeans, my hands slipping under as I explore his bare chest. He shudders under my touch, and that only turns me on more. He lifts the hem of my dress, hauling it up my body, and I release my hands, allowing him to pull it off me. I stand before him in my matching black lace undies and high heels.

He drinks his fill, his gaze raking me from head to toe, and I'm on fire from the intensity of his focus. "You are so beautiful, Rachel. Absolutely stunning."

His dark eyes are cloaked in desire as they lock on mine. I grab a fistful of his shirt, pulling him from the hall toward the bedrooms. He stops in the living room, pushing me up against the wall and kissing me so hard I feel it all the way to my toes. Overcome with lust, I snatch his shirt, yanking it apart with force. Buttons pop, flying all over the place. I toss the ripped shirt aside and dip my head, licking a line from the top of his jeans all the way up his chest. He tastes and smells divine. So masculine. So earthy and musky, and I need to feel him in my hands. I pop the buttons on his jeans and slide my hand inside, wrapping around him. He gasps. "Shit." Grabbing the back of my head, he aligns our mouths once again. I shove his jeans and boxers down, as our kissing grows more and more frantic. Honestly, I think I'd crawl inside him if I could. My body's on fire, and I'm moaning and writhing against him with reckless abandon.

Without warning, he steps out of his jeans, kicking them away, and grips my hips, lifting me up and effortlessly throwing me over his shoulder. I yelp as he swats my butt. "I am going to fuck you until you pass out," he promises, and I bite my lip hard as my pussy pulses in expectation.

He stops outside his door, gently placing me back on the ground. His eyes are almost fully black with desire as he stands before me utterly naked. He's magnificent. His body is a work of art. All defined curves, sharp lines, and carved angles. I want to lick every inch of him, and that thought rattles me.

Brad is changing me, and that scares me as much as it enraptures me.

He drags the tip of his finger under the strap of my bra, pulling it down one arm. Then he moves to the other side, doing the same. Bending his head, he runs his mouth across the swell of my breasts, and I stumble, my legs almost going out underneath me. Quick as a flash, he unclips my bra and flings it aside. He stares at my tits, and my nipples harden under his smoldering gaze.

"I have been fantasizing over your tits, but, fuck me, Rach, my imagination didn't do you justice. You're gorgeous." He lightly traces the tip of his finger over one breast and then the other.

It's like they are hotwired to my pussy, and I almost come on the spot. I have never been so aroused, and so needy. "Brad, I need you inside me. Now."

He kicks the bedroom door open with the back of his foot, never taking his eyes off me. His look turns serious. "I want this, Rachel. I want this really badly. Do you?" My mouth has gone dry again. I nod. "I need you to say it, beautiful. All joking aside, are you sure? I might die of the worst case of blue balls if you back out, but I won't hold it against you."

I wrap my arms around his neck, pressing my body flush against his. "I want this. I want you. I want you to fuck me until I pass out."

His mouth crashes down on mine, and that's the end of all conversation.

Chapter Nine

Brad

When I wake the next morning, I'm immediately conscious of two things. One: my body aches everywhere—a combination of tired muscles from the game and a delicious achy feeling from the mammoth sexathon with Rachel. And, two: the gorgeous creature I spent hours worshiping last night is still here, curled into my side, looking totally angelic in slumber. Her head is resting on my chest, and my arm is wrapped around her naked back. Our legs are tangled in each other and the sheet.

I rarely let girls stay over, preferring to call an Uber and escort them outside once the dirty business is over. But I was insatiable last night, and I couldn't bear to part with Red. I guess we both fell asleep from sheer exhaustion at some point.

She stirs, and little wisps of hair flutter across her brow. I take a quick moment to study her before she wakes up, opens her mouth, and hostilities resume, as I've no doubt they will. Her skin is flawless and a gorgeous creamy color, her cheeks flushed a little from the heat. Her lush mouth is slightly parted, and her lips appear still swollen from my kisses. Her long lashes are thick and lustrous as they flicker open. The hand on my chest moves southward, and my erect cock throbs with need. You'd think after five rounds last night, I'd be all out of juice, but, I'm learning, with Rachel, there appears to be no such thing. There's no denying the powerful attraction between us.

"Oh, fuck."

My little firecracker is fully awake. I clear my throat. "Morning."

She scrambles away from me, like she's just been electrocuted, grabbing the sheet up under her arms to hide her naked breasts.

It stings, and I switch to defensive mode. "No need to act all shy now, Red. I've seen all the goods." And some. Memories of last night, unhelpfully, flood my brain, and there's no disguising the bulge under the sheet.

"Shit, what time is it? I'm meeting Lauren and Faye at eleven."

"It's just past ten."

A flurry of expletives leaves her kissable mouth, and I chuckle.

"I need to get dressed." Her eyes dart around my room, and a tiny frown creases her brow. Her lips purse as she remembers the trail of clothes we left in our wake.

I fling the covers off and stand up, stretching my arms out over my head as a massive yawn rips from my mouth. Out of the corner of my eye, I spy Rachel doing her best not to look at me. I smirk, and her eyes narrow to slits. "See something you like, Red?" I wink.

"Can you at least put some boxers on?"

"And ruin my fun? I happen to like watching you squirm."

She sticks her tongue out at me, and I laugh. "Now I'm just remembering all the things you did with that tongue last night." Her cheeks inflame, and, shit, is feisty no-bullshit Red actually genuinely embarrassed?

She bounces back quickly. "A gentleman wouldn't be such an ass the next morning, but I guess I should've known to expect this from you." She folds her arms across her chest and glares at me.

Rachel's already made her feelings perfectly clear through her actions, so I'll make this real easy for her now. Besides, it's better to be *the rejecter* than *the rejected*.

"Chill the fuck out, Red. We had sex. Big deal. It's not like anything's changed. You're a great fuck but still a complete pain in my ass." I turn my back on her rapidly reddening face and walk to my dresser, removing a clean pair of boxer briefs.

When I turn around, she is standing behind me with the sheet wrapped around her body and her hair sticking out all over the place. The urge to grab her and kiss her is riding me hard. Fuck this girl. She is a temptation I don't want or need.

"You're still a dickhead, and I'm blaming last night on temporary insanity."

"I'm blaming it on wild monkey lust. No point in lying to oneself, Red." Smirking, I mess up her hair, knowing it will totally piss her off.

She slaps my hand away, and, if looks could kill, I'd be ten feet under by now. "I don't care what you call it, but it should never have happened. It's never happening again."

I rub a hand over my erection, preparing to finish this off. "Drop to your knees and we'll call it quits." I'm an asshole. I know it. But it's far too easy to wind her up. And I'd much rather deal with her anger than face facts, because this girl stirs too many emotions in me, and I've too much crap going on in my life right now to add to it. Having her hate me is the best policy. Never mind that I already want a repeat of last night. Red is right about one thing. That shit ain't happening again.

My cheek stings as she slaps me across the face. "You're a despicable human being. Truly despicable. Is this the way you treat every girl after sex? No wonder you have such a rep on campus." I shrug, refusing to allow those words to infiltrate the armor around my head and my heart. "Stay away from me, dickhead. I mean it this time. And if you dare breath a word of last night to anyone, I will string you up by the balls and castrate you slowly, inch by inch, until you're begging me to stop."

A loud throat clearing startles both of us. I jump back, and she screams. Our heads jerk to the door. Ky is lounging against the doorframe with a knowing look on his face. He dangles a lacy black bra from the tip of his finger. "I think this might belong to you." He offers it to Rachel, and she walks toward him, snatching it away with a horrified look on her face. Ky produces a bundle of clothing and hands it to her. "Your dress?"

Her face has turned puce, and I take pity on her. Grabbing a pair of sweatpants from my dresser, I walk to the door and push Ky aside. "Let's give the girl some privacy." I close the door behind me and follow Ky to the kitchen.

"Dude, please put those on." He gestures toward my sweats. "Eating breakfast with your giant boner staring me in the face is not my idea of a pleasant Sunday morning."

I get dressed and saunter to the coffee machine, switching it on. A new layer of stress heaps on top of me as I turn to face my friend. He reads my expression instantly. Sitting in a chair at the kitchen table, he drops his head in his hands. I watch him silently. After a couple minutes, he looks up at me. "Look, about last night..." He trails off, clearly at a loss for words, and I get it. I don't have a fucking clue what to say either.

I pour two black coffees and hand one to him, slipping into the seat across from him. "Do you want me to move out?"

"What?" He looks surprised. "No. Of course not."

"It's not like we even see all that much of each other anyway. I doubt you'd even miss me."

He curses, dragging a hand through his hair. Dark circles line the space under his eyes. Either he had trouble sleeping or he also indulged in a late night sexathon. "I've been an ass."

I almost fall off my chair. "What?" Now it's my turn to act confused.

"Rachel tore strips off me last week for leaving you alone, and Faye has been nagging me too." He scrubs a hand over his chin. "I haven't been a very good friend to you, Brad, but I'm going to try harder if you'll do the same." He doesn't need to elaborate on that statement. I know what he's alluding to.

"What do you think I'm trying to do?" I arch a brow, gesturing toward the bedroom with a nod of my head at the precise moment Rach makes an appearance.

The look of hurt on her face is hard to miss.

Aw, shit. I didn't mean for her to hear that. For it to be misconstrued. I stand up. "Rachel, I didn't me—"

She slams past me. "Save your breath, dickhead. I've heard just about enough from you today." She tosses a quick glance over her head. "See you later, Ky." Offering me one last glare, she storms out of our apartment, and the door almost lifts off the hinges.

"Jesus Christ, Brad!" Ky sighs in frustration. "You've just made things a million times worse. Now, Faye is going to be fucking pissed. You can't bone her friend and then treat her like a piece of trash."

I stand there incredulously although I don't know why. "Everything doesn't revolve around you and your fucking girlfriend! And I'm not the only asshole around here!"

He jumps up. "You know what? Screw this shit. I came over here as a peace offering, hoping we could go to the track and iron out our differences, but there's really no point. Not when you seem to enjoy hurting the people you profess to care about. I've got better things to do with my Sunday." Grabbing his hoodie, he stalks out of the apartment without uttering another word.

I slump in my chair, wondering how the hell I'm managing to fuck up my life so spectacularly.

I return to bed and sleep for a couple hours. The smell of Rachel's perfume lingers in my room, infuriating me at the reminder of my latest fuck up. Any enjoyment from last night is erased by the ugliness that was today. I strip the covers off my bed and add them to the laundry pile before making my bed with fresh sheets and opening both windows to air the room out. As if removing every trace of her will fix my broken brain. Then I mope around the living room for hours, feeling sorry for myself, trying to evict all the memories of last night from my mind. But it's futile. Every touch, every caress, every blissful sensation is imprinted on my mind, and it replays on a continuous, torturous loop until I can stand it no more. I need to get out of here.

I change into running shorts and a sleeveless top and go outside. I decide to head to the Malkin Athletic Center to pound the treadmills. It might help calm me the fuck down. I start off jogging at a gentle pace, only picking up speed as I enter the Harvard grounds. When I run past one of the upperclassmen residential houses, two figures standing in the shadows snag my attention. I stop running, concealing myself behind the nearest tree as I watch Rachel and Keven Kennedy talking animatedly. She is gesturing wildly, and she looks upset. His big hands land on her shoulders, and I go rigidly still. He is peering deep into her eyes as he talks, and a sour taste floods my mouth. Slowly, she nods. He slings an arm around her shoulders and ushers her around the front of the house. He opens the door for her, and she steps inside.

I don't move for at least a couple of minutes, wondering what the hell is going on between them. I shouldn't care. It's none of my business, but I've lied enough to myself. It bothers me that something might be happening between them. That she'd leave my arms and run pretty much straight into his.

I should be happy. I was deliberately horrible to her because I didn't want her to catch feelings.

Problem is, I already have. I've just been in denial. Fact is, this last week, the only Irish girl occupying space in my head is Rachel.

That should be a welcome relief, but it isn't.

I bark out a laugh as the irony of the situation jumps up and slaps me in the face.

Am I trapped in a different love triangle with another Kennedy brother?

Probably would serve me right for treating Rachel like shit this morning.

I need to get out of here. Standing around wondering what she's doing with Keven in his room isn't going to help clear my head. Turning around, I backtrack and head for Cambridge. I have a familiar route I run, and I set off at a fast pace.

Sweat coasts down my spine, gluing my top to my back as I run. My feet pummel the sidewalk as I race through Cambridge like there's a knife-wielding maniac on my heels. I weave around the foot traffic, ignoring the shouts and curses leveled at my back. The busy streets and sounds of the city help drown out the disquieting thoughts in my head.

After an hour, I slow down in a quieter part of town. I approach a street vender and buy two bottles of water and a couple protein bars.

I knock back one bottle of water, tossing the empty container in the nearest trash can, before I start walking back toward our apartment. A delicious gentle breeze wafts over my skin, and I pour the second bottle of water over my head, welcoming the cold rivulets as they trickle over my hot skin.

I'm passing by a narrow alleyway when a hand darts out, latching onto my arm. Caught unawares, I drop my water bottle as I'm yanked sideways. It rolls to the ground, falling over the edge of the curb. I swivel around, ready to put up a fight, and come to a screaming halt at the sight that confronts me.

The woman falls back, urging me to follow with her eyes.

My heart is thrashing around in my chest, beating so fast and so out of control as I walk silently behind her. She stops behind a smelly dumpster and turns to face me with tears streaking across her cheeks.

A lump the size of an apple is wedged in my throat, and I want to say something, do something, but I'm rooted to the ground like a mute. I can only stare at her, drinking her in.

Is this real, or am I projecting? Is my imagination playing the cruelest prank?

She looks different, but it's still her. Thinner than I recall, but she looks real. Whole. Alive.

She reaches up and cups my face, and her touch does funny things to my insides. It is her. She's really here. I blink excessively, still rigid as a statue. Her gaze never leaves mine. So much love shines in her eyes, and the lump in my throat expands. I don't even realize I'm crying until she swipes at the tears quietly trailing down my face.

Finally, I find my voice. "Mom?" I croak. "What are you doing here?"

Chapter Ten

Rachel

"I've changed my mind. I don't want the app," I tell Keven, holding out my hand for my phone.

"Are you sure?"

I nod. "Yeah. I don't want to know where he is at every minute of the day. I only need to know if he comes anywhere near me."

"If you let me install the app, I can set it to notify you if he comes within a certain range. You can just ignore it the rest of the time." He leans back in his chair, crossing one leg over his knee, as he studies me. "And you're hidden. He won't be able to find you, so the tracking app is only precautionary."

I'd like to believe that, but *he's* resourceful too. And he told me he'd never let me go. That I'd never be free of him. A familiar weight presses down on my chest. I draw deep breaths, in and out, willing my heartrate to slow down.

Kev is still watching me with those shrewd all-seeing eyes of his. I can tell he's curious, and, if I know him at all, he's probably already digging.

Not that he'll find anything. On the surface, *he's* squeaky clean.

My secret is safe, unless Kev's developed an app which can dig through my brain.

Then I'm in serious trouble.

"No," I reconfirm. "I don't want the app." I can't tell Kev how anything connected to *him* is impossible to ignore. That app would sit on my phone like a blaring beacon, calling out to me, taunting me, demanding I check. And I'm trying to forget him. To forget what he did. To overcome the many ways in which he tried to ruin me.

But he hasn't ruined me. I'm finally fighting back. And I'm getting better. I'm healing. He might have destroyed my childhood, and robbed me of my innocence, but he's not taking my future. *I'm a survivor, and I'm going to get through this. I'm strong enough to do it.* I repeat the familiar mantra over and over in my head. I need to keep reminding myself of the important things.

And I've already taken such a huge step in moving here.

What I've asked Kev to set up is self-preservation.

Having a link to his whereabouts on my phone would be the opposite of that.

The less I know, the better.

I rest my arse on the edge of the desk. "I know I'm asking a lot, but could you just monitor the app and have it notify you if he lands on American soil?"

He leans forward, placing his elbows on his knees. "That's a mighty big ask."

I open my bag and withdraw my purse. "I can pay you more."

He stands up. "That's not what I meant, and I'm not taking any more of your money. I meant we need to narrow the search field. How about I set the tracker to notify me if he gets within a twenty-mile radius of Cambridge?"

Bile swims up my throat, and a powerful shudder rips through my body at the thought of him coming anywhere near me again. "Make it fifty miles."

Kev doesn't miss the way my entire body trembles. "Rachel." His voice is uber-soft, as if he's speaking to a frightened child. Perhaps that's what I still am. "I know we don't know each other all that well, but I meant what I said before. You can trust me. You can tell me what's going on, and I won't tell anyone. I swear." I look everywhere but at him. He tilts my chin up with one finger, forcing me to look at him. "I won't judge. I can see how scared you are and I'm doing my best to help, but it would be easier if I knew exactly why you're so frightened of him."

I'm mortified when huge tears pool in my eyes. *God, what is wrong with me?* I'm blaming the dickhead. He's raising tons of surface emotions, and I'm ill-equipped to deal. "I can't, Kev," I whisper. "And I do trust you, so much, but I haven't told anyone, because if I talk about it, it'll only become more real, and I'm trying really hard to put it behind me."

Without hesitation, he pulls me into his arms, and it's like déjà vu. Man, Kev gives the best hugs ever. I know Faye thinks Kev is the most guarded of the Kennedys, but that hasn't been my experience. There is something about him that makes it almost too easy to talk. We spent a good bit of time together the summer before last, and, although everyone thinks all we did was hook up, we actually spent most of our time talking. That one night he spent in my place was one of the best nights of my life. We spoke about second chances and needing a do-over without either of us explaining the reasons why. He didn't pry, and I didn't push, and it was perfect. I know everyone thinks we slept together, but we didn't have sex. I had the best night's sleep I'd had in years, cocooned in his warm, protective arms.

Kev's a fantastic kisser, and he makes me feel safe and cared for, and a part of me wishes it could be more than that. But it won't ever be. He isn't interested in me like that, just like I'm not interested in him like that.

And he doesn't make my body tingle and come alive the way the dickhead does.

Irony is a bitch. To pick up feelings for a dickhead like Brad is idiotic, even more so because he's in love with my best friend. I don't know what possessed me to throw caution to the wind last night. Deep down, I knew I was going to get hurt and that it'd only confuse things further.

Hearing him tell Ky I was some kind of experiment to help him get over Faye was a savage kick in the teeth. And a major blow to my do-over efforts. Last night had been magical. The first time I've been with a guy and really and truly let myself go. Let myself feel things and not be drunk or numb or self-conscious. With the way he adored my body, and the words that poured out of his mouth, I thought he had felt it too. I'd felt cherished and desired, but it was an illusion. A cruel joke. The universe's perverted way of messing with me further. I was a damn fool. I was just another handy fuck to him, and the acknowledgment hurts. A lot. I'm in a whole world of pain today, and I've no one to blame but myself. I knew it would backfire on me, but I ignored all the warning signs, giving in to unprecedented lust.

My self-worth is in the toilet again. That blanket of self-loathing is back, and it feels like I've regressed a few months.

It'd be easy to blame the dickhead, but this is all me. I've got to stop letting guys get to me so much. I need to develop thicker skin.

"I'm worried about you," Kev says, still holding me against his chest.

I wriggle out of his arms, desperately needing to get a grip. "Don't be. I'll be fine. And you're helping me enough."

He looks pensive. "Does Faye know?"

I shake my head. "I told you. No one knows."

His eyes soften. "I'm probably the last person you'd expect to suggest this, but what about speaking to a therapist? They are anonymous and they won't judge." I start shaking my head, but he continues on. "My brother was very reluctant too, but I know it's helped him. It could help you too."

I know Faye actively encouraged Ky to pursue therapy to help him deal with all that crap surrounding his bio dad, and she's mentioned it several times to me over the years. She saw a therapist for years over the trauma arising from stuff that happened to her in school in Waterford, and she has spoken about how much it helped.

There were times when I really wanted to go speak to someone like that. Someone neutral who could help me make sense of what was happening. But I couldn't speak to a therapist, because they'd involve the police, and it'd break my mother's heart. I can't do that to her. I can't destroy her.

So I continue to keep *his* secret.

And hope that I'm strong enough to rise above my past.

I've got to be.

Because if I can't put it behind me, he's already claimed my future too.

Chapter Eleven

Brad

I haven't stopped hugging her. I'm afraid to let her go in case she magically disappears. I'm still scared it isn't real even though I know it is because her body is warm and comforting against mine. "I've missed you so much, Mom." I crush her to me, her head barely meeting my chest.

"Oh, honey. We've all missed you so much. I've been so worried." She manages to pry herself out of my clinging clutches. Both her hands move to my face, and she cups my cheeks firmly. "It's great to see you looking so well. You're all grown up. Look at you?" She steps back, casting an admiring glance over me. "So healthy. So handsome." She grabs my hands in hers. "I'm so proud of you and happy you stuck to your goals. Not a day went by when I wasn't thinking about you. Leaving you behind was the hardest decision I've ever had to make, and it was all so rushed, and I worried I didn't impress on you enough that it was extremely difficult to go without you, but I didn't want your father's crimes to derail your future. I didn't argue with your rationale because I loved you so much. I hope you know that."

Although there were plenty of times, when I was depressed and upset, when I convinced myself Mom didn't love me as much my sisters—how could she when she left me behind without much protest—I'm not admitting that now. I won't add to her worries or her guilt. Deep down, I've always known my mother loves me. We've always been super close, and those times when I doubted her was only because I was hurting so much. Missing her so much. "I know, Mom. I've always known."

A loud clatter at the entrance to the alleyway has her anxiously scanning her surroundings. I glance over my shoulder. "It's okay. Someone just knocked over a trashcan."

She gulps, pulling the hood of her jacket up over her head again. "Can we go somewhere to talk? Not your apartment. I don't trust that you aren't being watched."

I don't know if the Feds are still tailing me, but I'm not taking any chances. "Don't worry. I've got you covered." I remove my cell and tap out a quick message to Ky. Even though we are barely even speaking, I know he won't let me down.

I need ur help. Can u come get me?

The phone rings not even a minute later. I pick up, lowering my voice and cautiously looking around.

"What's happened? Are you in trouble?" he asks, before I've even had a chance to speak.

"I'm fine, but I need you to come get me. It isn't safe to explain over the phone. Come alone. As quick as you can."

"I'm already on the move. Hang tight."

"Kyler?" Mom whispers, and I nod.

We don't talk much as we wait. I can tell Mom is too scared to talk in public, so we just embrace, and I'm enjoying recouping some of the missed hugs from the last two and a half years.

My phone vibrates with a text.

One minute.

I take Mom's hand and turn her around. "Come on. Just keep your head down, and let me guide you."

Kyler's large black Range Rover pulls up in front of the alley, and I tug on Mom's hand, running toward it. I open the back door and help her up before sliding in beside her. Kyler's eyes almost bug out of his head. "Mrs. McConaughey?"

"Hello, Kyler," Mom says with a shy smile. "Thank you for coming to get us."

"Of course." He looks completely shocked as his eyes flit to mine.

"Can you get us out of here?" Even though the windows are dark glass, I scan our surroundings, half-expecting the Feds to make an appearance. My foot taps nervously off the ground.

He nods, thrusting the car into gear and gliding out into the traffic.

"Where are Emma and Kaitlyn? Are they okay?"

She laces her fingers in mine. "Your sisters are safe. They are with your Aunt Cora."

My stomach lurches to my toes. "Mom, is that wise? Wouldn't that be one of the first places the Feds would look?"

Ky looks at me through the mirror, sharing my concern.

A resigned world-weary look appears on her face. "We're hiding in their basement room, and we arrived in the dead of night a week ago. No one saw us arriving, and I've hidden in the trunk of your uncle's car every time I've gone out, which hasn't been much. I only ventured out to find you. I've been watching and waiting for the right moment to reach out."

I slide my arm around her shoulders, holding her close to my side. "I'm going to fix this. I'm going to keep you safe."

Kyler looks at me again, and an unspoken communication passes between us. I nod my agreement. He punches a button on his phone and a dial tone rings out. His dad picks up a few seconds later. "Kyler."

"Hey, Dad. I need your help. I'm en route to Mom's house as we speak. Can you call her and let her know and then meet us there with Dan?"

"Sure, but—"

"I'm fine, we're all fine," Kyler preempts, "and I'll explain everything when we arrive. I'll be using the special entrance."

"Okay. I hear you loud and clear, son. Consider it done. Drive carefully." He cuts the call, and Ky presses his foot down on the accelerator.

"Special entrance?" I inquire, raising a brow.

He grins. "You'll see."

Mom is trembling beside me, and any trace of humor fades. "Don't worry, Mom. Alex and James will help us. We can trust them. They took me in and helped with school and college and my sponsorship. They're good people."

Even though Ky and I were joined at the hip, our parents were never overly friendly. Sure, Dad played golf with James on occasion, but they were never close. And Mom barely knows Alex because she wasn't around for school runs or parent-teacher meetings, and it's not like they had much in common. Alex was too busy running her multi-billion-dollar fashion empire.

"It seems I have a lot to thank them for, and I don't want to bring trouble to their door."

"My parents will want to help, Mrs. McConaughey, and Dan is one of the finest attorneys around."

"Thank you," Mom whispers. "And please stop calling me Mrs. McConaughey. We're all adults here, and I'm good with Danielle."

Kyler grins. "Okay, Danielle."

"Thanks, man." My words are suffused with gratitude. I could live ten lifetimes and never fully repay Ky and his family for all they have done for me.

"You're my family, bro. No matter what is going down between us, that will never change."

Another shared look passes between us. I reach forward and squeeze his shoulder. No more words are needed.

"I'm just going to call Faye real quick. She'll only worry otherwise." He makes the call, discreetly updating Faye without mentioning names or specifics.

I'm surprised when Ky bypasses the main entrance to his mom's house, driving around the rear of the vast estate. He stops the car in front of an open section of the woodland which rims the perimeter of their property. Pulling a fob out of the glove box, he presses a button, and I watch, with my mouth hanging open, as the trees part, revealing a hidden iron gate. The gate glides open, and Ky maneuvers the car into a dark tunnel. When the gate clangs shut behind us, a row of spotlights light up the ground in front of us.

"What the hell, dude?" It's like something from a James Bond movie.

He chuckles as he slowly drives forward. "Dad went a little overprotective after everything that went down last year, and he hired this guy that used to work for the CIA or Homeland or something to build a secret entrance to the property." Up ahead, a long tunnel awaits. Spotlights embedded in the floor flicker on, one at a time, lighting our path. "He's also building a fully-equipped underground bunker complete with every luxury known to man, as well as impenetrable panic rooms with supplies and direct communication to local authorities. He has a fulltime team of security guards watching the property and keeping an eye on all of us, and he's learning how to shoot and fight. It's his new pet project, and he's like a little kid on Christmas morning."

"Good God," Mom exclaims, drooping a little in her seat.

"It seems like we definitely came to the right place."

Ky laughs again. "One hundred percent. I think Dad fancies himself as a modern-day Batman. I'm just waiting for him to show up in a cape one of these days."

Tires screech as the Range Rover rounds a bend. Ky slows down as we enter a largish garage with bare stone walls and an angled, vaulted ceiling. As I look around in amazement, I'm inclined to agree with Ky's dramatic statement. His dad's superhero aspirations are most definitely showing.

James Kennedy is waiting off to the side, lounging casually against the side of a blacked- out SUV with his feet crossed at the ankles.

We all exit the car at the same time, and James's eyes pop wide the instant he sees Mom. He pushes off the SUV, walking toward us with urgency. "Hello, Danielle. I wasn't expecting to see you." His hand is outstretched, and his tone and expression is surprised yet friendly.

"It's good to see you, James, and I'm sorry to show up unannounced."

He waves his hands about. "Not at all. Brad is basically an adopted member of this family, and that means you are by default. Family is everything to Kennedys. Whatever you need, you've got it."

A lump forms in my throat again, and Mom looks teary-eyed. "I don't know how I can ever repay you for all you've done for Bradley."

"Honestly, that's not necessary. We're glad to help. Speaking of which, Alex is waiting upstairs, but I think it's best if we meet down here. Work is still underway on this facility, but the west wing is completed. We can move there and talk in complete privacy."

James calls Alex and then we follow him out the back of the garage and down a long well-lit passageway. He stops in front of a heavy-duty door, typing in a code on the wall-mounted keypad. There's a click, a ping, and then the door slides open to reveal plush living quarters bathed in a soft glow from the overhead lighting.

"Full lights on," James commands, and the room bursts in glorious brightness. He turns around, with his arms thrust out, grinning. "This is pretty cool, right?"

"Damn straight." My jaw is so slack it's practically touching the floor. This part of the annex is open plan with a large living area, kitchen to the far right, and a dining room at the end. The space is painted a soothing blue-gray color, and a few carefully placed modern paintings hang on the walls. The furniture is all high end and sophisticated yet comfortable looking. A large fake window displays a serene woodland scene. The air feels light and the temperature is just right.

There are no words.

"We have four en suite bedrooms, a living room, gymnasium, games room, dining room, and fully-equipped kitchen in this annex." He eyeballs Mom. "It's completely private and safe. I'm guessing you need a place, Danielle, and you are welcome to stay here for as long as you need to."

Mom looks around in awe. Then she looks up at me and bursts into tears. I don't hesitate to bundle her into my arms. "It's okay, Mom. Don't cry. Everything is going to be okay." Her entire body is quaking against mine, and I hold her tighter, pressing a kiss to the top of her head. "Thank you, James. Thank you so much."

He nods, just as Alex enters the room with Dan Evans, the Kennedy's attorney. She strides toward Mom with purpose. "Danielle?" Shock is splayed across her face.

Mom sniffles, wiping her eyes and shucking out of my embrace. "How are you, Alex?"

Alex doesn't hesitate, leaning in and hugging Mom like they are long-lost friends instead of mere acquaintances. "How are *you* is more to the point? How did you come to be here?"

"Why don't we sit down and have some coffee?" James proposes, gesturing toward the long oak table in the far corner of the room.

Ky is already fiddling with the expensive coffee station in the kitchen. I help Mom into a seat and join my friend in the kitchen. We work silently and efficiently, loading a tray with cups, a coffee pot, cream, and sugar. Ky opens the cabinet, and I'm not surprised to find it well stocked. He removes a couple packets of cookies, adding them to the tray.

I take the empty seat beside Mom, automatically holding her hand.

"Why don't I ask you a few questions, and we can take it from there?" Dan suggests.

I pour a coffee for Mom, adding a drop of cream and one sugar into the cup before handing it to her. She smiles at me before nodding at Dan. "Sounds like a plan."

Removing her sweater, she hangs it over the back of the chair and folds her hands in her lap. "Fire away." She holds her head up high, looking Dan directly in the face. "What do you need to know?"

"Where is your husband?"

Chapter Twelve

Rachel

"Try not to worry. Ky said everything was okay, and he's been texting you all night," I repeat, trying to reassure Faye for, like, the millionth time as we make breakfast together. It's the start of another week, and we need to be out the door within the hour. We were both idiots for signing up for early Monday morning classes. Faye's concerned because Ky took off yesterday evening, and she hasn't seen him since. All we know is Brad was in some kind of trouble, and they went to the Kennedy house in Wellesley where they stayed last night.

"I know," she sighs, slathering lashings of butter on her toast. "I just wish he could tell me what's going on. Not knowing is killing me."

"What about his classes today?" I plop my butt in a chair.

"They aren't going which is also concerning. Ky doesn't like to skip, and Brad needs to keep a clean slate so he doesn't fall foul of his football coach."

"Whatever's going on must be important then," I muse, and it's totally the wrong thing to say to little Miss Worry Wort.

She stops chewing mid-munch, and a new layer of anxiety creeps over her face.

"Relax, Faye." I reach out, squeezing her hand. "They are big boys, and they know how to look after themselves."

"What happened Saturday after we took off?" Lauren asks once we are seated side by side in the lecture hall, waiting for the prof to show. I fill her in quickly, giving her the clean-sanitized-non-hookup version of events. I'm too embarrassed over how easily Brad played me to admit I slept with him, and the less people who know about my humiliation, the better.

"That girl was such a bitch to do that, whether it was true or not."

"I know. It was mean and spiteful, but the Kennedys always draw those kind of gold diggers."

"I kinda felt sorry for Brad."

I pin her with a disbelieving look. "You did? Why?"

"He looked really embarrassed and genuinely remorseful, and I doubt it meant anything." I snort. Can't help it. Her eyes probe mine. "You don't agree?"

"No. Everyone knows he's in love with Faye. It's been going on for years."

She taps a pen against her lips. "Weird. I didn't see that at all. The only girl he had eyes for"—she looks pointedly at me—"was you."

I flip my notepad open as the prof enters the room. "I think you were seeing things."

"Nope. I'm very observant. In fact, it drives Gavin mad. He says I'm always looking at everyone and everything going on around me and that I constantly ignore him. Which is why I noticed Brad looking at you when he thought no one was watching. Or maybe he wasn't aware he was doing it, but, every so often, his gaze would flit to you as he was talking to Kyler. I think someone's crushing on you." There's a teasing glint in her eye.

"Well," I whisper, lowering my voice as the professor calls for quiet. "Even if that was the truth, I'm definitely not crushing on him. He's an annoying fuckwit, and he makes me want to pull every last hair out of my head."

Liar. Liar. Pants on fire.

"Uh-huh." Lauren grins. "You keep trying to convince yourself of that."

I sigh. I'm fooling no one. Least of all myself.

My phone pings just as I'm entering the second last class of the day. The text is from Faye, so I open it up immediately.

Need 2 talk 2 u urgently. Ring me now.

Turning around, I offer up apologies as I maneuver a path through the people pouring into the room. When I'm back out in the hall, I find a quiet spot and call my friend.

"Can you get home now?"

"Why? What's wrong?"

"I can't say over the phone, but I wouldn't ask if it wasn't urgent."

"Ky's back?" I'm guessing this is something to do with whatever is going down with Brad.

"Yeah."

I hate ditching class, it's not in keeping with the new-me, but friends take precedence.

Always.

"I'm leaving now. Be there as soon as I can."

I'm not altogether surprised to find both Brad and Ky waiting with Faye when I step foot in our apartment a half hour later. I deposit my backpack on the floor in the living room and walk to the fridge, grabbing a bottle of water.

No one speaks, and it's all very cloak and dagger. They wait for me to get settled before Faye clues me in. "Brad's mom is back in the country," she admits, surprising me.

While I'm not privy to all the ins and outs of Brad's family history, I know enough to understand it's risky for her to be back on American soil. My gaze bounces to his, and the look he gives me is a mixture of exhilaration and sheer terror. But it's genuine, and there's a lot to be said for that. I return my attention to Faye, nodding for her to continue.

"Brad's dad is still overseas, and if the government find out she's back, they'll most likely arrest her. For now, she's going to stay in hiding, but we need to get Brad's sisters from his aunt's house and bring them to Wellesley so they can all be together while Dan is figuring out the best course of action."

"Who's Dan?" I ask.

"My parent's attorney," Ky confirms. "He's going to try and find a loophole they can work with."

I clear my throat, resurrecting my lady balls, and look at Brad. Ignoring the sting of his rejection, and the fact I know how hot he looks stark naked, I speak up. "I'm really happy that your family is back, but I don't see what this has to do with me?"

He leans forward in the chair, propping his arms on his knees. "The Feds were watching me at one time, and we don't know if they still are. They know I'm close with the Kennedys and Faye, too, so it's hard to find someone who isn't on their radar."

"So, you need me to ...?"

"Drive to my aunt's house, pick up my sisters, and deliver them to Wellesley." He has the decency to look sheepish. My brows climb to my hairline. "I know it's a big favor to ask, but you're the only one the Feds aren't aware of. I could ask one of the guys on my football team, but then I'd have to fill them in on everything, and I can't take that risk. I know I can trust you, and I'll be coming with so you won't have to do this on your own."

"You say that like it'll sweeten the deal, but the thoughts of you and me, alone, in a car for any amount of time is about as enticing as eating raw kangaroo testicles."

Faye scrunches her nose, grimacing. Brad doesn't see the humor, scrubbing his tense jaw with a look of growing panic on his face. Thing is, of course, I'm going to do it. I'd be a heartless bitch not to, but that doesn't mean I can't take advantage of the opportunity to make Brad squirm a little. He deserves it.

His head lifts, and he pierces me with a solemn expression. "Look, I've been a complete jerk to you, I get that—"

"Try backstabbing, self-serving, arrogant, slimy dickhead," I interject.

I catch Ky's eye, and he winks. He's enjoying a little payback too.

Brad swallows a whole tub of humble pie. "So, I've been a back-stabbing, self-serving, arrogant, slimy dickhead, and I know you owe me nothing, but I'm begging you, Rachel, please, please do this. Do it for my mom and sisters, not for me."

I pretend to inspect my nails. "What's in it for me?"

Faye gasps, jumping up. "Rach, what the hell has gotten into you?"

I level her with a "butt out" look, and she clamps her lips shut. Not before showing me her middle finger though. I smother the laughter waiting to bubble up my throat.

"What do you want?" Brad asks, ignoring Faye's unwanted intervention.

I wrack my brains for something good, and then it comes to me. I'm struggling to hold on to my composure as I speak. "You'll allow me to take a photo of you naked, holding a carefully placed sign confirming you're a—"

"Backstabbing, self-serving, arrogant, slimy dickhead," he supplies for me with a sigh.

"Corrrrect. And you'll allow me to post it online or anywhere around campus that I choose."

Faye sniggers, and I know she's cottoned on.

"Fine." He stands up. "Agreed."

"Sit down. I'm not finished," I demand, really getting into the spirit of it now.

He grits his teeth, and a muscle ticks in his jaw. Reluctantly, he sits back down. "What else?"

"And I want five orgasms."

Faye falls off the side of the couch, convulsing with laughter. Ky has a hand over his mouth, struggling to keep his cool.

But I'm not done yet.

"All in the one night, and you will do exactly as I tell you." I tap a finger off my chin. "Like my own personal sex slave."

Brad smirks that infuriating smirk of his, and I'm ready to take him down another peg or two. "I've no problem agreeing to that." He leans back, locking his hands around the back of his head, grinning nonstop.

"And you're not allowed to come."

He smirks again. "I hate to break it to you, Red, but it's not like you can stop me."

"Wanna bet?" I arch a brow and he shoots an amused look my way. "You'll be fully clothed, I'm not laying a finger on you, and you'll pleasure me exactly as I tell you. If you are close to coming, I'll throw a bucket of ice water over you." He blinks profusely, and the grin slips off his mouth. The other two are howling with laughter at this stage. "And if that fails, there's always a male chastity belt."

His expression is a mixture of disbelief and mounting horror. "That's not a thing."

"Is too."

"And how would you know?"

"I might've had cause to Google it one time."

"You're totally fucked in the head, and you can't do that! That's complete torture."

I fold my hands in my lap, giving him a smug grin. Oh, it's cruel, but I'm getting perverse pleasure out of this. "Exactly."

"Sadist," he mumbles under his breath.

"Oh my God, Rachel, remind me to never get on your bad side." Ky laughs, pointing a finger in Brad's direction. "Shit, man. She has you by the balls."

"Fine. I'll agree to your terms. Can we make a move now?"

He stands up again, and I pull myself to my feet, arching my spine in a regal fashion. "Shake on it." I extend my hand, and Faye titters.

His handshake is warm and firm, heating me upon contact. He pulls away, his expression turning all business-like. "Now it's my turn to have the floor." His look challenges me to argue, but I've had my fun. "Okay, so this is how it's going to go down. You'll drive Ky's Range Rover out of the garage with me in the cargo hold and head toward the I-95. There's an abandoned gas station just outside of Dedham where you can pull in. Provided no one is following us, I'll drive the rest of the way. Before we reach my aunts, I'll hop back in the cargo hold, and you can drive to her house."

"Okay. Let's go then."

Ky and Faye walk to the underground car park with us. Ky is explaining how the controls work, while Faye and Brad are talking in quiet whispers behind us. "I'll be fine. I was driving my uncle's tractor when I was barely out of nappies."

His brow puckers.

"Diapers," Faye explains, "and I think that's a slight exaggeration. Although"—she turns to grin at Brad—"I hope you have an iron constitution because you're going to need it with Rachel's driving."

I playfully shove her. "Hey! I've been driving way longer than you, and I've never been in an accident."

Faye plants her hands on her hips. "And how many penalty points do you have on your license?"

I flap my hands about. "They don't matter. They were only for speeding."

"God, help me." Brad makes the sign of the cross, shaking his head.

I send him one of my special death-destroyer looks. "Shut your gob, and get your cute butt in the boot."

"You think my butt is cute?" He opens the rear door of the SUV, smirking again, and my fists involuntarily ball up at my sides. It's instinctive at this stage. That smirk of his always rubs me the wrong way, and I hate that he knows that and uses it at will to piss me off.

"I think you're a butthead. Now get in the *cargo hold*." I fake an American accent, and he chuckles.

He climbs into it, putting his delectable butt way too close to my face. I'm pleading involuntary reaction to what I do next. I whack his butt hard and then squeeze his cute buns a little. He stumbles, loses his balance, and tumbles head-first into the cargo hold. He whacks his head off the side, emitting a volley of colorful expletives. "What the actual fuck, Rachel? Are you actually *trying* to kill me?"

I raise my hand to the door. "If I wanted to kill you, I'd do a better job of it." I smirk, giving him a dose of his own medicine. "Now, stop being such a drama queen, it's only a little bump." My grin turns devilish. "I'll try to keep to the speed limit, but I'm making no promises." Before he can protest, I slam the door shut, smacking my hands together in satisfaction. I fucking love messing with his head.

Love it. Love it. Love it.

"Wow. You really want to make him sweat," Faye says, leaning back against Ky. He has his back to the wall, and his arms are clasped around her waist.

"He deserves it for being an asshole."

"When are you going to let him off the hook?"

"About five minutes before we get to Wellesley."

Faye snickers. "Cruel bitch."

"If the cap fits, girlfriend." I grin wickedly as I hop up into the Rover.

They come over to the window. "Be safe, and please slow down," she beseeches.

"I'll be careful. I promise."

I thrust the stick into gear and start backing out of the parking spot.

"Try not to murder my friend," Ky hollers.

"That's one promise I cannot commit to," I shout out, revving the engine and flooring it out of there.

Chapter Thirteen

Brad

Shit, Faye wasn't kidding. Rachel is a lunatic driver. I'm thrown all over the cargo hold as she maneuvers the car like it's a fucking tank and we're being chased by an enemy hell-bent on our destruction. I roar at her, but she ignores me. Her self-satisfied chuckles drift my way, and I know she's enjoying this immensely.

I slam to the front of the cargo hold as we come to a screaming halt, instinctively placing my hands over my face in a self-protective gesture. My breathing is erratic and my heartrate is elevated to near-coronary territory. It's a wonder I didn't crap my pants.

A waft of welcome cool air drifts over me, and I blink my eyes open. I hadn't even realized I'd closed them.

"Time to get out, dickhead," she purrs, as if I haven't just endured a near-death experience.

"Holy fuck, Red," I exclaim, accepting her hand and letting her help me out. I make a grab for her shoulder as I stand on shaky legs. My limbs are trembling in shock. "That was insane! What idiot thought it was a good idea to give you a driver's license?"

She laughs. Actually laughs. The bitch.

"Shit yourself, did ya, big guy?" She wiggles her brows, and her glee is obvious in the extreme.

"Very fucking nearly," I admit, shaking my head in disbelief. I hold my palm upright. "Give me the keys. You're not going near the steering wheel again."

She drops them into my upturned palm, grinning like an idiot. "Poor baby," she teases, pinching my cheek. "Can't handle a little rough play."

I send her a cocky grin, knowing she hates when I look at her like this. "I think we both know the truth on that score."

"Hasn't anyone ever told you arrogance is a most unattractive trait?" she retorts, flouncing over to the passenger side door without waiting for my response.

I decide to make her sweat a little, because I haven't forgotten that I still owe her for earlier. Without replying, I settle into the driver side seat, pushing it back to accommodate my longer legs. I switch the engine on, smoothly steering the car out into the traffic. Once we are back on the highway, heading in the right direction, I relax a little. "So, Rachel, about the other night."

Her head pivots to mine, and her eyes narrow to slits. "I'm not going there."

I glance at her quickly, planting a fake innocent mask on my face. "Why not? We're consenting adults, and we both enjoyed ourselves." She opens her mouth to say something, no doubt something derogatory and argumentative, but I cut her off first. "Don't even attempt to deny that. All those naughty moans and cries you made would only make a liar of you. And let's not forget that dirty, filthy mouth of yours." I can vividly remember every crude, dirty word that came out of her mouth and how it ramped my arousal into orbit.

Blood starts heating down south, and I squirm a little in my seat. The purpose of this line of questioning is to aggravate Rachel, not to turn me on, I silently remind myself.

Her cheeks flush, and she bites down on her lower lip, and my cock twitches to life. Subtly, I part my legs a little, hoping she doesn't notice the slight movement or the growing bulge in my jeans.

"So your little experiment worked then?" She spits the words out, and there's no missing the animosity behind them.

I frown. "I'm not with you."

She swivels in her seat, staring at me. I take a quick sideways look at her, almost shrinking from the venom in her expression. But I detect a note of hurt at the back of it. "I heard what you said to Ky. I should've realized I was part of your little trial."

My brows knit together. "Still not following you."

"Why doesn't that surprise me." Kicking her shoes off, she lifts her legs and rests her feet on the dash. Her dress slides down her thighs a little, giving me plenty of access to her gorgeous, toned legs. My gaze locks on, and I almost forget I'm driving. "Keep your eyes on the road, dickhead, or we'll both be toast."

Her biting words, and the blast of a horn, snap me out of my lusty haze. "Don't flash me your panties then!" I hiss, exaggerating in a feeble attempt to explain my behavior. I'm grouchy because she's somehow gaining the upper hand again, and that pisses me off.

"I didn't flash my panties!" she screeches. "I only put my feet up on the dash. You are the one who seems to have a problem keeping your eyes off me."

I can tell she's pouting without even looking at her. "Don't flatter yourself, sweetheart," I snap. "You don't have the monopoly on great legs. Faye definitely gives you a run for your money in that regard," I tack on the end, completely on the spur of the moment. I watch her face fall in the mirror, and I feel like the biggest jerk on the planet. I want to take it back. To tell her I didn't mean it, but I can't make the words come out of my mouth.

She lowers her feet to the floor and crosses her arms over her chest. "Which is exactly the point I was making," she says in a much calmer voice than I'd expect. "All the drinking and getting laid is so you can forget her. You told me as much in Nantucket. What I failed to realize the other night was that I was lumped into that category too. If I'd known, I would've said no."

I want to tell her she's wrong. That it couldn't be further from the truth. That she's the first girl in a very long time to capture my attention and consume my mind. The first girl that's made me stop thinking about Faye. I want to tell her that, but I can't. Because I still haven't worked out *why* I think like that, *what* it means—if anything—and *what*, or *if*, I want to do anything about it. So, like a coward, I say nothing.

"God, you really are a dickhead," she says a few minutes later when it's clear I'm not refuting her claims.

"I promised you a good time and I delivered. I never promised anything beyond that."

"Yeah. You're a man of your word." Sarcasm drips off her tone.

I rub a tense spot between my brows. "Can we talk about something else? Anything besides us."

She looks out the window, ignoring me, and I figure my punishment is to suffer the rest of the journey in silence. Any other time, I wouldn't give two shits about that. But today I need the distraction of conversation. I'm excited about reuniting with my sisters but apprehensive about it all going smoothly. I won't relax until we're with Mom in Wellesley.

After about ten minutes, she finally speaks, although she doesn't look at me. "I guess you must be delighted your family are back."

"I am, but I'm worried too."

She twists her head around. "We'll get your sisters out safely, and I've been watching through the mirror. I can't see anyone following us that looks suspicious."

I haven't either, and I've been keeping a keen eye out too. "I'll only chill when they are safely with Mom."

"How did they get here? I imagine it must've been a risky journey."

"If they'd been traveling under their own names, sure."

Her eyes pop wide. "They traveled under false aliases?"

I nod. "It's how they got out of the country in the first place. Dad clearly knows some dodgy fucks. They all have fake passports and it's how Mom and my sisters were able to leave and come back without being spotted." It's still unbelievable, as if my life has become an episode of *CSI* or *Criminal Minds*.

"What are your sister's names? And how old are they?"

"Emma is twelve, and Kaitlyn is"—I have to stop and calculate it in my head. She was Emma's age the last time I saw her—"fifteen. Shit. She's just turned fifteen." I gulp over the new wedge of emotion in my throat.

"And it's been nearly three years since you've seen or spoken to both of them?" I nod. "That's rough."

I nod again, my Adam's apple jumping in my throat. "Do you have any brothers or sisters?" I ask, realizing I know very little about Rachel's family other than her parents won big on the lottery a few years back and they are getting a divorce.

She looks out the window again. "One brother. Alec is three years older than me."

"Are you guys close?"

She shrugs, still looking out the window. "Not especially. He's been away at college the last few years so I haven't seen that much of him either way."

"Faye told me your parents are getting divorced. I'm sorry about that."

"It is what it is. I can't say I'm overly surprised or upset about it."

"Is that why you moved here?" I indicate, pulling the car over into the next lane.

"What's with the twenty questions?" She twists around, and there's a strange look on her face.

"No reason. Just making small talk. If you're uncomfortable, we can talk about something else."

Her foot taps idly off the floor, and she's shifting around in her seat. "What about your dad?" she asks. "What's happening with him?" I grit my teeth, and my jaw locks. I turn off at the next exit. "It's okay if you don't want to talk about it. I understand."

"It's not that." I shake my head, following the line of traffic moving toward our destination. "It just makes me so mad."

Air whooshes out of her lungs. "I can relate."

I flip my eyes to hers, and we share a look. "Dads are supposed to protect you, not hurt you and throw you into the line of fire."

My chest constricts at her words. More for what she's not saying.

She straightens up, as if realizing she's said more than she should. "This isn't about me." I catch the warning. "Tell me about your dad."

"He's still hiding abroad," I start telling her the story Mom told us. "Mom was fed up of life on the run, and she wanted to put down roots for the girl's sake, but Dad has to keep moving in case the authorities catch up with him. He's on the FBI's list of Most Wanted so they had to keep moving to avoid detection. Mom put her foot down. She missed me, and she wanted the girls to have a normal life. She gave him an ultimatum: turn himself in or she would leave by herself. When she woke the next morning, he was gone."

"Shit," Rachel says. "That's awful."

"He's a selfish asshole." I'm seething. Mom just wasted almost three years of her life, and risked her freedom, for nothing. "I used to think he was the best dad ever, but he's a selfish coward who only puts himself first. What man thinks he can steal millions and not get caught? What man refuses to face up to his actions and does that to his family?"

"He's either in denial or narcissistic."

"Or a bit of both," I acknowledge, as I drive straight through the main thoroughfare. Aunt Cora lives in a small, private neighborhood on the outskirts of town. I pull the car onto the shoulder and put it into park. "We're almost here," I say, turning to face her. I wipe my sweaty palms over my jeans. "You keep straight until you come to a T-junction. Then take a left, the next right, and it's the fourth last house on the left-hand side. It's the big white two-story house with the American flag out front." She looks at me curiously. "Both my cousins are in the marines." I open the door the same time she does. "Pull the car into the driveaway and around to the left, as far as you can go." I look up at the dark nighttime sky. "If anyone is watching the house, hopefully we can get in and out before they have time to do anything about it."

I climb into the cargo hold, trying to pretend my heart isn't trying to beat a path out of my chest. "Try not to kill me before I get to my sisters," I joke.

Her expression softens. "I'll drive slow, promise."

"Thanks for doing this, Rachel. I owe you."

She surprises me by reaching out and taking my hand. "It's okay. I'm glad I could help, and it's going to be fine. Your sisters will be so happy to see you, and you're going to be a family again." She smiles, squeezing my hand briefly before moving away.

As she closes the door, I lie flat on my back, my knees bent, praying she's right. Because this is only the start of a new battle.

Chapter Fourteen

Rachel

I do as Brad asked, driving slowly and carefully, and pull into his aunt's driveway, bringing Ky's Range Rover around the side of the house. I kill the engine when I can go no farther, parking in front of the three-car garage. I quickly jump out and go around back to let Brad out. He scrambles out as a light turns on inside the house, throwing both of us into the spotlight. Cursing, Brad grabs my hand and pulls me with him, racing toward the back of the house.

A large man with a mass of thick gray hair and a fierce expression steps out onto the back porch as we reach it. He's got a shotgun pointed right at us, and I almost pee my pants. His shoulders slouch, and his expression softens when he spots Brad. "Quick, inside," he says in a gruff voice, scanning the surroundings over our heads as Brad ushers me into the house.

A small, petite woman with long gray hair pulled into an elegant ponytail paces the kitchen floor in front of us. "Oh, Bradley, thank God," she rasps, rushing Brad and pulling him into her arms. "We got such a fright when you pulled up. I've been so worried about your mother. Please tell me she found you?"

Brad wraps his arms around his aunt. "It's okay, Aunt Cora. She did, and she's safe with my friends. I'm sorry you were worried, but we couldn't risk calling."

The back door snicks shut unexpectedly, and a little whimper flies out of my mouth. I don't think I'm cut out for all this sneaking around shit.

Cora's gaze lands on me. Extracting herself from Brad's arms, she smooths a hand down her plain pink shirt and steps toward me. She clasps my hands in hers. "I'm so sorry, my dear, I didn't realize Bradley brought a friend."

"This is Rachel," Brad says by way of introduction. "She came with me because I was afraid I might have a tail."

"Nice to meet you." I smile at her kind face. "Although I wish it was under different circumstances."

"We all do," the man says, carefully placing his rifle down on top of the counter. "I'm Jonathan by the way, but my friends call me Jon." He pats me gently on the shoulder, sending me a reassuring smile.

"Where are they?" Brad butts in, the urgency transparent in his tone and the expression on his face. "Where are my sisters?"

His aunt's face lights up. "This way. Emma hasn't stopped asking for you from the minute she got here."

"She hasn't?" The sheer vulnerability on Brad's face is doing funny things to my insides. Does he think his sisters haven't missed him as much as he obviously missed them?

Jon unlocks a wooden door to the basement, flicking the switch on the wall and tramping down the stairs. We all follow silently behind him. It's a workroom of sorts. Tons of tools hang from shelves and nails on the wall, and boxes of supplies line the floor. He guides us to a smaller, less conspicuous door at the back of the open space. He raps three times on the dirty door, unlocks the padlock, and then steps aside to let Brad enter first. He nods for me to follow him.

"Brad!" a girlish voice calls out in excitement. The sounds of racing footsteps approach. I hang back as a small girl with long blonde hair throws herself at Brad. She's sobbing and clinging to him. He lifts her up with ease, hugging her to him as he swings them both around. Tears flood his eyes, falling freely down his face, but his smile is as vast as the Atlantic Ocean. My heart soars at the sight, and tears threaten my eyes.

"Pumpkin," he croaks out. "I've missed you so much."

"Me, too, Brad," she cries. "I missed you every single day." She wraps her legs around his waist, and he holds her up. Pressing his cheek into the top of her head, he looks at me with unbridled joy and relief. It's contagious, and I find myself grinning back at him.

"Kaitlyn," Cora calls out, gesturing toward the corner of the room. I lift my head up, only noticing his other sister now. "Come say hi to your brother." She's nearly as tall as Brad, and her hair is the same shade of blonde. She has it cut in a short bob with both sides tucked behind her ears. She's wearing tattered jeans that have clearly seen better days and a long, loose patterned T-shirt with a charcoal gray hoodie.

She pushes up from the couch, sauntering toward us with a wary expression. Brad places Emma's feet on the ground, squeezing her hand before walking toward his other sister. "Munchkin," he murmurs, tentatively pulling her into a hug.

Kaitlyn is stiff as a brick in his arms. "Don't call me that. I'm not a little girl anymore, Brad."

Easing back, he places his hands on her shoulders. "No, I can see that." He skims his sister's face. "You've changed so much. You're so tall, and you cut your hair."

"It wasn't by choice," she snaps.

"Kaitlyn." Cora's voice carries a silent warning.

"I guess we've lots to catch up on," Brad says calmly, but the way his voice falters a little tugs my heartstrings. I can't even begin to imagine what life on the run was like, and Kaitlyn is obviously battling some demons, but taking it out on Brad isn't fair. He's been through his own hell.

"I'll give you the short version," she says, her sneer matching the sarcasm in her tone. "Dad's a selfish prick, and Mom's too weak to stand up for herself. She'd rather subject us to shady lowlifes and drag us all round the world, rather than tell the man she married that he's a scumbag criminal who deserves to rot in hell for what he's done."

"Don't sugarcoat it or anything, Kaitlyn," Brad retorts, jerking his head in his younger sister's direction.

"Screw you, Brad. What the fuck would you know about it? You held on to your lifestyle while we were slumming it." She pushes away from him, folding her arms angrily over her chest.

A muscle clenches in Brad's jaw, but he doesn't retaliate. He just stands there, taking the abuse hurled at him. That doesn't sit right with me.

"Contrary to what you believe, it hasn't been all rainbows and unicorns for your brother either," I interject, feeling pissed and protective on Brad's behalf. "And I don't care what you've been through, you need to watch your tone."

Yeah, I'm so not analyzing that.

She narrows her eyes at me. "And who the fuck are you to tell me anything?"

"Don't, Rachel." Brad turns pleading eyes on me, and I reluctantly seal my lips shut.

I want to speak up for Brad because I know he hasn't had it easy, but his sister is still young, and she's clearly been through an ordeal too. That thought throws water over the smoldering flames of my anger. "We should make tracks. It's getting late."

He nods, and his eyes express gratitude. "Can you pack up your things, girls. We're getting out of here."

"Where to?" Kaitlyn asks, still scowling.

"Mom's in a safe place, and I'm bringing you to join her."

The girls pack their things, and we say a quick goodbye to Cora and Jon. I promise to text them once everyone is safely in the house in Wellesley. Brad climbs in the cargo hold, and the girls cower on the floor of the backseat as I reverse the Range Rover out of the driveway. Once I've gone a few miles and I'm sure no one is following us, I pull over and let him out.

Before I can walk away, he snags my wrist and pulls me to him. His mouth is soft and warm as it collides with mine. I know I shouldn't kiss him back, but it's too difficult to resist. Especially when his kiss is sweet and adoring, and I'm sensing how much he needs this connection, so I don't bother fighting something both of us want even if we're opposed to articulating it. We mutually part lips a couple of minutes later. He presses his forehead to mine, and my hands automatically grip his waist.

"Thank you, Rachel," he whispers. "For putting yourself on the line for me."

I look into his sincere eyes, and he plants his lips against mine for one last, brief moment, and, dear Lord, that feather-soft kiss unravels me. There's something so tender in the gesture, and in his gaze, and it affects me on a soul-deep level. This is the side of him Faye has spoken about. A side I've only caught fleeting glimpses of up to this point. A side

I was reluctant to believe existed. I can keep dickhead Brad at bay, but a softer, kinder persona? I don't know how I'm expected to resist. The thought unnerves me for a whole heap of reasons.

I touch my fingers to my lips, savoring the lingering tingle from his caress. How he can manage to convey so much with one tender kiss is unreal, but I know I'll be replaying it in my mind later. I imagine this is what it's like for Faye every time Ky kisses her. For the first time, a pang of envy jumps up and bites me, and I don't know what to make of it.

We part without another word, climbing into the car, and Brad wastes no time getting back on the road.

"Hey," he says a little while later, extracting his iPhone and handing it to me. "I still have all your songs, Munch—Kaitlyn. How about some Katy Perry?" His handsome face is expectant as he looks through the mirror at his sister.

I plug his phone into the docking station and switch it on.

"She's lame."

I've never been a huge Katy Perry fan, but I feel a sudden urge to defend her considerable talent; however, I bite my tongue. The last thing Brad needs is me and his sister at loggerheads.

He scratches the back of his head. "Eh, okay. I have tons of other stuff on there if you want to look? I've got lots of current music if that's more your scene?"

Kaitlyn slouches in her seat, scowling. "Yeah, 'cause I spent the last three years downloading songs on my imaginary iPhone," she drawls. "Get real." She stares out the window, her shoulders hunched over, looking like she's carrying the weight of the world, and I feel for her.

Brad looks so lost and unhappy, and I reach out, touching his knee. "What about you, Emma?" I turn and look at his youngest sister. She's twelve, but she's hugging a battered, dirty white teddy bear to her chest like he's her best friend in the world. I suppose he probably has been in recent years. The thought makes me unbelievably sad. I have some experience of losing precious childhood years. It's not anything I'd wish on my worst enemy. "Would you like to listen to some Katy Perry?"

She sends me a small smile. "Do you have "Roar"? I always liked that one."

"Coming right up, Pumpkin," Brad says, winking at his little sister, and I can almost see the tension seeping out of his pores.

The rest of the journey passes by quite quickly. Emma is a little sweetheart, and it's blatantly obvious how much she missed her brother and how much she looks up to him. She chatters away, singing along to some of the songs and introducing me to Snowy—her well-worn teddy bear.

I see a totally different side to Brad as he interacts with his little sister, and a pang of some emotion I can't decipher hits me square in the chest. I can already tell Brad is a great big brother, and his sisters don't realize how incredibly lucky they are to have him. This is further evidence of the side of his personality he's previously kept hidden from me. I don't miss the concerned glances he shoots his other sister's way. Kaitlyn is sullen and silent the entire journey, refusing to engage in conversation even though Brad tries relentlessly to include her.

If ignoring people was a skill, she'd hold the black belt. But I'm trying not to be judgmental. I have no idea what horrors she's been through.

Brad doesn't bother getting back in the boot again. We figure if we've gotten this far that we're not being tailed. Still, I don't take a proper breath until we are safely in the tunnel of the secret entrance onto the Kennedy property and the gate is sealed shut behind us.

"What the hell is this place?" Kaitlyn asks, looking lively for the first time. She sits up straighter in her seat, forgetting to be sulky in the face of such an unbelievable sight. I'm with her on that front. Brad had burst out laughing when he saw the shocked looks on both our faces as the trees parted, revealing the hidden gate for the first time.

"It's like the Batcave!" Emma shrieks, jumping up and down in her seat. "Are we going to live in Wayne Manor?"

"Don't be such an idiot," Kaitlyn snorts. "You're old enough to know Batman isn't real."

"What?" Brad feigns shock. "Batman isn't real? Shut. Up. Dude."

I laugh, and Emma sniggers. Kaitlyn rolls her eyes.

Faye and Ky are waiting for us when we park. The garage is well-lit and less creepy than I was imagining as Brad maneuvered the car through the narrow tunnel. A petite woman with a huge smile stands out front. If I didn't guess it was Brad's mom, I could tell by the eyes. Brad's are a carbon copy of his mother's. I stretch my arms over my head when I hop out, attempting to loosen my stiff limbs.

"Girls!" Brad's mom cries, running forward. She grabs both her daughters in her arms, hugging them firmly to her chest. Kaitlyn displays the same stiff posture with her mother, so it's obviously not just confined to her brother.

"Bradley." She reaches an arm out for Brad, pulling him into the family embrace. I scoot over beside Ky and Faye, watching the reunion with damp eyes. Faye and I share smiles.

"What happened to your head?" his mom asks, pressing her fingers to the bruised, raised bump on his forehead, courtesy of moi.

I silently curse.

Uh-oh.

I think I'm in trouble.

Chapter Fifteen

Brad

Mom frowns as she gently probes my skin. Before I can downplay it, Ky cuts in. "That's called foreplay," he quips, and I want to slap him upside the head. Judging from the glare Rachel sends his way, I'm figuring she shares my sentiment.

It might be commonplace for the Kennedys to talk so crudely in front of their parents, but my home was never like that.

"You never told me you had a girlfriend, honey," Mom says, scowling a little at Ky's word choice. If she were in her own house, I'm sure she'd have a few choice words in reply, but she's in his domain, and Mom's way too polite to put him in his place.

Even though the jackass deserves it.

Mom and I have completely different views on sexual entanglements.

Case in point. Mom hears foreplay and thinks girlfriend. I hear foreplay and think hookup. She'd be disgusted if she knew the truth about my sex life. She raised me to be respectful of women, and she's an advocate for committed relationships. She was at her happiest when I was going out with Rose, loving the fact I was in a steady relationship, despite how young we were. Dad was Mom's first and last boyfriend, and to say she's sheltered and completely ignorant of what it's like to be a single male on campus these days is an understatement.

Perhaps I'm a coward like my dad, but I don't want her to be disappointed in me so soon after she's returned home. There'll be plenty of time for that.

"Shame on you, Brad," Ky retorts, enjoying making me squirm.

I am so going to kick his ass for this. He has some inkling of what Mom's like, and he's milking this on purpose.

"When will I get to meet her?" Mom asks, planting her hands on her hips.

I'm across the garage in a flash, my hand covering Ky's mouth before he can dig an even bigger hole for me. Out of the corner of my eye, I notice Rachel elbowing Faye in the ribs.

But both our interventions are to no avail.

"She's right there, Mom," Emma pipes up, innocently pointing at Rachel. "Brad was kissing her outside the car earlier."

Shit. Didn't think either of my sisters had been paying attention to that.

Several pairs of eyes swivel in my direction. Ky folds his arms, surveying me with a smug expression. Mom turns around, smiling broadly at Rachel.

Holy clusterfuck.

Rachel looks at me with panic-stricken eyes. My gaze is pleading. "You owe me," she mouths, and I dread to think what new punishment she'll line up for this. Drawing a sharp breath, she takes a step forward. "Hi, Mrs. McConaughey. I'm Rachel. Brad's, um, girlfriend."

My breath of relief mingles with a layer of stress. *How the fuck did I end up with a fake girlfriend again?* I'm going to murder Ky for setting this in motion.

It's really late so we decide to crash here for the night. Alex and James appear, bringing takeout. After we've eaten, I help my sisters settle into their rooms. Kaitlyn is quiet as she takes in the plush surroundings of the gorgeous double room with en suite bath, but I'm figuring that's a positive thing. She left an innocent, cute little girl and has returned all grown up with an attitude to match. Instead of feeling pissed at her, I'm consumed with grief and sorrow. I spent the years we were separated worried about my family, but I never really stopped to think about what life must've been like for them. I think the fact she's so moody and grumpy is more than just normal teenage hormones, and I'm sick over the things she might've endured.

Although she's been prickly, I don't hesitate to grab her into a hug before I leave. It's one-sided again, but I don't care. I'll do whatever it takes to get through to her, to help her overcome the stuff she's been through. "I'm sorry things have been so shitty for you, Kaitlyn, but that's all behind you now. I'm here, and I'm not going to let anything happen to you, Mom, or Emma. I promise."

Slowly, her arms wrap around my waist, and a surge of emotion tightens my chest. She doesn't speak, but I don't need words. I just need her. I kiss the top of her head. "I'm staying upstairs. If you need anything, anything at all, just come find me."

She nods, giving me a small smile, and I feel like punching the air.

Emma is already tucked up in bed, with Snowy, by the time I make it to her room. Mom kisses her on the forehead and leaves. "Hey, Pumpkin." I tousle her hair. "You doing okay?" She nods, yawning. "I'll see you in the morning before I have to leave."

"I don't want you to go," she mumbles, fighting to keep her eyes open.

"I don't want to go either, but I need to talk to my coach and my professors. Then I'll be back and I'm going to stay for a while. That sound okay?"

She nods sleepily again, and I bend down, kissing her cheek. "Sleep tight, sweetie."

"I love you, Brad," she mumbles, and her small arms circle my neck.

"Love you too, Pumpkin." My heart is swollen to bursting point.

I stand in the doorway, watching her little chest inflate and deflate, in grateful relief. Words cannot express how happy I am to have my family back in my life.

"Sweetheart," Mom says, appearing behind me. "You should get some sleep. You've an early start."

"You have everything you need?" I whisper, turning to face her.

"I'm good, sweetheart. Go to bed. I'll see you for breakfast." I hug and kiss her before making my way upstairs to the main house.

Ky is waiting for me in the darkened living room. "Everyone else has gone to bed. I just wanted to make sure everything was good with your family," he says, as I drop down on the couch across from him.

"They're all good. Thanks so much, man. I don't know what we'd do without your family's support."

"No sweat. You'd do the same if the tables were turned." He stands up, stretching his arms out over his head. "I'm going to turn in. You're in your usual room." He fights a smirk as he looks at me. "I put Rachel in the guest room beside you, in case you want to kiss your girlfriend good night."

"Don't ruin my good mood, dude." I stand up, slapping him on the back.

We walk together, talking in hushed voices. "What? You have an issue with fake girlfriends now?"

I pin him with an "are you serious?" look. "Yeah, 'cause it worked out real swell the last time around." The smirk falls off his face, and he glares at me. "What the fuck do you expect me to say? Are you trying to piss me off on purpose?" I demand.

He stops, grabbing my elbow. "Of course not. I'm sorry. I guess I'm just tired and spouting shit."

I shrug his hand off. "Forget it. I don't want to fight with you."

We walk silently through the lobby and out into the corridor leading to the bedrooms.

"You could do worse you know," he whispers.

I sigh. "I know, and if things were different maybe it would lead somewhere."

He stops outside his room. "Don't close yourself off to it. I know you've a lot of shit on your plate, but she could be good for you, and I see the way you two are with each other. You can't deny you feel something for her."

I sigh again. "I feel something," I admit truthfully, "but I don't know what yet, and I can't go there. Mom needs me and my focus has to be on school, football, and my family. Maybe when things settle down..." I deliberately trail off, not able to vocalize the thoughts in my head. I'm thrilled Mom and my sisters are back, but they're not out of the woods yet, and there's still plenty at stake.

I'd be lying if I said I wasn't terrified.

I'm scared shitless of what the future holds, but I'm determined to step up and be the man my family needs. My father wasn't prepared to put himself on the line for the girls, but I am. Nothing means more to me than my family.

I'm still tossing and turning in bed an hour later. I glance at the clock, groaning at the time. I've only got five hours until I have to get up for the trip to Harvard. I need to try and smooth things over with Coach and the administration and buy myself some time off.

My phone pings quietly, and I reach over for it. It's a text from Rachel.

U awake?

Yeah. Can't sleep.

Me either.

My pulse throbs wildly. I tap out a reply before my head can talk me out of it.

Want company?

The three little dots appear, and my stomach is twisted into knots as I wait for her response.

My door is unlocked.

I'm out of the bed in record time, snagging my jeans off the floor and pulling them on. I pad in my bare feet to her door, quietly stepping inside.

The room is in darkness, but I can make out her form in the bed. She's sitting up with her knees tucked in to her chest. I walk to her side, perching on the edge of the bed. Her big brown eyes convey everything she wants. I lean in slowly, angling my mouth toward hers. She closes the gap, cupping the back of my head and pulling me to her. Our lips collide in an explosive kiss, and my fingers wind through her hair. Her mouth opens, and I slip my tongue inside, exploring her exquisite mouth as her tongue dances with mine. I'm rock hard already, and blood thrums through my veins in anticipation. Clawing at my bare back, she runs her fingers up and down my spine. She emits a gorgeous throaty sound as she leans sideways, pulling me with her. Our upper bodies are flush, but my legs are still on the floor.

Ripping my lips from hers, I stand up, dropping my jeans to the ground. "Move into the center of the bed," I command, and she obeys. I crawl over her, completely naked. "I need you naked, Red." My voice is heavy with desire.

Without speaking, she undresses, and my eyes skim over every luscious curve. Reaching over, she pulls a condom out of the bedside table and hands it to me. I pull it on and then lean down on top of her, trailing a line of kisses from her mouth to her neck and lower. I pepper kisses down her body, stopping to worship her glorious tits, teasing her nipples until the buds are taut. I continue my journey down her body, and my cock stiffens painfully. When I taste her, she arches her back off the bed, whimpering. My tongue goes to work, and I'm loving the way she's writhing and breathing at my touch. When she falls into ecstasy, I stay with her, lapping at her until she's completely sated. Then I position myself and dive into her in one smooth thrust.

I capture her gasp of surprise with my mouth. "Shush, beautiful. We don't want to wake the entire house."

I move slowly inside her, kissing her mouth and her neck, wanting to take my time. To commit every touch, every caress, every tremor to memory. She keeps a slow, steady pace with me. Her hands explore my body as we move together, and her legs wind around my waist. Our eyes connect, and we stare at one another as our breathing becomes more erratic, my thrusts more urgent. Still, we don't lose eye contact, and it's the most intimate moment of my life. I feel too much for this girl, and it scares me, but I can't look away. Can't ignore the connection or the way she makes me feel.

A second orgasm rocks her body, and my own release thunders through me. I bury my head in her shoulder as I come down from the high. Her legs relax, and I slide to the side, reality crashing down around us. Silently, I move to the bathroom and dispose of the condom.

I return with a cloth and help clean her up. She looks up at me uncertainly. I was planning to retreat to my room to question my sanity, but I don't want to fuck her and run. I don't want her thinking she was just another hookup when we both know what we've just done is way more than that. So, I slide under the covers, spooning her from behind. "Sleep, beautiful." I press a kiss to her temple and tighten my arms around her waist.

Chapter Sixteen

Rachel

Predictably, Brad is gone when I wake the next morning. At least I can avoid an awkward conversation. Last night was different. It felt like more than just meaningless sex, but what do I really know? Sex for me is usually something that's taken or expected. Inevitable and more about the momentary high than any real pleasure. But last night was completely different. It felt like Brad was making love to me, cherishing me in a way no one ever has before. I'm totally conflicted over it, so I'm glad he's not here, because I have no way of explaining it to myself, let alone to him.

I take a shower and get dressed in the clothes Faye gave me last night. I've only just slipped my shoes on when there's a knock on the door. "It's open," I quietly call out.

Faye pops her head in. "We're going to have breakfast in the Batcave with Brad's family. You in or out?"

I smile at her reference. "Sure. I'll come."

"So," she says as we make our way to the secret lair. "What's going on with you and Brad?"

I tuck my hair behind my ears. "I don't really know," I answer truthfully.

"Ky saw him coming out of your room during the night."

There's no point denying the truth. "Yeah. We slept together."

Her answering smile is expansive. "That's becoming a bit of a habit."

I scratch the side of my head. "I know, but I don't know what it means, if anything."

"What do you want it to mean?" she asks, stopping just outside the door to the annex where Brad's family are staying.

"I honestly don't know. I'm very confused." Truth.

"I think he likes you but he's afraid to admit it to himself."

"Maybe. And maybe that's where my head's at." I surprise myself with my forthrightness, but it's a pleasant surprise. In the past, I'd rather have yanked out all my teeth than admit to any sort of feelings.

We walk into the annex, and Faye heads straight for the kitchen to help serve up breakfast. The smell of bacon and eggs wafts through the air, and my stomach grumbles in appreciation. Brad is seated at the dining table with Ky, James, and Emma. Kaitlyn is nowhere to be seen, and Brad's mom is in the kitchen helping Alex.

Might as well get this over and done with. "Morning," I say, in an overly cheery manner, taking the vacant seat beside Brad. I'd rather that than face him across the table.

"Morning," Brad murmurs, not even looking at me. So, it's going to be like that. My stomach twists unpleasantly.

"Morning, Rachel," Ky says, leaning back in his chair, with a cheeky look on his face. "Sleep well?" His lips twitch.

I grab a piece of toast from the heaped plate in the center of the table. "Perfect. Thanks." I sink my teeth into the buttery toast and imagine it's Ky's head.

"So," James says, leaning forward with his elbows on the table. "When did you two become an item?"

I almost choke on my toast, and Brad visibly stiffens beside me. I open my mouth to admit the truth when Brad's mom walks to the table carrying a mammoth dish laden with crispy bacon and poached eggs. She places it down, her gaze bouncing between me and her son. "I'm interested to hear this story too."

She taps my shoulder affectionately before taking a seat the other side of Brad. I kick him under the table, and a trickle of sweat beads on my brow. His eyes lock on my face, pleading with me to keep the ruse alive. I'm not happy about it, but I'm guessing this is tied up with his mom, and he doesn't want to admit to the lie. Fine, but I'm not going to throw more lies on top of the pile. He can man up, considering he's the one who trapped me in this mess.

I plant a sugary sweet smile on my face as I lean in and kiss his cheek. "You tell them, honey. I'm sure your mum would love to hear you share the story."

Ky is struggling to maintain his composure across the way. Faye starts handing out plates and dishing out food, sharing a quick "what the hell" look with me. "It's a relatively new development," Brad starts explaining. "Rachel and I have met a few times these last couple of years, and we've gotten closer since she moved here for college. It just kinda happened naturally."

I reluctantly admire how smoothly he got out of that one, and he hasn't told any lies either. I've got to give credit where it's due.

His mom seems appeased by that too. She leans back in her chair, smiling at me. "I'm looking forward to getting to know you, honey. Any girl that has captured my Bradley's heart has to be special."

"Ugh," Kaitlyn says, materializing in the kitchen in her pajamas. She rubs sleepy eyes. "I think I'm going to vomit. Seriously, Mom? Can we not do this first thing."

I've got to agree with the girl. I'd give anything to terminate this conversation before it escalates.

"Kaitlyn." Mrs. McConaughey sounds exhausted as she utters that one word.

Brad stares at his sister, imploring her with his eyes. "Come eat with us before we have to leave."

The rest of breakfast passes uneventfully, and it's not long before the four of us are alone in Ky's Range Rover, heading on the quiet roads back to Harvard.

"We've got to do something about this fake relationship thing," I say from the back seat. Brad is sitting up front with Ky, while Faye is in the back with me. "I hate lying, and I should never have agreed to go along with it in the first place."

Brad twists around, eyeballing me. "You owed me."

I slant a look at him like he's crazy. "How the hell do you figure that?"

"For all the shit you put me through before agreeing to go last night."

I fold my arms across my chest. "I don't know what you're implying. I meant every word." I never did get a chance to tell him I was bluffing about the whole deal.

His eyes narrow suspiciously. "If you say so."

"I do."

A smug grin appears on his mouth. "Well, at least we've made some progress. Two orgasms down, three to go, and no male chastity belt in sight."

My cheeks flare up, and I cannot believe he just went there. Especially in front of our friends. Brad seems to have a natural ability to take something I consider special and transform it into something seedy. Last night meant something to me. Clearly, it didn't to him.

Before I can form an appropriate retaliation, Ky thumps him on the arm. "That's not cool, man."

"What? Rachel knows how to take a joke." He turns confused eyes on me. "Right?"

"Just shut up, dickhead." A piercing pain stabs me through the chest, and tears are threatening to spill.

"Aw, come on, Red. Don't be like that."

"Brad. I think that's enough," Faye snaps.

"For the record," I say a couple of minutes later, when the threat of tears has subsided. "I *was* only messing last night. Consider us quits, and the next time your mom asks me about us, I'm telling her the truth, so I'd suggest you fill her in first."

"Fine," he snaps.

The look Ky gives him would cause weaker men to cower, but Brad just glares right back.

I'm tempted to call him out on his hurtful, juvenile behavior, but I don't have the energy for this. And it hurts. More than I'd like to admit.

All conversation ceases for a while. There's an awkward vibe in the car, and I know everyone's feeling it.

Faye sends me sneaky glances every so often as I rest my head against the window. Her hand creeps over the leather seat, her fingers threading through mine. I can scarcely swallow over the lump in my throat.

I hate how Brad can take me from such highs to such lows. But I'm grateful for the reminder.

This is exactly why I avoid relationships.

I don't have the time or the mental capacity to deal with his rapidly changing mood swings.

I swear I'm not sleeping with him again.

He can go and fuck himself for all I care.

My phone vibrates in my pocket, and I remove it, swiping my finger across the screen.

I've a new text message, but I don't recognize the number. Figuring I've received a text in error, I open it up without thinking.

All the blood drains from my face as I read it. My stomach dips to my toes, and nausea swims up my throat. It's as if my heart's just stuttered in my chest.

You can run, but you can't hide. I'll be seeing you soon.

Chapter Seventeen

Brad

I'm watching Rachel through the mirror, and I can tell the instant she turns ghostly white. Her lower lip trembles, and her cell slips between her fingers, plummeting to the ground. I've great reflexes, and I lunge for the phone, my fingers curling around it before it hits the floor.

"Here." I hold it out to her, and she takes it from me with shaky hands. I gently touch her arm. "Hey, is everything okay?" Her eyes are swimming in panic when she lifts them to me. Nervous adrenaline courses through my system. I've only seen such naked terror one other time. On Faye's face when we were tied to chairs in the cabin and Courtney was holding us hostage at gunpoint. She'd been petrified, and I remember a similar look on her face.

What the hell just happened to Rachel to cause that same look?

Who the hell just texted her?

"Rach?" Faye looks anxiously at her friend. "Who is it? Is something wrong?"

Rachel stares ahead, as if in a daze. Faye unbuckles her seatbelt, and scoots over beside her. Her arm goes around her friend. "Who was the text from?"

Rachel turns rigidly still, and my instincts go on high alert. Faye looks at me with blatant concern.

"I, ah, can you stop the car, Ky. I need some air." Rachel's chest rises and falls in quick succession.

Ky pulls over to the shoulder and she hops out. Faye jumps out with her, keeping an arm around her waist as she throws up. I glance at the back seat where Rachel left her phone.

"Don't do it, man." Ky pins me with a look. "If she wants us to know, she'll tell us."

"She's scared stiff." I scrub a hand over my unshaven jaw. "I want to help."

"Stop being a douche then. Seriously, man. It's like you have foot in mouth disease, or are you doing that shit on purpose?"

"I don't know." It's the truth. It's like my internal settings are automatically set to self-sabotage mode.

We stop talking as the girls clamber back in. "Here." I pass her some tissues. "You okay?"

She nods, but her hands are still trembling as she clumsily fastens her seat belt. Ky shares a loaded look with Faye before easing the car back out into the traffic.

Silence engulfs us, and the only sound is the tap-tapping of Rachel on her phone. A few minutes later it pings with a new message. Rachel clears her throat. "No need to drop me off at college. I'm coming to Harvard with you."

Faye sits up straighter. "What's up?"

"Nothing." Rachel wets her lips, looking a little more composed. "I just have someone I need to meet."

Luckily, we reach campus while it's still early, because parking is a fucking nightmare most of the time, but Ky finds a vacant space and kills the engine. Rachel is out of the car before the engine's stopped humming. She gives Faye a quick hug, wiggling her fingers at Ky and me, and then she takes off running across the lot.

"What the hell is going on with her?" I ask, stepping outside.

"I don't know, but I don't like it," Faye replies, shutting the car door as she drags her lower lip between her teeth. "And you need to stop with all the mixed signals."

I shuffle on my feet. "It's not intentional. Shit just keeps popping out of my mouth."

Faye folds her arms across her chest. "Do you like her?"

I wish the ground would open up and swallow me. I lock my hands behind my head, scrambling for the right words.

Ky locks the car, and moves to Faye's side, taking her book bag and slinging it over his shoulder. He laces his fingers in hers.

"Well?" Faye demands, eyeballing me. She's not letting this go.

"I don't know," I admit truthfully. "I mean, of course, I like her, but I'm not looking for a relationship."

"Why not?" she bluntly asks, putting me on the spot again.

"I don't have time for a girlfriend."

"I'm calling bullshit on that," Ky interjects. "You make it sound like having a girlfriend is a chore or a responsibility when it's the complete opposite." He looks at Faye in his usual adoring manner. "Having someone on your side, someone you can talk to about all the shit, is in no way a chore. And you need that, man, because you don't confide in anyone."

I shove my hands in the pockets of my jeans, growing more and more uneasy by the second. "I *have* had girlfriends before."

"It's not like with Rose, man, you were only kids, and your other relationships were too casual to count. Don't disregard something that could be good for both of you."

"And it works both ways. I think Rachel needs you too."

"Don't," I hiss. "Don't put that shit on me. I don't know what's going on with her, and I'm sorry she seems to be dealing with stuff, but I can barely handle my own crap. How am I expected to support her?"

Faye shakes her head, and a disappointed look appears on her face. "I never took you for a coward, Brad, but it's like I don't even know you anymore." Her piercing eyes penetrate mine. "Do you even know yourself?"

And there's the million-dollar question.

I throw my hands in the air. "I don't know what you want me to say here, Faye. I'm clinging on by a thread in case you hadn't noticed. And I'm trying to do Rachel a favor by not involving her, and here you two are spouting all this shit at me. Enough already."

"Well then, stop sleeping with her!" Faye yells. "Rachel is trying to start afresh, and you're not helping if you're hurting her."

That sobers me up. "I don't want to hurt her. That's never been my intention."

"Well, you have. She won't ever admit that to me, because she's funny about guys, but I know my friend, and she has feelings for you. If you don't feel the same way, then you need to stay away from her. I won't forgive you if you mess her around."

"I hear you. I'll keep my distance." I sling my bag over my shoulder. "I've got to go. I need to find Coach. I'll catch you guys later."

I don't stick around, hotfooting it out of there. My heart is like a block of stone in my chest as I walk. No matter what I do, I can't help fucking everything up, and I'm getting sick of being in my own head.

I spend a couple hours with Coach and my advisor explaining my current home situation. Coach agrees to release me from training this week upon faithful promise that I'll be back next week. My advisor agrees to notify the relevant professors and arrange to have class notes and assignments emailed to me.

That should make me happy, but I'm still in a pissy mood as I walk through campus grounds. I'm passing through the quad when I spy Rachel leaving Kev's place again. Kev holds the door open for her, and they step outside. I dart behind a tree and watch.

Glutton. For. Punishment.

He has his hands on her lower back, and there's a concentrated look on his face as he talks. She nods slowly, and tears well in her eyes. He draws her into his arms, pressing his chin to the top of her head. Her eyes close as she wraps her arms around his waist. There's a familiarity and a comfort between them that indicates they are closer than I realized. Acid crawls up my throat, and I take off running, not able to witness another second of their togetherness.

I shouldn't care, but I do.

I return to our apartment and fix myself a sandwich for lunch. I turn the TV on to ESPN, watching highlights from the Patriot's last game as I eat. At some stage, I obviously fall asleep because I wake up a few hours later with a giant crick in my neck. I check my watch, cursing, and hop up.

I'll need to get on the road soon if I'm to avoid rush hour traffic. Yawning, I walk to my bedroom and start packing a bag.

The buzzer sounds in the kitchen, and I go to see who it is.

"Hi, it's Rachel. Can I come up. I have something to give you."

I press the button without responding and walk to the front door, leaving it unlocked.

"Brad?" she calls out a few minutes later.

"In here," I holler, stuffing the last few items in my duffel bag.

I smell the sweet, musky scent of her perfume before her presence is confirmed. I zip my bag and dump it on the floor before turning around. She's just wearing tight jeans and a plain white tank under an open pink-checkered shirt with high block-heeled shoes, but she manages to look completely ravishing. Her hair is loose but tucked behind her ears, and a light sheen of sweat dots her brow. She looks a little harried, and there's an uncertain expression on her face. I hate the thought that I probably put it there.

Bending down, she retrieves a multitude of shopping bags from behind her and walks into my room, almost buckling under the weight of her luggage. She deposits them at my feet before straightening up. "I thought your sisters might need some new clothes and things."

My eyes startle as I scan the vast amount of bags. "You went shopping for my sisters?"

She wipes her hands down the front of her jeans. "Um, yeah. I hope that's okay. I kinda needed to kill time, and I noticed they didn't have much stuff with them, and what they had seemed worn."

"You didn't go to class?"

She shakes her head. "Couldn't face it today, but I needed a distraction, and I love shopping so ..." She trails off, looking down at the floor, and she's like a different girl. Gone is the feisty, mouthy, confident girl I know. A huge surge of guilt waylays me. *Did I do this? Is this all on me?*

I take a step toward her. "You didn't need to do that, but thank you. I'm sure Emma and Kaitlyn will be very grateful." I slip my wallet out of my back pocket. "Let me give you something toward it." I can ill afford it, but it's not right that she's paid for it all.

Her head jerks up at that. "I don't want your money, Brad. You need it more than I do."

Ignoring the insult to my male pride, I remove all the cash in my wallet and hand it to her. "It's fine, and it's only fair. I had some spare cash leftover from my last student loan. Here, take it."

She steps back, clasping her hands behind her back. "I don't want it, Brad. I have more money than I know what to do with, and I wanted to do this for your sisters. It's a present from me. Put your money away."

She looks at me with steely determination, and I know there's no way I'm winning this battle. Stashing my money back in my wallet, I admit defeat. "Thank you. I'll find some other way to pay you back." I curse the instant the words leave my mouth, acknowledging how they could be misconstrued.

The Rachel I know would've had an instant retort on her tongue and a snarky expression on her face. But the stranger in front of me merely looks at the ground again. "Not necessary. I like that I'm in a position to help. We didn't have a lot of money growing up, and I'm lucky that I don't have to worry about it anymore."

Rachel's clearly in pain, and the urge to fold her into my arms and never let go is almost insurmountable. I purposely cement my feet to the floor because I don't think she'd appreciate the gesture. She just looks so lost, so forlorn, and so unlike herself, and my natural instinct is to protect her, to make her feel better. But I'm not her boyfriend, and I have no right to touch her without her permission. And after last night, and how I acted this morning, she probably wants nothing more to do with me, and I wouldn't blame her.

Last night was beyond incredible. I've never felt so much with any girl before, and it scared me. I can add coward and scoundrel to my resume, because, instead of confronting my feelings, I belittled her in front of our friends.

"I'm sorry," I blurt. "For what I said this morning. It was uncalled for and cruel, and I didn't mean to dismiss what we shared. I don't know what's wrong with me these days. I—"

"Forget it. It doesn't matter anymore." She starts backing toward the door. "We're cool, okay?"

No. It's not okay, but I don't want to push things and end up arguing again. "Okay."

"I'll see you around, I guess." She gives me a little wave and turns to leave.

I race after her. "Rachel, wait." She's already at the front door, but she stops, keeping her back to me. I maneuver in front of her. "I'm going back to Wellesley for the week. I want to be there for Mom as she deals with all the legal stuff, but it's not too far away. If you need me, need anything, all you have to do is call, and I'll come back."

"Why would I call you?" There's no malice in her tone or her expression. She's just stating a fact.

"Because I think you're going through something, and I want to help."

She shakes her head. "No, you don't. You just feel guilty now, but you've made your feelings perfectly clear. I think it's best if we stay away from one another."

"It doesn't mean we can't be friends."

"Yeah, I think it does." She looks sad. "But don't worry. I have someone I can depend on, and I'm fine."

An ugly ball of jealousy churns in my gut at the realization she means Keven. But I can't argue with her or defend myself, because my actions have sent her hurtling in his direction. And maybe it's best to step back. To let him support her. He's obviously better able to give her what she needs. If I care about her, and I realize I do, then I should step aside.

"Okay. I'm glad you have support, and my offer still stands. Call me anytime."

She sidesteps me, opening the door. "Thanks, but I won't."

And she might as well have driven a stake straight through my heart.

Chapter Eighteen

Rachel

"What's up with you?" Lauren asks, as we exit our last class of the day on Friday. "You've been acting weird all week."

"Nothing. I'm fine." I should just record myself saying it and press play anytime anyone asks. Faye has been on my case all week, and it's starting to piss me off. I know she means well, but she usually knows when to back down. Not this time. This time she's determined to unearth my secret. And I wish I could tell her, but I can't.

Last night, I spent three hours on my laptop searching for psychologists in the local area, and I have a couple of names saved in my phone. It's the closest I've ever come to seeking help, but I'm getting desperate. It feels like I'm losing my mind, and I'm scared out of my wits. Lauren is right in her observation. I know I'm acting crazy. The slightest noise has me jumpy, and on edge, and it's a wonder I haven't given myself whiplash with all the looking over my shoulder. I haven't relaxed all week, and I have barely eaten a thing. I can't stomach anything, and I'm surviving on nervous adrenaline, fresh air, and water.

I'm throwing myself into my studies, and I've been up late every night drawing designs and sewing until my fingers ache. It's the only thing that adequately distracts me. After a couple of nights of not sleeping—thrashing about in bed as the worst of my nightmares made an unwelcome return—I picked up a prescription for sleeping tablets. I took one last night and enjoyed three hours of solid, uninterrupted sleep before the horrific memories invaded my slumber.

Keven has stayed true to his word, contacting me daily with an update. He put a trace on the phone the text message came from, but he wasn't able to track down the sender or his location as the person covered their tracks too well. Kev says it's the work of someone who knows what they are doing, so I know *he* isn't doing this alone. All Kev could tell with certainty is that it's an American cell number and most likely the person is in the country.

I dry retched for an hour after that discussion.

I'm tempted to flee. *To take off again, but where would I go? And how long would it take before he'd find me again?*

No, running away isn't the solution.

Fucked if I know what is.

I almost took to the bottle the other night, but, somehow, I managed to resist. Returning to form would be so easy, but then all my hard work is undone, and I'm giving him power over me again. So, I've resisted but we're going out tomorrow night, and I'm infused with wild, reckless abandon. Perhaps, I should stay home, but I don't want to be alone, and I don't want to ask Faye to stay in again. Ky has been sleeping at our place all week, and they've barely left my side, because I begged her to stay in our apartment. She obliged immediately, but she knows I'm scared, and she wants to know the reason why.

"Rachel!" Lauren's concerned tone brings me back to the moment.

"What?"

She takes my elbow, steering me out of the building. "You haven't heard a word I've said."

I zip my jacket up as we hit the pavement. "Sorry. I was daydreaming."

"You know you can tell me anything, right? I know something's wrong, and I just want to be a friend."

I link my arm in hers. "And I love you for that, but I'm grand, honestly."

Filthy dirty liar.

She chuckles. "I'm so borrowing that word."

"You have my permission." I can't even muster a smile.

Her humorous expression withers and dies. "I know you have something on your mind. Is it Brad?"

I shake my head. "Nope. I've washed him right out of my hair." That's only half a lie. I *have* managed to avoid thinking of him too much, but that's only because all the other stuff is occupying my mind. At the moment, I have zero energy to figure out what's going on with Brad, and he hasn't contacted me all week, so I'm guessing we're both on the same page and I'm fine with that.

"Maybe you'll meet someone at the party tomorrow. Gav's bringing a few of his buddies along, and there's a couple of hotties in the group. You should let loose, and have some fun. Relieve some of that tension."

"I'm not interested." The words fly out of my mouth.

She raises her palms. "Okay. I get it. No running interference. Gotcha."

The party is on in the basement of some swanky three-story townhouse a fifteen-minute walk from Harvard. Some of the guys who play football with Brad live here, and they're celebrating their earlier win. Brad wasn't playing or even at the game. He's still back in Wellesley with his family. According to Ky, their solicitor has done some deal whereby his mom will give a statement in return for immunity from arrest. It's Brad's dad they want, and she's only a means to an end.

"Easy there, chicka," Faye tells me, eyeing my fresh bottle of beer. "You only picked at your dinner, and you know how it affects you when you drink on an empty stomach."

"I've got this. It's cool," I lie. I promised myself I could have a couple beers before we set out, but they're going down way too easy. I'm already on my third and nicely buzzing.

I just want to forget.

I can have this one night, and I won't spiral backward.

I'm still in control, I delude myself.

Faye and Ky are stuck to my side, and I hate that I'm cramping their style, but I'm not drunk enough yet to let them off the leash either. Every so often, I turn around, scanning the room. This type of a setup would be ideal. *He* could slip in and blend into the crowd and be upon me before I realized it, so, even though I'm well on my way to getting smashed, I'm not drunk enough to lose all sense of my priorities.

By the time Lauren, Gavin, and company show up, I've gone beyond the point of caring. She introduces me to the guys, and soon I'm in the middle of the group cracking jokes and laughing like I haven't a care in the world. In this moment, I don't. I fling my arms out as the music turns louder, swaying my hips in time to the beat.

"Hey, gorgeous." Large hands land on my hips, and I'm spun around. The guy smiling down at me looks somewhat familiar, but I can't yet place him. He's cute though with really broad muscular shoulders, dark brown hair that is curled at the front, and two massive dimples.

Man, I'm such a sucker for dimples. Before I know what I'm doing, my fingers are caressing the cute indents in his cheeks.

"I've zero issue with you putting your hands on me, but what the hell are you doing?" he asks, grinning.

"Exssamining your dimpless. They're ssspectacularr." I've a feeling I may be slurring my words a little.

He barks out a laugh. "Whatever turns you on, gorgeous." He grips my hips more firmly, and he starts moving us from side to side.

My hands land on his solid chest. "Nice." I trail my fingers up and down his chest and the ripped contours of his abs. "Very niccce."

He laughs again. "You're something else, but I like it. I like you."

I bat my eyelashes, running my hands up his arms and under his short-sleeved shirt, purring as I caress his huge biceps. "Biceps. Yum. Yummy." I nibble on my lip, swaying a little on my feet, and his large palm moves to my lower back, holding me in place.

"Want to take this somewhere more private?" he asks, and I nod without thinking.

Taking my hand, he leads me across the room. Faye is in front of me in a flash. "Where are you going?"

"Somewhere private." I wink and then giggle.

"I don't think that's a good idea." Her eyes narrow as she stares at the beefcake by my side.

"Me either. I think issa *great* idea." I giggle again.

"All righty. You heard the lady. If you'll excuse us." The beefcake wraps his arm around my waist, steering me forward.

Faye runs in front of him, slamming her palm into his chest. "She's drunk and she doesn't know what she's doing."

He glares at Faye. "She's a little tipsy, so what. Aren't we all?"

"Stop being a party pooper!" I peel her hand off his chest, trying to focus on her face, but it's blurry and I'm seeing double. "Go grab your guy and hazz some fun. I'll be back sssoon."

"Rach—"

"Christ, Faye! Would you just fucking quit it!" I grab her arm, pulling her off to the side, whispering in her ear. "I know what I'm doing, and I just want to forget, and cut loose, have a li'l fun. A mindless fuck is exactly what the doctor ordered. He's on the football team with Brad," I add, suddenly remembering why he's familiar, "and we're only going to be upstairs, so chill out. I know whass I'm doing. Go back to your boyfriend before he freaks out."

I grab the guy's hand and pull him forward. "Let's get this party started."

He leers at me, bringing my hand to his mouth and planting a wet kiss on my skin. "Your wish is my command."

I trot alongside him, teetering on my heels, vaguely aware of passing faces, hearing voices, and going up a couple floors. My head is spinning, and my stomach is churning, but my brain is beautifully fuzzy, and that's what I'm after.

The click of a door locking brings me back to the moment. I glance around. We're in a decent-sized bedroom. The walls are painted a dark gray, and the king-sized bed is dressed in shades of black and gray. The bed is unmade as he pushes me back on it, crawling over me and smashing his mouth against mine.

So much for subtlety.

He tastes like beer and stale cigarettes, and my stomach lurches. He's attacking my mouth like it's been a decade since he kissed a girl, and there's nothing tender or pleasant about the sensation. A meaty hand slides under my dress and up my thigh. Shoving my knickers aside, he thrusts a finger inside me without warning, and it hurts. Guess he's not much for foreplay either.

His breath is hot and heavy as his finger starts pumping in and out, and panic seizes control of my body.

What am I doing?

I *don't* want this.

Reaching down, I grab his wrist and yank on it, trying to turn my face to the side, away from his plundering mouth. His bulky frame presses down on me, and I can't get enough air into my lungs. "Stop!" I cry, tugging on his hand again. His finger stalls inside me, and he lifts his mouth off mine. I suck in greedy lungsful of air.

"What's wrong, babe?" His finger pumps inside me again.

"Gezz off me. I changed my mind."

"What?!" he growls, rocking his hips against mine, making sure I'm aware of how aroused he is. "You can't get me all worked up and then decide to fuck off. You want my mouth all over you, is that it?" Removing his finger, he moves up my body, and his mouth suctions on my neck, before quickly trailing lower. He tugs on the straps of my dress, yanking them down, and his lips slide over the swell of my breasts.

Panicking, I prop up on my elbows, throwing him off balance a little. The room spins. "Whoa." My vision is blurry, and I feel ill. Not that he seems to care. He lowers his face to my chest again. "Stop!" I plead. "I don't want to do thisss with you. I mazz a mistake."

He pushes me back down on the bed. "Just relax, baby. You're so tense." He starts tearing at my dress, desperate to get me naked. One side of my dress is ripped down, dragging my bra with it, exposing my left breast. He starts kneading my flesh roughly, his thumb pinching me, and a small cry leaves my mouth.

Flashbacks resurrect in my mind, and everything locks up inside me. "Please, stop," I ask in a quiet voice, all the fight leaving me in a rush as my past finally catches up to me.

"Just stop thinking, lie back, and enjoy. I'll have you begging for my cock in no time." His mouth crashes against mine as he frantically pulls at the other side of my dress. His breath reeks in the claustrophobic room, and the sounds of his slobbering, combined with the rough, greedy brush of his hands against my flesh, drags me firmly into the past, mentally kicking and screaming.

I ask him to stop again, but he ignores me.

It's as if my pleas have ghosted silently over his head.

As if my voice carries no tone or no weight.

As if I've resumed invisible status.

Horrific scenes return to haunt me. The hands pulling at my clothes are replaced with more familiar ones. The mouth brutalizing mine belongs to someone else. The body pinning me down exerts ultimate power, as *he* did time and time again.

I'm transported back to the very place I've been trying to escape, and I check out.

A rattling of the door handle barely snags my attention as he forces his tongue deep into my mouth. The sound of material ripping scarcely registers. Huge tears slide down my face, and my entire body is trembling, but I give up fighting. *What's the point?* He'll just take what he wants anyway. If I stay quiet and do as I'm told, it'll be over quicker. He pushes my thighs apart, burying his groin between my legs and emitting a guttural moan that twists my insides into knots. Acid churns in my gut, and nausea crawls up my throat, but I'm frozen in place on the bed, locked in the terrors of my past.

The door slams inward with a massive bang, crashing off the wall with a loud thud. Kyler storms into the room, followed by Keven and Gavin. The guy is ripped off me superfast, and Ky punches him in the face. Then Faye is there, pulling the ripped threads of my dress up, so I'm somewhat concealed, and cradling me in her arms. "It's okay. I've got you. You're safe."

I'm numb in her arms, clutching her shoulders and staring vacantly ahead. Sounds of scuffling and multiple curses filter through the room, but I barely hear it. Lauren crouches down in front of me, tears streaming down her face. She pulls off her cardigan and swathes me in it, buttoning it all the way to the top so I'm fully covered.

"I'm okay," I hear myself say in a monotone voice. "He didn't do anything to me." Well, not that much in the scheme of things. It could've been a hell of a lot worse.

"I'm getting her out of here," Keven says, lifting me into his strong arms. I rest my head on his chest as he walks with me, my stomach heaving with every jarring step. My surroundings blur, and my eyes spin in my head. Nausea churns at the base of my throat, and I clamp my lips shut.

As my eyes continue to roil in my head, I have one thought before my world turns black: I wish Brad was here.

Chapter Nineteen

Brad

I'm blatantly ignoring the speed limit, but I couldn't give two shits. I'd challenge any cop to pull me over and manage to restrain me. I can barely think over the red rage that's taken control of my body. I didn't hesitate when I received the call from Ryan, jumping in the car immediately. It was Ryan who tipped Ky off when he noticed Rachel going upstairs with Brady, and I owe him, big time. The closer I get to Harvard, the stronger my blood boils.

I try Ky again. I've been calling him incessantly, but he hasn't picked up so far.

But perseverance pays off.

He answers, this time, on the third ring. "You heard."

"Is she okay?"

"She's sleeping, but she seems okay."

Bile coats the inside of my mouth but I need to ask this question. "What did he do to her?"

"He was all over her when we bust into the room, and her dress was ripped, but I don't think it had gone very far, although we won't know until Faye talks to her, and that's if she even remembers. She was totally wasted."

Stars burst across my retinas, and the urge to hit something is strong. "Fuck! Fuck! Fuck! I should've been there. If I had, that asshole wouldn't have dared go near her."

"What are you going to do?"

"What do you think?"

"You need back up?"

"I'm good. Ryan and a few of the others will have my back."

"You sure about that? He's on the team too."

"Brady isn't well liked, and he's tried to pull this shit before. The guys take a dim view of any guy who tries to force himself on girls. Trust me, they'll willingly join in."

"Okay. I'll stay here then. Faye's upset, and she needs me. But if anything changes, just call and I'll be there. Don't be surprised if Kev has beat you to it. He was furious."

"I didn't know Kev was there. How the fuck did he allow this?" *How the fuck did you?* It's on the tip of my tongue, but I manage to rein it in. I'm saving all the venom for the douche who deserves it.

"He'd only just arrived, and, besides, I told you already they aren't seeing each other. She isn't his responsibility." That confirmation should please me, but, when it comes to Rachel and Keven, I don't think anyone but them knows what's going on.

"Just be careful. You don't need more heat on you."

Tell me something I don't know, but, in this moment, the only thing that matters is delivering punishment to the asshole who hurt Rachel. Consequences be damned.

By the time I reach the brownstone Brady shares with a few of our teammates, I'm practically spitting blood. I take the stairs three at a time, pummeling my fists on the door without mercy. Ryan opens up with a grave expression. He jerks his head upward. "He's hiding in his bedroom, but he knows you were coming. Grant and Fisher are with him, but everyone else is either with you or staying out of it. You sure you want to do this?"

"I'm sure," I snarl through gritted teeth. "But you don't have to. If Coach gets wind of this, there'll be hell to pay."

"I know, but if that was Chelsea, I'd want to pound his unapologetic ass into next week."

I nod. "Okay, let's do this."

I sprint up the stairs, fueled by angry adrenaline. Five of my teammates are waiting outside Brady's room, and they go quiet when I arrive. One by one we touch knuckles. "I appreciate this, but this is my battle, and my fists will be the ones flying."

"This douche has had this coming. It's not just your battle," Green speaks up. "He's shamed the team, and that reflects on all of us."

"Fair enough, but shit will get real if this gets out. Are you prepared for the fallout?"

The guys trade concerned expressions, and it's clear they haven't properly thought this through.

"Are you?" Green retaliates.

I don't need to think about it for long. I thought of nothing else on the drive here. "Yeah. Yeah, I am. He's not getting away with doing that to Rachel." I was weighing up the possible consequences on the drive over, and there's nothing that will stop me from teaching this pervert a lesson. Nothing.

Green slaps me on the shoulder. "Then I'm with you."

"We all are," Ryan supplies.

"Thanks, but only get involved if it's necessary. Agreed?"

They all nod. Now that's decided, I turn and face the door, hammering on it with my fists. "Open up, Brady. I know you're in there, hiding like the sniveling coward you are."

The door swings open. Grant and Fisher block the doorway, shielding the douche from sight. "Think this through, man," Fisher says, eyeing my clenched fists. "He didn't know she was yours, and it didn't go very far. He'll apologize to your girl tomorrow."

I don't bother correcting him. Whether she is or isn't my girl is beside the point. He has no right to treat any girl like that. If she was wasted, he should've known she was incapable of making a rational decision.

"I never fucking agreed to that!" Brady exclaims from behind.

Grant turns around. "Shut the fuck up, you idiot."

"I don't want to fight you," I tell Fisher, "but I will if you don't let me in that room. You know this isn't the first time he's pulled something like this, and it won't be the last unless we do something about it."

"Stop spouting crap, McConaughey," Brady says, elbowing his way in between the two guys. "We all know what this is about. You're just sore 'cause I had my hands and my tongue all over Irish. And she was fucking loving it too. You're clearly not satisfying her if she has to go elsewhere to get her kicks."

I lunge for the asshole, but Fisher holds me back. "You motherfucking asshole! I will kill you if you touch her again."

"Take a fucking chill pill, jerkoff," he sneers. "As if I'd go there again. If I'd known she was a drunken whore, I would have chosen more wisely. She was so wasted I could have stuck my dick anywhere and she wouldn't have complained. Would have too if that douche Kennedy hadn't butted in."

Grant curses, shaking his head as he steps out of the room. "That's it. You're on your own with this."

Fisher silently agrees, stepping aside and giving me free rein.

I crack my knuckles and launch myself at him.

I stagger up the steps to our apartment, cradling my sore ribs and biting back a moan. My hand throbs like a bitch, and I've a headache to end all headaches, but it was worth every ache. The guys held back, while Brady and I went head to head. Even with his superior bulk and height, he was no match for my vengeful aggression. He got a good few punches in too, but I managed to overpower him, pummeling my fists in his face as my rage spiraled out of control. The guys had to drag me off him, and I left him bloody and well-beaten. Hopefully, he'll think twice before pulling a stunt like that again.

I dump a ton of ice in the tub and climb in, packing it against my ribs and my hands.

After, I shower, washing away the last vestiges of blood, and crawl into my bed, aching and utterly exhausted. I pop a couple of pain pills, send a quick text to Ky, and promptly conk out.

It still hurts like a bitch the next morning when I finally wake. I've a couple of missed calls on my phone. I call Mom back first. "Sweetheart, is everything okay? You left so suddenly last night, and I've been worried."

Shit. I'm unaccustomed to having to account for my whereabouts with anyone, and I bolted out of the house the second I hung up on Ryan last night. All I'd said was that Rachel needed me, and I'd fled.

"Everything's fine, Mom." I try to disguise the wince as I pull myself upright in the bed. "Nothing for you to worry about, and I'm sorry I didn't text you last night. Guess I'm out of practice." Before, I never would have stayed out all night without texting Mom to confirm my whereabouts.

"Is Rachel okay?"

"She's fine." I hope. Swinging my legs out of bed, I stifle a groan as I clutch my throbbing ribcage.

There's a pregnant pause. "Well, I was calling to let you know that the meeting with the police chief has been brought forward to this morning. I'm getting ready to leave now."

Dammit. I really want to check on Rachel, and I want to be by Mom's side for this meeting too. *How to be in two places at once?* Before I make a call, Mom makes it for me. "I'd prefer if you weren't here, Brad. It's better that you're in the city."

"I want to support you, Mom."

"And you are, son, trust me, you are. But I'm not going to disrupt your life any more than is necessary. I want to keep you as far away from this as possible. If the media get hold of this, you need to be nowhere near it. James and Dan will both be with me, and it's not that big of a deal. I'm only giving a formal statement."

"What are you going to tell them?"

"The truth."

"All of it?"

"As much as I can without putting your father at risk."

I grind my teeth to the molars. She's still protecting him, even after everything he put her through. "He doesn't deserve your protection, and you don't owe him anything, Mom. He should have protected *you*." All week, I've bitten my tongue, but I can't hold back now. She needs to put herself first for a change. And if not for her, for my sisters. I don't see how any of us can put this behind us while Dad is still at large.

"When you love someone with every fiber of your being, you go to the ends of the earth to protect that person. Even if they've messed up.

I won't abandon your father or throw him to the wolves. Please don't ask that of me."

I don't agree, but this isn't the kind of conversation one has over the phone. "Okay, Mom. Good luck with the meeting, and I'll be back later. You can fill me in then."

"Of course, honey. Love you."

"Love you, too," I croak out. Mom always ended her phone calls like that, but it's been years since I've been on the receiving end of it, and it fills me with happiness to hear those words again.

An hour later, I pull up in front of Faye and Rachel's apartment building and park on the side of the street.

Faye opens the door to me, gasping when she sees the state of my face. Overnight, bruises have developed across my skin, complimenting the large cut on my lip. My face looks like something from a horror movie. She steps aside to let me in. Ky is in the kitchen drinking coffee. His eyes roam my face. "It's dealt with?" I nod.

"Are you going to get in trouble for this?" Faye asks in a hushed tone, pouring a mug of coffee and handing it to me.

"Thanks, and I don't know. Nor do I care. Someone had to deal with that asshole." Her look is contemplative, and then a slow smile graces her lips. I frown. "What?"

"Nothing." She sips her coffee, the secretive smile still intact.

"Is she here? Can I see her?" I ask.

Faye's smile fades. "I'll go ask her. Stay here." She puts her mug down and leaves the room.

"Rachel's not in a good place, Brad. She has barely eaten all week, and she's been throwing up most of the night. She was like a zombie this morning, and she's not even talking to Faye, so I wouldn't get your hopes up."

"This is my fault." I sigh.

"I honestly don't think it is. There's something else going on with her. Has been for years, but she refuses to talk about it, although

Faye is even more stubborn than she is, and now she's decided she's not backing down until she opens up. She's considering calling her parents."

"That would not be a good idea," a burly voice says, startling us. Keven Kennedy removes his jacket and flings it over the back of a chair.

"How the fuck did you get in here?" Ky asks.

"The door wasn't properly closed." He stalks to the counter, pouring himself a coffee.

His words regurgitate in my mind. "Why would calling her parents be a bad idea?"

He leans back against the counter, surveying me as he sips his coffee. "That's not for me to say."

I bite the inside of my cheek in aggravation. "If you know what has her so terrified you need to tell me." He arches a brow, crossing his feet at the ankles, and his unruffled demeanor is having the opposite effect on me. I'm strung tight like a bow.

"And why is that, Brad? Or is there something I don't know about the status of your relationship with Rachel?" He looks to his brother.

Ky straightens up. "We're all worried about her, Kev."

"I know, but I'm on it."

I push the stool away, and it scrapes noisily across the tiled floor. I stand to my full height. "What exactly does that mean?"

"I'm keeping her safe."

My fists ball at my sides. His calm, impassive expression and vague comments are rubbing me up the wrong way. "What's going on with you two?" I blurt, unable to stand it any longer.

"None of your business." Kev's throat works overtime as he drains the rest of his coffee.

The guy might be built like a tank, with biceps bigger than my head, but I could take him. "Screw you, Kev."

"Quit with the pissing contest," Faye says, marching into the kitchen. "Rachel doesn't need this grief." Her features soften as she looks at me. "I'm sorry, Brad, but she doesn't want to see you." A horrible crushing feeling presses down on my chest. She cringes a little as she turns to Keven. "She's been waiting for you. You can go straight in."

To be fair to Kev, he doesn't look smug or milk it in any way, merely nodding and walking out of the kitchen. Faye looks apologetic, and a messy ball of emotion churns in my gut. I need to get some distance, and there's nothing keeping me here now anyway. "I've got to go. Catch you guys later."

I don't wait for a reply, striding out of the apartment and slamming the door shut behind me. I've no right to my anger or my hurt, but I can't help how I feel. In the elevator, I bury my head in my hands, hating how fucking confused I am.

My phone pings as I step foot outside the building. It's a message from Coach asking to meet him in an hour. Dammit. Guess the cat's out of the bag. I sprint to my car, and power up the engine.

Time to face the music.

I took one look at Coach's face and knew I was in deep shit. He's just chewed me out for the last ten minutes without pausing for a breath. "You've got huge potential, McConaughey, but you're pissing it away. I don't want to do this, but I have no choice. You put Brady in the hospital with a concussion. The doctors are keeping him in for a few days, and he's unavailable to the team for at least a couple weeks. The last thing I want is to lose another key player, but I have to set an example. The administrative board takes a very dim view of violence in any form, especially where it's a teammate."

"If I can say something," I butt in when I find a gap in his tirade. "I'm not excusing my behavior or condoning it, and I'll take whatever punishment is deemed appropriate, but I didn't lash out for no reason." I update him on what went down last night and the other few incidents I was privy to where Brady overstepped the mark with girls. His face is stoic and unreadable as he listens.

He sighs, leaning back in his chair. "You boys are turning me old before my time," he mutters. "If what you say is true"— he raises his palm in warning when I open my mouth to speak. I clamp it shut again—"I'm not doubting you, but Brady needs a chance to respond to your allegations, and I'd like to talk to the others. If it's true, then Brady will be subject to disciplinary action, but I can do jack shit about that until he's released from the hospital. Until then, I'm sorry, son, but you're suspended for a month."

I hang my head, nodding, even though I'm pissed to be missing four crucial games.

"Keep your nose clean, kid. Steer clear of parties and trouble."

"Yes, sir."

He eyeballs me, and I squirm a little. "Okay. Now get the hell out of my sight."

I walk around campus like the aimless idiot that I am. Plonking down under a tree, I pull out my earphones and listen to music, blanking everything out as the melodic tunes waft through my eardrums. Whenever I take two steps forward in my life, something always seems to happen to drag me ten steps back. I used to pride myself on not letting anything get to me, but each curveball knocks my confidence back a notch until it's pretty much in the ground by now.

Sometimes I just want to get off this merry-go-round that is my so-called life.

Football has been my sanctuary, but I'm even messing that up now.

After a while, I get over my pity party for one and jump up, wiping bits of grass from the back of my jeans. I stroll through campus grounds, bypassing the parking lot and heading for my favorite coffee place. I need a quadruple espresso. Preferably injected directly into my bloodstream, but I'll settle for a black coffee through the mouth. Less effective, but it'll have to do.

I'm not sorry I did what I did. I knew the consequences, and it could be a hell of a lot worse.

No. My current melancholy comes mainly from the mess with Rachel. I've never been good with rejection, and her choosing to talk to Keven over me has left a really nasty taste in my mouth. Add that to my lingering feelings for her best friend, and you have the worst kind of emotional clusterfuck.

I snatch up my takeout coffee and exit the coffee place. I lean against the wall outside, resting my head back and staring at the sky above me. As if it contains the answers to my problems. The heat from the coffee warms my chilled hands, and I take a healthy glug, relishing the hot, pungent, bitter taste as it slides down my throat.

"There you are!" Faye is panting and out of breath as she lands in front of me. Crouching over, she rests her hands on her knees, struggling to recalibrate her breathing.

"What's up?"

"We've been calling you nonstop for the last hour. Ky would've come, but Kev said he wasn't to leave Rach unprotected."

"Sorry. Coach called me to a meeting, and I had my cell off."

"Crap. He knows?" I nod. "Well?"

I shrug. "The douche has a concussion and he's in the hospital. I'm suspended for a month."

"Oh no, Brad. I'm so sorry."

I kick at imaginary dirt on the sidewalk. "It doesn't matter. I'd still do it again."

Without warning, her arms wrap around me. I'm rigidly still at first. Consequence of always being on my guard around her, but gradually I relax, and it's nice. There's nothing sexual about it at all. It's a pure comforting gesture, as if she knew how much I needed this right now. "Thank you for looking out for my friend, and I'm sorry if you were hurt earlier." She eases back, her hands hanging loosely at her sides. There is barely an inch between us, but it's not uncomfortable. "She wasn't choosing Keven over you."

I try to hide my despondency, but I've exhausted all my reserves, and I can't do anything to disguise my true feelings. "Oh, Brad." She gently cups my face. "You care much more than you've let on, right?"

I shrug. It's all I have the energy for.

She bites on her lower lip, shuffling anxiously on her feet.

I bridge the gap between us, tilting her chin up with my finger. "What?"

She noticeably gulps. "This is all my fault. We never should ha—"

I put my finger to her lips, silencing her. "None of this is your fault. You did nothing wrong." She looks up at me with those big baby blues of hers, and I'm a goner. Her pouty lips part gently, and I melt. All logic escapes my mind, and my head is tilting downward before I even realize what I'm doing.

Her hands slam into my chest, and she shoves me back. "What the hell are you doing?"

I clamp a hand over my mouth, retreating to the edge of the sidewalk. My heart is pounding at an alarming rate. Fuck. *What the hell was I thinking?*

I wasn't. I think that's the point.

"Shit. I'm sorry, Faye." I rub the back of my neck. "I don't know why I did that."

She holds her head in her hands, and I feel like a piece of shit.

Time passes while we stand there in silence, not even looking at one another. I'm trying to find the right words to fix this, but they don't appear to exist.

She lifts her head, piercing me with a grave stare. "We don't speak of this ever. To anyone. Okay?"

I know how much it must be costing her to suggest this. "Are you sure?"

"No, but you've a lot on your plate, and your head isn't in the right place. There's no need to cause trouble when it was only a momentary lapse in judgment." She eyeballs me. "That's all it was, right?"

"Yeah." I don't actually know one way or the other so that doesn't really make it a lie.

Relief floods her face. "Okay. It's forgotten. We're good."

"Thanks." I shove my hands in my pockets. "What's so urgent that you came out looking for me anyway, and how did you know where I was?" I ask, remembering there was a purpose to this. Her look is apologetic, and I figure it out. "Keven." Even saying his name is starting to piss me off.

"Shit, Brad. I hate to land this on you when you've already had a crappy day, but there's no way of sugarcoating it."

Everything goes on high alert inside me. A whole avalanche of horrifying thoughts flit through my mind. "Give it to me straight."

"Your mom's been arrested, and it's all over the news."

Chapter Twenty

Rachel

I venture out of my bedroom when Faye returns, knowing I can't ignore Brad forever. Besides, Ky filled me in on what's happened with his mom, and I feel for the guy. No matter how weird things are between us, I want him to know I'm here if he needs me. My jaw hangs open when I cop a load of his face. "What happened to your face?"

"Nothing you need to worry about," he says in an uncharacteristic tender tone. "Are you doing okay?"

I nod, not wishing to articulate the lie. I'm disgusted with myself. Disgusted for losing control and letting *him* affect me so badly. Disgusted for letting myself down. For embarrassing my friends.

"You should report Brady to the police," he softly suggests.

"No." My tone is firm. "I was drunk, and I willingly went to his room, and besides he didn't do much. Not really."

Brad scowls, opening his mouth to argue no doubt, when a loud commotion erupts from the TV, distracting us all.

"I'll turn it off," Ky offers, raising the remote control in front of the screen. A news reporter is standing in front of the Wellesley Police Station, and the headline screams "Fugitive's wife arrested."

"No, leave it," Brad says. "I want to hear what they're saying."

Nothing nice, it seems. An angry mob crowds the footpath outside the police station where Brad's mom is still being held. Reporters are claiming she came in voluntarily to give a statement but was arrested for being uncooperative. They speak to some of the bystanders; many are victims, or related to victims, of Brad's dad's fraud. Emotions are running high, and people are understandably angry.

"Shit." Brad drags a hand across the top of his head. "Have you spoken with your father?" he asks Ky.

"Briefly. I told him we'd meet him at the station. We're to enter at the rear of the building for our own safety."

"You don't have to get dragged into this. I can go alone."

"Shut. Up. I'm coming with you. It's not up for debate."

"What about the girls?" His gaze jumps between Faye and me. "Should we ask Kev to come over?"

My cheeks flush. In my manic state earlier, I'd been borderline hysterical. Between being violated, and the threat the monster poses, I was on the verge of completely losing it. I begged Kev not to leave, but he had prior engagements and he had to go. He obviously said something to Ky, and now I'm embarrassed for overreacting. I need to calm down. Kev has tons of precautionary stuff in place. *He's* not getting to me without Kev knowing.

"It's okay. We'll be fine by ourselves. I was just freaking out earlier after you know..." I can't even say the words. It's humiliating how easily I put myself in a precarious position. It was stupid and dangerous, and I should've known better. It's as if all my hard work these past few months has been unraveling this week in the aftermath of that text, and I've got to get a grip.

Brad steps up to me with fury in his eyes. I instinctively take a step back, wondering what I've done to annoy him this time. His facial features immediately transform to concern. "I'm not angry at you. I'm angry at myself. I should've been there last night, and that asshole wouldn't have dared go anywhere near you. I'm really sorry, Rachel."

"You have nothing to apologize for." I take a step closer, lightly touching his arm. "I'm the one at fault for getting trashed and having such little regard for my own safety."

"No." Faye jumps in. "Neither one of you is at fault. That asshole is responsible. Yes, you were foolish in your actions, but when you said no, he should have respected your decision. He didn't, and that's why he's the only one to blame."

I don't want to debate it. I know the part I played, but arguing is only going to delay the guys, and Brad needs to leave. "You need to get out of here. Your mom needs you."

Surprising me, he bends down and kisses my cheek. "I haven't had a chance to say thanks for the clothes and stuff. My sisters were thrilled."

"Even Kaitlyn?"

His lips tug up. "Not that she'll ever tell you to your face, but, yes, even Kaitlyn. She couldn't conceal her excitement when she pulled the iPhone out."

That cheers me up enormously. "That makes me happy."

I can't discern his expression as he looks intently at me. From the corner of my eye, I watch Ky sweep Faye into his arms, dipping her down as he kisses her passionately. Brad and I stand in awkward silence, waiting for them to finish. Faye looks like she might melt into the floor when he finally lets her come up for air. Entwining her arm in mine, she swoons at her boyfriend before sending a cautious look at Brad. I frown, my gaze swinging between them.

"Come on." Ky slaps Brad on the back as if he's been the one holding things up. "Time to hit the road."

I take a long bath after the guys leave and change into clean trackie bottoms and a vest top. The buzzer chimes just as I step into the living room. Faye hops up, attending to it. "It's Lauren," she confirms when she returns, making a running jump for the couch.

"I didn't know she was dropping by, but her timing works. I can give her the dress." She looks back at me from her horizontal position on the couch. "And she still doesn't know?"

"Nope. I wanted to surprise her."

"She's going to love it. You're very talented, Rachel, and you should definitely show some of your designs to Alex."

Faye was the one who first planted the idea in my head of studying fashion design. When I visited her in Wellesley, I spoke to Alex and became really excited by the idea. I've always loved clothes, and the girls were constantly telling me I had a great eye for pulling an outfit together. Since my parent's lottery win, I've invested in a top-of-the-range sewing machine, and I have the best of materials to work with. I've made tons of stuff since then, and a lot of the dresses in my wardrobe are from my own collection. My long-term goal is to open my own fashion design company, probably specializing in haute couture or high-end women's fashion, but, in the meantime, I need to learn the ropes so the plan is to find a job after I graduate working for a leading fashion house and put everything I've learned to good use.

"I will when I have more pieces to show her. I've only got a few items worthy of showcasing."

"You're way too modest," she hollers to my retreating back as I walk to the front door to let Lauren in.

She envelops me in a humongous hug the minute I open the door. "How are you feeling?"

"I had an epic meltdown this morning, but I'm grand now. It could've been a lot worse."

She removes her denim jacket and silk scarf, placing them on the back of the couch. "I heard Brad put the guy in the hospital."

"What?" I shriek. Of course, I'd suspected Brad had gone after him when I'd seen the bruising on his face, but I'd dismissed it quickly. *Why would he jump in to defend me? Beat one of his teammates and risk sanction?*

"You didn't know?" Lauren asks, glancing between Faye and me.

"No one told me." I slant a stern look in Faye's direction.

"I wasn't sure how you'd react," she coolly replies.

I chew on the inside of my mouth. "Am I a sick bitch if I admit it pleases me?" I've always dreamed of having a guy to jump to my defense.

"Totally sick," Lauren agrees, smiling.

"Twisted and evil," Faye concurs, grinning too.

Lauren plops down on the reclining chair, and I perch on the edge of it. "Just admit it. You like him. There's no shame in that."

"I ..." I pause for a minute and then I think feck it. "I think, maybe, I might like him. When he's not being a dickhead."

"Ho. Lee. Shit," Faye exclaims. "I need to freeze frame this moment for posterity."

I swat the back of her head. "No need to get carried away. I said *might*. Emphasis on the word might."

"Yay!" Lauren says gleefully, clapping her hands. "We can go on triple dates."

I palm my forehead. "Crap. Now you're both going to gang up on me."

"Too right." Faye points her finger in my direction. "You deserve some love in your life."

I almost choke to death. "Steady on there. How did you get from *might like* to love? I think you two fell off the crazy tree and hit every branch on the way down."

Besides, I think Faye's forgetting the elephant in the room.

Brad's in love with her.

Time to kill this conversation. "I have something for you, Lauren. Come with me."

I'm nervous as I step into my bedroom. I hope she won't think this is overstepping the mark. "So, you know how you were disappointed that you didn't have time to make something yourself for the wedding?" Gavin's older sister is getting married next weekend, and Lauren is flying to Chicago on Friday with him to attend the wedding. She had wanted to create something herself but ended up buying an off-the-shelf number that I know she isn't mad about.

"Yeah. Between classes and work, I ran out of time, although that's really just an excuse." I quirk a brow, as she drops onto the edge of the bed. "I don't think my strength lies in fashion design. I get more glue on my hands anytime I've done a project, and I don't have your eye or your creative flair. I've been thinking of pursuing a career in merchandising as a buyer or something."

"I considered that too."

She rests back on her hands, sending me an incredulous look. "That would be an absolute travesty, and a waste of your talent. You were born to be a fashion designer."

A huge smile graces my lips. "You're so sweet, and I hope you don't mind, but I kinda *made something for you*." I whisper the last few words. Shock splays across her face, but I can't tell if it's happy shock or wary shock. "It's just I had tons of time on my hands this week, and I pulled together a few pieces, and this one had your name written all over it, but you don't have to wear it if it's weird or if you don't like it or ... yeah, shutting up now." I walk into my wardrobe without further ado and retrieve the green and black three-quarter-length dress. It has a full skirt and a snug bodice with tiny spaghetti straps that crisscross over the back. It's sexy and sophisticated without showing too much of anything.

"Oh my God, Rach." She almost runs to my side, her fingers gently caressing the slinky material. "This is exquisite." She's bubbling with enthusiasm. "Seriously, you made this for me?"

"Yeah. Is that okay?"

She flings herself at me. "Are you kidding? This is awesome! Now I won't have to wear that dowdy number from Macy's. Thank you so much!"

"Aw, I'm thrilled you like it," I say, as my phone buzzes on my locker. "Go try it on while I check that."

All my euphoria dissipates. It's the same every time my phone has pinged with a message this week. *Get over yourself, Rachel.* It's probably nothing. I can't keep thinking every text is from *him*. Anyway, Kev got me a new sim and triangulated the signal, or some such stuff. When I check the screen, I've received no new messages, and I scratch the side of my head. Then I remember my other mobile. The one I keep purely for communicating with my folks. They think I'm living in Spain, so Kev set this one to reroute to a location on the Spanish mainland just in case they check. I want it to look legit, to throw the monster off the scent. I open my bedside locker and remove it with trembling hands. Trepidation washes over me. Apart from the odd phone call and text message, I haven't had much contact with either of my parents. They're too busy swanning around the world with their much-younger partners and pretending they're teenagers again.

I flip the phone over and over in my hand, taking deep breaths to calm myself down. The screen confirms I have a new message. Drawing a brave breath, I tap into it, and my legs almost collapse from under me.

Nice try, but I've got your number. You know, I actually really like America. Think I might stay.

Chapter Twenty-One

Brad

I barely managed to sleep at all last night. When Ky and I arrived at the Wellesley Police Station, they refused to let me see my mother. I flipped out, and they almost locked me up too. James and Ky managed to calm me down. All it took was mentioning my sisters for me to sober up. Kaitlyn and Emma need me so I came back here last night and stayed with them. Dan is working on getting me in to see Mom today. I've been sick with worry all night.

"When's Mommy coming home?" Emma asks, as I place a plate heaped with pancakes in the middle of the kitchen table.

"I don't know that yet, Pumpkin, but I'm going to do everything I can to bring her home as quickly as possible."

"I can't believe she's still defending that asshole," Kaitlyn seethes, attacking her pancakes as if they'd done her some personal injustice.

"Watch your language, and this is not the type of conversation we should be having at the breakfast table." I subtly nod in our younger sister's direction.

"I know what an asshole is, Brad, and I know she's talking about Dad," Emma says very matter-of-factly, cutting her pancakes into four even-sized pieces.

"I don't want to hear that word coming out of your mouth again, and the situation with Dad is complicated."

"Is he going to go to jail? Because Kaitlyn said they were going to lock him up and throw away the key."

I shut my eyes and pray for patience. "We don't know what's going to happen to Dad."

Emma pauses mid-bite, looking thoughtful. Swallowing down her food, she looks up at me with so much trust in her eyes. "Daddy told me he made a terrible mistake, and he hurt lots of people who didn't deserve to be hurt." I nod, surprised he was so forthcoming with her and that he feels anything even close to remorse. That's not how I remember our last conversation. He was hell-bent on avoiding jailtime, on evading punishment of any sort. There was an arrogance in the way he spoke about being caught, like he was now part of some infamous gang of fraudsters. His attitude had sickened me to my stomach, and we fought bitterly. If I hadn't pretty much washed my hands of him then, I have now. Letting Mom and the girls go by themselves, knowing what they were most likely walking back into, is unforgivable in my book.

"He stole millions from people who trusted him, and he deserves to rot in prison," Kaitlyn unhelpfully interjects.

"For God's sake, Kaitlyn, can you keep your mouth shut unless you have something constructive to add. Emma doesn't need to hear this."

"You can't shield her, Brad. She stopped being an innocent the day Dad took us out of the country."

I hate that Kaitlyn's probably right, and it's something else to hate Dad for. "You may be right, but it doesn't mean I can't try."

"This way," Dan Evans says, steering us forward as we enter the police station. Mom's been held here overnight while the Feds and local police argue over her case. At least she wasn't transferred to prison, and that's something to be grateful for.

Once the relevant personnel are apprised, and the right paperwork is in order, I'm brought to a room with Dan, where Mom awaits. Her smile is sad as I walk toward her. Her hands are resting on top of the table, and the sight of her in cuffs brings tears to my eyes. I couldn't despise my father any more than I do in this moment.

I lean down and kiss her cheek, pulling her into a hug. The policeman standing guard inside the room pretends not to watch. "Are you okay? Have they been treating you well?"

"I'm fine, Bradley, and they have."

"Take a seat, Mrs. McConaughey," Dan says, all business-like. "We have a lot to get through."

I kiss Mom's cheek one more time before sitting across from her. Dan pulls out a wad of papers and starts leafing through them. Clearing his voice, he removes his glasses, setting them down on top of the paperwork. "Firstly, let me apologize for yesterday. It seems the agreement we had with the police chief was null and void when faced with joint objections from both the CIA and FBI. The fact is, you aided and abetted a criminal, and now you refuse to impart pertinent details that could aid his capture. If they can't get to him, they will happily make you the scapegoat. The administration needs a win in this case to appease the public in the run up to the presidential election."

"I understand all that." Mom is remarkably calm. Too calm for someone in her predicament.

"Then you understand that if you continue to refuse to cooperate they will lock you in a federal prison, and you'll be lucky to get out before you die?" He isn't pulling any punches, and I respect him for that.

"I can't sell my husband out."

Whatever tenuous hold I have on my emotions floats away. I lose it, and the words flow naturally from my mouth. "But you can sell your children out?" I lean across the table, trying to keep the rampant fury off my face. "You spoke to me yesterday about love and doing whatever it takes to protect the person you love. Doesn't that protection apply to your children? You're happy to leave Kaitlyn and Emma without any parents? Or you assume I'll step into that role? How the hell do we deserve that?!"

Dan places a cautionary hand on my arm, and I slouch in my chair, unable to even look my mother in the eye.

Tension is ripe in the air, and no one speaks.

After a bit, Mom asks in a timid tone, "What are they asking me to do?"

Dan wets his lips before speaking. "They want to hold a press conference for you to appeal to your husband to turn himself in. They also want the name of the person who supplied the fake passports and your husband's last known whereabouts."

Mom looks pleadingly at me, and her eyes are full of pain. Her face carries noticeable strain, but I'm not going to toe the line on this. I can't placate her. She needs to hear the ugly truth. "I understand you take your vows seriously, and that you love him, Mom, but he didn't show you the same courtesy, because if he did, then he wouldn't have asked you to run. He would have admitted his crimes and faced the consequences of his actions. That is what he should have done for his family, but he was selfish, and only thinking of himself. Look at what he has done to all of us. If you are feeling guilty about betraying him, don't. Because you haven't betrayed him, Mom. You stood by him, and you're still trying to protect him, but enough is enough."

"You've no idea how much it hurts me to hear you speak in such a way about your father." I feel like slamming my head repeatedly against the table. She reaches across the table for my hand, and I meet her halfway. "You are correct when you say he didn't make the right call when this first blew up. He should've stayed here and faced the music, but he's changed. You haven't seen him in a long time. He's not the same man. He's truly sorry for what he did, but turning himself in isn't going to get those people their money back."

"No, but it will give them some closure. Us, too."

I get up and walk around the table, kneeling down in front of her. "If Dad is at large, this will hang over all of us our entire lives. We'll never be able to move on from it. And what kind of life will he have? Always on the run. Constantly looking over his shoulder." I shake my head. "If he's changed, why didn't he return with you?"

"Because he's scared, sweetheart."

"Sorry, Mom, but that's just not good enough. He's a grown man with responsibilities and he left you and the girls alone to deal with the aftermath of his poor choices. You don't owe him anything. You owe it to yourself and your daughters to do the right thing. I think you should tell the police what they want to know and do the press conference."

"I want to do the right thing, I do but ..." Her voice wobbles and tears pool in her eyes.

"But what, Mom?"

"I'm scared, Bradley. Your father has kept me safe since I was nineteen. I don't know how to be without him."

I sigh, distraught at how the once-strong woman I used to know appears to have left the building. Mom is a shell of her former self.

Hell, we all are.

I wish I could find some sympathy in my heart for my dad, the man I used to admire so much, but it's damn hard when we're all messed up because of him. I stand up straight, putting my hand on her shoulder. "Don't be scared. I'm here, and I'll look after you and the girls. I promise. You are not doing this alone."

Tears spill down her cheeks. "I love you, honey."

I kiss the top of her head with fierce determination. "I love you too, Mom. And it's time to let him go. Time to do the right thing."

I sweep the moisture on her cheeks away with a brush of my thumb. Mom tucks her hair behind her ears and levels a firm look at Dan. "You heard my son. Set it up. I'm ready to talk."

Chapter Twenty-Two

Rachel

I'm quiet in the car the following morning as we drive to Wellesley for Brad's mom's press conference. When the call came in last night, and Ky explained, it took little persuasion to convince me to go with him and Faye, to provide moral support to Brad. I need to get out of the city and away from the constant threat of *him* turning up on my door. I didn't sleep a wink last night. After the text arrived, I made my excuses to rush Lauren out of the apartment, and then I locked myself in the bathroom and called Keven. It took him almost an hour to talk me down from the ledge.

I don't know how much longer I can keep the truth from him. If I don't give him something, I'm afraid he's going to go to Ky or Faye and force things out into the open. With my current fragile state of mind, that is the last thing I can face. The urge to flee is riding me hard again.

Keven broached the subject of a bodyguard again. When he first mentioned it a few weeks ago, I immediately dismissed it. The thought of someone following me everywhere, even if it's for my protection, creeps me out. Plus, I was afraid my friends would notice and start asking questions. But now I'm definitely considering it. If *he's* in the States, it's only a matter of time before he finds me. And I don't know how he's going to react. He made it clear I'm his. That I'll always be his. He won't be pleased that I've tried to cut all ties. That I've tried to outsmart him.

He's psychotic. I'm convinced of it despite my lack of qualification. And that terrifies me. Because he's unpredictable, and out of control, and I'm scared he might hurt me way worse than he already has.

I chew on the corner of a nail as I contemplate hiring a bodyguard.

"Shit." Ky cusses, scowling as we draw close to the hotel where the press conference is taking place. Swarms of people crowd the front of the hotel, blocking the entrance to the underground car park. Ky beeps the horn repeatedly, and it takes at least ten minutes before he can safely maneuver the car into the car park. Hands slam on the car as we pass, and protestors wave banners and shout at the top of their voices. Thank God for the dark windows, but it's still a flipping scary experience.

The hotel lobby is thronged with men and women and TV crews, but I keep my head down, letting my hair fall around my face. We join James and Brad in a private room off the lobby. A bunch of people in business suits converge in the corner, talking in low voices. "Where's Mom?" Ky asks.

"Alex stayed behind to mind the girls," James confirms, "and she thought it best she wasn't here in case her presence drew any more unwanted attention."

"Where's *your* Mom?" Faye asks Brad, looking all around the room.

Brad is smartly dressed in a white dress shirt with black trousers and a blue tie that brings out the vibrancy in his eyes. He looks like the quintessential all-American boy. Except for the multi-colored bruise on his cheek, which hints at a darker side. "She's being briefed by the police. Dan's with her." His eyes catch mine. "I appreciate you all coming. Thanks."

"No problem, man." Ky clamps a hand down on his shoulder. He's also similarly attired to Brad, while Faye and myself are both wearing appropriate knee-length dresses.

Ky's father leans in to me. "I think your boyfriend could use some TLC. The last twenty-four hours have been stressful."

Join the club.

I move to Brad's side, lacing my hand in his as I lean up on my tiptoes and kiss his cheek. His hand wraps firmly in mine, and he presses his mouth to my ear. "You don't have to keep up the charade. There are cameras and tons of press milling about the place. I'll tell Mom the truth."

I shake my head. "Not yet. She's got too much on her mind. Let things settle and then you can tell her. I don't mind keeping this going for a while longer." Truth is, I'm clinging to his hand and his side because he's my lifeline at the moment as much as I wish I was his. But I'm under no illusion in that regard. This serves a purpose for him, nothing more. "We should hide that bruise on your face," I whisper, tugging on his hand. "Come with me."

Carefully, we sneak out of the room, walking briskly to the bathroom. I pull him into a wheelchair accessible toilet and lock the door. I push the toilet seat down. "Sit there," I instruct, turning to wash my hands in the sink. I remove a makeup palette from my bag and face him. Tilting his chin up, I angle his head to the side.

"I'm glad you're here," he admits, surprising me.

"I was glad to get out of the city." I dab my brush in some concealer and press it against his cheek, expecting him to probe further, but he says nothing. "What's going to happen to your mom?"

"They've agreed to release her without charge after the press conference. The official line is that she was helping with their inquiries."

I blend the concealer with my fingers, and he flinches under my touch. "At least that's good." I step back, surveying his cheek from both sides. It's not perfect, but it's the best I can do. If I layer any more concealer on, it will look too noticeable. At least it isn't so blatantly obvious now.

"It is. Without the threat of arrest, she can move on with her life. Find someplace to live and decide what she wants to do."

"You're done," I confirm, moving back to the sink to wash the makeup from my hands.

He stands up, inspecting his face in the mirror behind me. Heat wafts from his body, stirring unwelcome sensations in me. "Nice job. Thanks."

I twist around to face him and suck in a shocked gasp. He's pressed right up against me at this angle, and his potent scent swirls around me, dazzling me in a nanosecond.

"Sorry." He steps back, creating some space between us.

I try to steady my beating heart. "I heard what you did to that asshole, and I wanted to thank you. You didn't need to do that for me, but I'm grateful."

He examines my face, his eyes intensely probing mine, and the air turns thick with electricity. "I never know what to expect with you. Most girls abhor violence and wouldn't approve."

"Well," I say, pushing off the sink. "I'm not like most girls, and my personal view is that violence against monsters doesn't count. What you did to him pales in comparison to what he would've done to me if the others hadn't bust into the room, so you'll never hear me criticizing you for that. I owe you."

He shakes his head. "Nah, I think that makes us even." His lips curve into a smile. "Although, I haven't forgotten I still owe you three orgasms."

"That was only a piss take, remember?"

He chuckles. "I can guess what that means, and you're not letting me off the hook that easily."

"Bradley." I plant my hands on my hips. "Are you flirting with me? Minutes before your mom addresses the entire nation? The entire planet?"

He takes my hand in his. "Fair point. It's not the time or place." He opens the door and peeks out. Pulling me out, he grips my hand firmly as we scurry along the now empty hallway. "But we're not done with this conversation."

The hell we aren't.

They are just about to start proceedings as we make our way to the front row. Faye and Ky have kept us seats, and I drop down alongside my friend while Brad runs up to the podium to wish his mom a last-minute good luck.

The press conference goes off without a hitch. Brad keeps a firm hold of my hand the entire time, but I don't mind. His touch is helping to flay the edge off my anxiety. When his mom wells up as she's imploring her husband to hand himself in, I watch Brad's jaw clench and his eyes turn glassy. I squeeze his hand and he turns to me, pressing a tender kiss to my forehead. The gesture tugs at my heartstrings, but I try not to read too much into it. This is an emotional time for him, that's all.

As the thought wafts through my mind, it registers that being with him like this doesn't frighten me in the way it usually does. Being with him, as his significant other, even if it's fake, feels natural.

Faye subtly nudges me in the ribs, and I look into her expectant face. She smiles at me, motioning in Brad's direction, and it isn't difficult to get her meaning. She's reading too much into this, same as me. Either she's forgotten that he's infatuated with her, or she's happily in denial. Not that I can blame her for that. If Brad moved on, it would alleviate the awkward tension and allow her and Ky to properly move forward. I know they're stuck in limbo while the situation remains unresolved.

But I can't ignore facts.

Brad has a thing for my best friend, and I don't want to be the backup plan or second-best. I've never properly entertained the notion of a boyfriend before, and I don't want to do that with a guy who doesn't see me as his everything.

The conference ends a few minutes later, and I hang back with Ky, Faye, and James Kennedy while Brad goes with his mom and Dan.

"He's into you," Faye whispers when Ky is busy chatting with his dad.

I shrug. "I thought you liked him?"

"Don't do this. Don't try and force us together. He doesn't know what he wants, and this is all for show, remember?" Her face drops, and she bites her lower lip. She's keeping something from me. "What don't I know?"

She looks over her shoulder at her boyfriend. He's still deep in conversation with his dad. "Not here." She takes my hand in hers. "Bathroom break," she mouths to Ky over her shoulder as she drags me to the toilets.

She locks us into the wheelchair accessible toilet, sitting down on the toilet seat and resting her head in her hands.

"What happened?" I ask, because I know something has.

"I swore I wouldn't tell anyone this, but I'm freaking out." She gulps. "I genuinely don't think he meant it, but Brad tried to kiss me yesterday."

My heart deflates, like a balloon that's been pricked with a sharp instrument. A piercing ache splinters my chest cavity, and my mouth is dry. "Oh." I drop my head.

"Ah, crap." She stands up, walking to my side. "You like him a lot more than you've admitted. I'm sorry. I shouldn't have told you that."

I lift my chin. "Of course, you should have. We're best friends. You shouldn't be afraid to tell me anything."

Hypocrite.

"Look, I am freaking out over it, but not for the reasons you're thinking. I'm terrified Ky is going to find out and read more into it. Because the truth is, I still don't believe Brad loves me. I believe he *thinks* he does, but it's the idea of what I represent more than anything. And we get on so well, and given everything he's been going through, it was only natural he'd kinda latch onto me. But that's all it is. I see the way he's been looking at you recently. He likes you a lot, but I think he's scared to face reality."

"No offense, Faye, but I think you're reading far too much into it because you want him to get over his infatuation with you, and I can understand why, but I don't think he cares about me that way. He likes fucking me, but that's all. And despite what happened this weekend, that's not me anymore. I want someone to love me for me. Not just for my body. And I want to be the center of someone's universe, like you are to Ky."

A tear rolls down my face. This is the most honest I've been with myself in a long time.

I *do* want that.

I see what my best friend has with her boyfriend, how much they love and support each other, and I want that for myself. I want my face to light up when my guy steps into the room. I want the feeling of safety and warmth when I'm enveloped in his arms. The contentment and happiness that comes from willingly sharing my bed with a guy who can be sweet and sexy, who knows when I need a hug, and when I need him to fill me up.

The admission almost knocks me over.

I wonder if deep down I've always felt like this but I was too afraid to want that for myself. Too afraid I wouldn't know how to be that for someone. Too afraid I'm damaged and incapable of offering all of myself to another person. Too afraid of relying on someone and being let down, because those closest to me have a habit of doing that.

But I want that with a guy. I want that for myself. I do.

Perhaps, in different circumstances, Brad could be that guy for me, because he has contributed to this realization, but he's too fixated on Faye to offer me what I need.

"And you will be." She pulls me into a mammoth hug. "You're one of the sweetest, kindest, most thoughtful people I know, and you deserve to be loved. And I want that for you, and it's wonderful to finally hear you acknowledging you want it too. I'm proud of you, Rachel."

When we rejoin the others in the lobby, Brad is back. "Everything okay?" he asks, his gaze flitting between me and Faye.

"Of course. Why wouldn't it be?" My tone is clipped, and the look I give him is harder than I intended.

He scratches the back of his head. "I'm going to return to the house with Mom, but I'll be heading back to Harvard later. I was hoping you might come with me? I know Emma would love to see you."

My instinct is to tell him to get stuffed, but I guess I love torturing myself because I find myself nodding. Ky and Faye bade us farewell. She has an assignment that's due in tomorrow, and she needs to complete it. So, I find myself traveling back to the Kennedy house with the others.

Brad's mom is quiet the entire journey, and I understand why. She's had to throw her husband under the bus to protect the rest of her family. The warring emotions are written all over her face. "I know that was hard, Mom, but you did the right thing," Brad quietly reassures her. "I'm proud of you."

She pats his hand but doesn't reply.

When we get back to the basement annex they are staying in, she hugs her daughters before retreating to her room for a nap. Brad goes to make coffee, leaving me with his sisters in the living room. Kaitlyn grabs me into a quick hug, startling me. "I know my brother thinks I'm a jerk, but I want to say thank you so much for the clothes and the stuff. I really appreciate it."

"You're welcome. I love shopping so it's not as if it was a big burden."

"I used to love shopping too."

"We should go shopping together," I blurt, before I have a chance to stop myself. Sometimes, it's easy to forget I'm only playing a role.

"I'd like that."

"Can I come too?" Emma asks, running over to hug me.

"Of course." I kiss her cheek. "Maybe we can grab a movie and some dinner too."

"That would be awesome," Kaitlyn says, and I spy Brad watching and listening from the corner of the room. "Can we go to the same store where you bought that blue dress? I totally adore it."

My cheeks flush with pride. "Actually, I made that one, and I figured you might like it. I knew it would suit your coloring and your height."

Her mouth drops open. "Get. Out! You did not."

"Rachel's studying fashion design, and she's incredibly talented," Brad says, handing me a coffee.

"How would you know?" I quirk a brow.

"You made that red dress you wore to the twenty-first, right?"

"Yeah, but how did you know that?"

"I have my sources. And you looked sensational in it."

My cheeks darken, and a smile graces my lips. I'd almost believe he meant that, except Faye's words from earlier still linger in my mind. He's been sleeping with me, yet he tried to kiss my best friend yesterday. I can't ever forget that. My smile fades, and he frowns when he notices.

We spend an hour with his sisters and chat briefly to his mom before it's time to leave.

Brad is quiet in the car, but I prefer that. Kicking off my shoes, I pull my knees into my chest and stare out the passenger side window. Strips of purplish navy streak through the fading daytime sky. The closer we get to the city, the more on edge I become. Today was a great distraction, but as we draw nearer to my life, all the fears and worries resurface.

"Are you hungry? There's a great diner just up the road I was going to stop at," he says, a few minutes later.

"Sure. I could eat." Anything to delay the inevitable.

Ten minutes later, we are sitting across from one another in a booth. "This reminds me of a chain of diners back home," I remark, sipping my sparkling water as my eyes skim over the décor.

"The burgers are to die for."

My stomach rumbles at the mention of food, though I doubt I'll be able to manage more than a few mouthfuls. The waitress approaches and Brad places his order. "I'll have the same," I tell her, not even bothering to look at the menu.

I take another sip of my drink as Brad leans over the table, wetting his lips nervously. "Faye told you, didn't she?"

I try to keep the hurt out of my expression as I look at him. "Yeah."

"It meant nothing. She caught me at a vulnerable moment, that's all."

I sigh, leaning back in my seat, as if putting a little more distance will give me perspective. "I don't care," I lie. "It's not like I've any investment in this except that I don't want to see my best friend hurt."

His eyes lower to the table. "I don't want to hurt her either."

"Maybe you should've thought of that before you tried to kiss her," I snap, instantly wishing I could claw the words back.

He grimaces at my tone. "I've hurt you, too. I'm sorry."

"You haven't hurt me. It's not like we mean anything to each other. I'm just an easy lay, right?"

His face pales, and he stretches his hand across the table, but I ignore it, tucking my hands under my butt so I'm not tempted. "I do not think of you like that." The waitress returns, placing our food in front of us, and no more words are exchanged until she's gone. "I'm sorry that I'm making a mess out of everything, but you—"

"Stop. Just stop talking. I've a pain in my head listening to this." I glare at him, as a myriad of confusing sentiments swamp me. "And I don't want to get dragged into this shit that's going on with you three. I've got enough on my mind as it is. The only reason I'm sore with you is because you're causing problems for my friend, and if Ky finds out, there will be hell to pay. But apart from that, I don't care. We fucked a few times. It was no big deal, and it meant nothing to me either, so just drop it. I'm not interested in hearing your excuses. I just want to eat my food and get home."

A muscle ticks in his jaw. "Fine. Message received."

We eat in awkward silence. Or at least Brad does. I can only stomach three bites before I push my food away. Brad insists on paying, and then we hightail it out of there. More silence engulfs us in the car, and I close my eyes, praying for this day to end.

My phone pings in my pocket the same time Brad's cell lights up. "Can you check that?" he asks in a curt tone, not taking his eyes off the dark road.

My palms are sweaty, and a little puke fills my mouth as I remove my phone. I don't think I'll ever be able to look at my phone again without heart-thumping fear taking hold of me. Drawing a deep breath, I open up the text, clicking on the link Faye sent.

"Pull the car over now." My voice brokers no argument.

Brad pulls into the hard shoulder. "What is it?"

"Your worst nightmare." I pass my phone to him, watching all the color leach from his face as he plays the clip. It's a YouTube video of him outside the coffee place with Faye, showing him clearly leaning in toward her for a kiss. It's already got over five thousand views.

He bangs his head off the steering wheel. "Fucccckkkkk!!"

"Faye says you need to go to your place. Ky has seen it and he's freaking out."

The tortured look in his eyes almost undoes me, but it's not my place to console him. He's an idiot for trying to kiss my best friend, in public of all places. "I'd prefer if you dropped me off first. This is nothing to do with me, and I don't want to get involved."

Hurt flares in his eyes as he restarts the engine. "Of course."

Sympathy wells inside me. Dammit. It's so hard to stay mad at him when he looks like a lost little boy whose whole world has just collapsed. I brush my hand over his arm. "I'm sure it'll be fine once he's calmed down and hears your explanation."

Brad snorts. "Don't you know him at all?"

Yeah, trouble is, I do, and I recognize my lie for what it is. An empty platitude. Ky is going to lose his shit, and this may well be the final nail in the coffin of their friendship.

But I've enough problems of my own to deal with.

So, I'm staying clearly in the neutral zone and minding my own business.

But you know what they say about best-laid plans?

Chapter Twenty-Three

Brad

I walk along the corridor toward our apartment with a heavy heart. Ky will not understand this. I know I wouldn't if I was in his shoes. And I can't deny I have feelings for his girlfriend, because I do. I shouldn't think about her or look at her the way I do, but sometimes I don't even realize I'm doing it. Rachel's gorgeous face swims into my mind, heaping another layer of anxiety onto the pile. The hurt on her face was obvious before, and I hate that I've dragged her into this mess.

Fact is, I have feelings for her too, but I can't decipher any of it.

It's official: I'm a complete mess.

Steeling my heart, I open the door to our apartment and step inside, bracing myself for the incoming assault.

I walk into the kitchen and stop. Faye is leaning against the far wall, and she's crying. Her eyes are swollen and red-rimmed, and she's hugging herself as if she's falling apart. I've done this to her, and I hate myself for it. But I'm angry at him too. *Why the hell is he taking it out on her?*

"Are you okay?" I ask, ignoring him. Her lips wobbles, and she sniffles, either refusing or unable to answer. I swing around to my best friend. "Why is she so upset? Why the fuck are you angry with *her*?" I know they have a "no secrets" promise, but that doesn't mean he should be taking this out on his girlfriend.

His menacing glare turns even darker. His voice is too calm when he speaks. "Are you for real?"

I drop my bag to the ground, squaring up to him. "I'm the only person you should be angry with. Faye has done nothing wrong."

"Oh, I'm plenty angry with you, believe me." His chest heaves up and down, and his fists are in knotted balls at his sides.

"Then take it out on me, but leave Faye alone."

He closes his eyes for a second. When he reopens them, I almost cower at the extent of the hatred and fury radiating from him. "You do not get to tell me how to treat my girlfriend. You have no fucking say in my relationship, and what has transpired between us is none of your business."

"The hell it isn't!" I yell, my own anger churning and bubbling inside me. "You've upset her, and I'm not okay with that."

"Because she was fucking defending you!" He starts pacing the floor, and I can't remember ever seeing him so rattled, so unlike himself. He would walk over hot coals for his girl, and I know she's the love of his life, but he seems to have forgotten that now. I hate that he's mad at her when it's all my fault. "And how can I be sure there isn't something going on between you two?" His gaze jumps between us, and a loud sob erupts from Faye's throat.

"What the actual fuck?" I shove his chest. "Are you fucking insane? She's crazy about you, and you two spend basically ever single second together, outside of class. When the hell would she have time to cheat on you with me?"

"I'm about two seconds away from beating your ass until you can't move." He shoves me, and I take it.

I step back. "Look, let's just calm down. For the record, nothing is going on between us. *Nothing*. It was a dumbass move on my part, but my brain had disengaged. If I was thinking clearly, I would never have attempted to kiss her. I swear. The last thing I want to do is cause issues in your relationship."

He snorts. "All you have *ever* done is cause issues in our relationship."

That pisses me off. The truth has a way of doing that. "I will accept blame where it's due, but don't go putting all that shit on me. You are the one who agreed to the fake relationship. You are the one who told me to pursue her when you went back to Addison. And it's you who has been insisting on us living together. That was all you. Not me. So, don't try and pretend like this is all my fault. You've contributed to this clusterfuck."

That pushes him over the edge. He charges at me, and I prepare for impact.

"Fucking quit it, bro!" Ky shoves me back, pinning me against the wall, his torso blocking my path. He slams his fist into the wall beside my head, and I raise a brow. "Don't," he warns, shaking his head. Anger burns fiercely in his eyes.

"Ky." Faye moves tentatively behind him.

"Don't, babe. Stay out of this."

She nibbles anxiously on her bottom lip.

"Get out of my face." I push his chest, and he stumbles back. I sidestep him, catching Faye's eye.

Ky growls. Then he punches me in the face. "Stop eye-fucking her!"

"What the hell?" I glare at him, rubbing my sore jaw.

"You think I'm blind?" He rages, pacing the floor in front of me. Faye looks like she wishes the ground would open up and swallow her. "You think I don't see the way you watch her every move? The way you mentally undress her with your eyes?"

Faye turns an off-white color.

It's on the tip of my tongue to say "it takes one to know one," but that's not an argument I can win. Ky has every right to look at his girlfriend like that. *Me?* Not so much. He's right, and if I was in his shoes, I think I'd have snapped a long time ago. "I can't help it. It's too difficult to be around her and not feel the way I feel." Faye looks horrified, and now I wish the ground would swallow *me* whole. Continuous rejection has me battered and bruised on the inside, and it's like my vital organs are shutting down, one at a time.

"I can't do this anymore, Brad." Ky stops in front of me, and all the fight seems to have left him. "I've tried really hard to be patient. Made countless excuses for your behavior because I didn't want to lose you. You're my best friend, dude, but this has to end. I never wanted to choose between the girl I love and the guy who's been like a brother to me practically my whole life, but you've left me no choice. If we continue like this, our friendship will be destroyed anyway. Maybe this is the right thing to do." He looks over his shoulder at Faye. "Maybe I should've done this all along."

Turning back around to face me, he sighs. A pained expression replaces the angry look on his face. "I'm sorry, but it has to be like this." His gaze penetrates mine, and there is so much conveyed in that one look, almost too much. My emotions are in a whirlwind, but I say nothing. There isn't anything I can say that will help make this situation bearable. He walks to Faye's side, pulling her into his arms and kissing the top of her head. "I'm sorry, babe. It's going to be okay. I promise." Silent tears drip down her face. "I'll move my stuff out this weekend," he says, over his shoulder. "I'll stay with Faye while I look for somewhere else to live."

Somehow, I manage to nod even though I'm disoriented and frozen. I hate the thought of this, but I need it too. I'm never going to get over her if she's so prevalent in my life.

They stop at the door, and Faye is talking frantically in Ky's ear. She's whispering so I can't hear what she's saying, but it's obvious they're arguing. I sag against the wall, dejected and beaten down. Faye rushes to my side, grabbing me into a hug. My arms hang loose by my sides, and I'm afraid to move a muscle. My jaw still aches, testament to Ky's intolerance of me. I don't blame him for it. He's put up with a lot—more than I probably would have. Faye is sobbing into my shoulder, and I hate that I've put us through all this pain. I want to wrap my arms around her and kiss her pain away.

But she isn't mine to console.

She'll never be mine.

And I wish my heart could accept that reality instead of foolishly clinging to nonexistent hope.

She may not be mine to love and cherish, but she's still my friend, and I hate to see her so upset. I tap her lightly on the shoulder. "Hey. Don't cry. It's going to be fine. Ky is right. We all just need some space."

She lifts her head up, and her red-rimmed tearstained eyes cut through me like a knife. "Will you be okay?"

"I hope so." I offer her my best effort at a smile. "Don't worry about me. I brought this on us, and it's my responsibility to make this right."

"This sucks." She sniffles.

"It won't be forever." I hope. My eyes meet Ky's, and there's not even a hint of a promise there. "Go on, sweet Faye." I kiss the top of her head, closing my eyes as I commit her scent and the feel of her against me to memory.

Ky growls, and I reckon that's my five-second warning. Opening my eyes, I remove myself from her embrace and walk into my bedroom, slamming the door behind me, without looking back at either of them.

I don't know how long I stay in the dark, lying on my bed, curled into a ball, and rocking like a crazy person. I'm completely anesthetized on the inside. This isn't the kind of dazed-delirious-happy feeling I get when I'm following Rach's temporary mind-numbing strategy. Nope, this is a sucky soul-empty kind of numbness, like all the life force has been drawn from me.

A knock at my door only mildly startles me. I don't respond in any shape or form. I'm incapable of moving any part of my anatomy.

The door swings open, and Rach's hot body fills the doorway. One look at her face and I know Faye has spoken to her.

"Go away."

"Brad." She takes a step toward me.

"I'm not in the mood for sex." That's more than a little unfair, but when I'm hurt, I lash out.

"That's not why I came." Her eyes bore a hole in my skull as she walks toward the bed, her gaze never wandering from mine. She walks to the other side, and I hear her toeing her shoes off. The bed dips when she slides in beside me. She curls her body around me from behind, and warmth infuses my frozen bones.

"What are you doing?" I ask, remaining stationary.

"Being a friend."

"That's not who we are." I thought we were drifting into that space, but her earlier comments drove the point home. She doesn't have feelings for me. Not in that way.

"Who are we?"

Damn good question. *Two lost souls sharing our pain and hot sex, or two idiots feeding each other's grief? Or was it becoming more than that?* Who the hell knows. "I don't know," I honestly admit.

"Me either," she whispers.

"You don't have to do this."

"I know. I want to."

"Why? You hate me."

She takes forever to reply, and I wonder if she's nodded off to sleep. "You hate me too, and I don't work well with conscious feelings, you know that," she admits. "But Faye told me what happened earlier, and I couldn't stop thinking about you. I didn't want you to be alone, so here I am."

"What does it mean?"

"Fecked if I know."

That brings a smile to my face. I reach around for her hands, pulling them closer to my waist. Her body squashes against mine, and it feels nice. Soothing. I hold onto her hands, rubbing circles on her skin. "Thank you. I'm glad you're here."

"Me too."

We don't speak after that, but it's a relaxed silence. We stay wrapped around one another, and the stifling pain in my chest loosens a little. My eyes are shuttering, and I'm on the verge of unconsciousness when she calls my name. "Hmm?"

"For the record, I don't hate you anymore. I don't know if I ever really did," she whispers.

"I don't hate you either," I mumble, and then slumber claims me, and I drift off into the welcoming darkness.

Chapter Twenty-Four

Rachel

I wake up the next morning feeling more rested than I have in weeks. At some point during the night, I peeled my dress off. Now, I'm curled around Brad, dressed in only my underwear. His leg is on top of mine, trapping me, and his arms are wrapped firmly around my waist. His body heat envelops me, pacifying me, and I feel safe here with him like this. An idea starts forming in my mind.

He moves, unconsciously thrusting his erection into my leg, and my core pulses with need. I could touch him, and I know things would escalate, but our relationship is messed up enough as it is. And after what went down last night with Faye and Kyler, that is the last thing either one of us needs.

The thought douses my igniting arousal, and I wriggle out of his grip, sliding out of the bed. He turns over, his hands reaching for me even in sleep, mumbling my name. That does something strange to my insides. I watch him for a few minutes. He looks so content in sleep, no worry lines or hints of concern marring his face. Air trickles from his slightly parted lips, and he snuggles deeper into the pillow. His bare chest and arms are a work of art, and it's no surprise he has girls crawling all over him. One day, he's going to make some girl really happy.

I pick my crumpled dress up off the floor, holding it out in front of me to inspect it. It's in a million creases and not the freshest smelling. Tiptoeing to Brad's dresser, I remove one of his T-shirts and slip it on.

In the kitchen, I remove ingredients for an omelet and get to work. Soon, coffee is brewing and the delicious smells of eggs, cheese, onion, tomato, and herbs infiltrate the air.

Brad appears in the doorframe, wearing low-hanging trackie bottoms and nothing else. He scratches the top of his head as he walks to the counter, yawning profusely. "Something smells good."

"I hope you like omelet?"

"I'm ravenous," he admits, rubbing a hand over his delectable stomach. "Whatever you're offering, I'm buying."

I'm not sure if he meant to be intentionally flirtatious, but that's the way it comes off. Still, I'm not complaining. I was hoping things wouldn't be awkward after last night, and so far, so good.

His gaze rakes over me from head to toe as I fiddle with the coffee pot. "Is that my shirt?"

"Um, yeah. Hope you don't mind?"

His eyes zone in on my bare legs, and his tongue darts out, licking his lips. "Not a bit. You can wear my shirts any time you like." His lips turn up at the corners, and there's a mischievous glimmer in his eyes.

Time to shut this—whatever *this* is—down.

He sits on one of the stools, and I hand him a mug of steaming coffee. "How are you feeling today?" I prop my elbows on the marble top, looking across the island unit at him.

"I'm a bit pissed, to be honest."

I quirk a brow before turning around to plate the omelets. I don't respond until I'm sitting across from him, and we're both tucking in. "Pissed at who?"

He stops mid-bite. "Myself." I urge him to continue with my eyes as I eat. "My feelings for Faye have always been complicated, but she's his girl, and while it's hard to be around her sometimes, I've always known there was a line. I honestly don't know why I tried to cross it, and now I've lost my best friend and her in the process."

I put my fork down, carefully choosing my next words. "Do you love her?"

He takes a few mouthfuls of his breakfast while considering his reply. My chest tightens painfully the longer the silence continues.

He peers intently into my eyes, gulping. "Yes, but I'm not sure it's the right kind of love or the way I would feel if she was the one."

The tightness in my chest expands at his confirmation, and I hate the feelings his words invoke in me—jealousy, anger, hurt. I'm such a novice with this stuff. I concentrate on my food, shoveling mouthfuls into my gob in an attempt to avoid speaking. I'm not sure what might come out if I do.

Reaching across the island, he places his hand on top of mine. "I don't mean to upset you. I'm just trying to explain what's in my head, and it's not a surprise that it's come out all jumbled. What I'm trying to say is I have certain feelings for her, but I don't think it's the way I'd feel if she was the love of my life, and a lot of how I feel for her is tied up with all that stuff that happened between me and Ky before Faye was even on the scene." He averts his eyes. "I harbor a lot of resentment toward him." His chest heaves.

I tilt his face around so we're looking at one another. "I don't know all the details, and I'm not asking you to tell me, but I can understand that to a point, and you shouldn't feel guilty about how you feel."

He takes my other hand in his. "I've never admitted that to anyone, and you've no idea how much guilt I'm carrying for so many things, and how much I hate myself sometimes for the mistakes I've made. For not being a stronger, better person."

"I understand that more than you know."

"Maybe, one day, we'll be able to tell each other."

"Maybe."

Silence stretches between us as we hold hands over the island unit. "About what you said last night," he says, clearing his throat. "I've never hated you, Rachel. I've been going around angry at the world, and for whatever reason, I took the brunt of it out on you. I'm sorry. I never meant to hurt you or make you feel less important than you are. I wish I could take back so much, but I can't, so all I can do is try to make it up to you. I'm so grateful that you came here last night. Faye's your best friend, and considering what's gone on between us, I wouldn't blame you for hating me."

"I meant what I said last night, and I'd like a fresh start. I'd like it if we could be friends."

He smiles. "I'd really like that too."

My shoulders relax, and I smile back at him. "I'm glad, because I've had an idea, and I wasn't sure how to broach it with you."

"Shoot."

"How would you feel if I moved in here with you?" His eyes are out on stilts. "Just as friends," I rush to add. "Strictly platonic."

"You'd do that for me?"

I nod. "You're going to need someone to help with rent and bills and stuff."

"You don't need to do that. I'm sure I can find someone else to move in."

"I doubt it. Not this early in the semester."

"It doesn't make sense. You own that apartment, so why would you move in here and pay rent? I appreciate what you're trying to do, but I'm not a charity case," he says, through gritted teeth.

I think I've just offended his precious male pride. Boohoo. "It's not about the money, and you know how I feel about that. I'm not being entirely selfless either. There is an ulterior motive. I don't particularly want to live with a couple, especially not those two. As much as I love them to death, they can't keep their hands off one another, and it's bound to get awkward. I'll feel like I'm in the way. This way, Kyler can stay with Faye and not have to worry about finding a new place, you don't have the hassle of trying to locate a new roomie, and I don't have to wear earplugs to bed every night." I bite down on my lip. "Unless you plan to have female company, which is totally fine, and I'll just make myself scarce then."

"You won't have to worry. I'm finished all that."

"Yeah?"

"Yeah."

An uncomfortable silence gathers in the space between us. "I, um." I remove my hands from under his, wrapping my arms around my waist. "If we're to do this, then the ground rules should be really clear. Our arrangement is strictly friends only. No sex. No kissing. Just normal roommates."

"I can do friends, but are you sure you want to move in here?"

"Yes." What I haven't articulated is how much safer I'll feel here, off the grid, with Brad's protection.

"Okay, then, roomie." Brad extends his hand, and we shake on it. "Let's do this."

I return to my apartment an hour later and start packing up my things. When Faye surfaces from her bedroom, I explain my decision.

"I don't want to drive you out of your own apartment." She sinks down on the bed alongside me.

"You're not. I made this decision, and you know I'm right. It's best for everyone."

"The plan was that we were going to live together, not that we'd both end up living with boys."

I shrug. "Circumstances have necessitated a change in plans. We couldn't have predicted that."

A wave of sadness washes over her face. "I feel so bad about all this." She looks me straight in the eye. "I know you have feelings for him, and it's like *I'm* messing up whatever potential is there."

"Stop it. Stop beating yourself up over it. It is what it is. Brad and I are strictly friends only from here on out."

Her frown deepens, and I elbow her in the ribs. "Stop that! Honestly. I'm grand, and you have nothing to feel guilty for."

"He doesn't love me, Rach. I'd bet my life on it. He just doesn't know what he's feeling."

"He tried to kiss you, Faye." I hate how much it hurts to say that.

"Honestly, Rach, I could've been any girl and he would've done that."

"That's not making me feel any better."

"What I mean is, he needed comfort in that moment, and I was the one there. It was purely situational. It wasn't because he wanted to kiss me."

Faye glances anxiously over her shoulder. "I don't want Ky to hear me talking about this, he's pissed enough as it is, but I'm glad you're moving in with Brad. He needs someone on his side. He needs someone watching out for him," she says, in a deliberately low tone of voice.

"I know, and, in a funny way, I think I need him too."

"There's nothing funny about that, and maybe this is just what you two need to sort out your feelings for one another."

Perhaps Faye's right, but I'm not entering into this arrangement to progress things with Brad. I have more urgent concerns that demand my focus.

I'm waiting outside Kev's building, checking my watch every few seconds. He's late. He told me to meet him here at six, and it's now seven minutes past, and he's still a no-show. I take out my phone to call him when he come's bounding around the corner. "Sorry I'm late. One of the TAs pulled me aside after class and I got delayed."

"No sweat."

"Come on," he says, panting like he ran the whole way here. "Let's go up to my room and talk."

As we enter his apartment, Kev does a quick check to ensure his roomie is out before speaking. "Something's not adding up, and it concerns me." He prods the door shut with his booted foot.

"In what way?"

"So, you know I have a trace on the guy's passport, bank accounts and cards, social media, cell, and online activity?" I nod, as rampant panic blossoms in my gut. "According to that text you got, all indications pointed to him being in America, but my reports show he's still in Ireland."

I release the breath I'd been holding. "That's a good thing, no? It means he isn't here."

Kev scrubs a hand over his stubbly jaw. "I'm not sure. Either he's bluffing to scare the shit out of you or he's got someone else using his identity and he's traveling under a fake one, because all activity on that profile shows minimal travel that's confined to Ireland. It's too neat. I don't trust it."

My stomach coils into knots. "It's possible to do that?"

"Pretty much anything is possible if you've got money and the right contacts."

"He has plenty of money."

"And money can buy you the right kind of connections." Kev leans forward in his chair. "I don't want to worry you unnecessarily, but I wanted to make you aware of my suspicions. I'm going to dig deeper. Hopefully, the text was just a ruse, and he's still in Ireland, and you've got nothing to worry about."

But as I walk to the apartment, I'm in a daze, understanding I've got a shit ton to worry about. Because if there's one thing I know about *him*, it's that he won't hesitate to use his money to find me. If Kev suspects he's on to us, and that he's using fake identification to move around undetected, then I'm ninety-nine percent certain that's exactly what he's doing.

He's here, and it's only a matter of time before he finds me.

Chapter Twenty-Five

Brad

It's the night after Rachel moved in, and I'm cooking dinner when she returns home looking like she's got the world's problems on her shoulders. "I hope you like spaghetti and meatballs," I call out, as she drops her keys, purse, and jacket on the island behind me.

"Anything sounds good after the day I've had."

"Want to talk about it?"

"Nah, just college crap and other stuff."

I stir the sauce, placing a lid on top as I move to the fridge and pour two iced waters. I hand one to her.

"Thanks," she says, chugging it back.

"Dinner will be about fifteen minutes, so why don't you take a bath or a shower and relax. I'll call you when it's ready."

"Actually, a bath sounds lovely. Good idea." She hops up. "I'll get changed."

While she's in her bedroom, I move to the bathroom, turn the water on, and fill the tub with some scented bubble bath Faye left here. The room fills up with steam and the scent of jasmine. I light a few candles and retrieve a couple of fluffy towels from the cabinet.

"You didn't have to do that," Rachel says from behind me.

I straighten up, shrugging and trying not to stare at her tempting bare legs. She's wearing a silky black and pink robe that clings to her curves and reaches just above her knee. Her hard nipples jut out through the fine material, instantly stirring my lust. "It's no big deal." I rush past her, anxious to get out of here before I do something stupid like strip her of that robe and jump in the tub with her.

I knock on the bathroom door about ten minutes later. "Dinner's ready, but take your time. I'll keep it warm."

"I'll be right out," she shouts through the closed door. I press my forehead to the doorframe as sounds of water sloshing about feeds my overactive imagination. Streams of steam creep out under the bottom of the door, and I conjure up vivid images of her standing in the tub, her skin damp and flushed as beads of water trickle down over her tits and farther south. I'm already hard as a rock and questioning the decision to let her move in. She was pretty adamant about the "friends with no benefits" arrangement, and I don't want to disrespect her in any way. I haven't always treated Rachel right, and this is a golden opportunity to make amends.

Meaning, no fantasies of taking her to my bed.

Adjusting myself in my jeans, I walk back to the kitchen computing calculus equations in my head. Anything to replace the images of a wet, naked Rachel in my mind, because I'm desperate to diffuse the bomb in my pants.

Rachel only picks at her dinner, and she's quieter than usual as we eat. "You don't like it?" I ask, clearing away the plates.

She hops off the stool. "It was yummy, but I haven't had much of an appetite recently." I've noticed she's looking thinner, and the black cotton jersey dress she's wearing is loose around her waist and hips. I don't want to pry, so I swat my curiosity aside. "Leave that," she says, taking the plates from my hands. "You cooked. I'll clean."

"Yes, ma'am." I salute her. "You're the boss."

She rolls her eyes, but her mouth twitches in a half-smile.

I stroll into the living area, flopping lengthways on the leather couch. I flip on ESPN.

Rachel joins me a few minutes later, gesturing toward the game on the screen. "I hate that you were suspended because of me."

I shake my head. "Not because of you. Because of that asshole, and I knew there would be hell to pay if I was caught. I have no regrets, so you shouldn't either."

She is quiet for a bit. "Do you miss it?"

"Yeah, but I'm only suspended for a few weeks. I'll cope. At least it's given me time to catch up on course work, and spend time with my family."

"How's your mum?"

She sounds so like Faye when she says that word. A pang of regret lances me on all sides. I've been purposely trying not to think about Kyler and the fact we're not even on speaking terms anymore. "She's doing okay. I know she still feels like she's betrayed my dad, but it was the best way for everyone to move on. I'm going house hunting with her this weekend. Aunt Cora has loaned her enough money for six months' rent."

"What's she planning on doing?"

"I'm not sure if she's given that much thought yet. She's focused on getting the girls enrolled in school this week and then finding somewhere to live, and then, I guess, she'll figure out the rest."

"And there's been no news of your dad?" I shake my head. "Do you think he'll turn himself in?"

I snort. "Not a chance. Unless they catch up to him, I doubt we'll ever see him again."

"Maybe he'll surprise you."

"I don't really care, either way." And I don't care much for the direction this conversation has taken either. "If you don't have plans on Saturday, do you want to come to Wellesley with me? I know Mom would love to see you."

She cringes a little.

Shit. Why did I go there?

"It's totally cool if you don't want to come, and, don't worry, I'll tell her we're not really going out so you don't have to visit anymore."

She pulls her knees into her chest, causing the material to slide down, exposing a decent amount of her thighs. It takes gigantic effort not to ogle her naked flesh.

"No, it's not that. I like your family, and I don't mind hanging out with them. It's just that, I, ah, already made plans to have lunch with Kev on Saturday."

"Oh." I swallow the bitter lump of jealousy constricting my airwaves. "No problem." I turn my attention back to the screen. Neither of us speaks for a few minutes, until I can stand it no more. "What's going on with you and him?"

"We're just friends."

"You seem to spend a lot of time together."

"He's helping me with something."

I turn over on my side, staring at her. "In what way?"

She squirms a little. "It's not something I'm comfortable discussing."

She has no issue in discussing it with him it seems. I don't know what expression appears on my face, but it obviously gives the game away. "And I haven't told him much either. He knows enough to help me but that's it."

"It's none of my business." I return my gaze to the TV.

She sighs, getting up and walking over to the couch. She perches on the edge by my legs. "Look, I don't want us to get off on the wrong footing, and I don't want us to start arguing either, because, honestly, I can't deal with that shit right now. Nothing is going on with Keven Kennedy, nor will it be. We're friends, and that's the end of it."

"Friends who had sex." It's like I've got word vomit. I just can't help myself.

"I never slept with Keven."

I sit up straighter. "What? But Ky said—"

"That he stayed in my place one night during their Irish vacation? Yes, he did, and we slept in the same bed, and we did some stuff, but mainly we just kissed and talked. Contrary to popular opinion, I don't sleep with every guy I come into contact with."

"I didn't mean to imply you did. Not that there'd be anything wrong with it. I'm hardly in any position to judge, but I'm surprised." Pleasantly so, but I'm not admitting that.

"Anything else you want to know about Kev, because I'd rather he wasn't a source of tension between us?" There's a slight edge to her tone.

"No, and I'm sorry for prying."

"No harm, no foul," she says good-naturedly before returning to her seat. I miss her closeness instantly, but I'm in no hurry to analyze that. Steering clear of girls for the time being seems like the best plan of action.

The next week goes by fast. Rachel and I are both busy with college, and she goes to yoga two nights a week with Faye, while I hit the gym most nights, but we always make it back in time to share dinner together. We've settled into a routine, and it's much easier living with her than I thought it'd be.

Yes, I still have inappropriate thoughts about her, and the morning I found her in the kitchen wrapped in only a teensy towel tested my control to the limit, but, so far, the friends thing is working out.

I like having her here, and I know I'd be lonely without her.

I've heard her crying in her sleep a couple of times. I've wanted to go check on her, but she guards her privacy fiercely, keeps her secrets locked inside, and I don't think she'd appreciate me acknowledging I know her fears are disturbing her at night. I'm hoping, in time, she'll come to trust me and let me in. Until then, I'll respect her need for privacy, and I haven't mentioned it.

It's my night to cook, and I've just put a pizza in the oven when the front door slams violently. Rachel storms into the kitchen, ignoring me and heading straight for the fridge. She grabs a bottle of white wine and pours herself a large glass. She drinks greedily from it before turning to face me.

"Bad day?" I know she's trying to abstain from alcohol, so something shitty must've happened to have her reach straight for the bottle.

"I've just seen something I'd really rather not have seen."

I grab a beer from the fridge and pull her out to the couch. "Sit. Tell me all about it."

She takes another greedy gulp of the wine. "Oh, fuck." I drink from my beer, waiting for her to calm down and tell me. "I just saw that bitch Callie hitting on Ky, and he wasn't exactly pushing her away."

"Come again?"

"They were outside the coffee place, and she had her hands all over him."

"I'm sure it's not how it looked. I've been on the receiving end of that, remember." I'm still getting funny looks on campus, and the rumor mill has been flying with all kinds of perverted crap about Faye and me including that Ky and I "share" her as our girlfriend. Anyone that knows Kyler Kennedy knows that shit wouldn't fly with him. Kev took the post down straightaway, but online discussion boards have popped up, and plenty of students have been gossiping over the situation. A few comments have suggested her relationship with Ky is just a cover so that she can date me in private. Which is utter garbage, because lots of girls can attest to my reputation on campus. I'd hardly have a girlfriend in private and screw around so publicly. More malicious rumors have said we've been cheating behind his back for years. No matter how quickly Ky gets Kev on the case, the minute he removes one thread, another pops up. I say let them fly and run their course. Nipping them in the bud is only adding more fuel to the fire.

"I know, but ..." She trails off, picking at a loose thread on the bottom of her shirt.

"But what?"

She takes another glug of her wine. "Faye is fairly certain Callie was behind the YouTube video, and she's made no secret of her attraction to him. What if she's got her hooks in him?"

I vehemently shake my head. "There's no way Kyler would cheat on Faye. I'd stake my life on it. He loves the crap out of her."

"Didn't he cheat on her with Addison?"

No. That was me.

I was the one who got crazy drunk the night I discovered my father was a fraud and let my best friend's girlfriend seduce me. Although we discovered afterward that Addison had planned the whole thing—as a warped means of isolating Ky from everyone he cared about—it still doesn't excuse the fact I slept with her while she was his. As long as I live, I'll never forgive myself for hurting my friend like that. The usual guilt threatens to waylay me, so I shake all thoughts of Addison aside. No good ever comes from thinking about that time.

"Not the same thing. He was protecting her, and it was before they became official. Kyler isn't cheating with Callie."

"You didn't see how cozy they looked."

I stand up as the oven timer beeps. "I don't need to. Kyler isn't screwing around on Faye."

If circumstances were different, I'd be on the phone straightaway telling him what Rachel saw so he could diffuse the shitstorm that's about to come his way, but I can't interfere anymore. I've got to stay out of their relationship, irrespective of how honorable my intentions are.

Chapter Twenty-Six

Rachel

Now that we're into the second week in October, the temps have dropped significantly. It's a lot colder than I was expecting, although the familiarity of the cooler weather is reassuring on one level. I've always much preferred colder climates anyway. Brad is a pretty chill roomie, and the arrangement is working out far better than expected—notwithstanding the fact I want to rip the clothes off his back and jump his bones on a regular basis. We haven't fought once during the two weeks we've shared living space, which has shocked the hell out of me. For the first time, I feel like I'm actually getting to know the real Brad. He's a dedicated student and devoted to his family. When he focuses on something, he gives it one hundred percent. He works out religiously every night at the gym, and I virtually lock myself in my bedroom until after he's showered. The sight of all that sweaty, glistening skin and rippling muscles cranks my desire to the max, and my trusty electronic friend is getting a thorough workout these days.

Thankfully, Brad seems to have shunned his party boy lifestyle, and he's at home most nights which I'm grateful for. I'm sure all the rumors floating around about him and Faye are contributing to his hibernation, along with the desire to avoid running into them on campus. Whatever the reason, I'm glad he's here every night because I'm still jumpy, and the only time I can relax is when I'm here with him. When I feel safe. He may not know it, but he's my protector, and I'm less on edge living here than I was in my own apartment. However, the thought of being here by myself still gives me the heebie-jeebies, and if I'm home before Brad, I'm on tenterhooks until he arrives. Kev is still on the case, and there's been no further developments or further text messages, but it doesn't reduce my anxiety much. *He's* plotting something, and that thought is enough to bring me out in hives. I've lost more weight thanks to my vanishing appetite, but I can't force myself to eat. My body's in a constant state of flux, and it's playing havoc with my health.

We are both back late Friday night. I've just spent the last hour chatting to Faye, relieved to hear that everything is hunky-dory between her and Ky. Not that I was ever truly worried— Faye and Ky are as tight as any couple can be. And that whole incident with Callie turned out to be exactly as Brad said it would be.

"Hey, you okay if we get takeout tonight? My treat," Brad asks as I flop down on the couch beside him.

Kicking off my shoes, I massage my tired feet. "Sure, but only if you let me pay half."

"Rachel." His tone carries an appropriate level of censure.

"Brad." I cross my arms over my chest and feign ignorance.

"You can't keep paying for everything. You're wounding my male pride."

"Pfft. I'm not, and in case your ears aren't working correctly, I only offered to pay for *half*. I'm all for women's lib and equality."

"There's no point arguing with you, is there?" He stretches a hand around the back of the sofa.

"Nope, and I'm glad you've come to realize that." I swing my legs up on the couch and lie down flat.

He hovers over me a minute later, holding his hands behind his back, with an almost shy expression on his face.

"What?" I'm immediately on guard.

Drawing his hands around the front of his body, he thrusts a long-stemmed red rose at me. "This is for you."

I pull myself upright, bending my legs at the knees. I take it from him as if it's some strange alien offering. "No one has ever given me flowers before," I admit before I've had time to question the wisdom of it.

"Well, technically it's only one flower, but that's a damn shame. I can't believe none of your boyfriends ever bought you flowers."

I press my nose into the delicate petals, inhaling the soft, sweet scent. "I've never had a boyfriend." I don't know what's wrong with my mouth tonight—spewing honesty without provocation. Usually, I'm tight-lipped and, even when drunk, you'd have to pry the information from me in painful slowness. But Brad and I have been casually chatting every night, and it's becoming more natural to open up to him.

"What?" He sounds shocked as he lands his perfect butt on the edge of the sofa beside me. "You're kidding, right?" I shake my head. "Are all the guys in Ireland blind or braindead?" I shrug. "You're gorgeous, Rachel, and I can't understand how you've never had a boyfriend. Honestly, it makes no sense."

"I've never wanted or needed one."

He opens and closes his mouth. "And now?" His voice is clipped.

"Now is no different. Relationships complicate things, and I crave uncomplicated."

"I don't know, Rach. You've said that to me before, and I've been following your motto this last year, but it's not all it's cracked up to be. Don't you feel...empty? Lonely?"

His words resonate with me. It's only since I stopped screwing around and ceased all the drinking and partying that I've realized that's how I feel too. Alcohol and boys were a temporary numbing strategy, but the rest of the time I've felt like a shell of a person on the inside.

"Sure, but I'm used to it." I sound as if I don't care, as if my heart doesn't ache with loneliness.

After we've finished our takeout—and when I say "we" it's more like "he" because I barely touched the food—we break out the wine and share a bottle. I'm not usually a vino drinker, but I'm trying to avoid vodka and Brad's trying to stay away from beer, so wine it is. When the second bottle is emptied, I'm starting to feel buzzed. From the goofy, flushed look on his face I can tell he's feeling the same.

I hop up suddenly, swaying a little on my feet. "I've got an idea." I bound off to my room before he can quiz me, returning a couple minutes later with a box under one arm and a gleeful expression on my face.

I plonk the box down on the floor in front of him, sitting cross-legged. "Ever play Twister before?"

"Are you implying I had a deprived childhood or something? Of course, I've played Twister," he scoffs. "And you're going down, babe. Prepare to watch the master at work."

We spread out the mat and twirl the spinner, and soon we're both sprawled across the floor in extremely awkward positions. My head is presently under his body, and my butt is raised and virtually stuck in his face. Not that he's complained about the view. His hand is on the yellow square, alongside my foot, and his body is angled over mine. I'm fairly certain he can see down my top from this position, but I'm not losing sleep over it. It's not like he hasn't seen the goods before. Reaching out, I rotate the spinner, cursing like a sailor when it lands on "right hand green."

"Admit defeat," he teases.

My face is scrunched up in concentration as I try to figure out a way to maneuver my body without falling. "Never," I huff out.

"I'm the Twister champ, and the champ always wins. Ask Kaitlyn. She's never beaten me. Not even once."

"That's because your long legs and arms give you an unfair advantage. I'm going to complain to the manufacturers and get feminist movements on the case."

He snorts with laughter. "I think they might have more pressing concerns."

I make my move, twisting around and balancing precariously on one hand. "Ugh! Shit!" I stretch my elevated hand across the space under Brad, but my arm isn't long enough. I overextend, lose my balance, and fall backward. My leg swings around, taking his down, and we collapse in a tangled heap of limbs on the sheet. Brad is sprawled on top of me, and I'm practically crying tears of laughter.

He roars with laughter too until he registers the feel of my body underneath him. Jerking his head up, he peers into my eyes, and it's as if all the air has been sucked out of the room. My chest rises and falls as his gaze drifts to my mouth. Blood rushes south, and I'm instantly throbbing with need. There's no way he doesn't feel it. Not with the way his body is strategically aligned against mine. It's like unknown cosmic forces have conspired to tempt us. Propping up on one hand, he runs a thumb lightly across my mouth. Fiery tingles dance over my lips from that one soft touch, and I whimper. His chest is visibly pounding, and my heart is hammering against my ribcage. Searing need rips through me, and my brain shuts off as he lowers his mouth to mine. Our lips mesh, and I groan when I taste his welcoming, soft caress. His mouth moves expertly against mine, and he lowers his body again, pressing flush against me.

I think I could combust on the spot.

I curl my left leg around his waist, and he rocks his hips into me. I see stars, and the world explodes in a colorful burst of lust. He flicks his tongue at the seam of my lips, and I readily open for him. He explores my mouth with frantic need, and I grip the cheeks of his ass through his jeans, pulling him closer to me.

Visions of the hours we spent making love in his bedroom swim through my mind, and I'm more aroused than I've ever been in my life. His hand creeps up my shirt, his fingers caressing the expanse of skin, sending delicious tremors ricocheting all over my body. I arch my back when his mouth suctions to my neck, and he trails a line of hot kisses from my mouth to my jaw, down to my neck, and back again. I'm writhing and moaning underneath him, like some demonic lifeform has me possessed, and I want him inside me so badly. He palms my breast, rubbing the hardened peak of my nipple through my flimsy bra, and the sharp pinch snaps me out of my lust-fueled daze.

Shrieking, I place firm hands on his chest and push him away. He stumbles, landing flat on his back alongside me. "What's wrong?"

I scoot over to the space beside the couch, drawing my knees in to my chest. My breathing is ragged. "We can't do this."

He straightens up, sitting cross-legged across from me. "Why not?"

"Friends. The deal was friends only."

"What if I want to change the terms of our arrangement?"

I blink profusely. "What? Why?"

"We're attracted to each other, and we're getting along really well. Why not take things to the next level and see what happens?" He slants his head to the side. "No labels, no pressure. We can keep this casual."

I'm unsure if he tagged that suggestion on for his benefit or mine.

"I can think of one very good reason not to." His brows knit together as I scramble to my feet. I need to put distance between us before I throw caution to the wind and fling myself back into his arms. I look down at him, with my body screaming in silent protest. "You're in love with my best friend, and I want to be the champ too. I don't want to be second-best."

Chapter Twenty-Seven

Brad

She went to her room after that. I should have followed her. Should've told her she was in pole position, but I didn't. Because I don't want to lie—to either her or myself—and until I work out exactly what my feelings are toward Faye, I owe it to Rachel to keep my distance.

So why the fuck do I feel so miserable now?

I'm still tossing and turning in bed, unable to quell the maelstrom in my mind, a few hours later when I hear her shout out in her sleep. A minute later, a piercing scream rips through the still night air, and I flip the covers off, racing to her room.

Rachel is thrashing about on the bed, limbs flailing. "Stay away from me!" She lashes out at imaginary monsters as I cautiously approach the bed. "No! Stop it!" Very gently, I place my hand on her arm, and all hell breaks loose. "Don't touch me!" she roars, rearing up in the bed, her eyes fluttering open in panic. "I'll kill you. I will." She thrusts her clenched hand in my direction, and her fist impacts my jaw, sending me tumbling backward onto the floor. She jumps up, eyes blazing, panic etched all over her face. A look of sheer confusion transforms her features. She whimpers, clutching her arms around her waist as her gaze darts about the room.

Slowly, I scramble to my feet, raising my palms in a conciliatory gesture. "Rachel. It's me. It's Brad. I'm not going to touch you. I promise."

She swings her gaze in my direction, and her brow puckers. "Brad?" A choked sound rips from her throat, and her voice is laced with pain. Someone may as well have reached into my heart and crushed it to nothing. I've had my suspicions, but I don't need much more convincing than this: someone hurt Rachel, and when I find out who it is, they're going to wish they'd never been born.

She slithers to the ground, utterly shattered. Burying her face in her hands, she starts sobbing. Very slowly, I crawl to her side, sitting beside her, careful not to touch her even though I want to swaddle her in my arms and protect her. "You're safe, Rach. I'm here, and I'm not going to let anyone hurt you again."

She sobs even louder.

I sit beside her, listening to her anguished sobbing, wanting to help but clueless on how to do that. I'm hoping my quiet presence by her side is offering some comfort. She cries for ages, and each sob is like someone taking a knife to my skin and slicing me open. I've just decided to endure Ky's wrath and call Faye when she leans her head on my shoulder, and the sobs become quieter and more sporadic. "Brad?" she whispers in a croaky voice.

I risk reaching my arm around her back, pulling her in closer. "Yes, Red?"

"Will you stay with me tonight?" Red-rimmed bloodshot eyes stare into mine. "I won't have any more nightmares if you're holding me."

I press my lips to her forehead. "Of course." I help her to her feet, tucking her into the bed while I grab some bottles of water from the kitchen. When I return, she's lying on her side, facing the window, with her back to me. I put a bottle on her bedside table and crawl into bed behind her. Very slowly, I wrap my arms around her, careful to keep a gap between our bodies. She curls back, snuggling into me, and I relax, knowing she's okay with this.

"Did I hurt you?" she whispers a minute later.

"No. I'm fine," I reply, deliberately ignoring the dull ache in my jaw. That girl's got a killer left hook, but I don't want her feeling guilty, especially when it wasn't really me she was lashing out at. I kiss the top of her head. "Go to sleep, beautiful. I've got you."

She laces her fingers through mine. "Thank you," she whispers.

The next morning, it's as if nothing happened during the night. I'm awake before her, my insides all knotted up at the thought that someone hurt the girl in my arms. She stirs, yawning and stretching her body out in the bed. She twists around, giving me a shy smile. "Morning."

"Morning." I sweep her hair back off her face. Although her eyes are still a bit swollen, she looks rested. "How are you feeling?"

"I'm good." Her smile widens, but it doesn't quite meet her eyes.

"Do you want to ta—"

"I'm thinking poached eggs and bacon for breakfast. That sound good?" she interrupts me, throwing the covers off and jumping up.

I'm looking to her for guidance, and I don't want to push her, so I follow her lead, as much as it pains me to remain in the dark. "Sounds perfect. You want some help?"

"Nope. Why don't you grab a shower while I cook?"

"Is that a polite way of telling me I smell?" I joke.

Her nostrils twitch. "Now that you mention it ..."

"Don't push your luck, Red, unless you want to get into an intimate conversation about bodily smells?" I fling the covers off and stand up.

Her cheeks flush as her eyes drop to the noticeable bulge in my boxer briefs. Shit, forgot that's all I'd been wearing when I bust into her room last night.

She lets her hair hang around her face, hiding her expression. "Definitely not up for that kind of conversation at this hour on a Saturday morning. Go shower. You have ten minutes."

"Yes, boss lady." I give her a saucy wink, and she shakes her head before leaving the room.

Over breakfast, I ask her what her plans are for today. She shrugs. "Nothing much. I'll probably fit in some studying and maybe meet with Faye and Lauren for lunch."

"Cool." I remove our plates and take them to the sink. "I'm going to do a couple hours in the gym and squeeze in some studying before heading to Wellesley later to view a few more houses with Mom. I'm planning on staying there tonight. You wanna come with?"

A customary look of fleeting panic skates over her face. I've noticed the same look every time I leave the apartment. Rachel is terrified to be by herself, and, after last night, I need to know why. If she won't or can't tell me, then I know someone who might.

I walk to her side, gently palming her face, determined to make this easy for her. "Come with me. Please."

The relief is evident on her face. "Okay, you've twisted my arm. What time are we leaving?"

"Around two?"

"Perfect. I'll be ready and waiting."

After suggesting she call Lauren to come over and study with her, I leave the apartment, happier in the knowledge that Rachel's not alone. I text Kev on my way to ensure he's there. Twenty minutes later, I'm knocking on his door.

"Hey, man." He jerks his head at me, standing aside to allow me in. "What's up?"

"I need to talk to you about Rachel."

He folds his arms over his chest, leaning back against the wall. "This is starting to get old, pipsqueak."

"Don't call me that," I snap, running a hand through my hair. "I'm not that little kid you can tease and beat on anymore."

"I never beat you."

"Don't you remember that time Ky and I followed you and Kade to that party? I seem to recall a few punches being thrown."

He chuckles. "Man, you two were so obvious, and a few slaps hardly counts."

"Much as I'm loving this trip down nostalgia lane," I deadpan, "I'm here to talk about Rachel. I know someone hurt her, and that she's fucking terrified of something, and I'm figuring they're connected. Every time I think she's going to confide in me, she retreats, and I'm back to square one. I know you're helping her with something, and I want to know what you know."

He sighs, scrubbing a hand over his taut jaw. "I can't betray her confidence, bro. That's not how I roll."

"Even if it's in her best interests? I want to help protect her, but it's hard when I don't know what I'm up against."

"I'm glad you care and that she's living with you now. I don't want to see anything happen to her either but it's not my place to tell you. All I can say is there is someone from her past she has asked me to keep tabs on, and I'm concerned that person has followed her here. As for what went down, I'm as clueless as you. She won't tell me either, but it looks like it's some sick shit."

"I'll say. She broke down in my arms in the middle of the night. She's hurting so much and I want to kill the fucker who did this." I crack my knuckles for extra emphasis, and a muscle tenses in my jaw.

He scrutinizes my face. "Me, too. Look, how about this? We stay in contact, and if there's anything suspect to report, we group our efforts. We can do that without betraying Rachel's confidence."

"Yeah, let's do that. All I care about is keeping her safe."

"Stick to her side, and if you notice anyone suspicious hanging around, let me know."

I open the door and step outside. "Will do."

"One final thing." He stretches his arms above his head, holding onto the doorframe. "If *you* hurt Rachel, I'll be the first one lining up to kick your ass."

I nod. "Understood, but that's not going to happen."

"Don't fuck her around. I mean it."

"For fuck's sake, Kev, there's no need to drill the message home. I got it, and I'm not going to hurt her. I care about her, and I want to protect her. Why the fuck do you think I came here?"

"Chill, bro. Just making sure. I care about her too."

"Later." I walk away before I say something I'll regret.

Rachel has her jacket on and a bag at her feet when I return to the apartment. "I made you some lunch," she says, holding out a square box. I open the lid, my mouth watering at the homemade wrap and chocolate chip cookie. "In case you didn't get a chance to grab lunch."

"I didn't, and thanks." Without thinking, I lean in and kiss her cheek, and it feels like the most natural thing in the world. I walk to my room to grab a few things, noticing she's placed the rose I gave her in an elegant, long-necked clear glass vase and it's holding center stage on the small coffee table. For some reason, it lifts the melancholy mood I've been in since my visit with Kev.

I chomp on the wrap as I drive while Rachel skims through the music collection on my iPhone. She puts on some Katy Perry, and I smile. No matter what my sister Kaitlyn says, every time I hear this song, I still think of her as a rambunctious twelve-year-old bopping her head as she sang along, every lyric committed to memory. I hate that I've missed so much time with my sisters. That I missed out on a crucial part of her teenage years. That I wasn't with them to help her deal with shit. The more I look back on it, the more selfish I feel. I didn't want to give up my dream of going to Harvard and playing college football, but I should have sacrificed that for my sisters. They needed their brother, and I abandoned them.

I don't know how or if I'll ever be able to make it up to them, but I won't stop trying.

"Do you miss your family?" I glance momentarily in Rachel's direction. She's staring out the window, tapping her knee up and down to the beat of the music.

Her kneel stalls. "Honestly? Not really." She doesn't look at me, fixated on the view outside the window.

She doesn't talk about her family much at all, but I get the sense she isn't close to them, which I struggle to understand based on my own experience. "It must've been lonely growing up."

She turns around, and there's a weird expression on her face. "Jill and Faye were more like my family growing up. We used to go to Faye's house after school to do our homework and study, because both Jill's and my mum worked. Faye's mum didn't, and she was like our surrogate mum. She always welcomed us with open arms. I loved hanging out in her house."

"I've always thought you were more like sisters than best friends. Your relationship with Faye reminds me of the one I have with Ky. Or had," I add, with a tinge of sadness. I haven't heard from my buddy in weeks, and I miss him. It reminds me of the months we spent without talking after all that crap went down with his ex. That was a bleak period in my life for a few reasons.

"Your friendship will recover." She places her hand tentatively on my knee. "It's too important to both of you to lose."

"I can't tell if you're right, but I hope you are." I stop at the gates to the Kennedy property, inputting the security code.

We're both quiet as I drive up the long driveway, but it's not an uncomfortable silence. Rachel's hand still rests on my knee, and I like it there.

When Mom comes running out of the house, flapping her hands in the air, I slow down in front of the main entrance. Rachel and I share a look before getting out. She threads her hand in mine, and I'm grateful. The tearstained look on my mother's face is shredding my heart to pieces. "What's wrong, Mom?"

"It's your father," she rasps, tears streaming down her face. "He's turned himself in."

Chapter Twenty-Eight

Brad

"What?" I'm stunned as I stare at Mom, her words bouncing around my brain. "He actually did it?"

She nods. "He traveled on a fake passport, and when he arrived at Logan Airport, he turned himself in to the airport police."

"Where is he now?"

"We don't know, but Dan is trying to find out."

Mom's already cancelled the viewing appointments, so we stay holed up in the Kennedy house awaiting further news. Kaitlyn stomps around the place with a sulky look on her face, but we haven't said anything to Emma yet. We need to find out what's happening before we can fully explain it to her.

Rachel helps Alex fix dinner while I hold Mom's hand on the couch. Understandably, she's on edge. There's some sci-fi movie for kids playing on the TV in the background, but Emma and Keaton Kennedy—one of the triplets and Ky's younger brother—are the only ones engrossed in it.

After dinner, Rach sits beside me on the couch while we idly listen to Alex and Mom chatting about kids growing old and leaving the nest. "Want to watch a movie in the home theater?" I whisper in her ear. This house is the bomb, and it comes complete with a home movie theater, as well as indoor and outdoor pools, a massive basketball court, and private gym. Not to mention the woods and additional properties at the rear.

"Yes, please. This conversation is giving me gray hairs."

I chuckle, pulling her up and clasping her hand in mine. "We're going to watch a movie. Let me know if you hear anything." I kiss Mom's cheek.

"How are you feeling about the news?" Rachel asks as we walk through the lobby.

"I don't know."

"Are you surprised?"

"Yeah. I really didn't think he'd do it. I figured I'd never see him again."

"Will you meet with him?"

Air releases from my mouth in a noisy burst, and an ache spreads across my chest. "I haven't decided. I think I need to let the news settle and then work out how I feel and what I want to do."

Sounds of giggling greet my ears as we round the corner and enter the large games room. Kaitlyn is squirming on the couch, swatting at Kent Kennedy as he reaches for her. "Stop it, Kent! I told you I'm ticklish."

"And you should never have admitted that. The million-dollar question is where are you most ticklish?" His tone is suggestive in the extreme as he grabs her shirt and pulls her to him.

I'm on top of him before I've even registered the fact my feet have moved across the room. I yank him up by his shirt. "What the actual fuck do you think you're doing?" I yell. "She's off limits to you! If you have laid one finger on her, I swear to God, I'll beat your ass all the way into town."

"Oh my God, Brad, stop! You're freaking embarrassing me!" Kaitlyn shrieks, trying to drag me away from Kent.

Rachel intervenes, unclenching my fists and releasing Kent. She tugs me back a few steps, whispering calming words in my ear. Kent smirks before deliberately raking his gaze over my sister from head to toe. I lunge for him again, but Rachel reacts fast, putting herself in between us. "Chill out, Brad. Seriously, you're going to have a heart attack if you don't calm down." Kent smirks again, and a red layer coats my eyes as I glower at the little shit. Kent is the resident delinquent, the brother most out of control, and I'm damned if I'm letting him anywhere near my sister. I still remember the time Faye and I had to call Ky to drag Kent out of a foursome. We caught him naked with three college chicks, and he was only fifteen at the time. He's always been reckless, and he's been cautioned for shoplifting on several occasions. If it wasn't for the Kennedy connections and wealth, he'd probably be in juvie by now.

"Has he touched you?" I bark at Kaitlyn, and she flinches.

Her cheeks turn bright red. "No. We're just friends, and you're making a big deal out of nothing."

Ignoring him, I work hard to calm myself down before facing my sister. "He is trouble, and you are to stay away from him. He's too old for you anyway." The triplets turn eighteen next month, and Kaitlyn won't be sixteen until next year. "Have I made myself clear?"

"Screw you, Brad. You're not the boss of me."

"Fine. I guess I'll just have to have a word with Mom then." I send a death glare in Kent's direction. "Once I fill her in on your past, she'll have your balls in a cage, and her head on a leash." I point at my sister while my eyes stay firmly locked on Kent.

His Adam's apple jumps in his throat. "Let's not be too hasty here. No need to scare the shit out of your Mom. I'll stay away from Kaitlyn. I promise."

"And you expect me to take you at your word?"

"Don't be an asshole, Brad." The smirk drops off his face. "I won't touch her."

"Thanks a heap," Kaitlyn says, shoving me aside before storming out of the room. I crick my neck from side to side, trying to loosen the tension in my muscles. Rachel runs her hand up and down my spine, and her touch helps soothe me.

"She's fifteen, Kent, and she's just been through hell. She's vulnerable, and if I hear you've taken advantage of her, I won't be responsible for my actions. I don't care if you're Ky's brother or not. I will beat the ever-loving crap out of you," I warn.

"And I'll help him," Rachel adds, sliding her arm around my waist.

Kent looks nonchalant. Honestly, I think nothing gets to that kid. "Are you two fucking now?" He gestures between us.

"None of your business, and stop deflecting," Rachel snarls. "And what about Whitney? I thought you two were together."

"She lives in New York, so it's not an exclusive thing. Besides, I wasn't doing *anything*."

"The hell you weren't." Tension coils in my stomach at the thought of his grabby hands anywhere near my little sister.

"Let it go," Rachel implores. "Kent knows he'll get an ass kicking if he dares even look funny at Kaitlyn. Right?"

"Message received," he barks, scowling. "So, you can drop it."

"Come on," she takes my elbow, dragging me in the direction of the theater room.

"Oh, and Rach," Kent says, calling after us. I throw my eyes to the ceiling, already sensing where this is going. "If you get tired of the asshole, you know where I am. I'm always up for a good time." He rocks his hips, making an obscene gesture with his hand.

"You're disgusting, and hell will freeze before I'll let you put a hand on me." She levels him with a grave look.

"Now you're just being cruel. I know you don't mean that." That dude's ego is through the roof—he genuinely believes his own press, and he has a ton of growing up to do.

She lifts her eyes to the ceiling, before ushering me forward. "Goodbye, Kent," she calls out over her shoulder.

We watch a couple of movies before Rachel says she's tired and we retreat to bed.

Separately.

I was going to ask if she wanted me to sleep with her again, but I've decided it's best to let her call the shots.

I'm only half-asleep when my door creaks open an hour later. A thin sliver of light from the hallway has me lifting my head and glancing at the clock. It's just past one a.m. I pull back the covers as the dark shape closes the door and tiptoes toward my bed. "Come here, beautiful," I whisper, patting the space.

Rachel slides into bed, and I immediately pull her in beside me. Her body curls into mine, and a whimper of contentment flies out of my mouth. A guy could get used to this. "Is this okay?" she whispers.

"I've been expecting you."

She snuggles into me, and I wrap my arm around her back. Her scent swirls around me, and I hold her even tighter. The more time I spend with her, the more my protective instincts kick into gear.

A few minutes later, she props up on an elbow, looking at me strangely. She tucks her hair nervously behind her ears as she wets her lips. "Brad?" she whispers.

"Yeah?" I run my fingers along the elegant column of her neck.

"Can you kiss me?"

I arch a brow, surprised she's breaking her own rule.

"It's just that—"

I cut her off with my mouth, brushing my lips against hers in a soft touch. "You don't have to explain, and it's hardly a chore." Her hands land on my chest, and blood rushes south. Things are stirring in my boxers, and I have a silent pep talk with my dick, tempering the expectations.

"I was only going to say I feel safe when I'm with you, and I know you've been staying in the apartment on purpose because you've sensed that. Thank you for doing that for me."

"Like I said, Red. It's not a chore, and if you're done talking, I'd like to claim that kiss now." She leans down, but I gently push her onto her back. I start kissing her neck, nibbling on the sensitive spot just below her ear. I'm trying to make amends with Rachel, starting with treating her how I should have from the start. That means putting her needs before my own and letting her see I'm genuine about taking things further with her. "I'm hard as a rock, babe, but I want you to ignore that. We're just going to kiss and cuddle." I deliberately look into her eyes, wanting to gauge her reaction. "Is that okay with you?"

"That's absolutely perfect. Now shut the fuck up and kiss me."

I grin as I lower myself down on top of her. I'm careful not to crush her with my weight, propping up on one elbow and keeping a small gap between us. My mouth is greedy as I drink from hers. My lips trace every inch of her mouth, and my tongue dives in when she readily opens for me. Her hands rest lightly on my bare waist, and the feel of her small, soft hands on my naked skin unravels me. My kiss is more insistent, and she meets me every step of the way, but I hold back from really letting loose even though I'd willingly chop off a testicle to go there. I don't know how long we kiss and innocently touch, but when we finally pull away, both our lips are swollen, and our joint ragged breathing is the only sound in the room.

She turns around so her back is to my front, pulling my hands firmly around her waist.

"Sleep, baby," I murmur, nuzzling her hair and curling my body around hers.

"Brad?" she whispers a minute later.

"Hhmm." I'm already in semi-slumber mode.

"I think I like, *like*, you."

Her words do something funny to my insides. Pleasantly funny. A goofy grin slips over my lips. "I think I like, *like*, you too."

We trade secretive little looks over the kitchen table the next morning at breakfast when we think no one's watching. Last night feels significant, like we've turned a corner.

"Fuck," Kent exclaims, waving his spoon between Rachel and me. "This is like Kyler and Faye part two. I'm gonna need a new puke bucket."

"Kent!" Alex hisses. "Cut that out or you can leave." She gestures subtly in Mom's direction. Mom has a hand to her chest as if she's having heart palpitations. I resist the urge to chuckle. Mom's so innocent sometimes, but it's endearing, and I wouldn't change her for the world.

Later on, Rachel is with me, Mom, and Alex when James and Dan arrive to update us. "Your father is being held under federal jurisdiction, and he's still undergoing questioning. Our understanding is that he's being detained in the FBI field office in Chelsea. I've submitted a formal request for visitation, but it's likely to be at least two or three days before that's granted," the attorney explains. "Usually, the FBI wouldn't keep a suspect for more than a couple of days or after the initial court appearance, but they have special grounds to detain him for longer."

I'm torn between staying and leaving, but I really can't afford to miss class, and tomorrow is my first day back at training. Coach will have my balls if I'm a no-show. Mom makes the decision for me, insisting we head back to the city.

Sunday night is a repeat of last night, with Rachel draped around me in bed, and while it involves a passionate make-out session, I keep my hands in a strictly PG-13 position, not progressing things until she's ready to go there. Which is kinda weird, considering we've already had sex several times. It's like we started everything backward, but I'm not complaining. I'm happy to take whatever she's offering.

It's Monday morning, and I'm feeling on top of the world. Rachel seems to be in a great mood too, openly kissing me on the mouth as I drop her off in front of her school. "I should be back before you finish yoga, so I'll fix dinner."

"Great." Leaning up on her tiptoes, she wraps her arms around my neck and kisses me more deeply this time. "A girl could get used to this you know," she whispers, and her cheeks flush.

"A guy wants a girl to get used to it," I whisper back, claiming her lips one final time. We've turned all domesticated, and the shocker is how much I'm loving that. I love going home and cooking, knowing she'll be back soon. Rooming with Kyler was completely different. The first year he had Faye over all the time, and I constantly felt like the third wheel. Then this year he's barely been home, preferring to hang out at Faye's apartment. I hadn't realized how lonely I'd become. Not that I'm blaming Kyler for that; it's my fault he had to tiptoe around me. "Scoot, before we're both late." I tap her lightly on the ass, laughing as she pouts.

I can't keep the grin off my face all day. There are no labels or anything, and I can't say I know exactly what's happening between Rachel and me, but, for the first time in ages, I feel like I belong in my skin. Like I finally recognize myself, and I'm comfortable with who I am. Things are moving forward, and I'm the happiest I've been in a long while. And that's saying a lot with all the Dad shit hanging over my head. His incarceration is front page news on every paper and the main headline on every single news channel. Hushed whispers and pointed fingers follow me around campus all day, but I ignore the gossipmongers and keep my head down.

My teammates cheer loudly when I appear in the locker room, and I'm jostled and slapped on the back so much I feel bruised. But it's good. Brady will be out for another week at least, so I don't have to deal with his skeezy ass yet. I'm hoping they find enough evidence to kick him off the team, but only time will tell.

My limbs ache as I limp off the field a couple of hours later. While I've kept up my gym sessions, it's no match for the rigorous training Coach puts us through. I hate that I've fallen behind, but I'll catch up.

Back at the apartment, I've just put some noodles on to boil when the buzzer sounds. Thinking it's Rachel and that she must've forgotten her key, I press the button to let her in. A few minutes later, there's a hard knock on the apartment door. Giving the noodles a quick stir, I sprint to the door and swing it open without checking.

A tall, dark-haired guy with familiar-looking eyes stands in front of me. "Hey, man," he says in a strong Irish accent. "I'm looking for Rachel. Is she in?" He peers behind me, and I move to block his view. I'm instantly on high alert.

"Who's asking?" I fold my arms and stare the guy down.

He laughs, extending his hand. "Sorry. I should've introduced myself first. I'm Alec. I'm Rachel's brother."

A layer of stress flitters away as we touch knuckles. "Good to meet you." I open the door wider. "Rachel never said you were coming."

"It's a surprise." He smiles as he steps inside, and he looks so much like her that I'm wondering how I didn't immediately make the connection. "You're Brad?" I nod, closing the door behind me. "She's told me all about you."

"Yeah?" I can't keep the shock from my voice. "What exactly did she tell you?"

He laughs again, sliding onto a stool at the counter as I return to the stove. "Yeah, I'm so not going there. Sibling code and all that."

"Fair enough. Have you eaten? There's enough here for three, and Rach should be back soon."

His smile turns to a frown, but he quickly disguises it. "No, I'm good. I had something to eat before I came here."

"You got someplace to stay?" I ask, trying to de-clump the noodles which are now sticking together in the pan. "Or do you need to crash here?"

"I've got a place. Already dropped my bags off."

The front door slams. "Something smells burnt!" Rach shouts from the hallway.

I lower the heat under the pan and twist around, smiling in anticipation of her reaction.

Rachel rounds the corner into the living space with a massive grin on her face. I know the second she notices our guest, because her face crumples, and she sways unsteadily on her feet. Her whole body starts shuddering, and there's a mixture of horror and disbelief on her face. I rush to her side as her brother stands up. "Baby, what's wrong?" I circle my arms around her waist, clutching her to me. She's shaking profusely, and tears cascade down her face.

"Hey, sis. Long time no see." Alec saunters toward us like there's nothing wrong with his sister's reaction.

Rachel clings to me, visibly trembling, but her eyes haven't left her brother.

He opens his arms wide. "Where's *my* hug?"

"Get out," she whispers, her voice barely audible.

"What's going on?" I tilt her chin up with my finger, forcing her eyes to meet mine. "What's wrong?"

"Make him leave." Her lower lip wobbles, and tears continue to course down her face. "Please, Brad. Get him out of here."

A cold, icy sensation crawls up my spine. Moving fast, I place her behind me, shielding her from him. My voice is like granite as I speak. "You heard her. Get the fuck out of here."

"Or what?" He steps up to me. "You'll make me?"

His face transforms in a split second, sending more chills creeping up my spine. A dark, deadly glare radiates from his eyes as he sends me a menacing look. "Move aside. I want to speak to my sister."

Rachel whimpers behind me, her fingers clinging to my shirt. Her body continues to tremble against mine. "No. She doesn't want you here. Get out or I'm calling the cops."

His eyes narrow to slits as he sizes me up. I ready myself in case he makes a move. Like a switch has been flipped, his features relax and he steps back, holding up his palms. "No problem. I'll go." He starts backing away. "But I'm not leaving, Rachel. Not until you speak to me. Remember what I told you the last time we spoke. That still stands. That will always stand. You can never outrun the truth."

"Go." I jerk my head toward the hallway.

"This time, man. You can have it this time." He stares at me and that unnerving feeling is back. He continues walking backward until he's out of sight. Taking Rachel with me, I walk out to the hall to ensure he's left. The door is wide open. As I watch him watching me while he waits outside the elevator bank, a silent storm brews inside me. I shut and lock the door, never taking my eyes off him until the door forms a solid barrier.

I pull Rach around in front of me, examining her face. Tears are cascading like a waterfall down her cheeks. "What did he tell you the last time you spoke?"

She gulps, swiping at her tears. Her voice is quaking when she speaks. "That I'm his. That I'll always be his, and no one else can have me."

Chapter Twenty-Nine

Rachel

"What?" Brad's face can't curtail his shock. "Why would he say that to you? You need to tell me what's going on, Rachel, because my mind has gone to a very weird place."

"That weird place is probably correct," I whisper.

He takes my arm, gently guiding me to the couch. "Wait there." I watch in a daze as he goes to the kitchen and turns off the cooker.

He returns with a bottle of water and a blanket. Sitting beside me, he tucks the blanket around me, but nothing can stop the chills that emanate from the very core of my soul. I sip the water, while my brain frantically scrambles to decipher the mesh of emotions cluttering my head and my heart. It's always the same when I'm confronted by my demons. When my tormentor appears in the flesh. Nausea builds at the base of my throat.

"Rachel, I know you haven't wanted to talk about this, but you've got to give me some answers. I want to protect you, but I need to know the truth. What did he do to you?"

Fresh tears spill from my eyes as I face him. The compassion and confusion on his face helps me decide. I'm tired of keeping this locked up inside. Tired of feeling like half a person. Like it's somehow my fault. As if I brought this on myself. And I'm so done with the hold he has on me. I used to think if I didn't acknowledge it, didn't speak about it, if I pretended like it didn't happen, then I could convince myself it wasn't real. But it's always been real. I've never been able to deny it. All my attempts at numbing reality have failed.

So, it's time to apply reverse psychology.

To free the secrets and lies.

I need to own them before I can overcome them.

And I want to, because I want to move forward in my life, to believe I have a future.

I clear my throat and slap a few invisible steel layers over my heart. "I was thirteen the first time my brother climbed into my bed in the middle of the night." My voice is eerily placid, like the calm before the storm.

Brad slides alongside me, and his arms close around my waist. "How old was he?" he asks through gritted teeth.

His touch, and his smell, give me the strength to continue. "Fifteen." I wet my lips as acid coats my mouth. "He kissed me, and when I tried to pull away, he told me not to be afraid of my feelings. That it was okay to want to kiss him and touch him." I look up into Brad's horrified eyes. "When I told him I didn't feel like that, he got so mad. He pinned my wrists down and told me to stop lying, that he'd seen the way I looked at him like I wanted him."

Another tear sneaks out of my eye, but I hastily brush it aside. I've shed too many of them over that monster. "I'd never looked at him like that. He was my *brother*, and I was still so ignorant of sex and boys. I didn't really have a clue, but I was scared. He'd always had this horrible temper, and he'd hit me on several occasions in the past. My parents never believed me when I told them the truth. As far as they were concerned, Alec was the golden child. The one kid who never gave them any problems. I was the one who got into trouble in school for always talking and giving cheek to the teachers. Alec had good grades and glowing reports from the teachers. He played football, Gaelic, and hurling, and when he joined secondary school, he was class captain and on the debating team. Everyone loved him." I'm rambling a little, but it's so hard to verbalize the torture I suffered at my brother's hands. I've never said the words out loud before.

"I bet everyone loved you too. It's impossible not to." His soothing tone is gentle, and I know he's trying to relax me, but there's no easing into this perverted shit.

I gulp back my panic and my fear. It's okay to let this out now. Brad knows. He may not be aware of the specifics, but he knows. There's a sort of beautiful freedom in emptying my head of the torment I've spent years trying to hide. "That night he only kissed me, but he slipped into my room again the next night, and he touched me down there. I had no idea what was happening, except that I knew it was wrong. I felt dirty. I couldn't stop crying, but he kissed my tears away. Told me it would be okay."

Brad weaves his fingers through my hair, kissing my temple, and I can tell how much of an effort it is for him to be tender in the aftermath of that revelation. "I'm so sorry, Rachel."

"Soon, he was creeping into my room at least every few nights, and things progressed quickly. He made me touch him, and his hands were all over me, inside me." I shudder as an intense bout of disgust and shame envelops me. "I hated it," I whisper. "I hated the way his hands lingered on places they shouldn't. I hated the way he made me feel. I begged him to stop, but he wouldn't. If I argued or tried to push him away, he pinned me down and took what he wanted anyway. My tears only seemed to turn him on more."

"Why didn't you tell anyone?"

"I was scared to tell my parents. Afraid they wouldn't believe me. I was the problem child after all. I thought of telling my friends, but Faye was going through her own shit, and Jill was far too innocent." I look away, biting on my lip so hard I draw blood. "I thought it was my fault, that I'd somehow led him on, and I was ashamed. I didn't want anyone to know what was happening in my bedroom at night."

"Did he ..." He stops, his jaw working overtime. He clears his throat. "Did he ..."

I cling to his arms. "He raped me after I got my period for the first time. Like he was waiting for me to officially be a woman when he forced his way inside me. I was fourteen, and he wasn't gentle. I cried the entire time and he kept his hand over my mouth to muffle my sobs."

Brad buries his head in my shoulder, and his entire body is shuddering. Hurt lances me on all sides. It's so hard to relive this. Especially after I've spent years trying to forget. But I've been fooling myself in thinking that I was coping. Shoving the hurt and the pain aside hasn't healed me.

It's only temporarily covered over the cracks. Now they're wide open and I'm bleeding. Like my heart has been savaged with a pickaxe and blood is oozing from the myriad of open wounds. A huge sob travels up my throat, and my chest is wracked with pain.

Brad lifts his head up, and his eyes are brimming with tears. "Oh my God, Rachel. I can't believe you've had to deal with that. I ..." He swipes away his tears. "I can't believe he did that to you. You're his sister. He should have protected you from monsters, not turned into one." He shakes his head. "I don't understand how your parents didn't notice *something*."

"Alec was clever, and my parents trusted him implicitly. He waited till my parents were asleep before coming to my room. Nights when my parents went out and left him babysitting were the worst. I remember begging my parents to hire a babysitter, but they always shooed my concerns away, insisting Alec was old enough and responsible enough to be left in charge. He'd have his hand in my knickers before the car even pulled out of the driveway. On those nights, he'd ply me with alcohol until I could barely see straight, and he'd force me to reenact scenes from pornos with him."

All the blood drains from Brad's face, but I don't stop talking. I can't anymore. The words are ready to erupt from my soul.

"I came to welcome that numb feeling. The alcohol anesthetized me to the things he did to my body. I became detached from myself. I liked to imagine I was a mute bystander. An emotionless droid just watching from the sidelines. I was barely living. I was in so much pain all the time. I was withdrawn and sullen, and my parents should have noticed but they were too busy with work and their social lives to pay attention to the signs. I was getting into more and more trouble in school and outside of it, and I began partying hard. I was regularly getting drunk and sleeping with guys. I needed to forget. Every second of every day he was with me. His cruel, taunting words echoed in my ear. His possessive caress left invisible fingerprints on my skin. I used to scrub myself red raw in the shower trying to erase the feel of him on me."

A potent shudder whittles through me, and Brad holds me even closer. "Sex became automatic. I slept with other guys because I thought if there were different hands on me, a different body inside mine, that I'd be able to erase the way my brother felt as he traumatized me. But it never worked. I'd have sex with some guy at a party, and then I'd hate him. Hate myself. I couldn't bear to look at the guy again. It was like the physical manifestation of my failure. My self-loathing and disgust were cranked to the max. Some days, I couldn't even face myself in the mirror. It's why I never entertained the idea of letting any guy into my life."

I peer into his eyes. I'm tempted to hold my next thought back, but there's no point in freeing my soul of this without being completely honest. "Until you. You're the first guy I've been with who makes me feel more than disgust and shame. The first guy who's brought me pleasure without all the dirty edges. The first guy to bring emotions to the surface. Perhaps it's because I've been trying to put it behind me. Trying to move on. To allow myself to feel things. To feel normal."

A pained look crosses his face. "Was I ... was I too rough with you? If I'd known ..."

I shake my head vehemently. "No, and don't do that. I don't want to be the victim in your eyes. I want to feel desired for all the right reasons."

"You are, believe me." He sweeps my hair away from my face, tucking it behind my ears. "Now isn't the time for this conversation, but I've always been attracted to you, Rachel. And if you think I haven't wanted to touch you, to hold you, and bring you to my bed these last few weeks, then you're wrong, because it's all I've thought about most days." His look turns tender. "And it's not just the physical connection. I've enjoyed living with you these last couple of weeks. Enjoyed getting to know you better, and I like what I see. I like you a lot, Rachel."

At any other time, his words would thrill me. But my emotions are in limbo. It's always been my best defensive mechanism. To bundle up all my feelings, squash them into an imaginary box, and seal the lid shut. There's more I need to say, but if I start thinking about feelings, I'll crumple. If I fall apart, I don't know if I can piece myself back together this time.

Ignoring his last comment, I continue. "He took photos of me. It's how he ensured my secrecy. He has hundreds, hell, probably thousands, of naked pictures of me. He said if I told my parents, told anyone, that he'd post them online, share them around school, and that he'd tell my parents I was prostituting myself on the side and he'd been trying to protect me. I knew they'd believe him. Mom was disgusted with the reputation

I was gaining around town, and it wouldn't take much for her to believe him. I was trapped, and so I remained his plaything until I turned sixteen."

"What happened at sixteen?"

"He went away to college, and I could finally breathe. Could finally start trying to repair the damage he had done. I signed up to self-defense classes and started digging for some dirt of my own. Turns out, he got his girlfriend pregnant, and he forced her into an abortion. My mother is totally against abortion, and she'd be sickened if she knew what he did. When he returned home for October midterm, I had a lock on my bedroom door and evidence of the abortion. I confronted him and told him to stay the hell away from me or I'd tell mum."

"I can't believe he had a girlfriend. I assume she didn't know what he was doing to you?"

"I don't think so, but I didn't really know her. He kept her away from me. Hardly ever brought her home. She went to a private school in the city center, and she mixed in different social circles, so she was a virtual stranger. At first, I thought he'd leave me alone once he had a steady girlfriend, but, if anything, his abuse accelerated. He got off on hurting me. He never left marks where anyone could see, but he became violent, and I learned to just shut up and lie there until it was over."

A murderous rage sweeps over his face. "I want to rip him from limb to limb, tear strips off his skin, and subject him to slow torture, over and over, until all he feels is pain."

"You'll have to get in line. I have thought of it, you know. I have money now. I've thought of having him killed."

"No one would blame you."

"Except then I'd never be rid of him. The memory of what I'd done, what I'd let myself become would haunt me forever. I'd be proving his point; that I'm sadistic and violent like he is. And I'm not. I'm not like him."

"Of course, you aren't. You have so much heart, Rachel, and even more so now I know your past. Don't ever let him make you feel that you aren't a good person. Because you're the best."

His words roll over me, like oil gliding over water.

He is quiet for a few minutes. "How did he react after you stood up to him?"

"He was furious, and, for the first time in years, I felt proud of myself. Proud that I'd finally had the balls to stand up to him. But that feeling didn't last long."

Brad runs his hands up my arms in a soothing motion.

"When he came home that Christmas, he started stalking me. He'd turn up at parties and watch me. I was still out of control, getting drunk and fucking random guys. He beat the shit out of all of them. Put one guy in the hospital. He'd drag me home in front of everyone. All they saw was the caring brother routine. The minute we'd get in his car, he'd jump on me, but my rage was enough to overcome the alcoholic coma. I fought him. Viciously. We both ended up bloodied and bruised, but he knew he'd never be able to rape me again. I was strong enough to fight back. But I was naïve if I thought his hold was only physical. It's way worse than that."

He presses a kiss to my temple, and his affection alleviates the battered edges of my damaged soul. "He told me if I breathed a word to anyone that he'd rape Jill and Faye." His face pales, but I go on. "He told me he'd kill any guy who dared think he could take his place." An incredulous laugh rips from my mouth. "He gave me his *permission* to fuck around. Said he understood I had needs and that he wasn't always there to fulfil them, so I could screw other guys, but no boyfriends. He told me I would never belong to anyone but him." I shake my head at the memory of that conversation. "I told him he was a fucking psycho and delusional if he believed I would ever think as he did. He said one day I'd stop resisting. That I'd come begging, and he'd be waiting. He said he owned me, and he had the power to make or break me. He told me he didn't care if I told Mum about the abortion. That it would pale in comparison to what he had to show her."

"Jesus Christ, Rach." Brad hugs me close to his chest. "He *is* a fucking psycho. No wonder you've been so scared."

"I felt so helpless after that. I thought of ending things a few times, but there was always this voice inside my head that said then he'd win. I almost completely lost it after Faye left for America. I never told her. Even after she dealt with her own stuff, because I didn't want to burden her with this, and I thought I was protecting her." I look into his eyes. "I could hardly tell her he'd threatened to rape her too. And I couldn't take the risk and confess. If anything had happened to her or Jill, I would never have forgiven myself. It was only when I visited Wellesley for the first time, and after my parents won all that money, that I began to think there was another way."

"I can't believe you've kept all this inside for so long." He cups my face. "You're so strong, Rachel. So unbelievably brave. And you're a fighter. You wouldn't be here otherwise."

"I reached a point where I wanted to change my life, and I decided I had to stop blaming him for the state I was in. *I'm* the one who let his actions destroy me. I had to convince myself that *I* still had control, and with money behind me, I could put my plan into action. I didn't tell my parents I was leaving the country until the very last minute. As it is, they think I'm in Spain. I couldn't tell them where I really was because they would have told him. Kev has helped me set up a false identity and masked my real identity."

"That's why I couldn't find you on Snapchat."

"I don't have online accounts. I lie and tell my friends it's just not my thing but it's a necessary precaution."

"But he still found you."

"Yes. I've had a couple texts from him in recent months. Kev set up tracking software to monitor his movements, but we believe he has someone else using his identity while he came here under a false one. Kev said whoever has set this up is an expert, so Alec has obviously done the same thing I've done: He's paid someone to find me, while I paid someone to hide me."

"What do you think his next move is?"

Butterflies go wild in my chest, and that nauseating sensation is back. "I'm worried you've just made yourself a target. He must think you're my boyfriend, and after what he's said ..." Tears spring forth in my eyes at the thought of anything happening to Brad.

"I can take care of myself," he coolly replies. "I meant what are his plans in relation to you?"

"Oh, that's simple." It's remarkable how calm I sound when I'm in bits on the inside. "He'll either kidnap or kill me."

Chapter Thirty

Brad

I swing into action even though I want to stay on the couch and cradle Rachel in my arms. But that asshole is completely psychotic and unpredictable, and I'm scared shitless for her. I put on the TV, place the water bottle in her hands, and tell her I'm going to fix this before moving into the kitchen and pulling out my phone. Every couple of seconds, she looks over her shoulder to make sure I'm still there, and it kills me every time. She's petrified but trying to put a brave face on things.

I waste no time bringing Keven up to speed. I know I can trust him to take her story to the grave, so I have no qualms in relaying her past. Kev is a guy of few words, so the stream of abuse and expletives feeding through the line tells me his feelings match mine. "I'll contact Dad's security guy and send a team to your apartment straightaway. They'll watch from a distance so she doesn't feel threatened, but he isn't getting near her again. Not on my watch."

"Not on our watch," I growl.

"Agreed. I'll also hack into the airport's server and see if I can find out which passport he traveled here on. If I can find the identity he's using, I can track his whereabouts, and then, hopefully, find where he's storing those photos."

"Good. I'm going to call Ky and Faye and ask them to come over. Faye knows this guy, and she might have some insight, and I think Rachel wants to tell her. To finally get it off her chest."

"Let's touch base again in the morning, and if anything happens during the night, call me."

"Will do."

I cut that call and make the next one with my heart in my mouth. This is the first time either one of us has initiated contact in weeks. Ky picks up after a few rings. "Hey."

"Hey. I hate to ask this when it's so late, but can you and Faye come over right now?"

Silence greets me initially. "Why?"

"This isn't about me. It's about Rachel. She needs Faye, and there's some stuff you need to hear too. How fast can you get here?"

The sounds of hushed conversation filter through the line. "We're leaving now. Be there soon."

I sit down on the couch, pulling Rachel onto my lap. I update her quickly and quietly. She looks even more anxious. "Are you worried about telling her?"

She nods. "I mean, I want to tell her. I've come close so many times, but I'm scared she's going to be mad at me for keeping this a secret for so long."

"She won't be mad at you." I kiss her cheek. "None of this is your fault. This is all on your brother." She looks away, and I tilt her chin up. "You didn't ask him to do what he did. He's a sick prick, and he's going to get what's coming to him." Potent rage swirls inside me again. I'm tempted to call Kev back and ask him to arrange a hit on the guy. I've no doubt Kev has those type of connections and that he could make it happen. I also know he wouldn't judge me, but it's just emotion speaking. Justice needs to prevail. Turning vigilante won't help Rachel move on from this.

"What if he hurts you or Faye or he uploads those photos online? Everything I've built here will be destroyed."

"Keven will find those photos. We're not going to let him hurt you again, and that's a promise."

Renewed tears shine in her eyes. "I can't thank you enough."

"Red, you don't need to thank me. I care about you, and I want to keep you safe. The thought of anything happening to you ..." I let my sentence trail off. I can't hit Rachel with anything else at the moment; she's way too fragile as it is. At least there is one positive to come out of today's events: I'm sure of how I feel about her. I'm crazy about this girl, and I'm going to protect her. I want to be her everything.

I've barely thought of Faye in weeks. In fact, since Rach showed up, Faye has occupied very little of my headspace. For the first time in years, I have clarity, and the resulting surge of relief is more than welcome.

The apartment door bursts open, and we both jump. "It's only us!" Faye calls out, and my heartrate returns to normal.

Faye comes into our line of sight first, Ky trailing a few steps behind her.

I look at her and ... feel nothing.

None of the usual angst and grief and turmoil lines the space between us. My smile is genuine as I haul Rachel to her feet, wrapping my arms around her body and keeping her close. "Thanks for coming."

Faye can't keep the smile off her face either until she looks closer at her friend. Her smile fades as she steps toward Rachel. "What is it?"

Rachel gulps, looking to me for reassurance. I nod, keeping my arms locked around her waist. "I need to tell you something," she says, eyeballing her friend.

Understanding appears on Faye's face. "Let's talk in your room." She extends her hand.

I reluctantly relinquish my hold on Rachel, feeling her loss the instant she steps away. She's at the edge of the room when she turns around and runs back toward me, flinging herself into my arms. I close my eyes, savoring the feel of her molded against me. Her mouth locks on mine, and we share a passionate kiss that manages to be both sweet and sexy. I don't open my eyes once, languishing in the smell, touch, and feel of her against me. I want a lifetime of kisses like this with Rachel.

Somehow, this girl has burrowed her way into my affections and wormed her way into my heart. Now that she's there, I don't want to let her go.

When we break apart, we peer deep into each other's eyes, and I sense she's feeling everything I'm feeling too. Despite what's gone down today, her expression is hopeful. I peck her lips quickly. "Go on. You can do this, and I'll be right here if you need me."

She hugs me once more and then she's gone. I'm staring after her like a loon.

Ky clears his throat. "Want to tell me what's going on?"

I nod, gesturing toward the couch, and he follows me. We sit across from one another. "Rachel told me about her past. About the stuff she's kept secret." I drag a hand through my hair, my heart suddenly feeling like it's weighed down with a ton of bricks. A sharp pain stretches across my chest.

"That's what she's telling Faye now?"

I nod. "Until she told me, Rachel hasn't spoken about this to anyone. It's some fucked-up shit, bro. Seriously, sick." He leans forward on his elbows, waiting for me to elaborate. I draw a long breath. "Her brother abused her for years, and he's done some crazy stuff to ensure her silence including threatening to rape her friends if she confided in them." All the color drains from his face. "He turned up here tonight." Ky bolts upright. "Rachel fell to pieces, but she finally admitted everything."

"Shit, man. That's ..."

"I know."

"I knew she had issues, but, fuck, that's horrific. Stupid question, but is she okay?"

"She will be."

He looks contemplative, and a strained silence wafts through the air. After a bit, he removes his phone and scrolls through his contacts.

"What are you doing?"

"Calling Dad's security guy."

"Already done." He looks up. "I called Kev before I called you. He's on it."

"Did you ask him to organize protection for Faye too?"

Shit. "Ugh. No." I scratch the top of my head. "Sorry. I didn't think of her."

He stares at me for a minute and then returns to his phone, tapping out a message, no doubt asking his brother to increase the number of bodyguards. Flinging the phone on the couch, he leans back and studies me.

"What?" All the tiny hairs raise on the back of my neck as he looks at me in that freaky way of his.

"I can't believe you didn't consider Faye. I thought you loved her." His words are clipped.

So, we're going there. Okay. Time to man up and fess up. I lean forward, staring him directly in the eye. "I thought I did too but I didn't. I don't."

He rubs at his lower lip, never taking his eyes off my face. "Keep talking."

I scrunch my shoulders up and down, trying to deflect the incoming stress. I'm way too sober for this conversation, but I'm not chickening out. I'm going to say what needs to be said. "I was pissed at you, man. In my eyes, you've always had things easy. You're better than me at motocross, and you always get the girl. While I never had feelings for Addison, it pissed me off that she used me to get to you. In my fucked-up mind, it was another example of how I'm always second-best in comparison to you." I pause for a breath, realizing I sound like an immature punk, but it's how I've felt for so long, and I owe it to my buddy to be completely honest with him. I want to fix things between us, and I can't until I get all this shit off my chest.

"When Faye came along, she was like a breath of fresh air. I liked her, but after it became obvious you were into her, it kinda became a challenge. I wanted her to choose me, to make me feel like I was as good as you. I should never have agreed to the fake relationship because it became too easy to imagine a relationship with her, and I liked the idea of it. When she made it clear she loved you, instead of accepting it and moving on, it's as if I channeled all my frustration and resentment into wanting her. I built something up in my head that didn't really exist."

His brow creases. "So, you're saying you didn't really love her, but you were doing it to exact some form of revenge?"

I cringe when he puts it like that. "Subconsciously, yes. I never set out to intentionally hurt you. In fact, I think, in a twisted way, I enjoyed hurting myself. Like it was a form of punishment for not being good enough."

"I think you should see my shrink. She'd fucking love you," he drawls, but he doesn't seem mad.

"That's probably not a bad idea. All the stuff with my family messed with my head too. It's like I was caught in this self-destructive bubble and there was no way out."

"Until Rachel?" His guess is right on the money.

"Yeah, and getting my mom and sisters back. And maybe waking up and realizing I was hurting you and Faye and making myself miserable for no good reason."

"But I saw the way you looked at her," he cuts in, a solemn expression back on his face. "Like you loved her."

"I think I did, a little, at the start, but not in the same way you love her, or in the way I would love her if she was the one. Mostly, I looked at her the way I wanted to look at someone."

"You've lost me."

It's so hard to explain this, when I'm only figuring things out myself. "I want what you have with her. I want to look at a girl like she rocks my fucking universe. Like everything starts and ends with her. I want to see my future mapped out in her eyes. I want to love her so much that I'd willingly slaughter everyone in the world to keep her safe."

"I would slaughter any fucker who threatened my girl, starting with Rachel's brother," Ky agrees.

"Don't think the thought hasn't crossed my mind. The only thing keeping me from going after his perverted ass was the girl sobbing in my arms. She needed me more than I needed vengeance."

"Things seem solid between you."

I shrug. "I guess, but we haven't spoken about it, and I don't want to put that pressure on her."

"But you want it? You want that with Rachel?"

I can't believe we're having this conversation. We've turned into two pussies, but all I can do is smile. "Yeah. Yeah, I really do."

The look of utter relief on his face is impossible to miss. He scrubs a hand over his jaw. "And you don't love my girlfriend?"

"I don't love her any more than a friend, and I'm so sorry for what I've put you through. I've been a shitty friend, and I wouldn't blame you if you wanted nothing more to do with me."

"Tempting as that is, motherfucker, I've missed your grumpy face."

"Likewise, douche." We're both grinning as we stand up, and I pull him into an awkward hug. As quickly as we joined, we pull apart.

"That was a pussy move. Don't do it again," he jokes.

We shoot the breeze for the next hour, talking quietly in between watching the game on the TV, but Rachel is never far from my thoughts.

When the girls emerge from Rachel's bedroom just after midnight, with their arms wrapped around one another, they have matching red, tearstained faces. I mute the TV and open my arms for Rach. Faye slides onto Ky's lap, burying her face in his shoulder. I pull Rachel onto my lap, rubbing a hand up and down her back. "You okay?"

She sniffles, but her features look more relaxed than earlier. "Surprisingly, yes. I never thought telling people the truth would give me such a sense of ... relief. I mean, it's hard repeating everything, but it's kinda therapeutic too. And you were right."

"I usually am."

She fights a smile. "She wasn't cross at all. She totally understood even though she wishes I hadn't shouldered the burden alone."

"Did she have any inkling?"

She shakes her head. "No, but she said my brother always gave her the creeps."

I tuck her hair behind her ears. "It's late, and it's been a difficult day. Why don't we go to bed, and we can make more concrete plans in the morning?"

"I'd like that." A yawn slips out of her lush mouth.

I stand up, holding her close to me. "You're staying with me." I want to be crystal clear on that fact. There's no way I'm leaving her alone tonight. Not after the day she's had. Her answering smile is radiant, and I bask in the glow.

"We're calling it a night," she tells Ky and Faye. "You should stay. You can have your old room, Ky."

Faye whispers in his ear. "We'll do that, thanks," he confirms.

Faye hops up, pulling Rachel into her arms. Her tears well up again, and she talks in a low tone. "I love you like a sister, Rach. I always have. I know you have Brad, but if you need me during the night, come get me. I may not have been there for you when all that was going down, but I'm here for you now."

"I know, and I love you too." Her voice is thick with emotion. Ky and I share a look, and it feels good to be back on the same page.

My cell pings in my pocket and I remove it, opening the text from Keven.

I'm downstairs. Buzz me up.

"Kev," I mouth to Ky as I walk to the kitchen and press the button to let him in. The girls are still huddled together, whispering, hugging, and crying as Ky and I discreetly wait for Kev in the hallway. I steal to the door, unlocking it in slow-mo so the girls don't hear.

I spot a guy in the corner of the corridor, blending into the shadows. He nods subtly in our direction, and I breathe a sigh of relief. Thank fuck for the Kennedys, their money, and their connections. The elevator chimes and the doors slide open. Kev's face is an unreadable mask as he strides toward us. Ky and I exchange another look. Calling at this hour of night doesn't bode well, and I'm bracing myself for the next hit.

He slips quietly into the apartment, closing the door over after him. "Where's Rachel?" he whispers.

"The girls are in there." Ky gestures over his shoulder, also whispering. "What's going on, Kev?"

"I've discovered something, and I think she needs to hear this."

"No." It's hard to sound authoritative when whispering, but I think Kev gets my message. "Unless it's life or death, we're not upsetting her any more tonight. She's dealing with too much as it is."

"I want to know," Rachel says from behind me, and I curse under my breath.

A muscle clenches in Kev's jaw. Ky shuts the door firmly. "Let's talk in the living room."

I walk to Rachel's side and she instantly leans into me, lacing her fingers in mine. At any other time, I'd mentally fist-pump the air, but this situation is too serious for competitive bullshit.

Kev stands in front of her, and his features soften. I've never seen him look so demonstrative. "I hate what happened to you, and I'm so fucking sorry that I failed you."

She touches his arm. "You didn't fail me. Not at all. You've done so much to help me these last few weeks, and you have nothing to be sorry for."

I wish I had been the one protecting her, but I don't blame Rach for turning to Kev. He had the skills she needed, and I was being a jackass, so it's no surprise she didn't look to me. But I'm going to make sure I'm the one keeping her safe from now on.

"You doing okay?"

"I'm as well as can be expected, better, maybe. I'm so glad it's all out in the open. I don't feel so alone."

Her words cut holes in my heart. I kiss her temple. "You're not alone. We're all in this with you now."

She grasps my hand, and we move into the living area. The four of us sit down, but Kev remains standing. Faye looks exhausted, resting her head on Ky's shoulder. I slide my arm around Rachel's back, virtually gluing her to my side. If Kev's about to drop another bombshell, I'm going to help keep her together.

"I've been doing some digging, and I've discovered some information I felt you needed to know." He rubs the back of his neck. "I presume you weren't aware that your brother has been expelled from college?"

Rachel jerks upright. "What? Like properly expelled. Not just suspended?"

"It appears so."

"Why?" Her voice is calm and low.

Kev's face contorts sourly, and I strengthen my hold on her. "Your brother is under criminal investigation for rape."

Chapter Thirty-One

Rachel

"According to the police report I read, one girl has alleged she was raped after he drugged her on a date, but I've discovered an online student forum where other girls are claiming the same thing happened to them. This is going to snowball, and everyone is going to find out who he really is," Kev explains.

"That's why he changed his identity and came here. It's as much to do with staying out of jail as it is about finding me," I supply.

"Don't underestimate your importance to him. Not with the things you've told me he said," Faye says. "I'm no expert, but he's clearly mentally unsound, and there's no telling what he'll do."

"Which is why all three of you have been assigned bodyguards," Kev confirms. "He's not getting anywhere near any of you."

I slide off the sofa and walk to Kev, circling my arms around his waist. "Thank you so much."

"Hey, you don't need to thank me. This is what we do for family, and you're a part of that now in the same way Brad is. We look after our own."

I take my time in the bathroom getting ready for bed as my mind churns at a hundred miles an hour. It's a wonder I haven't thrown up, considering how sickened I feel.

"Red, you okay in there?" Brad softly calls out.

I finish brushing my teeth and open the door. "I'm okay. Just thinking."

He's standing before me in form-fitting black boxers, all ripped and muscular, looking like he just stepped off the pages of *Sports Illustrated*. Damn. He's one fine specimen of manhood. There isn't an ounce of fat anywhere on his magnificent body. I lick my lips and my libido starts singing. After the day I've had, the fact I can feel anything even close to lust is testament to the magnetic pull of this gorgeous guy.

As I continue ogling him, I notice the growing arousal in his pants, but he makes no reference to it or the fact I'm shamelessly treating him like eye candy. Silently, he takes my hand and steers me to the bed. Once I'm all tucked in, he slides in beside me, immediately pulling me in close to his side.

A layer of stress is alleviated at the bodily contact. Brad feeds my body, mind, and soul. While now isn't the time to define what we mean to each other, after what he said earlier, I'm pretty confident his feelings for me are genuine.

"What are you thinking?" he asks in a hushed tone after a little while.

"Do you want the smutty or non-smutty reply?"

He laughs quietly before his voice turns grave. "I want a truthful reply. You've dealt with a lot today. No one would fault you for caving under the strain."

I sigh deeply. "I think I was holding my own until Kev showed up. Now I'm feeling massive guilt."

He twists on his side, and I do the same so we're facing one another. "You have nothing to feel guilty about."

"I want to believe that, but is it the truth? If I'd spoken up about what my brother was doing to me, then he'd never have had the chance to hurt those other girls. That means I'm partly responsible."

"No, you're not." He vehemently shakes his head. "You couldn't speak up because he threatened you and threatened people you love."

"I should have been braver, Brad. I should've done the right thing."

"You were young, Rachel, and hurting so much. You did the best you could, and it's not your fault that those girls were hurt. The only person responsible for that is your brother."

"Maybe." I nibble on my lip, deep in thought. A few minutes pass in silence. His fingers weave in and out of my hair and I love how it feels. Heat creeps up my neck and onto my cheeks. "Can I ask you something?" I whisper before I lose my nerve.

He palms my cheek. "You can ask me anything, anytime."

My cheeks stain a deeper shade of red. "Will you make love to me?" He looks torn, and then his expression turns pitiful. "Don't. Don't look at me like that."

"Like what, beautiful?"

I remove his hand from my face. "Like I'm damaged goods."

"That's not what I think. I just don't want to hurt you."

I prop up on one elbow, and my hair tumbles over one shoulder. "I've never had a healthy, normal attitude to sex because he stole that from me. But with you I feel desirable, and I feel things the way I should feel them. You make my body come alive, and I need that now, Brad. I need to feel desired. I need your touch to erase the memories of his touch." I put my hands on his chest. "I wouldn't dream of asking you this if I thought you weren't into it, but"—I deliberately focus on his straining erection—"you clearly are because I haven't even touched you and you're fit to burst out of your boxers. If you're saying no out of some misguided sense of protection, know you'd hurt me more by refusing than you ever could by sliding inside me."

He smashes his lips against mine, reeling me in flush to his body. "I'm sold, babe. I'm all yours, and I'm going to worship your body for as long as you need me to."

Those are the last words spoken for a very long time. Slowly and carefully we remove the rest of our clothing until we're both naked. He takes his time, kissing, licking, and nipping his way down my body, lavishing my breasts with care and attention, and I'm moaning and writhing underneath him. The blissful sensations he's evoking in me are all I'm thinking about, and it's exactly what I need.

He's a solid block of velvety smooth muscle in my hand, and my strokes are slow and deliberate until he gently pushes me down on my back and goes to town on me with his mouth and his fingers. My climax rattles through me a few minutes later, and it's the most intense, most orgasmic, experience of my life. Then he's suited up and sliding inside me, and that wonderful pressure is quick to build again. I can feel every inch of him inside me as he thrusts, and the look of lust in his eyes no doubt mirrors my own.

He kisses me passionately, and my hands explore his gorgeous body. I wrap my legs around his waist, urging him to go faster, but he maintains a steady slower pace, caressing every morsel of my skin with his mouth and his fingers. Tears flood my eyes at the tender way he worships me. He kisses me softly, telling me he understands and he feels it too. My body is awash with heightened sensation, and I don't think I'll ever get enough of the way he makes me feel.

Finally, he picks up the pace, thrusting harder and faster, and my second release rockets through me. Then he's falling over the edge with me, muffling his shouts of ecstasy by burying his face in my shoulder.

After we've cleaned up, we lie naked, clinging to one another, and I've never felt safer or more cherished. I want to tell him how deep my feelings go, but I'm scared he'll run for the hills, so I say nothing, content to drown in his tender embrace, and gradually I fall asleep.

I wake sometime in the early morning, still wrapped around Brad. He's snoring gently, and I smile. Small strips of light filter into the room between the gaps in the window blinds, highlighting the sleeping beauty at my side. Brad's presence is as potent in unconsciousness as it is when he's awake. And I'm not just talking about how good-looking he is. It's like he has this aura around him, this magnetism, that envelops me and coddles me, making me feel safe even when he's asleep.

My thoughts quickly return to the events of yesterday, and I weigh everything up as I press my cheek to his chest and circle my arms more snugly around his waist. In his sleep, he presses a kiss atop my head, and that gesture brings tears to the surface again.

By the time he rouses an hour later, I have my mind made up.

I wait until we are all seated around the table, eating breakfast, before I tell them what I've decided.

"I'm booking a flight to Ireland today," I blurt, and all other conversation ceases. "I'm going to tell my parents what he did, and I'm going to speak to a solicitor."

"Are you sure, Rach?" Brad asks, worry lines forming around his eyes.

"One hundred percent. I'm not shying away from this, and I'm sick of being the victim. I'll only be able to properly move on if I've stood up for myself and I've lodged criminal charges. If I don't, I'll continue to carry this around with me and his hold will be unbroken."

All three heads nod in understanding.

"And I need to do this before he hurts anyone else. If my testimony can help put him away, then I owe it to his future victims to do this. I might not have been able to stop him from hurting those girls on campus, but I can damned well ensure it doesn't happen again."

Chapter Thirty-Two

Brad

After a bit of back and forth, we decide to travel to Ireland tomorrow morning. Before Rach could protest, I told her I was coming and she could forget about raising any arguments because there was no way I was letting her do this alone. Faye and Ky insisted on coming too, and Ky's dad, James, is flying us there in his private jet. While he isn't privy to all the facts, he knows enough, and he's already lined up an appointment for Rachel with a top legal firm in Dublin.

I'm on my way across campus to a meeting with Coach when I bump into Callie. Ky confirmed Kev had identified her as the source of the YouTube video, and it's time to put her straight. She's with two other girls, sitting outside the SOCH, when I approach. Her customary scowl appears when she notices me. "Well, well, look what the cat dragged in." Sarcasm drips off her tongue, but I ignore it.

"Can I talk to you for a minute?"

"No. I've nothing to talk to you about."

I sling my book bag over my shoulders and level a no-nonsense look at her. "Fine, I don't care if I have an audience. I don't know if you're pissed because I called out another girl's name while we were screwing or if you deliberately set out to fuck me as a means of getting close to my best friend, but I don't care either way."

Her eyes dart to the ground momentarily. Bingo. This was a setup all along, and it makes this easier to say.

"This ends now. Kyler is madly in love with his girlfriend, and there's nothing you can say or do that will change that fact, and, honestly, even if he wasn't, he wouldn't look twice at you. He hates malicious, jealous bitches, and he knows exactly how to take your type down." She glares at me, and her two friends are sitting there with their mouths hanging open. "I don't care what you think you know or what else you are planning, because if you make any move, we will come after you with the entire weight of the Kennedys behind us. Any skeletons you have will be unearthed, and we will make your life hell. So, consider this your final warning. Stay away from me and mine, or you'll be fucking sorry you didn't." I grab the straps of my bag. "Now you have a nice day." I can't help grinning.

She flips me the bird, shouting insults as I walk away, but I honestly couldn't care less.

I'd like to say my meeting with Coach goes as well, but that would be an outright lie.

"No, you do not have my permission." Coach strains against the table, glowering at me. "You are only just back from a month's suspension and now you want to take off on vacation to Ireland?"

"It's not a vacation."

"Well, whatever it is, it isn't happening. If you want to retain your place on the team and hold onto your scholarship, you will not miss a single training session, and you will be at the game on Saturday."

"I am committed to the team, but my girlfriend needs me." I don't bother explaining that she's not officially my girlfriend because that wouldn't help my cause. "I can't let her go there by herself because she needs my support."

"What is more Goddamned important than football?" He slams his clenched fist on top of the table.

"I wish I could explain, Coach, but it's private, and I don't want to betray Rachel's trust."

"Then my answer remains the same. Be at training tomorrow night or you're off the team. Permanently."

My heart sinks as I stand up, but my resolve is unwavering. Rachel needs me, and that's more important that football.

I half-expect lightning to flash through the sky and strike me dead at that thought.

I nod. "Thank you for listening."

He calls out when I reach the doorway. "Don't do it, son. Don't throw your life away for some bit of skirt."

I turn and pierce him with a glare. "She's not some bit of skirt. She's someone I care a lot about, and if the tables were turned, she'd be there for me." The magnitude of the moment isn't lost on me. I'm not even contemplating pulling out of the trip, because nothing or no one is going to stop me from being there for Rachel. I know I'm most likely throwing away my future, but I honestly don't care. At present, the only thing that matters is being there for the one girl who matters.

I stop outside Coach's office, leaning back against the wall as the acknowledgment slaps me in the face.

I don't just care about Rachel.

I love her.

"Are you sure Coach was okay with you missing practice?" Rachel asks for the umpteenth time the following morning as we load our bags in the back of Ky's Range Rover. I stifle a yawn, understanding why we need to leave at the butt crack of dawn, but hating it all the same. At least, I can sleep on the flight.

"Yes. It's fine, so stop worrying." I kiss her cheek, deliberately avoiding the penetrating stare Ky is leveling my way.

At the airport, the girls take a quick shopping detour while Ky and I grab coffees. We've got thirty minutes to kill before our flight departs. The instant my butt lands on the seat in the coffee shop, I spill my guts. Might as well get in there before he does. "Before you ask, no, Coach didn't approve this trip. I'm off the team and my scholarship is in jeopardy if I don't turn up to training tonight."

"Fuck. That sucks, bro."

I snort out a laugh. "That's a fucking understatement, but I don't have any regrets. This is more important." He nods, and I take a sip of my drink. "You're not to tell Rachel."

"Agreed."

The girls return ten minutes later, and we head to the departures gate.

Once on board the plane, we settle in as James steps out of the cockpit to greet us. Rachel is almost frothing at the mouth. It's her first time on a private jet. "Oh my God, Mr. Kennedy. This is unbelievable." Her eyes are like saucers as she takes in the plush cabin with the leather seats and rich walnut tables.

He grins. "Call me, James, please. Mr. Kennedy makes me sound so old."

"You *are* old," Ky pipes up.

"Practically ancient," Faye agrees, failing to smother her grin.

"We'll just call you ole crusty balls," I add in, and everyone bursts out laughing.

James arches a brow, making a point of looking at his watch. "You know, I do believe you're still in time to catch the commercial flight. First class is probably full by now, but you lot are happy to slum it in economy, right?"

"Funny, Dad."

"It's not smart to antagonize the pilot or wound his feelings. Don't say you haven't been warned." James's teasing grin tells us all is forgiven.

Rach nods off about halfway through the journey with her head on my lap.

"You can move her to the bedroom if you like," Ky whispers.

"Nah. I don't want to disturb her." Truth is, I love having her all snuggled into me. I listen to music, dozing a little, before waking her up when James starts the descent to Dublin Airport. Curious, I peer out the window, dismayed to find it's already dark out. This is my first time in Ireland, and I wish I was here on vacation. These next few days are not going to be easy for Rachel, but I'm determined to do whatever I can to get her through this.

James is staying with us for the duration of our trip, rationalizing there was no point in returning to America only to have to return a few days later. Besides, he and Faye want to visit her parents' graves while they are here.

We check into our hotel and grab a quick bite to eat before setting out on foot for the lawyer's offices. It's early evening here, but James pulled some strings, and the lawyer agreed to a late meeting.

James is in his element pointing out various landmarks as we walk. I zip Rachel's coat up under her chin as another blast of icy cold wind swirls around us. A light smattering of rain hits the sidewalk just as we reach the law firm.

Rachel's knee bounces up and down while we wait in a small reception area on the second floor. I wind my fingers in hers and press a soft kiss to her lips. "It's going to be okay."

"I think I'm going to regurgitate my dinner any second now," she admits. My thumb starts rubbing soothing circles across the back of her hand. "Will you come in with me?"

"Of course." If that's what she needs, I'm there.

Ten minutes later, a tall, thin, distinguished man with sandy blond hair steps out to greet us. James introduces himself first, explaining that he wants all fees charged to his personal account. Rachel is shivering beside me, too paralyzed to even argue, which is most unlike her. The man introduces himself and shakes Rachel's hand before asking her to follow him into his private chambers. I take her hand and lead the way. Faye pecks Ky on the lips and skips after us.

Once the three of us are seated, the attorney—who happens to be the managing partner and one of the most experienced lawyers in the firm—leans back in his seat and asks Rachel to explain the reason for her visit. Faye and I sit on either side of her, and I take hold of Rachel's hand as she starts to tell her story. The attorney listens attentively, his face impassive as Rachel talks. She breaks down a couple of times, and he hands her a box of tissues. Walking to the long sideboard resting against the wall, he fetches her a glass of water. Rachel silently hands a tissue to Faye, and it's only then I notice she's crying too. I send her a sympathetic look.

The whole time Rachel talks, my heart is cracking wide-open again. It isn't any easier to hear this stuff the second time around, but I'm so proud of her for opening up, especially in front of a stranger.

There's an awkward silence after she's finished talking. The attorney clasps his hands in front of him on the table. "I'm very sorry that happened to you, Ms. O'Kelly. Very sorry indeed, and if you want to take legal action now, you have a couple of different options. You can take a civil case for compensation or we can pursue a criminal charge."

"I'm not interested in compensation. I'm not after money, I want justice."

"Okay, well then, we should pursue this matter as a criminal case. There is no statute of limitations in the circumstances, but it will be up to the DPP to decide whether or not to prosecute. Given what you've told me, your age, and the fact that the perpetrator is your brother, I believe this case will be taken very seriously. However, as a certain amount of time has passed, and there is no physical evidence we can use, and you didn't confide in anyone, it will come down to your word against his."

"What about the new allegations that have been made against him in Cork?" Rachel asks. "Does that add weight to my case?"

He nods. "It might, but I can't confirm that until we investigate. I'll instruct one of our solicitors to contact UCC and the gardai in Cork to ascertain the facts of that case."

Rachel retrieves some papers from her bag, sliding them across the desk to the attorney. "A friend found a list of girls who have also alleged my brother either raped or attempted to rape them. They haven't come forward yet, but perhaps they might be inclined to do so if they hear of my case."

He places the paperwork on top of a filing tray. "I'll have my team look into it. You will also need to lodge a formal statement with the gardai, but we can schedule a time to attend with you. If you like, my offices can set that up?"

After discussing various different aspects of the case, and agreeing that Rachel will provide a formal statement the next afternoon, we make our goodbyes and head out onto the busy street. Looking at my watch, I'm startled to realize we were in the meeting for over three hours, and it's past nine, local time.

Rachel is quiet as we walk hand in hand through the busy Dublin streets. James suggests stopping for food in an Asian fusion restaurant, but I can tell by Rachel's expression that she's not loving the idea. "We can go back to our room and order room service if you prefer?" I whisper in her ear. She looks up at me gratefully, and I address James directly. "We'll take a rain check. We're just going to order room service."

"Sure. No problem."

Faye pulls Rachel in for a hug. "Call me later if you need anything."

"I will, thanks." She's quiet as a mouse, and she looks exhausted.

"Mind yourself," Ky says, stepping in to hug her.

James's expression is compassionate as he watches me slide my arm around her waist and steer her away. We don't talk on the way back, and I sense there's a storm brewing in Rachel's head. She's been unbelievably strong these last couple of days, but I've been waiting for everything to hit her. I think we've reached that point.

I have only just closed the door to our room when she breaks down. Sinking to the floor, she buries her face in her hands and cries uncontrollably. Huge tears wrack her body, and she clutches her arms around herself as she rocks back and forth. I kick off my shoes and drop down beside her, circling my arms around her and drawing her body back into mine.

I hold her as she sobs for hours, and tears flow down my face at the sounds of her strangled, anguished cries. It's heartbreaking, but I'm glad she's letting it all out.

After she's cried herself dry, I lift her to the bed, silently helping her undress. I root out her pajamas and help her into them. She doesn't speak or acknowledge me in any way. She merely lifts her arms and her legs as required. My heart is aching for her. I tuck her in under the covers and place a bottle of water by her bed. "Do you want me to get you something to eat?"

She shakes her head. "I just want to sleep," she whispers.

I run my hand over the top of her head. "That's okay, baby. You sleep. I'll be right here."

Vacant eyes meet mine. "Don't leave me."

"I'm not going anywhere. I promise."

I sit up on the bed beside her, continually smoothing a hand over her hair until she falls asleep.

I sneak to the bathroom and use my cell to order some room service. Sandwiches and fruit and muffins. Stuff that will keep should she wake during the night and want something to eat.

Faye texts me a while later asking how she is, and I confirm she's sleeping. We arrange a time to meet for breakfast, and I decide I might as well go to bed too. It's late enough, and we had an early start. Plus, the different time zones are messing up my internal clock.

Mercifully, I fall asleep quite quickly, holding Rachel in my arms.

When I wake the next morning, as the alarm on my cell goes off, I find Rachel sitting up in bed munching on some fruit. "Hey." I rub my sleepy eyes and sit up, leaning against the headboard. "How long have you been awake?"

"Not too long." I'm glad to hear her sounding more like her usual confident self. "I was starving when I woke."

"I thought you might be so I ordered a few things for you last night."

"That was very thoughtful." She leans down and kisses me softly on the lips. "Thank you. Thanks for taking care of me."

"I'm glad I was here for you."

"Me too." She lays her head on my chest, and I circle my arm around her waist. There is nowhere else I'd rather be than with this girl in this moment, and it's more than just being a shoulder to cry on. I want to be her everything and for her to think of me in the same way.

I'm not sure exactly how it happened but Rachel is my person.

My only hope is that I'm hers too.

Chapter Thirty-Three

Rachel

"Let's get this over and done with," I confirm, after we've all finished breakfast. James and Ky aren't coming with us today. I felt it best to go to this meeting with my parents with just Faye and Brad. It was difficult enough getting both my parents to agree to be in the same place at the same time on such short notice without adding any extra fuel to the fire. If I rocked up with a group, they would be instantly suspicious, and this meeting is going to suck balls as it is.

I hope they've taken my request on board and not brought their new partners. I could do without that shitstorm.

I've reserved a private suite in an exclusive five-star hotel just off Grafton Street for the meeting. My dad is already in the room when we arrive. "Hey, chick," he says, pulling me in for a hug the second I step foot inside. "It's so good to see you. I've missed you."

The familiar scent of his aftershave is reassuring. I smile up at him, noting the few new strands of gray peppering his thick dark hair and the additional fine lines around his eyes. He's wearing black trousers and a light blue shirt and tie, and he looks just like he did every day when he was leaving the house for work. He quit his customer service job in the insurance company the day my parents received confirmation of their lottery win, and he hasn't done a day's work since then, but I guess old habits die hard. "I've missed you, too, Dad." I cling to him, and it's as if I've regressed ten years, and I'm a desperate nine-year-old craving her dad's attention.

"I expected you to be more tanned," he admits, giving me a quick once-over. "Or has the temperature dropped that much already in Spain?"

I cringe, hating that I lied. I know it's going to hurt him, but I can't get into it until Mum arrives so I divert his attention instead. "Dad, you remember Faye?" I pull my friend over by the hand.

Dad looks up, only noticing Brad and Faye for the first time. "Of course, I do. How are you? It's been a while." He gives her a quick hug.

"I'm good. America is treating me well."

He frowns a little. "You coordinated your trip?"

Brad intervenes this time, stepping forward. "It's nice to meet you, sir." He extends his hand.

Dad shakes it firmly, eyeing him curiously. "And you are?"

"I'm Brad." He sends me a quick look. "I'm your daughter's boyfriend."

His words thrill me silly, but I shouldn't let it go to my head. He's only doing for me what I did for him. I know he cares about me. He couldn't do all he's done and not care, but I can't jump the gun and assume he wants to be my boyfriend or that he's even considered it, no matter how badly I want to call him that.

I startle myself with the revelation, but I can't disguise the truth. I'm really into Brad, and, for the first time, I want to experience a proper relationship. To have what Faye has with Ky.

Dad scratches the top of his head. "But you're American. I don't understand."

Mum's arrival saves my bacon this time. She rushes into the room with a loud squeal. She has her hair dyed bright blonde, and judging by her flawless complexion and smooth forehead, I'm guessing she's had some cosmetic work done. She's thinner than I ever remember her being. Dressed in skinny jeans, a flimsy coral-colored blouse, and a fitted black jacket, she could easily pass for a woman ten years younger. A patterned scarf is casually draped around her neck, and she's wearing expensive-looking wedge-heel boots. She dumps her coat on the back of the chair and approaches me. I blink a few times as she grabs me into a squeezing hug, wondering if this glamorous creature is actually my mother.

I can still remember how dowdy she looked in that hideous navy-blue uniform she had to wear for work at the supermarket. I also remember the day of the lottery win when she gleefully set fire to it in the back garden.

"You look beautiful, honey," she tells me, her gaze raking over me appreciatively. "And this is gorgeous. Is this one of your creations?" She fingers the black and red kimono-type jacket I'm wearing. I nod. "It's stunning. My baby's so talented."

"What kind of a get-up is that?" Dad asks with a note of derision in his tone as he gestures toward her outfit. "You look like mutton dressed as lamb."

"And you wouldn't know good taste if it jumped up and bit you in the face," my mother retorts.

"Please don't do this," I plead. "I have something I need to tell you both, and it's not going to be easy, so can you agree a truce? Please. For me?"

My parents glare at each other. Dad is the first to relent. "I can agree to that if your mother does."

"Fine," she snaps, looking away. Her eyes spark with interest as her gaze lands on Brad, and her bad mood temporarily evaporates. "Hello. I don't believe we've met. I'm Rachel's mother." She offers her hand to him.

Brad shakes it. "Nice to meet you. I'm Brad. I'm Rachel's boyfriend."

Mum scans him up and down in a none-too-subtle manner, and I cringe again. *What the hell has gotten into her?* Turning to me, she grins. "I approve. I approve a lot." She winks, and I cringe for a second time. This is so embarrassing.

"Geraldine! You are making a holy show of yourself," Dad cuts in.

"What would you know," she scoffs. "You're nothing but an old fuddy-duddy."

It saddens me so much that things have come to this between them. Yes, my parents didn't have the best marriage, but it's not like they were constantly bickering. They seemed to like each other enough while we were growing up, although I don't recall many PDAs or loving gestures. But there weren't many rows either.

If there's one negative to winning all that money, the end of their marriage is it. Or maybe it's a positive, because they clearly weren't happy with one another, and if money was the only reason why they didn't separate sooner, then the lottery win was a blessing in disguise. Even if I hate that thought. I don't think anyone wants to see their parents split up and go their separate ways. Or watch as they snipe at one another with barely concealed hatred.

My family is as dysfunctional as they come, and that thought makes me sad. I know my revelation is going to devastate them, and it could be the very thing to rip us apart irreparably. Guilt waylays me, but I push it aside. It's not my fault we're here. That's all on Alec.

Brad sends me an apologetic look while Faye takes matters into her own hands. "You two are a disgrace," she says. "Your daughter needs to speak to you about something very serious, and all you can do is take pot shots at one another. You should both be ashamed of yourselves. Are you interested in hearing what Rachel has to say, or should we just leave you to it?" Planting her hands on her hips, she shoots them a frosty glare.

Both my parents look suitably chastised, and I seize the opportunity, grateful for my friend's intervention. "Let's sit down. I think you'll need to be seated for this."

I sit in the middle of Brad and Faye on one leather couch while my parents sit on the one across from us—at opposite ends, naturally.

"The first thing I have to tell you is that I'm living in Boston with Faye. I lied about being in Spain." They don't need to know I'm currently living with Brad. That will only divert the conversation from the main topic, so I feel justified in telling this tiny white lie.

Dad looks confused. "Why on Earth would you do that?"

"The *why* is the main reason I'm here today. This is not going to be easy for me to say or for you to hear, but I've kept this secret hidden for years, and I need to tell you what I should have told you years ago but was too afraid to say."

Brad and Faye take my hands, interlacing our fingers. Both my parents notice.

I'm already quaking on the inside, and my heart is banging around my ribcage in panic. Bile floods my dry mouth. It's now or never. Drawing a huge breath, I kick this off, deciding to go straight for the jugular because there is no way to ease them gently into this. "Alec abused me for years from the time I was thirteen. He raped me repeatedly, and he was violent and sadistic. I lied to you because I fled to America to try and have a normal life, and I didn't want you telling him where I was. But it was all to no avail, because he's followed me there and he's threatened me and my friends. He's ... he's psychotic, and he needs to be locked up."

Both my parents stare at me with shock splayed across their faces. My heart is still doing an energetic samba, and I can't ever recall being so nervous.

"What?" Dad croaks, finally breaking the silence. He peers into my eyes. Eyes that are rapidly filling with tears. "Is this true?"

"Yes. I would never make up something as appalling as this."

"Oh my God." He clamps a hand over his mouth as horror fills his eyes. Mum is staring blankly ahead, and you could cut the tension with a knife. "Why didn't you tell us?"

Mum seems to snap out of whatever daze she's in. "Don't tell me you actually believe these lies?" She sends an incredulous look at my father.

Brad and Faye stiffen beside me, but I can't say I'm overly surprised. In any argument, Mum always took Alec's side. *Always.* No matter what he did, she always believed his version of events. It still hurts that she doesn't believe me though.

"You think Rachel would lie about something like this?" Dad shouts. "Grow up, woman. You've always been blind where that boy's concerned. I knew there was something not quite right about him."

"What?" I croak.

Dad props his elbows on his knees. Pained eyes meet mine. "I've seen glimpses of rage over the years that scared me, but I had no idea he directed any of that toward you. I had no idea that was going on. You say since you were thirteen?" I nod. "How often?" he whispers after a bit, as mum harrumphs, mumbling under her breath. She crosses her arms and glares at me.

We both ignore her.

"He crawled into my bed at least twice a week. It went on until he left for UCC. When he came home on breaks, he would try, but I took self-defense classes, and I fought him off."

Tears pool in Dad's eyes. "I cannot believe he did that to my little girl, and under my roof. I'm so sorry, Rachel."

"Liar!" Mum seethes, jumping up. "Why are you lying about this? Your brother is a good boy. He always has been." Her eyes dart wildly around the room, and she starts pacing, tugging on the ends of her hair like she always does when she's preoccupied.

I stand up, holding my chin upright. "It saddens me that you don't believe me, but it's not entirely unexpected. This is one of the reasons why I didn't come to you at the time. That and the fact he took hundreds of naked photos of me and threatened to expose me. He also said he'd rape my friends if I told anyone."

She stops pacing, showering me with a look of horrified disgust. Quick as a flash, she closes the gap between us, jumping in front of me before I've had time to even acknowledge her movement. She slaps me across the face, and I stagger back, my cheek stinging. My lower lip wobbles, and a few tears slip out of my eye, but I wipe them away. She's not going to break me. Everyone is on their feet now. Brad wraps his arm around my waist and pulls me back, shielding me. Faye takes my hand, and Dad hauls Mum back. "Are you insane, Geraldine? If you assault my daughter again, I'm calling the gardai."

"You don't have to worry about that," she fumes. "I'm leaving." She grabs her designer bag and coat and turns to level another scathing look in my direction. She jabs her finger in the air. "You have a lot to answer for, young lady, and we did not raise you to be so deceitful. I don't know what game you're playing, but I will not allow you to destroy your brother's reputation." She shakes her head, and a mix of dismay, repulsion, and anger contorts her face. She's still shaking her head and muttering in disgust, as she strides toward the door.

Hurt is a flaming inferno inside me, and I shout at her retreating back. "Mum, you should know that a girl in Cork has filed a case against him for rape. You might not want to believe me, but it's hard to deny the truth when a stranger confirms your son is a monster."

I probably shouldn't have said that, but her absolute refusal to believe anything bad about him has left a bitter taste in my mouth.

The door slams shut, and a horrid silence fills the room. Dad opens his arms. "Come here, honey."

I don't hesitate, throwing myself at him. The floodgates open and I sob into his chest. He sobs with me. Faye and Brad go into the other room, giving us privacy.

After we've both calmed down, we talk some more, and I tell him about my meeting with the solicitor and what I have planned. He apologizes for not noticing, for not being there for me, reassuring me that he will be there for me now. "I will support you and your decision to formally deal with this, but I can't abandon your brother either. I hate him for what he's done to you, and I don't know if I'll ever be able to look him in the face again, but he's my flesh and blood too, and he's clearly sick." His voice chokes up, and he buries his head in his hands. "He needs to be punished for what he's done, but I can't leave him to deal with that alone."

I try to imagine what it must be like to be in Dad's shoes. To have to decide between your two children, and I know it can't be easy. Dad accepted my words as truth immediately, and he's going to stand by me. He supports the need for justice, but he wants to let his son know he will support him too. *Should I hate my father for that? Or can I find it in my heart to understand?*

I just don't know if I can. My emotions are a jumbled mess. "Dad, he violated me. Robbed my innocence. Did horrible things to me. Things I will never be able to tell another living soul because I cannot even form the words to describe it." Dad's face turns a ghastly shade of pale. "I know he's your son, and I'm trying to imagine what it's like for you. I'm not going to ask you to choose, but I don't know that I can absolve you for supporting him either. It's not like he's going to be alone. Mother will mollycoddle him like she always does." I can't disguise the hurt and the anger in my tone.

Dad grasps my hands. "I'm trying to do the right thing here, but I don't know what that is," he admits.

"I know, Dad. I know you are." I place a hand on his shoulder.

Brad pokes his head in the room. "Sorry to interrupt, but we're due at the police station in an hour, and we need to leave shortly."

"I'm ready." I don't have the energy to continue this conversation, and I need to find some reserves to get through the next ordeal. I stand up, eager to get the next stage over and done with before my strength fails me.

Dad lifts his head. “Can I come?”

“If that’s what you want.”

He stands up, pressing a kiss to the top of my head. “I’m your father. I should be there, and I want to be there.”

My afternoon in the police station is harrowing, and it’s nighttime again by the time we leave. There is already an arrest warrant out for my brother in connection with the Cork investigation—which, it turns out, my parents had only just been made aware of—so they are going to amend the details to include questioning in my case. The female officer who took my statement was lovely, and she assured me she’s going to include a personal recommendation when the file is sent to the DPP.

For now, it seems there isn’t much more that can be done. My solicitor will work with the police to build the case, and they will keep me updated via email and phone. I’ve one final meeting in the solicitor’s office in the morning, and then we are returning to the States in the afternoon.

Dad bids me farewell, promising he will come and visit me in Boston. I know he’s going to have words with Mum, and probably contact Alec, but that’s nothing to do with me now. “If you need me, honey, at any time, no matter what, you just call, and I’ll be on the next plane.”

“Thanks, Dad.” At least I can count on one parent.

“Are you sure you can’t stay longer?”

“I can’t miss any more classes, and I’ve a big project due in next week.”

“Okay, chick.” He hugs me fiercely. “Ring me tomorrow night so I know you arrived safely.”

Assuring him I will, we say our final goodbyes and part ways. I’m in a weird funk after that. We have a rather subdued meal in the hotel followed by a few drinks in the bar. Our other bestie, Jill, arrives with her boyfriend, Sam. They both live in Dublin and are attending Trinity College, which is only a short walk from our hotel. After initial casual conversation, us girls retreat to a quiet corner of the bar where I proceed to tell Jill everything. Like Faye, she’s always known I was holding something back, but she had no idea it was this.

She holds my hand firmly in hers, listening without interruption. Tears flow freely down her face. When I’ve finished explaining, she pulls me into a hug, almost squeezing me to death. Faye leaves us alone for a bit, and we talk through everything. By the time she leaves, I'm drained but happy that I've repaired my relationship with her and happy the most important people in my life know the truth now.

It's after midnight by the time we retire to our respective bedrooms. I'm exhausted the second my head hits the pillow, and I fall asleep almost straightaway.

Faye, James, and Ky visit the graveyard the next morning while Brad accompanies me to the solicitors. The meeting is difficult as the team who are working on my case ask me more sensitive and intimate questions, but I do my best to answer them honestly, and Brad's hand in mine the entire time keeps me grounded.

I only start breathing normally when we leave the building, and I know it's behind me. For now. The months ahead will be challenging, but I'll take it one step at a time.

Brad flags down a taxi, and we go to the airport to meet the others.

As I step foot on the plane, I'm sad to be leaving Ireland behind. Even though I've made a new life for myself in America, and being home reminds me more acutely of the horrors of my past, returning to Boston fills me with trepidation.

Because my brother is in the wind, and I know he's gunning for me.

With what I know now, I can tell he's more unhinged than normal, and that scares me worse than anything has ever scared me in my life.

Chapter Thirty-Four

Brad

We got in late last night, and then we were both out early this morning—I headed to the library to catch up on some assignments, and Rach went to meet Lauren to work on their project. It's the first time all week that I haven't spent every solitary minute of each day with Rachel, and I'm missing her something special. I want to tell her how I feel. That I love her and I'm in this for the long haul. To promise her I'll be there to support her through the next few months, but I'm afraid it's too much heavy with everything else she's dealing with. I've been letting her set the pace, so perhaps I should continue to let her do that, but I want to make this formal between us.

I want her to know I've fallen for her, and she's my whole world.

But I'm not sure she can handle it, and I don't want to pressure her.

These thoughts are still churning through my mind in the afternoon as I make my way toward the stadium for the game. Chances are Coach is going to toss me out on my ass, but I'm going to give it a go. I'm hoping he might've cooled down by now.

No such luck.

"McConaughey!" he barks out the instant I land at my locker. "You're off the team, and you've no business in here."

I open my mouth to beg—I'm not opposed to groveling if it'll help—but he holds up a meaty palm in front of my face. "Don't want to hear it, son. Everything that needed to be said was said on Tuesday. You've left me no choice."

"Coach, I rea—" Ryan is cut off with one vicious look. I pick my bag up and walk back out of the room. My former teammates are silent as I pass them, but they all nod in my direction, and I can tell by the expressions on their faces that they're feeling this with me. Until I come to Brady. He's leaning back against the locker with his arms folded and a smug grin across his face. Typical. He goes around sexually assaulting girls, and he's allowed back on the team. Apparently, there isn't enough evidence to kick him off the team, let alone charge him with anything.

If this had been a few months ago, I'd be virtually suicidal walking out this door. But a lot has changed since then. Perhaps, I didn't really want the whole football career as much as I thought I did. Maybe that was something else I latched onto at a time when most other things in my life were a mess.

I've just reached my car when Ryan catches up to me. "Are you okay, man?"

"I'm fine." I unlock the door and throw my bag inside. "Not like I can do much about it."

"Coach will come around."

"I really don't think he will, but I'm not going to regret it. Rachel needed me, and if I had to do it again, I'd still go to Ireland with her."

"I don't get why you can't come clean with him." I haven't told Ryan what the trip was about, but he knows it was to do with police and legal stuff and that it was important. "I'm sure if he knew the facts, he would be more lenient."

"I'm not divulging Rachel's secrets, and I'm not asking her to do that either. She's already had to repeat that shit to plenty of strangers, and it's taking a toll on her."

Ryan leans back against my car, smiling. "You're really into this chick."

"I am. I'm crazy about her, and Coach can kiss my ass."

He slaps me on the shoulder. "I hope it all works out." He starts backing away. "Better get back before he kicks me off the team for sneaking out. Later, dude!"

Faye and Ky are in the apartment when I return a short while later, but they leave as soon as I'm back. I know they were only keeping Rach company in my absence. "I got takeout," I confirm, swinging the brown paper bag in front of her face.

"Thanks." There's no hint of a smile on her face.

I put the bag on the counter and reel her into my arms. "Bad day?"

"I don't want to be afraid, Brad, because that gives him power over me, but I spent the whole day looking over my shoulder. I hate that no one knows where he is. That he's planning on ambushing me when I least expect it. It has my stomach tied into knots."

"He's not getting near you, babe. I've spoken to Nate"—that's Rachel's assigned bodyguard—"and he assured me you would never be out of his sight."

"I know, and he was really great, today. So discreet that no one even noticed, but whenever I looked around I could see him, and that did offer some comfort, but I'm still petrified. I'm such a wuss."

I cup her cheek. "You're the least wuss-like person I know." That raises a small smile. "You're incredible, Rachel. You've been through hell, but you keep fighting, keep getting back up. You're my hero."

She looks at me like I've grown an extra head or something. "Are you high?"

I laugh. "High on love." The words come out all by themselves, and I stiffen, worried at her reaction.

She goes rigidly still, and my heart is jumping in a wild panic in my chest. "You don't have to pretend anymore," she whispers, averting her eyes. "You've been amazing, Brad. So amazing that I know I wouldn't have gotten through this without you, but you don't owe me anything anymore. We're even-steven."

That pisses me off. "Do you really think that?" I tip her chin up so she's looking directly at me, and I note the old Rachel determination burning fiercely in her eyes.

"Truth time?"

"Please."

"I want to believe that you like me as much as I like you, but there's still that thing with Faye and—"

I place a finger to her lips, killing those words. "There is no thing with Faye. There never really was. She was right; I was projecting stuff onto her. I don't have those kinds of feelings for Faye. Maybe, at the start I did a little, but not anymore. Not for a long time. I've been envious of what her and Ky have, because I've always been more of a relationship kind of guy."

Her eyes almost bug out of her head, and my lips curve up. "I know. It's hard to believe because I've been such an ass these last couple of years, but it's the truth." To hell with it. I'm going to go with my gut and tell her I want her. "And I want a relationship with you. Really badly, Rachel. I want to stop pretending and start living my life with you."

The confidence in her gaze gives way to a mixture of awe, fear, and vulnerability. "Even after everything? Knowing I'm broken?"

I curl my hand around her neck. "You're not broken, baby. You're hurt, and you need time to heal, and I will give you as much time as you need. I will do whatever it is you want me to do, but if you feel the same way I do, don't shut me out. Give us a chance. Give me a chance, and I'll prove I'm worthy of you."

She circles her arms around my neck, beaming at me. "You've already proven that and more. I feel so much for you, Brad, and that terrifies me. I've never done this before, and I'm afraid I won't be any good at it, and you deserve the best because you're a pretty awesome guy."

My grin is so wide it threatens to split my face. "I am?" I puff out my chest, and she slaps it.

"I can see I'll have to rein your ego in."

"You can rein anything in, baby. Anything. I'm down with whatever you want to do to me."

"Why doesn't that surprise me?"

I kiss her after that, and we don't move for ages, both content to just kiss and hold each other. After, we eat cold takeout in bed and watch Netflix, and I can't remember ever feeling happier in my life.

I nuzzle her shoulder, pressing a searing kiss to her neck.

"What was that for?" she asks, turning away from the screen.

"Because you make me so freaking happy, Red."

She curls around, snuggling into me. "The feeling is definitely mutual, dickhead."

I chuckle. "I think I'll have to punish you for that, and you definitely need to find a new pet name for me. Dickhead doesn't quite convey the right tone."

She thrusts her bare leg through mine, and my cock hardens. "What kind of punishment did you have in mind?" she purrs, instantly going there with me.

"The kind where you're on your back, completely naked, and I'm sliding inside you."

"Hell yeah," she says, sitting up and whipping her top off. She's not wearing a bra. "That's my kind of punishment."

In the blink of an eye, she has her pajama shorts off and she's lying under me completely bare. "Well?" She fake glares, tugging on the hem of my shirt. "What are you waiting for? Get naked and punish me!"

Chapter Thirty-Five

Brad

I "punished" her three times last night and twice this morning, in bed and in the shower, and I'm still insatiable. I don't know what it is about this girl, but I just can't get enough. She's laughing and joking with me while she cooks pancakes from scratch, and it feels so natural to be with her like this.

"How did you learn to cook?" I inquire from my position on the stool. I'm facing the stove so I have a fantastic view of her gorgeous ass, and my eyes have been glued to her shapely butt for the last five minutes. She's wearing cut-off denim shorts that fit her perfectly and a cropped off-the-shoulder white top. Although she's wearing a bra, her nipples are hard and poking out through the flimsy material, and I've had a raging boner the entire time I'm watching her. I suspect that may become a problem in social settings, but in this moment, nothing could be more perfect.

We're on the same page, and she appears as happy as I am.

I'm on cloud nine.

Sign me up for the pansy-ass club. I'm right there with Kyler and Kalvin. Good for a repeat subscription.

It's the most amazing feeling in the world.

"*Santa* gave me a cookbook when I was six, and Mum and I made every recipe in the book at least a few times over." She sweeps hair off her face, and a melancholy look appears in her eyes. "That was when she had time for me. Before she had to go out to work. After that, I used to cook with Faye and her mum sometimes, and I did home economics in school. I've always found cooking therapeutic. A lot like sewing," she muses.

"You're good with your hands," I say with a saucy grin.

Her eyes narrow suspiciously. "Are you flirting with me?"

"I'm always flirting with my girlfriend because she's smoking hot."

She abandons the pancake mixture, racing to my side and throwing herself into my lap. "Would you think I'm one of those stupid, giggly girls if I tell you that you calling me your girlfriend is doing funny things to my insides?"

"You couldn't be stupid if you tried, and giggles are good." I kiss her mouth quickly. "Giggles are great." I don't need a crystal ball to know there hasn't been much frivolous laughter in Rachel's past.

She rests her forehead against mine. "How did I get so lucky with you."

"Hey. Stop stealing my lines." I ease back, staring into her eyes. "*I'm* the lucky one." I wind my hands through her hair. "I'm crazy about you, Rachel. Like head over heels crazy."

"Ditto, babe." She kisses me slowly and sweetly, and I never want to let her go.

When she wriggles off my lap, I scowl, and she laughs. "Don't be like that. I want to make my boyfriend pancakes to show him how much I care."

My stomach rumbles at the same time my cell rings. "They do say the way to a man's heart is through his stomach," I tease, removing my phone from the pocket of my sweatpants. "Mom? Is everything okay?" I hate that that's become my usual greeting, and I long for the day when I can just say "Hey, Mom" without hesitation.

"That depends on your interpretation." She pauses. "Your father wants to see us."

My blissful mood evaporates in a puff. I drag a hand across my bare chest. "When?"

"This afternoon, if you can make it."

"The girls too?"

"Yes, but I'm not letting Emma in to see him. She's too young, and I don't want her in a place like that."

"She's twelve, Mom. I think that's old enough to make her own decision."

"I'd rather see what's involved first and see what state of mind your father is in before I broach the subject with her."

"Fair enough. What about Kaitlyn?"

"She doesn't want to see him." I can understand the sentiment. Part of me doesn't want to see him either, but I have some stuff I need to get off my chest.

"That's her choice, and I can't say I'm surprised. Rachel is making breakfast, but we could be on the road in an hour. I'll come get you."

"Not necessary. The Kennedy chauffeur is taking me. I'll meet you there. I'll send the coordinates to your phone." Three hours later, I'm standing outside the FBI office in Chelsea with Rachel, waiting for Mom. She bundles both of us into a hug when she arrives. "Are you ready for this?" she asks, squeezing my cheek.

I shrug. "As ready as I'll ever be."

"Thank you for coming with me. I couldn't do this without you." She grips my hand.

"You're worried he's mad at you?" I guess, and she nods. "I won't let him take it out on you. I promise."

We enter the building, and once we've signed in and gone through the security gate, a young woman with dark curly hair steps forward to greet us. "Mrs. McConaughey. I'm Agent Tori Kendall. We spoke on the phone."

Mom shakes her hand. "This is my son, Bradley, and his girlfriend, Rachel."

I get enormous pleasure out of hearing that word, and it's as if I'm back in high school and the girl I'm crushing on has agreed to go steady.

We both shake the agent's hand, and then follow her up two flights of stairs and out into a long carpeted passageway. "Your husband is being kept here temporarily, but he'll be transferred to a federal penitentiary within the next few days. I'll make sure you're notified of the new location."

"Thank you," Mom says in a quiet voice.

We come to a halt outside a gray door with a hatch on top. Agent Kendall slides it open, briefly looking in. "He's inside. You can go in when you're ready. I'll wait here." She faces Rachel. "You can take a seat there, miss." She points at the two chairs propped against the wall behind us.

Mom removes her coat, wordlessly handing it to Rachel. Rachel squeezes my hand, before leaning up on her tiptoes to kiss me. "Good luck," she whispers. "You got this."

"Ready?" I grip Mom's hand, and she nods. I open the door and we step inside.

The room is a small square. With drab gray walls, a scuffed tiled floor, and only a table and four chairs, the bleakness of the environment matches my mood. Absolutely nothing could've prepared me for the man in front of me, though. Dad always prided himself on his appearance. As a leading stockbroker, he had to look the part. His closet was stuffed full of designer suits and shoes, and he was always immaculately dressed and perfectly groomed.

The man sitting on the chair across the table doesn't even look like the same man. His once short, dark hair is now almost fully gray, and it falls to his shoulders. A thick layer of gray stubble lines his jaw, and the wrinkles around his mouth are more pronounced. The orange jumpsuit hangs off his scary-thin frame. Dad went to the gym religiously every morning before work, and he was always in tip-top shape. This person barely even resembles my father.

Mom tugs on my elbow. I wasn't aware that I'd stopped moving. I'm rooted to the spot, staring in disbelief at a man I once looked up to. A man I tried so hard to impress. The man I wanted to be when I grew up.

"Bradley." His deep voice and piercing blue eyes are about the only familiar things. He stands up, beseeching me with his eyes. I walk to the empty chairs across from him and pull one out for my mother. Once she's seated, I drop down beside her, placing my hands, palm-down on the table. His Adam's apple jumps in his throat, and he sits back down, looking a little dejected. "It's good to see you."

"Is it?" My tone is harsh.

"Yes. I've missed you. I'm glad to see you looking well. The agent told me you're at Harvard and playing for the Crimsons?"

"I am at Harvard, but I'm not on the football team anymore."

"You're not, honey?" Mom turns questioning eyes on me.

"Coach didn't approve of my trip to Ireland with Rachel. Told me he'd kick me off the team if I went."

"You threw it away for some girl?" Disappointment is obvious in Dad's tone.

"A. She's not just *some* girl. And, B, I choose to protect her rather than selfishly serve my own interests. Not that I expect you to understand. Instead of admitting your crime, you dragged my mother and sisters half-way around the world and you left me behind without a second thought. You destroyed our family because you were too gutless to do the right thing."

I half-expect my mother to jump to my father's defense, and I'm hugely surprised when she doesn't.

Dad gulps. "You're correct. I was a coward, and I should never have done that. There are so many things I wish I'd done differently, but I panicked, and I made the wrong call."

Mom said he was remorseful, but it still doesn't explain everything. "If that's really true, why didn't you return when Mom did? You left them to travel by themselves. Anything could've happened to them!" My voice raises an octave.

Dad shakes his head. "I had people watching them every step of the way. They were never in any danger."

"You did?" Mom asks.

"Yes, sweetheart. I could never have lived with myself if anything had happened to you or the girls."

"I'm not buying it." I lean back in my chair.

"I don't blame you, son. I've messed up, and I will spend the rest of my life paying for that, but I hope, in time, you can come to forgive me."

"You left me."

"I know, but you were adamant you had to stay behind, and your reasoning was sound."

"It doesn't matter." I hate that my voice wobbles, and I pause to compose myself. "You didn't even try to convince me to go."

"Would you rather I had?"

This is the hard part. The part where my selfishness comes to the fore. I could lie, but then I'd be no better than him. "No," I quietly admit. "But that doesn't mean I don't feel guilty or hurt at being left behind."

"Oh, sweetheart." Mom cups my cheek. "You have nothing to feel guilty about. You did nothing wrong. It wasn't wrong to want to stay behind and try to make something of your life. If you hadn't, you wouldn't have been here to help me. I could not have gotten through the last few weeks without your support.

"For what it's worth, I'm sorry, Bradley. I'm so very sorry for letting you down." Dad looks me straight in the eye as he apologizes. "For letting the whole family down. I'm trying to do the right thing now."

"That won't give those people back their money."

He hangs his head. "I know, and I feel terrible about that. I've handed over the contents of the offshore accounts I held onto," he admits, wincing.

"What accounts?" I ask through clenched teeth.

"I had money stashed abroad. How else were we expected to live?"

Any empathy I was starting to feel is gone in a flash. "That wasn't your money to keep!" I hiss. "You stole it!"

"Well, I've given it back. It's nowhere near enough, but it should offer some small compensation to the clients who lost money." He looks to my mother. "I begged them to allocate some to you, but they appropriated it all. I'm sorry."

"I wouldn't have taken it, and you know that," she replies. "God knows we had enough arguments over that money while we were overseas. We will manage without."

Dad hangs his head again, mumbling, "I'm sorry."

I stand up. I'm done with this. I said what I came here to say. I offer one last parting statement. "I'm glad you handed yourself in, Dad, but you've a long way to go to convince me you're genuinely sorry." I turn away, looking down at Mom. "Are you coming?"

She shakes her head. "You go. I need to speak to your father in private."

I don't look back, and he doesn't say anything as I exit the room. Rachel is on her feet instantly, holding my hand and pulling me down on the chair alongside her. "Well? How did it go?"

"Exactly as I expected."

"I'm sorry." She rests her head on my shoulder.

"Don't be. It felt good to get that stuff off my chest, but it's hard to see him like that, and to know it's all his own fault. I used to think he was so strong when I was a kid, but I've never known anyone so weak."

Agent Kendall looks at the floor, doing a piss-poor job of pretending she's not listening, but I don't care. "My biggest fear is that I'll end up just like him."

Rachel jerks her head up, grasping my face in both hands. "That's not even remotely possible. You're a million times the man he is. You're good, through and through, and the most amazing man I know. You couldn't be him even if you tried."

Her words do wonders for my mood. I close the gap, kissing her deeply, my fingers sifting through her hair. Her feather-soft touch unravels me in the best possible way.

I hear the soft tread of footsteps as Agent Kendall quietly steps away.

I could kiss Rachel all day long and never grow tired of it. As her lips caress mine unashamedly, she pours everything into it, letting me know how she feels. My heart is full to bursting point, and I pull her closer to me. The craving to touch her intimately is almost more than I can bear. Unprecedented emotion swirls inside me as we keep kissing. It's not the most romantic setting, and maybe I should hold back, but I want her to know the full extent of my feelings. "I love you, Rachel," I whisper in her ear. "I love you so Goddamned much."

Her eyes turn moist. "Brad," she whispers in that sexy, husky voice of hers. "I love you so much too."

I kiss her again, and there's nothing soft or tender about this kiss. This is pure raw emotion mixed with potent need.

"I've never told any boy that before," she whispers against my lips.

I cup her face. "That makes me incredibly happy. I've never said it to anyone before and genuinely felt it. No one has ever made me feel the way you do." My thumb rubs along her swollen lower lip. "I want you to know I'm not messing around, Rach. I know we didn't get off on the right foot, but I'm one hundred percent committed to this. I'm all in."

"I'm right there with you. I can't imagine being with anyone else."

The door creaks open, and we break apart. The second Mom closes the door behind her, she bursts out crying. I'm on my feet straightaway, pulling her into my arms. "What did he say? I'll kick his ass."

She shakes her head, tears clouding her vision. "He didn't do anything."

I arch a brow in confusion. "I just asked your father for a divorce."

Chapter Thirty-Six

Rachel

Brad was subdued after his mother delivered the bomb, and I can only imagine the crap going through his head. We've both had quite the week. When Ky suggests hitting a local club in Cambridge, it sounds like the perfect antidote, even if we are up early for class in the morning, and the thought of being exposed in public brings me out in giant hives. But I'm not going to cower and hide in our apartment forever.

At the club, we bump into some of Brad's football mates, and I overhear a conversation that has my blood boiling. I'm not going to confront Brad and make a show in front of his friends, so I pull Faye with me to the bathroom and grill her the second we step foot inside. "Did you know Brad is off the football team?" I don't know much about relationships, but communication is key, and not telling me something like this is huge. I'm hurt and pissed off with him.

"Yeah. It sucks."

"Why?"

"Why does it suck?" She washes her hands and runs a brush through her hair.

"Why was he booted out?"

She spins around. "He didn't tell you?" She rolls her eyes. "Of course, he didn't. He didn't want to burden you after all the stuff you were dealing with this week."

That sounds like Brad, and the edge fades off my anger. "I hate that. He's been there for me, and I want to do the same for him."

"I'm so happy you guys made it official."

"Don't change the subject," I hiss.

"I'm not. We'll get back to that, but I want you to know how happy I am for you. I've seen the way you two have been looking at each other all night. Even when you're not with each other, your eyes are like laser beams scanning the room. I love it. I love that you're experiencing what I'm experiencing. Isn't it the best feeling in the world?"

"I know what you're doing, you know." I drill an imaginary hole in the side of her skull.

"I don't know what you're talking about." She feigns innocence, and I harrumph.

"I can read you like a book. You're making sure my head is in the clouds so that I won't go all raging bull on his ass."

"Is it working?"

"It might be."

She slings her arm around my shoulder. "Good. Keep that in mind, and don't be angry."

"I am angry! The guy I love kept something ginormous from me! I know I'm a relationship virgin, but even I know that's not a good thing." Faye starts bouncing on her heels and clapping her hands like an enthusiastic seal. "Dude, what the hell are you on, because I so need me some of that?"

"You said you love him," she squeals.

"Oh that." I wave my hands in the air, as if it isn't a huge deal. "That's old news."

"Has he told you he loves you?" Her eyes pop wide, and I swear she's holding her breath in anticipation of my reply.

The biggest smile breaks out across my face. "He did." Tears well in her eyes. "Hey."

She sniffles. "Don't mind me. It's just, you are two of my most favorite people in the world, and this is the most amazing news ever." She hugs me. "I'm so, so happy for you, Rachel. Brad is an amazing guy, and I trust him one hundred percent to look after you. Ky and I already see the difference in him. These last few weeks, he's been the guy I first met. The sweet, genuine, thoughtful guy who helped me settle into my new life. You've no clue how freaking happy I am for you."

"No, I'm feeling it. Believe me." But I can't fault my friend for her exuberance. "And screw you for eradicating my anger. Now I want to go out there and jump his bones, not tear him a new one."

"Good, because when you hear what I have to say, that's what you'll feel like doing anyway."

She proceeds to tell me how Coach gave him an ultimatum and he ignored it to come to Ireland with me. She also tells me he received a letter confirming his scholarship funding will be cut from next semester.

I can't believe he sacrificed all that for me.

I'm blown away by it.

No one has ever done anything so selfless for me before, and my heart is about to explode.

I race for the door, and Faye laughs her head off behind me. I shove my middle finger up at her before I rush outside.

Back in the club, my eyes scan the room, frantically searching for my man. I find him standing in a circle with a few of his friends, and I make a beeline for him. I throw myself at him, and he almost loses his balance with the unexpected move. But my guy has awesome reflexes, and he snags an arm around my waist to steady me. "Careful there, Red."

Uncaring that we have an audience, I grab his face and smash my lips to his. A chorus of wolf whistles ring out. "You're so stupid," I say, in between peppering his face with kisses. I press my body against him as my hands trek a path up his delectable chest. "And part of me wants to kill you." I continue caressing his lips. "But I can't be mad at you. Not when you sacrificed your place on the team for me." He holds me firmly against him, kissing me back with the same fervor. We only break apart when shouts of "get a room" ring out. We're both panting and grinning like idiots. "I fucking love you." I say it loudly, wanting his friends to hear but not expecting him to say it back.

"I fucking love you too." His confident declaration brings tears to my eyes again. This man has sacrificed his own future to support me through one of the most difficult weeks of my life. And he's happy to trade in his man-card, to declare his feelings in front of his friends, without a second thought. I cannot believe he's mine. That I got so lucky.

And after everything he's done for me, it's time for me to repay the favor. I'm not sure how, but I'll figure out a way to fix this.

The week goes by superfast, and I'm grateful. The more time passes, the less concerned I am over my brother. I know he's still out there, and I have to be on my guard, but I'm not obsessing over it and hiding myself away. I've stayed behind in college most nights this week because the group project we're working on needs to be handed in by Monday. There goes any Halloween plans this weekend. Brad insists on collecting me every night, and I love coming out of the building and seeing him waiting for me. It never fails to make my heart race and my blood pressure soar. The weekend after next, we're moving into my apartment. Faye was insistent. It makes no sense that we're living in Kyler's apartment while they are living in mine. And considering my brother already found me here, it's not any safer than my apartment, so I relented, and we're going to swap.

On Thursday, after class, I make the trek across town to Harvard, happy in the knowledge that Brad is at the gym and I won't risk bumping into him. He's a creature of habit, but I roped Ky in just in case my man decided to surprise me at home. I made an appointment earlier on in the week so Coach is expecting me.

He's very polite, holding a chair out and offering me a beverage. I decline, preferring to get to the point straightaway. I tell Coach outright why Brad came to Ireland with me, sparing him the salacious details, but leaving him in no doubt as to what happened to me and how much I needed Brad by my side. I explain I didn't know he would lose his place on the team or I would never have let him do that. "He sacrificed his lifelong dream and his future for me, and I'm here to ask you to give him a second chance. I'll do anything if you can reverse your decision and let him back on the team." He says nothing for a couple of minutes, staring off into space. He sits up a little straighter, clearing his throat. "That's a terrible thing that happened to you, and I can understand now why he wouldn't tell me."

"I wouldn't have had any issue if he did, but he was respecting my privacy and trying to protect me."

"I can see that."

"He's an amazing person, as I'm sure you've already seen, and it doesn't seem fair that he should miss out."

He sighs, scrubbing a hand over his jaw. "I can give him his place back on the team. That's not irreversible, but I doubt the scholarship funding can be reassigned." He looks apologetic. "I'm real sorry. I wish I had known. All I saw was a guy who was more interested in puss—in girls than football, and I was mad as all hell because he's a great player, and popular with the team, but I thought he wasn't committed."

"It doesn't matter about the scholarship. I've already paid his fees for the rest of the year, so if you can give him his place back on the team, that would be perfect."

"You have?" I nod. He smiles for the first time. "Alrighty then. Consider it done."

Now it's my turn to smile. I hold out my hand. "Thank you so much, Coach. I really appreciate this, and I know Brad will too."

He shakes my hand. "Thank you for telling me."

"Can you keep the info about his fees to yourself? I haven't had the chance to tell him myself yet." And I'm not sure how to broach that subject. He's a bit touchy when it comes to money.

"No problem."

"I'll get out of your hair then." I rise, walking to the door.

"I can see why he's so enamored with you," Coach says as my fingers curl around the handle of the door. "He's a lucky son of a bitch."

I turn to him one last time. "Believe me, I lucked out too."

I'm in a fantastic mood as I make my way to the apartment. I told Brad I was going out with Faye tonight and that I'd meet him at home. I call into the local store to pick up ingredients for my special homemade curry. I plan to butter Brad up with food and sex before I steer the conversation to his fees.

My bodyguard, Nate, had waited outside the store for me, but he's nowhere to be seen when I leave. I'm not overly concerned. He sometimes goes to check out the apartment before I set foot inside.

I'm humming my favorite song, and in my own little world, when I let myself into the apartment, closing the door behind me. The place is in darkness, and a weird sensation crawls over me. I try to shake off my paranoia. Dropping my keys, mobile, and bag on the hall table, I kick off my shoes and walk into the living space carrying my bag of shopping. I flick the light switch and nothing happens. I press it up and down, and still nothing. My pulse starts throbbing wildly in my neck, and all the tiny hairs lift on my arms. While the lightbulb could need replacing, I instinctively know that's not the case.

The bag plummets to the ground as I spin around and run back to the hall. My hands are shaky as I fumble in the dark for my phone. I grab onto it, only for it to slide through my fingers and fall to the floor with a dull thud. My heart is in my mouth as I sink to my knees, feeling around the floor for it. An icy chill filters through the air, and blood thrums in my ears.

He's here.

I know he is.

I can feel his presence.

A little whimper flies out of my mouth as I jump up. Screw the phone. I'll just have to take my chances. I figure he's done something to Nate; otherwise, he never would've gotten in here. My phone was my best chance of calling for help, but I feel him closing in, and I just need to get out of here now. My fingers are clumsy as I fumble with the lock on the door.

I've only pulled the door open a smidgeon when a heavy weight crashes into me from behind. The door slams shut with a massive wallop, and every bone in my body rattles as pressure is exerted on me from behind.

"Leaving so soon, sister dearest," Alec growls, yanking me back by the hair. Ignoring the stinging pain in my scalp, I ram my elbow back into his gut, and he stumbles, but his hold doesn't loosen enough. Something cold and jagged pushes against my exposed neck, and I freeze. "Don't try anything, or I'll slice that pretty neck wide open."

With the knife pressed to my throat and one arm around my waist, he drags me back into the living room. "Do you know how unhappy I am with you?" His breath is hot on the side of my face as he leans in close to me. "Do you, Rachel?"

"Fuck you."

A sharp sting pricks my throat, and a trickle of blood starts oozing down my neck. "I wouldn't upset me any further, little sis. I'm furious with you, but I don't want to hurt you even though you've done your best to hurt me. Why'd you do that, Rachel? Why'd you hurt your only brother? The only person who will ever love you so completely? Does our past mean nothing to you?"

I want to tell him to go to hell, but I'm too afraid he'll cut me again, so I decide to play along. "You know that's not the truth. It matters, but this isn't the way to win me over."

"Why did you go to the gardai? I had it under control! That girl was going to accept a payment and withdraw her allegation, but now you've come forward and all these other girls are coming out of the woodwork. I'm royally screwed, thanks to you."

"I'm sorry." My entire body is quaking with fright. Blood continues to seep down my neck.

"Do you really mean that?"

"I do. I'm really sorry." In my head, I'm trying to calculate how long it'll be until Brad returns, but I know it's got to be at least twenty minutes. If I can just keep him distracted until then.

"Prove it."

Every muscle locks up in my body. "What?"

"Prove you're sorry. Prove you love me and not that American asshole."

I attempt to smother my mounting panic. "How?" My voice squeaks, and I hate how scared I sound.

"Down on your knees. Suck me off."

Oh, dear God. I'm going to be sick. I'm quaking all over.

Removing the knife from my throat, he turns me around, forcing me to my knees. My eyes have adjusted to the darkness, and I can detect the wicked gleam in his eyes. He holds the knife over my head, while his other hand fumbles with his belt. "Don't try anything or I'll gut you like the squealing pig that you are."

My heart is beating so rapidly I fear it'll give out.

His jeans and boxers drop to the floor, and he wraps his free hand around his hard length. Tears are coursing down my face. Horrific memories are bouncing around my mind, and I'm that frightened little girl again. I don't want to put my mouth anywhere near him, but I figure this might be my only chance to escape. It's risky, because he could impale me with the knife, but I've got to try something.

He grabs the back of my neck, jerking me forward. Closing my eyes, I take him in my mouth, say a silent prayer, and bite down really hard.

He lets out an almighty roar, and there's a clang as the knife flies out of his hand, across the room, dropping to the floor. He sinks to his knees, cupping himself as he screams in agony. "You fucking bitch! I'll kill you! I'll fucking kill you! Whore!"

I scoot away from him, shaking and crying as he continues to shout expletives. I'm paralyzed with fear, my brain having returned to a very dark place. A sliver of light starts pushing through, and I snap out of it. I'm not that same girl, and he's not going to win. This is not how my life ends.

Scrambling to my feet, I race toward the door. Blood is thrumming in my ears, and nausea floods my mouth. A line of sweat coasts down my spine.

I have the door halfway open, and one foot outside, when I'm thrown forward with force. He has a tight grip on my right ankle, and his nails are digging painfully into my flesh. My face whacks against the side of the door, and I scream as agonizing pain shoots through me. Stars blur my vision as I slam face-first into the ground. I'm only semi-conscious as Alec drags me back by my foot. My head is spinning and there's a metallic taste in my mouth. My nose throbs like a bitch. Dumping me in the living room, he hobbles to the door and closes it again.

I'm rolling around on the ground, clutching my aching body, dazed and in pain, with blood dripping down my face and my neck. My vision blurs in and out, and I'm seconds away from passing out.

I will myself to get up, but I can't make my limbs move. They won't cooperate. A loud sob bursts free of me.

I am going to die here today.

There's nothing I can do to stop it.

My sobs turn to anger as he presses himself down on top of me, reaching for the hem of my skirt. "You fucking bitch. I'm going to make you pay for that, and then I'm going to kill you and leave you here for your precious Brad to find. We still have fourteen minutes until he returns, and that's more than enough time to do what I need to do."

Tears spill out of my eyes at the sound of material ripping. He rips my skirt right up the middle, and a blast of cool air flitters over my skin. I try to buck him off, but it's a feeble attempt at best.

I go to that place.

That special empty space in my head where no one can hurt me, and I prepare myself.

I've no doubt he means what he says, and I can't fight it anymore. I have no energy left.

As his hands wander to places they shouldn't, my last conscious thought is of Brad and how awful it's going to be when he comes home to find me like this, dead on the floor.

Chapter Thirty-Seven

An hour earlier

Brad

Something's wrong. I feel it in my bones. I can't explain it, but from the minute I arrived at the gym, I couldn't concentrate. After a half hour, I take a break and ask my bodyguard to check in with Nate. His cell rings out repeatedly, and I don't waste another second. I sprint to the locker room and remove my own phone, dialing Rachel's number.

"What's up?" Ky asks, bounding into the room behind me.

"I can't reach Rachel, and her bodyguard isn't picking up either."

"Fuck! Let's go!"

We grab our bags and run all the way to the parking garage. Ky floors it, tires squealing as he drives like a maniac out onto the dark road. I call Kev on the off chance he's close by. He doesn't pick up either. Ky calls the guy in charge of the security team asking him to send more resources to the apartment. Then he calls Faye in case they happen to be together and are just ignoring their phones. She confirms my worst fears. She hasn't seen Rachel at all today which strikes fear into the heart of me. Rachel told me she was meeting Faye after classes ended, but she obviously lied.

Where the hell was she, and where the hell is she now? All Ky knows is that she was doing something to surprise me, and he was supposed to make sure I stayed at the gym.

Kev calls back a minute later. He calls up the tracking app on her phone as I speak. "She's in the apartment," he confirms.

"What about her brother?" I barely recognize my voice. Panic is doing a number on me.

"I haven't been able to trace his new identity, so I've no way of knowing where he is. I'm getting in my car now."

"How far away are you?"

"About twenty minutes."

"We're closer," Ky confirms. "We'll meet you there."

"Pedal to the metal, brother," Kev says.

"Already on it."

I keep trying Rachel the entire trip to the apartment. Ky doesn't try to reassure me, and I appreciate that. Hearing him say she'll be fine would offer no comfort in this moment. I'm fucking terrified that I'm going to walk into that apartment and find her gone or dead. My insides are twisted into knots.

Ky drives like a maniac, weaving in and out of traffic. We make it to our apartment block in record time. As soon as he swings the car into the garage, we both jump out, not even bothering to close the doors.

Ignoring the elevator, I push through the door to the stairs, taking two steps at a time. Nervous adrenaline pushes my limbs to the limit. Ky removes a gun from the back of his sweatpants as we step out onto our floor. My eyes dart to his in silent question. "I got this after the cabin. I didn't want to be caught unawares again. I have a permit."

"I don't give a fuck about permits. I'm just glad you have it."

We're running toward our apartment door when a loud scream perforates the otherwise still air.

"Rachel!" I fumble in my pocket for the keys. Inserting it into the lock, I turn it and nothing happens. I jiggle the key again, but it doesn't move. "Fuucckkkk! He has it locked from the inside."

"Stand back," Ky instructs. Holding the gun in front of him, he shoots the lock out and I kick the door open.

The hallway is dark, and all the lights are off in the apartment. Sounds of scuffling bounce off the walls. I round the bend into the living room and screech to a halt. It's fucking pitch-black, but I can still make out the two forms on the ground. He has her pinned to the ground, and his hands are around her throat. I don't think. I just act.

I charge at him, knocking him sideways, and we wrestle on the floor, both grappling for the upper hand. "Showtime, asshole," he croaks, before headbutting me. Black spots mar my vision, and a stabbing pain pierces my skull. He climbs off me and I lift my foot, angling it at his crotch, but my vision is fuzzy and my aim is off. My foot glances off his hip, and he laughs.

"Hands up, perv, or I'll shoot." Kyler steps around Rachel, pointing the gun at her brother. The crazy motherfucker charges him, and the gun flies through the air before he can get a shot off, landing somewhere in the darkened room. They both go down, swinging fists.

I crawl over to Rachel. She's lying flat on her back, and she's naked from the waist down. I strip off my sweater and cover her lower half. Tears are streaming down my face. A large red stain darkens the front of her cream blouse, and blood is smeared across her neck. Her eyes are closed and she's so still. "Oh my God, Rach. No! Please, baby, please be alive." I bring my trembling hand to the side of her neck, and I almost collapse when her pulse thrums against my fingers.

A loud crash diverts my attention. Alec has slammed Ky into the wall, and I watch in horror as my best friend collapses on the floor, out cold. Alec turns around slowly. He's also naked from the waist down, and the sight of his semi-hard dick, and his sneering, arrogant face, flips a switch inside me. I lose it, launching myself at him as I roar. He lands a punch to my stomach, but I barely feel it. I swing at him, glancing the left side of his face.

We go at it, punching one another, each trying to gain dominance, but we're pretty evenly matched. I throw another jab at him as the blare of approaching sirens fills the room. He starts backing up toward the door. Hell to the no. The only way he's getting out of here is in cuffs or a body bag.

I make a grab for his shirt, and he makes a stupid mistake, stumbling as he tries to duck out of my reach. He loses his balance and falls to the floor. I jump on him, fists swinging, digging my knee firmly into his naked groin as he yelps in pain. His hands swing wildly, but I have him pinned, and I rain blows down on him. He stops fighting back after a bit, but I continue to pummel him, raining shots on him in pure rage. Blood spurts out of his mouth, spraying me, and I want to keep going. To make sure he doesn't ever get back up, but I don't want to join my father in a jail cell either.

I force myself up off him, wiping blood from my own mouth as the pounding of footsteps grows louder. Shapes hover in the doorframe.

"Hold your hands up where I can see them, son," the police officer says, his eyes squinting to take in the scene in the dark. Strips of light leak in from the open doorway and the corridor behind, illuminating Ky and Alec lying bleeding and unconscious on the floor.

"It's not what it seems," I tell them, holding my hands up in case they shoot me. "This guy broke into my apartment, and he tried to kill my girlfriend. He knocked my friend unconscious." I jerk my head in Ky's direction. "Can you call an ambulance, please. My girlfriend is unconscious too."

"Already on its way." They don't lower their weapons. "Lock your hands behind your back and walk slowly toward me."

"I told you I didn't do this."

"Until we can verify that, you are under arrest."

"I'm not leaving this apartment until that piece of shit is removed. I'm not leaving him anywhere near my girlfriend. There's a warrant for his arrest in Ireland, and you can check with the local police, the Irish authorities were already in contact with them. His name is Alec O'Kelly."

The police officer inches toward me but hollers over his shoulder. "Weiss! Call that in. See if it checks out."

"Brad?" The small voice behind me is like music to my ears.

"Baby?" My voice is choked, and I daren't turn around in case the cop shoots me. "Don't come any closer," I warn her, keeping hawk eyes on her brother. It wouldn't surprise me if he was only pretending to be unconscious. In horror movies, the baddie always jumps up and makes a last-ditch attempt.

"Point the gun at *him*!" Rachel's voice is frantic. "He broke in here and tried to rape and kill me. My boyfriend stopped him."

That seems good enough for the cops. The officer swings his gun at the floor, and a second cop bends down over Rachel's brother.

I whirl around, walking with purpose toward my girlfriend. She's slouched against the wall, clutching my sweater around her hips, clearly injured, but she's holding herself upright. Gently, I wrap my arms around her, and she folds into me, crying. "It's okay. I've got you, baby. It's over. He can't hurt you again."

I'm holding Rachel's hand in the ambulance, and I haven't taken my eyes off her the entire time. The medics have temporarily bandaged her neck, and she's hooked up to a drip. Ky, thankfully, came around a short while after Rachel did. While he was claiming he was fine, the medics insisted he needed to get checked out, so he's on his way to the same hospital in a different ambulance. Kev is with him, and Faye is on her way in a taxi.

Rachel smiles, and it amazes me. She's so resilient. So brave. Already, it's as if a cloud has lifted and her face is brighter, less strained. "How did you get there so fast?"

I cringe at the raw, throaty sound she makes as she speaks. Finger marks have left an obvious imprint on the exposed skin around her neck. Every time I think of that bastard trying to choke her, I want to go back in time and kill his psychotic ass. But Rachel needs me to be calm and in control. "I had a sense something was off. I couldn't shake the feeling, and when we couldn't reach Nate, I just knew something had happened. We left immediately."

Her eyes turn moist. "You saved me."

"You saved me first, Red." I thought it was my family who was healing the broken pieces of my heart, but all along it's been this fierce, strong, feisty Irish girl who's been healing me. No doubt my family have played a part, but Rachel has been the driving force whether she knew it or not. "I was lost, but you found me."

"We found each other."

I hold her hand to my mouth and plant a gentle kiss on her skin. "Let's never lose sight of that."

At the hospital, Rachel is whisked away to be examined, and I wear a line in the tiled hallway, pacing back and forth. Kev is slouched in a chair, listening to someone on his phone. He gets up, clenching his jaw as he walks toward me. "That was dad's security guy. They found Nate in an alley near the apartment with his throat slit."

I stop pacing, running a hand through my hair. "Shit, he's dead?" Kev nods. "Rachel's gonna be really upset when she hears that." Although she hadn't known her bodyguard that long, I know she liked and respected him.

"I knew him. He was a good guy. I wish I'd killed that motherfucking pervert when I had the chance."

You and me both, buddy. I hope Alec rots in a jail cell for the rest of his miserable life.

Kev walks off to get coffee while I resume pacing the hallway. A few minutes later, Faye comes racing around the corner, almost crashing into me. "Whoa!" I grip her upper arms to steady her.

"Is he okay? Is Rach?"

"They're fine. They're both fine."

Kev returns carrying two cups of coffee. "I was with him in the ambulance," he says, handing her his coffee without question. "He didn't stop bitching and moaning. I'd say there's absolutely nothing wrong with him, but they are taking necessary precautions."

"I just asked at the desk, and he's being released as soon as the paperwork is processed," I confirm.

A half hour later, Ky strolls toward us with a relaxed grin. He pulls his girl into his arms, kissing the top of her head.

"I was so worried, Ky." Faye squeezes the hell out of him.

"I'm perfectly fine, except for a splitting headache and a bump on the back of my head."

A nurse steps forward carrying a clipboard. "I'm looking for Mr. McConaughey and Ms. Donovan."

"That's us," I supply, gesturing between myself and Faye.

"Rachel is asking for you."

We follow her down the corridor and around the corner. Rachel is in a private room, sitting up in bed munching on tea and toast. Faye gasps at her obvious injuries, holding a hand over her mouth. The cuts and bruises on her face and her neck will heal. I'm more concerned about the scars we can't see.

Rach holds out her arms, and Faye hugs her with tears falling down her face. "I was so freaking worried. I'm sure the taxi driver thought I was a mental case."

"I'm okay. It looks worse than it is."

"Is it?" Faye sits back, glancing quickly at me as I sit down on the other side of Rachel. I thread my fingers in hers.

"Yes. He didn't rape me, although he tried. I was trying to fight him off when Brad and Ky got there. Then he panicked, and that's when he started choking me."

A rap on the door interrupts us. A nurse walks in with the police officer who was on the scene. I assume he's here to take a statement. "Can't it wait until the morning?" I ask before he's even opened his mouth. "She's been through an ordeal and she's exhausted."

"We're not here to take a statement. That *can* wait for the morning, given the circumstances. I need to inform Ms. O'Kelly of an update in the case."

"Whatever you have to say can be said in front of my boyfriend and my friend." Rach pulls her knees in to her chest, and I can see her bracing herself. I sit up beside her, wrapping my arms around her shoulders.

"Alec O'Kelly was your brother?" He isn't disguising his disgust.

Rachel nods and visibly shudders. I pull her in closer to my side. "Was?" she asks what we're all thinking.

"Your brother tried to wrest the gun from my colleague in the ambulance on his way here. In the melee, the gun was discharged, fatally wounding him. I've sent notification to the Irish authorities to contact your parents, but I thought you would like to know."

"He's dead? He's really dead?"

"Yes, miss." He coughs. "I'm sorry for your loss."

"I'm not." Her jaw flexes, and I massage her stiff shoulders. "I stopped looking at him as my brother a long time ago. To me, he was only ever a monster, and I'm not going to lie and say I'm sorry the monster is dead."

He nods in understanding before backing out of the room.

Faye and I exchange a look. I don't blame Rachel for her thoughts. I'm not sorry the sick bastard is dead either, but it's not as cut and dried for my girl. She is angry and hurting now, but I wonder how she'll feel when those sentiments subside.

All I know is, whatever she goes through, I'll be right by her side helping her to deal with it.

"I mean it," she adds in a less defiant tone. "I know my parents will be upset, and I'm upset for them, but I finally feel ... free."

I kiss her temple. "I'm glad, baby. I'm glad you're no longer burdened."

She looks up at me and smiles shyly. "We don't have to hide or constantly look over our shoulder. We can just be a normal couple now."

I kiss the end of her nose. "I love the sound of that."

Faye quietly leaves the room.

"I love you." She presses a chaste kiss to my mouth, wincing a little.

I sweep my thumb gently across her cheek, careful not to hurt her. "I love you, too, Rachel, and I can't wait to do normal with you."

Epilogue

5 weeks later

Rachel

"Where are we going?" I ask for the umpteenth time, taking one last glance in the mirror. I'm wearing a silver and purple Rachel O'Kelly creation, and I feel like a million dollars. It helps that I have the most delectable arm candy tonight. I glance up at my guy, falling in love with him all over again. Brad is wearing a tailored black suit with a pristine white shirt and a purple tie to match my dress, and he looks fit. So bloody fit. He's letting his hair grow out again, and it's longer on top, more like the way he wore it when we first met. I love running my fingers through his hair or tugging on the strands when we're in the middle of hot sex.

He tweaks my nose. "Not telling until we get there no matter how many times you ask."

I can't be mad. Not when he's gone to so much trouble to organize a six-week-anniversary date. I thought girls were the ones to swoon over stuff like that, but Brad puts me to shame. He made me breakfast in bed this morning, showered me with new sexy lingerie and flowers, and told me he was taking me out for dinner later. All he said was to doll up. I've been trying to bribe him in all manner of ways all day, but he's been stubbornly tight-lipped.

"It must be some place fancy if you have to wear a suit."

He winks, holding out his arm. "It is."

I grab my bag and my coat and loop my arm in his. "I'm starving, so I hope it isn't one of those pretentious places where they give you a quarter-sized dinner and charge you ten times the price."

He throws back his head, laughing, as we exit the apartment. "I thought you didn't care about spending money."

"I don't mind spending money, but I'm opposed to spending it foolishly."

"I still can't believe you did it," he says, pulling me into the elevator.

I roll my eyes. "For the love of God, man, just let it go." I think Brad was secretly pleased I took care of his fees for the year, but every so often, his manly pride gets the better of him. He's yet to realize I've cleared all his student loans too, but that argument can wait for another day.

"I *am* going to pay you back." He kisses the top of my nose. "That's a promise."

As if I'm taking a penny off him, but I'll play this charade. "If it makes you feel better. Fine."

I wave to the concierge as we walk through the lobby. Brad stops me at the door, insisting I put my coat on. "It's freezing out, and I don't want you getting sick on our anniversary." He tugs my collar up around my neck, ensuring I'm wrapped up tight. I'm wearing my hair up for the first time tonight, and I'm glad the scars on my neck have healed and that there are no obvious signs of what happened.

The rest of the scars are a work in progress. I'm seeing a great therapist, and he's helping me work through everything, but I've a long road ahead. You can't heal years of hurt overnight, but with the support of Brad, my friends, and my therapist, I feel hopeful I can get through it. And now my dad is moving here too, and I'm overjoyed. Both my parents were devastated at Alec's death, but where Dad has come to terms with it, and he's trying to come to terms with what Alec did to me, Mum continues to deny reality. She hasn't spoken to me since that meeting in Dublin, and I don't know if we'll ever be able to repair our relationship.

For now, I'm glad for my dad. He broke things off with his girlfriend and he's moving here to be with me. That means more to me than he'll ever know.

We haven't been able to locate the photos Alec had of me, and I'm hoping it's something my brother took with him to the grave. Kev says they're probably stored on the hard drive of his laptop, but I've no desire to verify that. They haven't surfaced, and they're unlikely to now, and I'm happy to draw a line under it. Thoughts of my brother create the usual maelstrom of emotions inside me. I thought it'd be cut and dried now he's gone, but it hasn't turned out like that. Not all my memories of him are bad, although for years I couldn't see anything but the torment he inflicted. Since his death, everything has risen to the surface, and I'm struggling to deal with so many confusing emotions.

"You okay, babe?" Brad gently clutches my face. Concern shines from his eyes, and I push all thoughts of my brother aside. Brad's taken such amazing care of me these last few weeks, and every day I fall more and more in love with him.

"I'm perfect—I'm with you." I lean up on tiptoes and kiss him. "You're so romantic, and I love it."

He captures my lips in a searing hot kiss. "You make me want to burst into song and serenade you," he admits with a bashful smile.

All my lady parts rejoice, and my heart starts beating a new rhythm. My grin is huge. "Keep talking like that and I'll never let you go."

He pushes out into the cold night air, tucking me under his arm. "I'm never letting you let me go."

My laughter falters when I see the stretch limo waiting outside our building. The driver has the door open for us. "Oh my God. You did all this?"

He smiles proudly, helping me into the car. Once inside, he pours two glasses of champagne. "Our six-week anniversary is definitely something to celebrate."

"It is," I agree, trying to banish thoughts of the last time I was in a limo drinking champagne with Brad. I'd been out of my face, and he'd held my hair as I puked into the ice bucket. That feels like a lifetime ago now. Here's hoping tonight ends on a more positive, and a more romantic note. I'm wearing the sexy purple lingerie he bought me, and I'm on a countdown until he's stripping me out of it. My body hums in excitement, and I'm already aroused at the thought. "And if this is what you do for six weeks, I can't wait to see what you pull out of the bag at six months."

"Or six years." He chinks his glass against mine, leaning down to kiss me.

I think I'm probably rocking a "deer in the headlights look" if his chuckle is any indication. He blows me away with these grand gestures and grand declarations, but the small things he does, on a daily basis, are equally impressive. Whether it's leaving an umbrella out for me on rainy days, running to the local store to pick up my favorite smoothie before he leaves for Harvard, or running me a bath when I'm late home from college, Brad is the most thoughtful man I've ever met.

And so far removed from that angry, bitter guy I first met.

My boyfriend is the sweetest, sexiest man to walk the planet, and I'm the luckiest woman in the world.

"I meant it when I said I was in this for the long haul. I'm in this for life, Red."

I gulp, overcome with emotion. And it's not like this is the first time I'm hearing this. Brad wastes no opportunity to tell me how much I mean to him, and I cherish the words each and every time he says it. "I haven't scared you away?"

He takes my glass, putting it down. Taking my hands in his, he sears me with a solemn look. "I think we can both agree we've seen each other at our worst, and our lowest points, and the fact we are both still here speaks volumes. There is nothing you could say or do that will change my feelings for you. I love you, Rachel." He brings the tips of my fingers to his mouth and kisses them. Love practically oozes out of his body as he devours me with an adoring look. I inwardly swoon. I will never get enough of how well he loves me. "I love you for life."

Tears blur my vision, but they're happy tears. "You're my whole world, Brad, and I can't imagine you ever not being in it. I love you for life too."

Brad

Her words infuse my body with warmth and happiness, and I want to bottle this feeling and never forget it. It's not easy for her to express her feelings, but when she does, it's always worth the wait. I cocoon her in a hug, just needing to feel her in my arms.

I'm so proud of my girl. These last few weeks have been difficult, but she's faced them with strength, resilience, and grace. Quite simply, I'm in awe of her.

I don't let go of her the rest of the short journey, but she makes no protest, happy to snuggle into me as we sip champagne and watch the world float by outside the window.

Her eyes are out on stalks when we reach our destination. Ky's dad helped me pull some strings to get a reservation here. La Grotte Secrete is the most sought after dining experience in the whole of Boston. Nestled in the basement of an old eighteenth century building in the harbor district, it has a private side entrance with an enclosed underground garage which guarantees absolute privacy arriving and leaving. The hefty price tag, and six-month waiting list, ensures it's an exclusive restaurant frequented only by the rich and famous. You won't find any paparazzi shots of celebs dining here, and it's a big attraction for those seeking an elitist dining experience that offers complete privacy from prying eyes. At least, that's what James and Alex told me. They've eaten here a few times, and they said the food is also to die for.

The maître' d approaches us with a welcoming smile, taking both our coats. Then he leads us through the dimly lit restaurant to our table. The ceilings are low, and the walls are a rustic stone with original stone tiles on the floor. A grand piano sits on a slightly elevated platform in the center of the room, and a woman in an expensive ball gown is tinkling away softly on the keys. The mood is romantic, and I couldn't have chosen a more perfect setting. Rachel deserves to be cherished and spoiled rotten, and I'm just the man for the job.

Secluded tables and booths are built into crevices around the edge of room, offering heightened discretion. Our table is at the back, nestled into a private corner. Two candles cast romantic shadows over the walls and the tabletop as we slide into our booth.

A bottle of non-alcoholic champagne is already on ice. "Compliments of Mr. and Mrs. Kennedy," the maître' d confirms.

He leaves after he hands us our menus. "Wow. This place is something else." Rachel's eyes are lit up like a Christmas tree.

"Only the best for my girl."

She snuggles into my side, kissing my cheek. "You are setting the bar high."

"You deserve it, beautiful."

"We need to take a selfie." She whips out her cell, and I groan. She digs me in the ribs. "Don't be a party pooper. Your sisters will love this."

I can't begrudge Rachel this. For so long, she's had to hide. Now, she revels in the things most of us take for granted. Like uploading a selfie on social media like any normal college student. I lean in for the shot, wrapping my arm around her. There isn't anything I won't do for her, and I'm already firmly under her thumb, and proud to admit that.

"So," she says a minute later after she's tucked her phone back in her purse. "Has your mum told you about her hush-hush project yet?"

"Nope. It's all very mysterious." Mom has entered into some new secret business venture with Alex Kennedy. They are both super excited about it but keeping it completely confidential until they are ready to launch.

"I'm so happy for her. She deserves it."

I am too. My family is living in the Kennedy's Cambridge brownstone. Alex insisted they move in as their family use the apartment so infrequently now. Both my sisters are settling into their new schools, and I love that they are so close to us. Every Wednesday we go there for dinner. My family adores Rachel almost as much as I do.

Life is good. Better than good.

Football and school are both going well, and things are finally back on track with Faye and Ky. It's been years since I've been this happy. The only blip on the radar is my dad. His court case is coming up soon, and I'm not relishing all the renewed media attention. I haven't been to see him since he was moved to the penitentiary, but I know I can't avoid him forever. In the meantime, I'm trying to find forgiveness in my heart.

But I don't want to think about my dad. Not now.

Not when I have the most gorgeous female on my arm, and she's looking at me like I hung the moon in the night time sky. "Me too. Things are finally looking up." I take a drink of the fizzy liquid, filling my mouth before leaning in to kiss Rachel. She opens her mouth, and the liquid transfers from my mouth to hers.

She grins at me, licking her lips. "Now I'm imagining all kinds of ways we can use that champagne."

A little dribble of the amber liquid leaks out of the corner of her mouth, and my tongue darts out, lapping it up. Her eyes sizzle with desire, and my eyes darken. My pants instantly stretch tight. One look at my hot girlfriend is usually all it takes. Rachel has an indisputable talent when it comes to turning me on. "If you're imagining the same things I'm imagining, then I'm in. I'm *all* in."

Her tinkling laughter does funny things to my insides. Her eyes sparkle with lust and giddiness, and she looks at me like I'm her everything. It's my mission in life to make Rachel laugh every day and to replace all the horrible memories with new happy ones.

Ky always said when you meet *the* girl you'll just know. I thought he was full of it, but now I know better. Rachel and I didn't have a traditional start, and there's been nothing normal about our relationship, but we're stronger for it. I know there will never be another girl for me. If it was up to me, I'd be on one knee right now, but I have to take things slow. She still has a lot of things to figure out, and she'll be in therapy for a while but she's healthy, happy, safe, and most importantly—all mine—and I intend to keep it that way. To love her so completely that there's never any question that we are made for one another. She brightens up my life in ways I could never have imagined, and when I look at my future she's all I see.

Life doesn't get much better than this.

After a sumptuous dinner, packed with more laughter and kisses, we get ready to leave. When I go to pay the check, I discover James has already taken care of it. I should be mad, but I'm in too much of a good mood. As she slides out of the booth, Rachel lifts her dress, flashing her purple panties at me. Looking up at me through hooded eyes, she licks her lips in a provocative manner, and I can't wait to devour her in the limo. There's no way in hell I'll be able to wait till we get back home.

I take her elbow, steering her through the restaurant in front of me, using her body to disguise the massive boner in my pants.

A familiar voice captures my attention as we move through the crowded floor. Discreetly, I scan the tables to my left, in the direction of the voice, squinting in the dim light. My eyes narrow on Kaden Kennedy. He's leaning over a table, spooning food into his date's mouth. He is focused singularly on the woman across from him, so he doesn't notice me staring. The look in his eyes is one I haven't seen from him before.

But I recognize it, because I've seen that same look on Kyler and Kalvin, and it's similar to the look I have when I gaze at the only girl who matters.

Kaden is in love, and my curiosity is piqued because his date is not the cute redhead he usually has on his arm. No, this woman has long, rich, thick chocolaty-brown hair that is styled in sleek waves, resting on her bare shoulders. She angles her head to the side, as Kaden cups her face, and I try to mask my surprise.

Because I know that woman.

Every red-blooded male at Harvard knows that woman.

Professor Garcia is the youngest, hottest, smartest female professor on campus, and it's no secret that most of the guys who sign up to her class do so purely to drool or to collect ammo for the spank bank.

It's not the first time I've seen Kaden with her, and my instincts weren't wrong. I'd sensed something was up, and it appears I was right. As Kade leans over the table and snares her lips in a scorching hot kiss, I wonder how long it's been going on.

And whether her husband knows she's having an affair with one of her students.

Seducing Kaden is the next book in the series, and it's a standalone new adult forbidden romance AVAILABLE NOW.

Subscribe to The Kennedy Boys Newsletter to stay updated with the series and to read exclusive bonus scenes and advance samples of future books. You will also be the first to hear of discounts, sales, and reader giveaways. You can subscribe to the newsletter here.

Keep reading for details of *Inseparable*, my standalone new adult romance, now available in e-book, paperback, and audiobook format. Read the description, check out the cover, and read an exclusive sneak peek!

If you need to talk to someone regarding sexual assault, please call the National Sexual Assault Hotline in the US at 800.656.4673. If you live outside the United States of America, please contact your local support services.

Inseparable

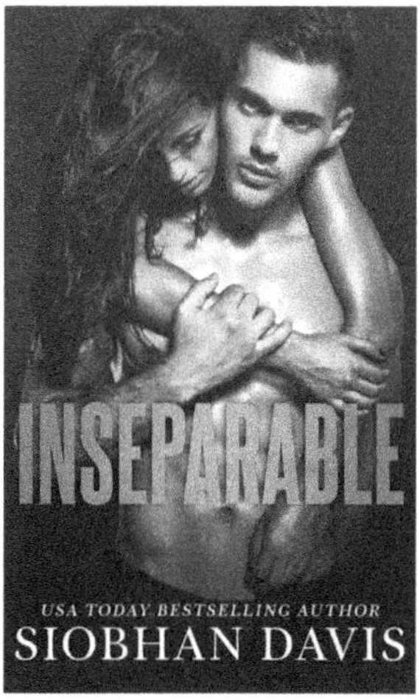

A gritty, angsty, friends-to-lovers standalone romance from *USA Today* bestselling author Siobhan Davis.

A childhood promise. An unbreakable bond. One tragic event that shatters everything.

It all started with the boys next door...

Devin and Ayden were my best friends. We were practically joined at the hip since age two. When we were kids, we thought we were invincible, inseparable, that nothing or no one could come between us.

But we were naive.

Everything turned to crap our senior year of high school.

Devin was turning into a clone of his deadbeat lowlife father—fighting, getting wasted, and screwing his way through every girl in town. I'd been hiding a secret crush on him for years. Afraid to tell him how I felt in case I ruined everything. So, I kept quiet and slowly watched him self-destruct with a constant ache in my heart.

Where Devin was all brooding darkness, Ayden was the shining light. Our star quarterback with the bright future whom everyone loved. But something wasn't right. He was so guarded, and he wouldn't let me in.

When Devin publicly shamed me, Ayden took my side, and our awesome-threesome bond was severed. The split was devastating. The heartbreak inevitable.

Gradually, Ayden and I grew closer. We graduated and moved on with our lives, but the pain never lessened, and Devin was never far from our thoughts.

Until it all came to a head in college, and one eventful night changed everything.

Now, I've lost the two people who matter more to me than life itself. Nothing will ever be the same again.

Inseparable

RELEASING JANUARY 8, 2018.

TURN THE PAGE TO READ AN EXCLUSIVE ADVANCE SAMPLE.

Prologue

Present Day - Angelina

Life is just a flow of interconnecting moments in time. A combination of well-thought-out actions and spontaneous reactions. A sequence of events and people moving in and out of your personal stratosphere.

At least, that's how I've always viewed it.

Like a squiggly line veering up and down with no apparent pattern. Plotting the highs; pinpointing the lows. Showcasing the happy times. Highlighting the mistakes and the resulting consequences. Calling into focus all the myriad of things I should've done differently if I had known.

When I was a kid, I was obsessed with the notion of time—making a beeline for the fortune tellers every year when the carnival descended on the wide, open grassy field just outside town. I saved my pocket money all year round so I could have my fortune told. The idea that you could see into the future, to know what was around the corner, held an enormous fascination for me.

I wanted to make something of my life.

To dedicate myself to a profession that helped others.

To know happiness awaited me.

To receive confirmation that the two most important people in my life would always be in it. Because even the thought I could lose Ayden or Devin always sent horrific tremors of fear rushing through me.

For as long as I can remember, it had always been the three of us. Best friends to the end. The awesome-threesome. Forever infinity. It was a friendship more akin to family. A meeting of minds and hearts and promises. A connection so deep that we swore nothing or no one would ever come between us. We committed ourselves in a secret bond when we were twelve, and the commitment was imprinted on my heart in the same way it was inked on my skin.

I could never have predicted what was to come.

That I'd be the one to destroy everything.

No fortune teller *ever* told me that.

For years, I've thought of nothing but the what-ifs, and obsessed over so many questions.

What if a fortune teller had told me what would come to pass?

Would things have been different?

What would I change?

Would I have had the strength to stay away from my two best friends? To forge a completely different path in life? To deny something that was intrinsically a part of myself? Could I slice my heart apart knowing it was the right thing to do?

For years these questions have plagued me.

But I'm too afraid to confront the truth even though it's front and center. Even though I carry it with me like a thundercloud, hovering and threatening but never opening up, never letting the storm loose.

Some truths are far too painful to acknowledge out loud.

As if to speak the words would confirm what I already know about myself.

That I'm weak, selfish, and not at all the person I thought I was.

Perhaps that's why we don't have that cognitive ability—to see the future, to know what lies ahead. I've thought of it often. If it's evolution. If at some time in the future humans will be able to sense the path of their destiny. To alter their fate. To assume full control over every aspect of their life with conscious decision.

For now, all I've got is that squiggly line and a huge helping of regret.

What good comes from continually looking back? From locking myself in the haunted mansion of my past? Meandering with the ghosts of guilt and shame? For a girl who spent her happy youth so focused on the future, it's a very sorry state of affairs. But I'm stuck in this washing machine that is my so-called life. The faster it churns, the more I lose myself. So, I try to stop time. To stand still. To numb myself to my reality. To blank out feeling and emotion. To close myself off. To never allow another human to imprint on my heart or to see into the black, murky depths of my soul.

The honest truth is, if I'd had a crystal ball—if I'd known what was going to happen—I still wouldn't have changed a thing.

Because I would've missed those high points. Those happy memories that are the only thing keeping me alive right now.

If that's what you can call my current existence.

And that makes me the most selfish, conceited liar on the planet.

END OF SAMPLE

Glossary of Irish Words and Phrases

The explanation listed is taken in the context of this book.

Arse » Ass
Bedside locker » Nightstand
Bloody » Damn
Boot » Trunk/Cargo hold
Car park » Parking lot
Cooker » Stove
Cop a load » Get a look at
Cop the fuck on » Come to your senses
Cough up » Provide
Deep Fat Fryer » Deep Fryer
DPP » Director of Public Prosecutions. This is the government body that decides whether a legal case will proceed to court or not.
Fecked » Fucked
Fella » Guy/Dude
Fit » Hot
Flippin » Frigging
Footpath » Sidewalk
Gaelic & Hurling » National Irish Sports
Gardai » Police
Get up » Outfit
Gob » Mouth
Grand » Fine
Guts me » Upsets me
Hammered » Wasted/Drunk

Hob » Stove
Jelly » Jello
Knickers » Panties
Loaded » Wealthy
Lift » Elevator
Making a holy show of oneself » Embarrassing oneself
Mobile/Mobile phone » Cell
Mum » Mom
Out of my face » Drunk/Wasted
Piss take » Joke
Press » Cupboard/Cabinet
Ride » Hot/Hottie
Secondary School » High School
Solicitor » Attorney
Top of the Range » Top class/top notch
Townhouse » Brownstone
Trackie Bottoms » Sweat pants
Trashed » Drunk/Smashed
Trousers » Pants
UCC » University College Cork
Wardrobe » Closet

Acknowledgments

Massive thank you to all my readers for embracing this series and helping to ensure it remains an international bestselling series. I hope you continue to enjoy reading stories in the Kennedy Boys world. I am committed to writing the rest of the boys' stories, and I will share details of impending release dates in my newsletter and on my Facebook page. However, release dates are subject to change depending on reader demand. The next book in the series is Seducing Kaden, and it's currently available in e-book and paperback format. Forgiving is the next release, slated for publication in early 2019.

As always, I couldn't produce these books so quickly without a wonderful team who supports my efforts. Thanks to my editor, Kelly Hartigan; my assistant, Lola Verroen; Fiona Jayde, and Robin Harper, for the graphics; and Tamara Cribley for the formatting. Huge thanks to my amazing beta readers—Sinead, Deirdre, Angelina, Jennifer, Danielle, and Dana. Your insightful feedback always helps me polish each title to perfection, and I'm so grateful for your time, commitment, and enthusiasm for this series. I also have to thank my street and ARC teams and bloggers the world over who help spread the word. To all my amazing author friends—thank you for the encouragement and advice, and I'm so honored to be a part of this wonderful community. Lastly, thanks to my long-suffering husband and my two gorgeous boys who are so supportive of my writing career even if they see very little of me these days and they tend to survive on convenience foods and takeaways. I'm very lucky to be able to live my dream, and I don't ever take it for granted. None of this would be possible without the support of everyone I've mentioned on this page, so thank you all from the bottom of my heart.

About the Author

USA Today bestselling author **Siobhan Davis** writes emotionally intense young adult and new adult fiction with swoon-worthy romance, complex characters, and tons of unexpected plot twists and turns that will have you flipping the pages beyond bedtime! She is the author of the international bestselling *True Calling*, *Saven*, and *Kennedy Boys* series.

Siobhan's family will tell you she's a little bit obsessive when it comes to reading and writing, and they aren't wrong. She can rarely be found without her trusty Kindle, a paperback book, or her laptop somewhere close at hand.

Prior to becoming a full-time writer, Siobhan forged a successful corporate career in human resource management.

She resides in the Garden County of Ireland with her husband and two sons.

You can connect with Siobhan in the following ways:

Author Website: www.siobhandavis.com
Author Blog: My YA NA Book Obsession
Facebook: AuthorSiobhanDavis
Twitter: @siobhandavis
Google+: SiobhanDavisAuthor
Email: siobhan@siobhandavis.com

Books By Siobhan Davis

TRUE CALLING SERIES

Young Adult Science Fiction/Dystopian Romance

True Calling
Lovestruck
Beyond Reach
Light of a Thousand Stars
Destiny Rising
Short Story Collection
True Calling Series Collection

SAVEN SERIES

Young Adult Science Fiction/Paranormal Romance

Saven Deception
The Logan Collection
Saven Disclosure
Saven Denial
Saven Defiance
The Heir and the Human
Saven Deliverance
Saven: The Complete Series

KENNEDY BOYS SERIES

Upper Young Adult/New Adult Contemporary Romance

Finding Kyler
Losing Kyler
Keeping Kyler

The Irish Getaway
Loving Kalvin
Saving Brad
Seducing Kaden
*Forgiving Keven^*
*Adoring Keaton^*
*Releasing Keanu^*
*Reforming Kent^*

STANDALONES

New Adult Contemporary Romance

Inseparable
Incognito
*When Forever Changes**

Reverse Harem Contemporary Romance

*Surviving Amber Springs**

ALINTHIA SERIES

Upper YA/NA Paranormal Romance/Reverse Harem

The Lost Savior
The Secret Heir
The Warrior Princess
*The Chosen One^*

* Coming 2018
^ Release date to be confirmed.

Visit www.siobhandavis.com for all future release dates. Release dates are subject to change based on reader demand and the author's schedule. Subscribing to the author's newsletter or following her on Facebook is the best way to stay updated with planned new releases.

CPSIA information can be obtained
at www.ICGtesting.com
Printed in the USA
LVHW11s0307241018
594625LV00001B/245/P